017

"Readers rejoice! The Mackenzie brothers return as Ashley works her magic to create a unique love story brimming over with depth of emotion, unforgettable characters, sizzling passion, mystery, and a story that reaches out and grabs your heart. Brava!" —*Romantic Times* (Top Pick)

"A heartfelt, emotional historical romance with danger and intrigue around every corner . . . A great read!"
—*Fresh Fiction*

"A wonderful novel, filled with sweet, tender love that has long been denied, fiery passion, and a good dash of witty humor . . . For a rollicking good time, sexy Highland heroes, and touching romances, you just can't beat Jennifer Ashley's novels!" —*Night Owl Reviews*

THE MADNESS OF LORD IAN MACKENZIE

"Ever-versatile Ashley begins her new Victorian Highland Pleasures series with a deliciously dark and delectably sexy story of love and romantic redemption that will captivate readers with its complex characters and suspenseful plot."
—*Booklist*

"Mysterious, heartfelt, sensitive, and sensual . . . Two big thumbs up." —*Publishers Weekly* "Beyond Her Book"

"A story full of mystery and intrigue with two wonderful, bright characters . . . I look forward to more from Jennifer Ashley, an extremely gifted author." —*Fresh Fiction*

"Brimming with mystery, suspense, an intriguing plot, villains, romance, a tormented hero, and a feisty heroine, this book is a winner. I recommend *The Madness of Lord Ian Mackenzie* to anyone looking for a great read."
—*Romance Junkies*

"Wow! All I can say is *The Madness of Lord Ian Mackenzie* is one of the best books that I have ever read. [It] gets the highest recommendation that I can give. It is a truly wonderful book."
—*Once Upon A Romance*

"When you're reading a book that is a step or two—or six or seven—above the norm, you know it almost immediately. Such is the case with *The Madness of Lord Ian Mackenzie.* The characters here are so complex and so real that I was fascinated by their journey . . . [and] this story is as flat-out romantic as any I've read in a while . . . This is a series I am certainly looking forward to following."
—*All About Romance*

"A unique twist on the troubled hero . . . Fresh and interesting."
—*Night Owl Reviews (Top Pick)*

"A welcome addition to the genre."
—*Dear Author*

"Intriguing . . . Unique . . . Terrific."
—*Midwest Book Review*

Berkley Sensation Titles by Jennifer Ashley

THE MADNESS OF LORD IAN MACKENZIE
LADY ISABELLA'S SCANDALOUS MARRIAGE
THE MANY SINS OF LORD CAMERON

PRIDE MATES
PRIMAL BONDS

PRIDE MATES

JENNIFER ASHLEY

BERKLEY SENSATION, NEW YORK

THE BERKLEY PUBLISHING GROUP
Published by the Penguin Group
Penguin Group (USA) Inc.
375 Hudson Street, New York, New York 10014, USA
Penguin Group (Canada), 90 Eglinton Avenue East, Suite 700, Toronto, Ontario M4P 2Y3, Canada
(a division of Pearson Penguin Canada Inc.)
Penguin Books Ltd., 80 Strand, London WC2R 0RL, England
Penguin Group Ireland, 25 St. Stephen's Green, Dublin 2, Ireland (a division of Penguin Books Ltd.)
Penguin Group (Australia), 250 Camberwell Road, Camberwell, Victoria 3124, Australia
(a division of Pearson Australia Group Pty. Ltd.)
Penguin Books India Pvt. Ltd., 11 Community Centre, Panchsheel Park, New Delhi—110 017, India
Penguin Group (NZ), 67 Apollo Drive, Rosedale, Auckland 0632, New Zealand
(a division of Pearson New Zealand Ltd.)
Penguin Books (South Africa) (Pty.) Ltd., 24 Sturdee Avenue, Rosebank, Johannesburg 2196,
South Africa

Penguin Books Ltd., Registered Offices: 80 Strand, London WC2R 0RL, England

PRIDE MATES

A Berkley Sensation Book / published by arrangement with the author

PRINTING HISTORY
Leisure Books mass-market edition / February 2010
Berkley Sensation mass-market edition / July 2011

ISBN: 978-0-425-24504-0

BERKLEY® SENSATION
Berkley Sensation Books are published by The Berkley Publishing Group,
a division of Penguin Group (USA) Inc.,
375 Hudson Street, New York, New York 10014.
BERKLEY® SENSATION and the "B" design are trademarks of Penguin Group (USA) Inc.

PRINTED IN THE UNITED STATES OF AMERICA

10   9   8   7   6   5   4   3   2   1

ACKNOWLEDGMENTS

Many thanks go to my editor Kate Seaver and all those at Berkley who helped make *Pride Mates* again available for readers.

Special thanks go to Theresa A. and Kerrie D., two defense attorneys extraordinaire who answered my many questions in minute detail. They helped me understand how a defense attorney spends her days and what kinds of challenges a female in the field might experience. I am extremely grateful to them for their time and knowledge; any errors in the book are mine. Also many thanks to my editor Leah, who once again didn't flinch when I presented her with my idea for a brand-new world. Working with her is always the greatest pleasure.

For more details on the series, please visit the Shifters Unbound pages at www.jennifersromances.com.

CHAPTER ONE

A girl walks into a bar . . .
No. A human girl walks into a Shifter bar . . .

The bar was empty, not yet open to customers. It looked normal—windowless walls painted black, rows of glass bottles, the smell of beer and stale air. But it wasn't normal, standing on the edge of Shiftertown as it did.

"You the lawyer?" a man washing glasses asked. He was human, not Shifter. No strange, slitted pupils, no Collar to control his aggression, no air of menace. Well, relatively no air of menace. This was a crappy part of town, and menace was its stock-in-trade.

Kim told herself she had nothing to be afraid of. *They're tamed. Collared. They can't hurt you.*

When she nodded, the man gestured with his cloth to a door at the end of the bar. "Knock him dead, sweetheart."

"I'll try to keep him alive." Kim pivoted and stalked away on her four-inch heels, feeling his gaze on her back all the way.

She knocked on the door marked "Private," and a man on the other side growled, "Come."

I just need to talk to him. Then I'm done, on my way home. A trickle of moisture rolled between Kim's shoulder blades as she made herself open the door and walk inside.

A man leaned back in a chair behind a messy desk, a sheaf of papers in his hands. His booted feet were propped on the desk, his long legs a feast of blue jeans over muscle. He was a Shifter all right—thin black and silver Collar against his throat; hard, honed body; midnight black hair; definite air of menace. When Kim entered, he stood, setting the papers aside.

Damn. He rose to a height of well over six feet and gazed at Kim with eyes blue like the morning sky. His body wasn't only honed; it was hot—big chest, wide shoulders, tight abs, firm biceps against a form-fitting black T-shirt.

"Kim Fraser?"

"That's me."

With old-fashioned courtesy, he placed a chair in front of the desk and motioned her to it. Kim felt the heat of his hand near the small of her back as she seated herself, smelled the scent of soap and male musk.

"You're Mr. Morrissey?"

The Shifter sat back down, returned his motorcycle boots to the top of the desk, and laced his hands behind his head. "Call me Liam."

The lilt in his voice was unmistakable. Kim put that with his black hair, impossibly blue eyes, and exotic name. "You're Irish."

He smiled a smile that could melt a woman at ten paces. "And who else would be running a pub?"

"But you don't own it."

Kim could have bitten out her tongue as soon as she said it. Of course he didn't own it. He was a Shifter.

His voice went frosty, the crinkles at the corners of his eyes smoothing out. "I'm afraid I can't help you much on the Brian Smith case. I don't know Brian well, and I don't know anything about what happened the night his girlfriend was murdered. It's a long time ago, now."

Disappointment bit her, but Kim had learned not to let discouragement stop her when she needed to get a job done. "Brian called you the 'go-to' guy. As in, when Shifters are in trouble, Liam Morrissey helps them out."

Liam shrugged, muscles moving the bar's logo on his T-shirt. "True. But Brian never came to me. He got into his troubles all by himself."

"I know that. I'm trying to get him *out* of trouble."

Liam's eyes narrowed, pupils flicking to slits as he retreated to the predator within him. Shifters liked to do that when assessing a situation, Brian had told her. Guess who was the prey?

Brian had done the predator-prey thing with Kim at first. He'd stopped when he began to trust her, but Kim didn't think she'd ever get used to it. Brian was her first Shifter client, the first Shifter, in fact, she'd ever seen outside a television news story. Twenty years Shifters had been acknowledged to exist, but Kim had never met one.

It was well known that they lived in their enclave on the east side of Austin, near the old airport, but she'd never gone over to check them out. Some human women did, strolling the streets just outside Shiftertown, hoping for glimpses—and more—of the Shifter men who were reputed to be strong, gorgeous, and well endowed. Kim had once heard two women in a restaurant murmuring about their encounter with a Shifter male the night before. The phrase "Oh, my God," had been used repeatedly. Kim was as curious about them as anyone else, but she'd never summoned the courage to go near Shiftertown herself.

Then suddenly she had been assigned the case of the Shifter accused of murdering his human girlfriend ten months ago. This was the first time in twenty years Shifters had caused trouble, the first time one had been put on trial. The public, outraged by the killing, wanted Shifters punished, pointed fingers at those who'd claimed the Shifters were tamed.

However, after Kim had met Brian, she'd determined that she wouldn't do a token defense. She believed in his innocence, and she wanted to win. There wasn't much case law on Shifters because there'd never been any trials, at least none on record. This was to be a well-publicized trial, Kim's opportunity to make a mark, to set precedent.

Liam's eyes stayed on her, pupils still slitted. "You're a brave one, aren't you? To defend a Shifter?"

"Brave, that's me." Kim crossed her legs, pretending to relax. *They picked up on your nervousness, people said. They know when you're scared, and they use your fear.* "I don't mind telling you, this case has been a pain in the ass from the get-go."

"Humans think anything involving Shifters is a pain in the ass."

Kim shook her head. "I mean, it's been a pain in the ass because of the way it's been handled. The cops nearly had Brian signing a confession before I could get to the interrogation. At least I put a stop to that, but I couldn't get bail for him, and I've been blocked by the prosecutors right and left every time I want to review the evidence. Talking to you is a long shot, but I'm getting desperate. So if you don't want to see a Shifter go down for this crime, Mr. Morrissey, a little cooperation would be appreciated."

The way he pinned her with his eyes, never blinking, made her want to fold in on herself. Or run. That was what prey did—ran. And then predators chased them, cornered them.

What did this man do when he cornered his prey? He wore the Collar; he could do nothing. Right?

Kim imagined herself against a wall, his hands on either side of her, his hard body hemming her in . . . Heat curled down her spine.

Liam took his feet down and leaned forward, arms on

the desk. "I haven't said I won't help you, lass." His gaze flicked to her blouse, whose buttons had slipped out of their top holes during her journey through Austin traffic and July heat. "Is Brian happy with you defending him? You like Shifters that much?"

Kim resisted reaching for the buttons. She could almost feel his fingers on them, undoing each one, and her heart beat faster.

"It's nothing to do with who I like. I was assigned to him, but I happen to think Brian's innocent. He shouldn't go down for something he didn't do." Kim liked her anger, because it covered up how edgy this man made her. "Besides, Brian's the only Shifter I've ever met, so I don't know whether I like them, do I?"

Liam smiled again. His eyes returned to normal, and now he looked like any other gorgeous, hard-bodied, blue-eyed Irishman. "You, love, are—"

"Feisty. Yeah, I've heard that one. Also spitfire, little go-getter, and a host of other condescending terms. But let me tell you, Mr. Morrissey, I'm a damn good lawyer. Brian's not guilty, and I'm going to save his ass."

"I was going to say *unusual*. For a human."

"Because I'm willing to believe he's innocent?"

"Because you came here, to the outskirts of Shifter-town, to see me. Alone."

The predator was back.

Why was it that when Brian looked at her like this, it didn't worry her? Brian was in jail, angry, accused of heinous crimes. A killer, according to the police. But Brian's stare didn't send shivers down her spine like Liam Morrissey's did.

"Any reason I shouldn't have come alone?" she asked, keeping her voice light. "I'm trying to prove that Shifters in general, and my client in particular, can't harm humans. I'd do a poor job of it if I was afraid to come and talk to his friends."

Liam wanted to laugh at the little—spitfire—but he kept his stare cool. She had no idea what she was walking into; Fergus, the clan leader, expected Liam to make sure it stayed that way.

Damn it all, Liam wasn't supposed to *like* her. He'd expected the usual human woman, sticks-up-their-asses, all of them, but there was something different about Kim Fraser. It wasn't just that she was small and compact, while Shifter women were tall and willowy. He liked the way her dark blue eyes regarded him without fear, liked the riot of black curls that beckoned his fingers. She'd had the sense to leave her hair alone, not force it into some unnatural shape.

On the other hand, she tried to hide her sweetly curvaceous body under a stiff gray business suit, although her body had other ideas. Her breasts wanted to burst out of the button-up blouse, and the stiletto heels only enhanced wickedly sexy legs.

No Shifter woman would dress as she did. Shifter women wore loose clothes they could quickly shed if they needed to change forms. Shorts and T-shirts were popular. So were gypsy skirts and sarongs in the summer.

Liam imagined this lady in a sarong. Her melon-firm breasts would fill out the top, and the skirt would bare her smooth thighs.

She'd be even prettier in a bikini, lolling around some rich man's pool, sipping a complicated drink. She was a lawyer—there was probably a boss in her firm who had already made her his. Or perhaps she was using said boss to climb the success ladder. Humans did that all the time. Either the bastard would break her heart, or she'd walk away happy with what she'd got out of it.

That's why we stay the hell away from humans. Brian Smith had taken up with a human woman, and look where he was now.

So why did this female raise Liam's protective instincts? Why did she make him want to move closer, inside the radius of her body heat? She wouldn't like that; humans tried to stay a few feet apart from each other unless they couldn't help it. Even lovers might do nothing more than hold hands in public.

Liam had no business thinking about passion and this woman in the same heartbeat. Fergus's instructions had been to listen to Kim, sway her, then send her home. Not that Liam was in the habit of blindly obeying Fergus.

"So why do you want to help him, love?" he asked. "You're only defending him because you drew the short straw, am I right?"

"I'm the junior in the firm, so it was handed to me, yes. But the prosecutor's office and the police have done a shitty job with this case. Rights violations all over the place, but the courts won't dismiss it, no matter how much I argue. Everyone wants a Shifter to go down, innocent or guilty."

"And why do you believe Brian didn't do it?"

"Why do you think?" Kim tapped her throat. "Because of these."

Liam resisted touching the strand of black and silver metal fused to his own neck, a small Celtic knot at the base of his throat. The Collars contained tiny programmed chips enhanced by powerful Fae magic to keep Shifters in check, though the humans didn't want to acknowledge the magic part. The Collar shot an electric charge into a Shifter when his violent tendencies rose to the surface. If the Shifter persisted, the next dose was one of debilitating pain. A Shifter couldn't attack anyone if he was rolling around on the ground, writhing in agony.

Liam wasn't sure entirely how the Collars worked; he only knew that each became bonded to its wearer's skin and adapted to their animal form when they shifted. All Shifters living in human communities were required to wear Collars, which were irremovable once put on. Refusing the Collar meant execution. If the Shifter tried to escape, he or she was hunted down and killed.

"You know Brian couldn't have committed a violent crime," Kim was saying. "His Collar would have stopped him."

"Let me guess. Your police claim the Collar malfunctioned?"

"Yep. When I suggest having it tested, I'm greeted with all kinds of reasons it can't be. The Collar can't be removed, and anyway it would be too dangerous to have Brian Collarless if he could be. Also too dangerous to provoke him to violence and see if the Collar stops him. Brian's been calm since he was brought in. Like he's given up." She looked glum. "I hate to see someone give up like that."

"You like the underdog?"

She grinned at him with red lips. "You could say that, Mr. Morrissey. Me and the underdog go back a long way."

Liam liked her mouth. He liked imagining it on his body, on certain parts of his anatomy in particular. He had no business thinking that, but the thoughts triggered a physical reaction below the belt.

Weird. He'd never even considered having sex with a human before. He didn't find human women attractive; Liam preferred to be in his big cat form for sex. He found sex that way much more satisfying. With Kim, he'd have to remain human.

His gaze strayed to her unbuttoned collar. Of course, it might not be so bad to be human with her . . .

What the hell am I thinking? Fergus's instructions had been clear, and Liam agreeing to them had been the only way Fergus had allowed Kim to come to Shiftertown at all. Fergus wasn't keen on a human woman being in charge of Brian's case, not that they had any choice. Fergus had been pissed about Brian's arrest from the beginning and thought the Shifters should back off and stay out of it. Almost as though he believed Brian was guilty.

But Fergus lived down on the other side of San Antonio,

and what he didn't know wouldn't hurt him. Liam would handle this his own way.

"So what do you expect from me, love?" he asked Kim. "Want to test *my* Collar?"

"No, I want to know more about Brian, about Shifters and the Shifter community. Who Brian's people are, how he grew up, what it's like to live in a Shifter enclave." She smiled again. "Finding six independent witnesses who swear he was nowhere near the victim at the time in question wouldn't hurt either."

"Oh, is that all? Bloody miracles is what you want, darling."

She wrapped a dark curl around her finger. "Brian said that you're the Shifter people talk to most. Shifters and humans alike."

It was true that Shifters came to Liam with their troubles. His father, Dylan Morrissey, was master of this Shiftertown, second in power in the whole clan.

Humans knew little about the careful hierarchy of the Shifter clans and prides—packs for Lupines—and still less about how informally but efficiently everything got done. Dylan was the Morrissey pride leader and the leader of this Shiftertown, and Fergus was the clan leader for the Felines of South Texas, but Shifters with a problem sought out Liam or his brother Sean for a chat. They'd meet in the bar or at the coffee shop around the corner. *So, Liam, can you ask your father to look into it for me?*

No one would petition Dylan or Fergus directly. That wasn't done. But chatting about things to Liam over coffee, that was fine and didn't draw attention to the fact that the person in question had troubles.

Everyone would know anyway, of course. Life in a Shiftertown reminded Liam very much of life in the Irish village he'd lived near until they'd come to Texas twenty years ago. Everyone knew everything about everyone, and news traveled, lightning-swift, from one side of the village to the other.

"Brian never came to me," he said. "I never knew anything about this human girl until suddenly the police swoop in here and arrest him. His mother struggled out of bed to watch her son be dragged away. She didn't even know why for days."

Kim watched Liam's blue eyes harden. The Shifters were angry about Brian's arrest, that was certain. Citizens of Austin had tensely waited for the Shifters to make trouble after the arrest, to break free and try to retaliate with violence, but Shiftertown remained quiet. Kim wondered why, but she wasn't about to ask right now and risk angering the one person who might help her.

"Exactly my point," she said. "This case has been handled badly from start to finish. If you help me, I can spring Brian and make a point at the same time. You don't mess with people's rights, not even Shifters'."

Liam's eyes grew harder, if that were possible. It was like looking at living sapphire. "I don't give a damn about making a point. I give a damn about Brian's family."

All right, so she'd miscalculated about what would motivate him. "In that case, Brian's family will be happier with him outside prison, not inside."

"He won't go to prison, love. He'll be executed, and you know it. No waiting twenty years on death row, either. They'll kill him, and they'll kill him fast."

That was true. The prosecutor, the county sheriff, the attorney general, and even the governor wanted an example made of Brian. There hadn't been a Shifter attack in twenty years, and the Texas government wanted to assure the world that they weren't going to allow one now.

"So are you going to help me save him?" Kim asked. If he wanted to be direct and to the point, fine. So could she. "Or let him die?"

Anger flickered through Liam's eyes again, then sorrow

and frustration. Shifters were emotional people from what she'd seen in Brian, not bothering to hide what they felt. Brian had lashed out at Kim many times before he'd grudgingly acknowledged that she was on his side.

If Liam decided to stonewall her, Brian had said, Kim had no hope of getting cooperation from the other Shifters. Even Brian's own mother would take her cue from Liam.

Liam had the look of a man who didn't take shit from anyone. A man used to giving the orders himself, but so far he hadn't seemed brutal. He could make his voice soft and lilting, reassuring, friendly. He was a defender, she guessed. A protector of his people.

Was he deciding whether to protect Brian or turn his back?

Liam's gaze flicked past her to the door, every line of his body coming alert. Kim's nerves made her jump. "What is it?"

Liam got out of his chair and started around the desk at the same time the door scraped open and another man—another Shifter—walked in.

Liam's expression changed. "Sean." He clasped the other Shifter's arms and pulled him into a hug.

More than a hug. Kim watched, open-mouthed, as Liam wrapped his arms around the other man, gathered him close, and nuzzled his cheek.

CHAPTER TWO

Kim made herself close her gaping mouth and turn away. None of her business if Liam Morrissey was gay. Seriously disappointing, but none of her business.

The second man held Liam in a tight hug, then with a thump of fists on backs, they released each other. Liam smiled—man, how gorgeous was he when he smiled? He had his arm around the second man's shoulders.

"Sean, this is Kim," Liam said. "She wants me to help her with Brian."

Sean had dark hair and blue eyes like Liam, and a body as honed, but his face was harder, his look sterner. He had a stillness in him that wasn't in Liam, as though something had happened to him that he'd never quite gotten over.

"Does she now?" Sean was saying. "And what did you tell her?"

"I was about to explain when you barged in without warning me. What if I'd thought you were a Lupine? I'd have taken your head off."

"Your sense of smell's that bad, Liam, that you'd mistake your own brother for a wolfman?"

"He's your brother?" Kim asked in a shaky voice.

"My brother, Sean Morrissey."

Kim's face heated. "Oh."

Liam still had his arm firmly around the other man. "Why? Who'd you think he was?"

Kim tried to control her embarrassment. "I thought you were a couple."

Liam burst out laughing, a warm sound. Sean smiled slightly. "Are all humans this crazy?" he asked Liam.

"They're all that ignorant," Liam said. "I've decided to let her talk to Brian's mum."

Sean's smile faded, and he and Liam exchanged a look that held caution, warning. Because they didn't trust humans? Or something more?

Both men focused on Kim again. No one could look at someone like a Shifter. They saw everything, missed nothing. She found that having two equally good-looking men give her the once-over wasn't bad, even if they were Shifters, potentially dangerous and potentially deadly.

"Sounds good," she made herself say. "Here's my card. Call me when you've set something up with her."

"I meant I'd take you around now," Liam said. "No time like the present."

"Right now? Without warning? Not always a good idea."

"She'll know we're coming."

Kim shrugged, pretending to share their nonchalance. Her years as a lawyer had made her anal—make appointments, keep detailed records, cover your ass on everything. Their casualness unnerved her.

And yet she sensed these men weren't relaxed at all. Liam and Sean shared another look, an unspoken warning, as if they were communicating something she couldn't hear.

But whatever. Kim had a job to do, and Brian had said that getting Liam's help was key.

She walked out the door Liam held open, her head up, trying not to melt when she passed between the two men's extraordinary heat.

They walked to Brian's house. Kim had been preparing to share the close space of her car with two Shifters, but found herself walking slightly behind Liam, with Sean behind her.

The house wasn't far. A couple of blocks, that was all, Liam assured her. *He* wasn't the one in the four-inch heels, she wanted to growl. Kim's shiny black pumps were great for office meetings, bad for hiking.

It wasn't a hardship following Liam, though. The man had a fine ass cupped by snug jeans, and he walked easily in the heat. No wonder people came to Liam with their problems—he looked like a man who'd invite you to rest your head on his shoulder while he made everything bad go away. His brother had the same height and build, the same strength, the same blue eyes, but Kim would gravitate to Liam if she had to choose. Sean had a wariness, a pulling back that she didn't sense in Liam.

The first block had a convenience store with a littered parking lot on one corner; another bar, closed, on the opposite end; and a boarded-up store and two bungalows left over from better times crammed in the middle. No one but the three of them walked here, and any street traffic sped through to newer and more prosperous parts of town.

Liam led Kim around the corner behind the derelict buildings. They passed through a wide-open gate in a chain-link fence and crossed a field. Kim winced and watched where she stepped, knowing her legs and feet would be open season for Texas chiggers.

When they reached the other end of the field, Kim stopped so quickly that Sean almost ran into her.

"*This* is Shiftertown?"

Liam grinned. "Not what you expected, eh, love?"

Kim had thought Shiftertown would be a slum, a ghetto of people not wanted in other parts of town. The houses were small and old, yes. The street itself was cracked and potholed because the city deemed repairs there a low priority. But Kim looked down the street at what appeared to be a beautiful and comfortable suburb. Every yard was green, with gardens or flower boxes running riot with summer flowers. The buildings were painted and in good repair, and most houses had deep porches filled with plants and furniture.

There were no fences anywhere. Kids played in yards and ran between houses without fear. One front yard sported a plastic wading pool filled with kids and a couple of dogs, while two moms watched from the porch steps. They were young women, casual in shorts and baggy T-shirts, legs stretched to the sun while the kids played. Everyone in the yard and on the porch, including the dogs, wore collars.

One of the women looked up and waved. "Good day to you, Liam," she called. "Hello, Sean." The other woman raised her hand in greeting but didn't speak. Kim felt the gazes of both Shifter women on her dark gray suit and stupidly high heels.

Liam and Sean gave them a casual wave back. The kids jumped up and down, and one sent a big splash of water over the edge of the pool.

"Look, Liam, I've got my own swimming pool."

"It's grand, Michael. You look after your brother now."

Michael turned to the littlest child in the pool, who was splashing happily. "I will," the older boy said seriously.

They moved on. The Shifters didn't hide in their houses, the way residents did in Kim's neighborhood. They roamed outside in the hot weather, working in the yard, looking after kids, talking to their neighbors. Everyone they passed waved or smiled at Liam and Sean, some greeting them, "Now then, Liam. How's your dad?"

By the time they reached the end of the block, Kim understood how Brian's mother would know they were on their way without Liam calling ahead. Every Shifter they passed noted Liam and Sean, every Shifter recognized Kim for the human stranger she was. Someone would be on the phone or running through the backyards to alert Brian's mother.

Brian had been living with his mother, Sandra Smith, at 445B Marble Lane, Kim knew from her files. She'd assumed the address meant an apartment or duplex, but it turned out to be a house set behind another house. A driveway ran past 445A and stopped at the garage of 445B.

Both houses had the look of the 1920s or '30s, low-roofed bungalows with brick-pillared porches, dormer windows, and separate garages. The front screen door opened as they approached, and a slender woman leaned against the doorframe.

"You've brought her then," she said.

Kim had never met Sandra Smith. When Kim first started putting together the case, she had requested that Sandra come to Kim's office and talk to her. Sandra had refused, and after a while had stopped answering the phone when Kim called. That was part of the reason Kim wanted to talk to Liam, to find *someone* who could help her build a solid defense for Brian.

"I hope you don't mind the intrusion, Mrs. Smith," Kim began as they approached the porch.

Sandra abruptly turned and went inside, the screen door banging behind her. Kim winced. This interview was not going to be easy.

Liam and Sean pushed past Kim to enter the house, no human custom of standing back to let a lady through a door first. Brian had explained the apparent rudeness to her. To a Shifter, letting a female enter a room or building ahead of a male was ludicrous. You couldn't be sure what danger lurked on the other side. The male checked it out and then gave the all clear for the female to enter. How could you protect your mate otherwise?

Kim followed them inside and stopped in surprise. Sean had taken Sandra into his arms, letting her lean against him while he rubbed his cheek on her hair. Liam moved to stand behind Sandra. *Very* close behind Sandra. He rested his chest on her back and both he and Sean murmured to her.

This was crazy. The way Liam had greeted his brother had made Kim think the two of them had something going on. Now she swore the brothers and Sandra were in a threesome.

Liam and Sean stepped away from Sandra, and Sandra wiped her eyes. Kim was struck by how young the woman looked, too young to have a twenty-five-year-old son. Sandra could be thirty, though her eyes spoke of a woman who'd seen far more of the world than Kim had.

"Can I get you coffee, Ms. Fraser?" Sandra asked, her voice shaky.

"No, no," Kim said. "Don't go to any trouble."

Sean smiled at Sandra. "I think a big pot would be grand, Sandra. I'll help you, shall I?"

Sandra softened under his look, and she and Sean walked to the back of the house to the kitchen. Sean went in first, then ushered Sandra in with his hand on the small of her back.

"What was *that* about?" Kim asked Liam.

"Sit down, Kim. You look all out."

She hadn't really expected him to answer. Kim collapsed to the sofa with a grimace and laid her briefcase on the coffee table. Her feet were killing her. She ran her finger inside her shoes, but it didn't do much good.

"Are you hurting?" Liam sat down next to her—right next to her, inside her personal space. "Let me see your feet."

Kim blinked. "Sorry?"

"I saw you limping. Get those ridiculous shoes off and swing your feet up here."

His eyes were so damn blue. Why did she suddenly long to feel his warm hands on her feet, on her ankles, up her legs under her skirt to where her stockings ended at bare thigh . . . ?

He was a *Shifter*. This wasn't right.

"I can't do that."

"You mean you won't."

"How do you think that would look? For the mother of the man I'm defending to come back in and find you giving me a foot massage?"

"She'd think it was the first sensible thing you did. You hide behind those clothes like they're a suit of armor. She'll not open up to you if you do that."

"But she will if I play footsie with you?"

Liam smiled a heart-thumping smile. "Get your damn shoes off, woman."

Oh, to hell with it. When in Rome . . . or Shiftertown.

Kim couldn't stop her groan of relief as she eased the heels from her feet. Liam patted his lap. Kim leaned into the corner of the couch and plopped her ankles on Liam's thigh.

"Is everything in Shiftertown backward?" she asked.

"Backward?"

"Men enter a room first, it's better to kick off your shoes on a stranger's couch than be businesslike, and you say hello by rubbing yourselves all over each other." Kim sagged in pleasure as he moved strong hands over her feet. "Ooh, that's good."

Liam's thumb traveled over her arch to her heel, his touch warm. Did the man know how to loosen tension, or what?

Another groan escaped her. "This is better than any day spa I've been to. You could make money doing this."

"Shifters aren't allowed in any profession where they touch humans." His voice went soft. "We might bite."

Kim didn't think she'd mind being nibbled on by him. Her nervousness about Shifters hadn't quite drifted away, but Liam was dissolving her fears little by little, at least about him. "I think I'd make an exception for you."

"Pheromones."

Her eyes popped open. "Sorry?"

"Sean and I felt Sandra's distress, and we calmed her down. She needed our touch. Like you need me rubbing your feet."

Kim thought about their caressing, group hug. "She must have been *very* distressed."

"She is. Why wouldn't she be?"

"Was Sean distressed when he came in your office? You hugged him too."

"Of course I hugged him. He's my brother. Don't you hug your brother or your sisters?"

"I don't have a family," Kim said. She couldn't keep the sorrow out of her voice. "Not anymore."

Liam gave her a look of open pity. "No wonder you're so tense. What happened to them?"

"I don't like to talk about it."

"Talk about it anyway."

Kim had always thought it best not to open up, but Liam's blue eyes and gentle voice pried something loose. "It's no big secret. My brother Mark died when I was ten. He was twelve. He was hit by a car while he was walking down to a corner store with his friends—a hit and run. My parents passed away a few years ago, within months of each other. Old age, is all. They had their kids late in life. So now it's just me."

The story was simple, easy to relate. Her grief had burned away to emptiness long ago. She lived in the big house she'd inherited from her parents, and it was—so quiet. She tried to cheer it up with weekend parties or office mixers, but the warmth never lasted. Her parents' neighborhood was one of standoffish elegance; no kids would dare splash in plastic pools in any front yard on her street.

Liam gently squeezed her feet. "I'm sorry for you, Kim Fraser. It's the hardest thing, losing a brother. It's like losing a part of yourself."

He was too right. Kim's next words came reluctantly. "When Mark was killed, I blamed myself. I know that's stupid. I was at a friend's house miles away, and I was ten years old—what could I have done? But I kept thinking that if I'd been there, I could have warned him, pulled him out of the way, kept him home altogether. *Something.*"

Liam's warm, relaxing fingers slid beneath each of her toes. "Sean and me, we had a brother. Kenny. We lost him about ten years ago. You always wonder, if you'd persuaded him to do something different that day, would he still be alive?"

"Exactly." After seventeen years, Kim had never found anyone who really understood, not friends or colleagues or the child counselor she'd been hauled off to. Now a Shifter she'd met an hour ago wrung the truth from her heart. "I'm sorry, Liam. About your brother."

He acknowledged the sympathy with a nod. "Did they ever get the bastard who hit Mark?"

Kim shook her head. "The police picked up a guy, but it turned out he didn't do it. Everyone wanted him to be guilty, wanted someone to blame, but I knew he hadn't done it when I saw him. He was so scared, and his wife was crying, and I said it wasn't him—but of course, how could I know? I was a kid and hadn't even been there. In the end, evidence came to light that cleared him. But everyone was pissed that he was innocent. They couldn't catch the real guy, so they wanted a substitute."

His hands slowed. "Is that when you decided to become a defense attorney?"

"No, I wanted to be a doctor." She grinned. "Or a dancer, I couldn't decide. I was ten. But I wanted the right guy to pay. I knew that if the wrong person went to prison, then whoever really did hit my brother would have hurt that many more people, you know?"

"Well reasoned for a ten-year-old."

"I thought about it. A lot. For a while, I couldn't think about anything else." Hence the child counselor.

"I know." He looked grim again.

Kim wanted to ask how his brother had died, but at that moment Sandra and Sean returned with the coffee. Kim tried to jerk her feet from Liam's lap, but he closed his hands around her ankles and held them fast. She glared, and he smiled back, showing her nice white teeth.

Sean set a tray on the table. It held the whole works: cups, a pot, cream, and sugar. No artificial sweetener. Kim wondered whether that was because Sandra didn't like artificial sweetener or whether Shifters never had to worry about their weight.

Sandra didn't look surprised or shocked that Kim had her stockinged feet in Liam's lap. She poured out a cup of coffee and handed it to Kim without comment.

"So, tell us, Kim," Sean said, as he sat down and took his cup, "is there any chance for Brian?"

Kim couldn't lie to them. "Brian's DNA was on the victim, Michelle, and in her bedroom, and now that everyone watches *CSI*, they figure DNA is the magic truth. But Brian says he'd been dating Michelle and had gone to her house, so of course his DNA would be there and on her too."

"Then what can we do?" Sandra asked, angry. "If this DNA has already convicted him?"

"We can prove he was nowhere near the scene of the crime that night," Kim said. "Which is why I'm here. Neither the private investigator I hired nor my journalist friend who's been following the case can find any information on his whereabouts that night. I mean, no information at all. Like he'd vanished for twenty-four hours. But I can't believe *no one* saw Brian or knew where he was going."

Hell, everyone on this street had known within minutes that Liam and Sean were taking the human lawyer to Brian's house. They probably knew Kim's full name and her favorite color by now. "I'm having the investigator look into Michelle's side of things—see if she had a jealous ex or an abusive father, or even a normally nice friend upset that Michelle was dating a Shifter. I'm trying to find any evidence the police overlooked in their zeal to arrest a Shifter."

"Your investigator came around and asked me questions." Sandra sounded pissed about it. "But Brian didn't tell me himself he was walking out with this girl, so how could I know?"

"But you might know something that can help," Kim said. "I'm sorry, I know this is painful for you, but Brian's clammed up about Michelle, so I have to poke and pry. I think getting him released is more important than keeping his personal secrets, don't you?"

"Is it?" Sandra had a bit of the same Irish lilt as Sean and Liam, but Brian didn't. He'd told Kim that his father came from a different clan, she guessed not an Irish one. Either that or his clan had lost their accent after living in Texas awhile.

Kim didn't really understand how the Shifter clans worked, though Brian had tried to explain a little. She knew that each immediate family belonged to a larger, extended family group called a pride, and *they* belonged to an even more extended group called a clan. Shifters never married within the pride, and tried to marry outside the clan. When a female married, she joined her husband's clan and pride, leaving her own. Kim had thought clans were based on what kind of animal the Shifter turned into, but Brian said it was more complicated than that. This Shiftertown was home to several clans, as well as several species of Shifters, and there was another Shiftertown with more clans on the northeast edge of Austin.

Liam's father, Dylan Morrissey, was more or less the official head of the Austin branch of his entire clan, but also the unofficial head of this Shiftertown, even over the other clans. But no, Kim couldn't talk directly to Dylan, Brian told her. He was off-limits to non-Shifters. She could petition him through Liam and Liam only.

Why not Sean? Kim wondered, glancing at Liam's brother. What position did he hold in the clan hierarchy? Officially and unofficially?

Sean helped himself to coffee and exchanged a glance with Liam. "So you need to find someone who was with Brian at the time in question?" Sean asked.

Kim could have sworn that Liam had nodded ever so slightly, as though letting Sean know it was all right to say this. Nonverbal cues were flowing thick and fast.

"An independent witness would be terrific," Kim said. "Someone without a grudge against Shifters. And preferably not a Shifter him- or herself."

"Tall order," Sean said.

"The girl is human," Sandra snapped. "What human will come forward and say my son didn't do it?"

She had a point. Kim knew that locating a witness was a long shot, but it would be a nice change to find something concrete. *Innocent until proven guilty* was not working in Brian's case. The fact that he was Shifter had already condemned him in most people's eyes. Kim had to exonerate him or he didn't stand a chance.

Liam started massaging the tops of Kim's feet, which made her tense limbs start to droop.

"I might be able to find out where Brian really was," Liam said. "You should have come to me about this right away, love."

"I didn't know that, did I? Like I said, Brian is the first Shifter I've ever met, and to get him to tell me that you, Liam, even existed was an amazing feat." Brian hadn't bothered to mention Sean.

"We don't like talking about ourselves," Sean said.

"I don't see why not. Shifters exposed themselves years ago, and everyone knows all about you. There's nothing to hide anymore."

She felt the three exchange another wordless communication, and it irritated her. It reminded her of being eight years old and watching her two best friends whispering and giving her gleeful looks, not letting her in on the secret.

A cell phone vibrated on Liam's belt. He looked at the readout, and without a word gently lowered Kim's feet to the floor. He stood and walked to the kitchen, closing the door, shutting them out.

Kim felt cold without his warmth beside her, even in the July heat. "Anything you can tell me might help," she said to Sean and Sandra. "Right now I can only win this case by tearing holes in the prosecution, and there aren't many holes. I need something that will stick a fork in the case and shred it."

Sandra drank her coffee, her gaze moving from Kim to the windows. Kim caught a glimpse of her sadness as she looked away, her near despair.

She's resigning herself to losing her son, Kim realized. Sandra thought there was no hope. She'd already started grieving for him.

Sean was watching Kim with an assessing look. She still wasn't sure about him, or where the haunted feeling she got from him came from.

"I don't like to lose, Sandra," Kim said briskly. "I want to see Brian walk free and the real person pay for his crime. I won't let you down."

Sandra didn't answer. Sean nodded at Kim. "I'm sure you won't."

Liam strode back into the room. Kim realized that the other two had said very little while Liam had been gone. Had he signaled them not to? And why?

Liam took up his coffee cup without sitting down and took a long swallow. He looked over the rim at Sean, who came alert.

"Everything all right?" Kim asked. "Did you get bad news?"

Liam clicked his mug to the tray. "No, an errand Sean and I need to run. I appreciate you coming all the way out to Shiftertown, Kim Fraser, but now it's time for you to go."

CHAPTER THREE

"What's going on?" Kim demanded as she strode down the driveway with Liam. "I just get you talking, and suddenly you're throwing me out."

Liam looked down at the fuming woman next to him. Sunlight danced on her black hair, the afternoon warmth making her smell good.

He was finding her enticing, even when she was mad as hell. When he'd announced the interview was over, she'd jammed her shoes on her feet, said a sweet good-bye to Sandra, and stalked out. Now as they walked back down the driveway, she glared at him.

"Sandra was uncomfortable," he offered. "She's not easy around humans."

"And you? Are you comfortable around us?"

"Not really. But more than she and Sean are."

"Is that why you work at a bar?"

Liam shrugged. "Humans like to see Shifters in bars.

It brings in business." She didn't need to know the real reason he worked there.

They'd reached the sidewalk in front of 445A. Kim swung to face him with hands planted on hips. "I'm trying to *help*. Why does Sandra believe Brian has no chance? *I'm* on the case."

Liam hid a smile. She was like a fox terrier determined to bring down a lion. He admired her balls, first in believing Brian's innocence, and second, for coming down to meet big, dangerous Shifters like him and Sean. She didn't realize *how* dangerous her pilgrimage was, and Liam wasn't going to tell her.

"And you on the case should be good enough?"

"I'm good, Mr. Morrissey. Michelle and her family will only get closure if the right guy goes down."

Liam lifted his hands. "I agree with you, love. It's not me you have to convince."

"Then why won't you tell me anything?" She regarded him with suspicion. "Something's going on. You and Sean know it. Sandra knows it. Hell, Brian knows it. I'm the only one in the dark. Help me out here."

Liam put his hands on her shoulders, and her blue eyes flickered with discomfort. Why did humans worry so much about touching? "We're grateful to you. You're the first human we've met who cares about Shifters. But you have to let me handle it from here."

If she didn't, Kim could die. Liam had already broken Fergus's rules by not placating her and sending her away at once, but Fergus could stuff it.

He couldn't tell Kim that he didn't know all that was going on, either. Sandra was hiding something, even from Liam, and it annoyed Liam that he didn't know what.

"You don't get it, do you?" Kim asked him. "I shouldn't have even come to talk to you, but I'm desperate. I have to be very careful about every point I have, so whatever you come up with will have to be checked and double-checked. It's not that I don't trust you, it's that I can't."

Liam circled his thumbs on her shoulders. "Well, you will have to trust me, sweetheart."

A shiver went through her body. She wanted to be touched; he could feel it. She needed it. But she fought it. *Humans.*

She glanced at his hands. "Has anyone ever told you that you're not PC?"

"Why, because I enjoy touching your soft skin and call you sweetheart? Or because I won't let you have it your own way?"

"What was the phone call you took about?"

"Oh, now you're prying into *my* business, are you? It was personal. Do you have a boyfriend?"

She blinked. "Talk about personal."

"Do you?" Liam repeated. "Someone special in your life?"

Kim pursed her lips as though she had to think about it. "Yes, a boyfriend. Sort of."

"Aren't you sure, then?"

"We don't go out much. We're busy."

"That's a tragedy."

She bristled. "Why?"

Liam leaned toward her. She smelled nice, this human. He liked her hair, all silky and curly, and he wanted to bury his nose in it.

"If I had someone like you, love, I'd be with her all the time. I wouldn't want her out of my sight. And I definitely wouldn't let her run around Shiftertown by herself. What is this man thinking about?"

Kim looked annoyed. "He doesn't know I'm here."

"He needs to take better care of you."

Indignation now. "He doesn't need to take care of me at all. I'm my own person."

"Maybe." Liam leaned closer, feeling his eyes change as he inhaled her scent. "But when you're in Shiftertown, *I* take care of you. No one will bother you here, I promise you that. They'll answer to me."

"I doubt I'll come to Shiftertown again."

"Even so."

Liam slid his arms around her and drew her close. She resisted. He traced patterns on her lower back and rested his cheek on her hair until she softened a little. He was right; her hair was silky and warm.

Kim started to relax against him, her body reacting to his. He needed to protect her. He'd made that decision the minute she'd walked into his office, to protect her from all other Shifters, most of all the leader of his own clan. "Everything will be all right now."

"Why do I want to believe you?" She sounded skeptical.

She had a nice voice, low and contralto. He imagined her whispering to him as she lay next to him in bed. Her hair would tangle on his pillow, and wouldn't she be pretty? He could understand keeping his human form for lovemaking if the human was Kim Fraser.

He straightened up and brushed a curl from her face. "Give me your cell phone."

"What for?"

"So I can admire the fine technology a human woman can afford to buy." He held out his hand. "I want to give you my phone number. What did you think?"

Kim pulled her cell phone out of a pocket of her briefcase and handed it to him. The phone was fancy, as he'd suspected, with all kinds of buttons and extras. Shifters were allowed to have only old models, recycled, most of the features disabled. Not that some Shifters didn't futz with them on the sly.

Liam started punching buttons. "I'm programming in my private number. For you only. If you need something, you call me. Any time of the day or night."

Kim watched as he tucked the cell phone back into her briefcase. "Anytime?"

"Anytime."

"What if I call every hour to check on your progress?"

"Then you do."

Her brows rose. "You trust me a lot."

"Because I'm asking you to trust me."

Kim chewed on her lip, making it red and cute. "I suppose I can see that." She held out her hand. "Thank you for your help, Mr. Morrissey. I'll be in touch."

Liam put his arm around her waist and turned her around. "I'm not leaving, love. I'm walking you back to your car."

"Why? It's only a few blocks away."

"I told you, when you're here, you're under my protection. Do you think that means I'd abandon you right here on the sidewalk?"

"I haven't the faintest idea what you mean."

"I mean I'm walking you to your car."

She made a noise of exasperation. "Whatever."

Liam wanted to laugh. She was adorable, his fox terrier. And determined.

And bloody inconvenient. The phone call had been from his father, telling Liam news he'd been waiting to hear. Ms. Lawyer needed to get out of Shiftertown. Liam and Sean suddenly had other things they needed to take care of.

Liam liked Kim's curves against his body as they walked, her narrow waist under his hand. She didn't try to break away from him, resigned, it seemed, to let him walk with his arm around her. As if they were a couple, in human terms.

Something warmed inside him, a space filling. Liam abruptly cut off the feeling. He could not afford to get involved with her. Protect her, yes; enjoy her, no. No matter how tempting she was.

Kim was breathing rapidly at their pace, her ridiculously

high heels slowing her down. He wished she'd kick off her shoes and peel off her stockings and walk barefoot in the grass. He imagined her strolling along beside him, shoes in hand, a smile on her face.

Too soon they reached her car, a black two-door Mustang. The car chirped as she pushed the button to unlock it.

Liam pulled her into another hug. Kim resisted again, but he scooped her against him, letting his mouth rest on the curve of her neck. She was warm, her skin salty, her pulse beating under his lips.

"Good-bye then, Kim. You take care."

He meant it. There was danger out there, and Brian's troubles were only part of it.

Kim took the card from her pocket that she'd tried to hand him earlier. "You'll call my office as soon as you have anything for me, right? Anything at all?"

Liam turned the card around in his fingers, savoring the feel of the raised letters of her name. "Of course, love."

"Even if you don't think it's relevant?"

He didn't bother to answer. Liam opened the car door for her, and Kim gave him a flustered look before tossing her briefcase inside.

Liam smoothed her hair from her face. He could stand all day looking at her, breathing in her scent, touching her sleek hair.

He let her go. He wasn't allowed to have her, no matter that he was hot and hard for her. She was beautiful, but not for him.

Kim gave him a smile, one that heated his blood, and slid into her driver's seat. She cranked the engine, let it roar to life, then reached over to switch the AC to high.

She rolled down the window, sending a trickle of cool air over his skin. "Thanks, Liam," she said. "I don't mean to sound ungrateful. I'm just worried."

"We all are, love." He stood up, patted the roof of the car. "You go on, now."

The window slid silently upward. Kim gave him one last nervous smile, then pulled the car onto the street. The taillights flashed red before she turned a corner, and then she was gone.

Liam might never see her again. The emptiness of that hit him.

No, that wouldn't happen. She was under his protection now. He had her phone number and her address. He'd make sure she'd need to speak to him again, and he'd make sure she had to see him in person to do it.

When Liam reached home after picking up Sean from Sandra's, their father Dylan was there. Three generations of males lived in the Morrisseys' two-story bungalow—father, two sons, and Liam's nephew, Connor.

Connor was twenty, tall and lanky, still a cub by Shifter standards. By human standards, he was old enough to go to college, and Connor had been attending a community college this year. Shifters weren't allowed to apply to the prestigious UT Austin, but it had been voted to allow them some college-level education. No degrees. Wouldn't want Shifters taking over professional jobs or learning enough to be a threat.

Connor's classes were out for the summer, and he passed the time catching up on DVDs. Laws forbade Shifters access to TiVo or premium cable for some reason, so movie rental outlets near Shiftertown did big business. Connor was watching *The Howling* and laughing his ass off.

"You'll have to go with him, Liam," Dylan said as soon as Liam walked in, continuing the conversation he'd had with Liam on the phone.

Liam gave a grim nod as he got himself a Guinness from the refrigerator. Dylan had told him that Fergus's trackers located a feral Shifter east of town, one that had slaughtered a Shifter woman and her cubs a few nights ago.

May hell rot all feral Shifters, Liam thought. He and Sean had found the bodies, a devastating sight that made his heart ache. As Guardian, it was Sean's duty to dispatch the feral, but Liam was looking forward to exacting some justice of his own. Besides, no way he'd let his brother face the attacker alone. Not after what had happened to Kenny.

"I'll go too," Connor said. He'd come silently out of the living room and leaned against the breakfast bar in the kitchen. "If it's a simple takedown."

Dylan gave Connor a look of compassion. Dylan's dark hair had gone gray at the temples in the last few years, finally making him look older than his sons. But a Shifter's eyes, not his human shell, betrayed his age. Dylan's eyes had seen much.

"No, Connor."

"I'm not a cub anymore, and I need to learn to fight these bastards."

Connor's father, Kenny, had been ripped to shreds by a feral Shifter. Their family had avenged the death long ago, but Connor had been too young to participate. The need for personal vengeance burned in him. But not only did Connor look twenty, he *was* twenty in human years. His fighting ability would take another decade or so to hone.

Liam drew his lanky nephew into a hug. "Like you said, lad, it's a simple takedown. We'll get him and go out for pizza." Liam kept his voice light, though he was buzzing with adrenaline. He was more than ready to get on with it.

Connor rolled his eyes as Liam released him. "You and Sean are so condescending it makes me sick. You have human scent all over you, Liam. What have you been up to?"

Sean grinned as he pulled a beer out of the refrigerator. "You should have seen him. He meets this human lady, and ten minutes later he's massaging her feet. He wouldn't leave her alone."

Liam threw his bottle cap at him. Sean snatched the cap out of the air and threw it back.

"She needs protecting," Liam said, catching the cap in turn and tossing it to the counter. "She's busting her ass for Shifters, the little idiot."

"Brave for a human," Dylan said. He was the only one in the room who didn't look amused.

"She's brave, but she's innocent. I scent-marked her so other Shifters will leave her the hell alone. They'll know that if they bother her, they answer to me. That goes for Fergus's thugs too."

Dylan watched him closely, and Liam pretended not to hold his breath as he drank his beer. Whose side would Dylan take? The clan leader's? Or Liam's? It was never certain.

Dylan gave Liam a slow nod. "If Fergus asks, I'll tell him I sanctioned it."

Liam relaxed. He went to his father and clasped his shoulder in thanks, then returned to the refrigerator. "We might as well eat while we wait. How about old-fashioned burgers on the grill?"

"Grand idea." Sean sauntered into the living room and threw himself on the couch. He crossed his feet and leaned his head back on his folded hands. "Make mine medium rare and put a slice of cheese on it, why don't you?"

Connor sprawled on the floor and took the DVD off Pause. "Rare for me, Liam."

"Gobshites," Liam growled, but he pulled the meat out of the freezer and stuck it in the microwave to thaw.

As he started up the grill outside and formed the burgers, leaving out all the onions and salt and crap that humans littered their meat with, he thought about Kim. How she smelled, how she felt. How her blue eyes could open so wide that her lashes curled against her skin. Her dark hair had gleamed in the sunlight, revealing golden highlights.

He wondered what she was doing now. Back at her office, hunched over a desk? Talking to Brian at the jail? Reading thick law books to see what she could do for a Shifter?

She'd go home soon. Liam had easily found where she lived when her secretary had contacted him earlier this week. A simple computer search had sufficed, even on dial-up—no cable modems for Shifters. Why the human government thought not allowing Shifters cable or wireless or good cell phones would slow down their communications, he didn't know. Humans had weird ideas.

What would Kim do when she got home? Peel off that severe gray suit, most likely. Would she wear sexy underwear beneath it? Did all-work-and-no-play Kim Fraser buy herself shimmering lingerie?

Liam pictured her in a silk camisole that barely contained her lush breasts, maybe bikini panties baring most of her butt. Or not a camisole, but a tiny lace bra that pushed her breasts up and barely covered her nipples. Stockings, not panty hose. With a garter belt. She'd walk around her house in that, loosening up after work, pouring herself a glass of wine. Or maybe she was a down-home Texas girl who'd reach for a cold beer.

Liam imagined the beads of moisture on the beer bottle in the humid summer evening. Kim's lips would skim the bottle's mouth until she upended it and poured a cool stream of beer down her throat.

He imagined it so vividly that Sean's and Connor's burgers traveled way past rare to well done before Liam could rescue them.

K im got out of her leisurely bath and went back to her bedroom with one towel around her torso and the other turbaned over her hair.

She'd gotten used to living by herself—unless Abel came over—no parents or siblings or anyone else. No dogs or cats, either, because she was gone most of the day, and she didn't want to subject a pet to so much neglect.

Or maybe she just didn't want to mourn when it grew old, died, and left another hole in her life.

Tonight she felt the emptiness. She'd tried to fill it by e-mailing her friend Silas, a Pulitzer Prize–winning journalist doing research for a documentary on Shifters, and then taking a luxurious soak. She'd tried to lose herself in a delicious novel in the tub, but her thoughts kept drifting and she gave up.

She reached for an emery board and started sanding her nails. Maybe she felt the emptiness because in Shiftertown she'd noticed the fullness. The kids playing in the front yards, neighbors waving at Sean and Liam, the easy bond between the two brothers.

She thought about how she'd spilled her guts to Liam and let him massage her aching feet. The rubbing had felt *good*. She could still feel his touch, the warmth, the sensual firmness of his strong fingers.

Even better had been his lips on her neck. The man was *hot*. She had no idea whether Shifters did it like humans, but she knew that if she were a Shifter woman, she'd be working to get him into bed.

Strangest of all, Liam had listened to her. Kim had told him more in ten minutes than she'd told Abel in the year she'd been dating him.

Did that say something about Liam or something about Abel?

Kim set down the emery board and picked up her cell phone. She punched Abel's number and listened to his phone ring.

"Yes?" he answered. He sounded rushed.

"Hey, it's me."

"Kim?" He sounded baffled. "What is it? Was I supposed to meet you tonight?"

"No. I just thought we could talk."

"Oh." Pause as he rustled something on the other end

of the phone. "Can I call you back? I'm in the middle of about ten things."

Kim waited for her anger to come. But she felt—nothing. "Sure."

"Tomorrow. Sleep tight, honey." *Click*.

"Yeah. Sweet dreams, babe." Kim keyed off the phone and dropped it on the table. Abel was a workaholic trying to make a name for himself at the firm. Of course he was in the middle of ten things. He always was.

Maybe it's time to cut that tie, a little voice in the back of her mind said. *Maybe it's beyond time.*

You know you didn't think that until you met Liam . . .

Kim picked up the phone again and scrolled to where Liam had typed in his name and number. It looked so normal, the four letters of his name, then an area code and seven-digit phone number like everyone else had.

You call me, any time of the day or night.

Had he really meant that? Or was it a mere platitude? *Call me, honey. Except when I'm busy, watching TV, out with my friends, or not interested in you right now.*

Just to be a pain in the ass, Kim pressed the button to call the number. One ring, and then Liam's warm voice filled her ear.

"Kim!" As though this was the best call he'd received all day. "You all right, love?"

"Yes, I'm fine," Kim said, her entire body warming. "I was . . ."

"Checking to see if I'd answer?" Liam's amusement came across loud and clear.

"Something like that. How's Sandra doing?"

"Better. Sean talked to her. You're not still working, are you?"

"I'm always working, Liam. Cases don't keep a nine-to-five schedule."

His chuckle sent a shiver down her spine. "You need to stop now and again, sweetheart. Take it from me. I know."

Kim realized. "Oh, you're at work now, aren't you? At the bar. I'm sorry, I shouldn't have interrupted."

"I told you, love. Anytime. You rest easy, now."

Take that, Abel. "Thanks, Liam. You too."

A pause. It stretched on.

"You still there?" she asked.

"Yes." He sounded suddenly subdued. "Good night, Kim. Call me again tomorrow, all right?"

She promised to, clicked off the phone, and held it to her lips. Her own boyfriend might or might not remember to call her back, but this Shifter had sounded happy to hear from her, even if he was up to his butt in bar receipts. She wasn't sure whether that made her feel good or lonelier than ever.

CHAPTER FOUR

Liam slid his phone into his belt as he mounted his Harley, waiting for Sean to join him. Kim's voice touched the raw sexual being inside him, the one that had wanted to unfasten her straining blouse buttons in his office. Even more warming was the thought that she'd made the choice to call him.

He'd stopped himself from asking, *What are you doing right now? What are you wearing? Or not wearing?*

Liam thought again of the directions to Kim's house he'd easily brought up on a computer search. Maybe after this takedown, he'd drive out there to check up on her. Maybe she'd let him in, and maybe he could persuade her up to her bedroom for another foot massage . . .

"Everything all right?" Sean asked as he straddled the bike behind Liam.

Liam shifted uncomfortably, willing his growing hard-on to calm down. "It's fine. Why wouldn't it be?"

"Because that thing in your pants looks painful."

Liam never found it easy to lie to his brother. "I was talking to Kim."

Sean started to laugh. He moved the sword strapped to his back to a comfortable position, then slid his arms around Liam's waist. "You have it bad, Liam. Give up the dream and go shag a pretty Shifter. Annie maybe."

Liam started the bike. "She works at the bar now. I never get involved with the help."

"I didn't say get involved. I said shag her. She's been happy to oblige you in the past."

"It's you she wants, Sean. I see her sweet gaze following your ass."

"Can we get a move on? I'd like to make this kill and be done with it."

Liam didn't reply. He knew Sean needed to calm his nerves, and stirring up his big brother was his favorite method.

Liam glided the bike, a Harley he'd bought for next to nothing and restored, into the street, then turned the corner and drove out of Shiftertown. He headed through crowded streets to the highway that would take them east out of the city. In his rearview mirrors, the skyline of downtown Austin glowed against the dark sky, the lit-up dome of the capitol a yellow beacon.

They turned down an inky-black road past Bastrop and rode across open country. Fergus's trackers had called right after Liam and Sean had finished their burgers, saying they'd followed the feral to some abandoned warehouses way east of town. The feral had made camp there, and the shit wasn't going anywhere, so could Sean and Liam please bestir themselves and come do their jobs?

If the trackers ran true to form, Liam knew they wouldn't show their asses if there was any kind of fight. They'd hightail it out of there as soon as Liam and Sean arrived. It was the trackers' job only to point the way, after all.

Liam parked well down the road from the warehouse, he and Sean doing the last stretch on foot. A chain-link fence surrounded the property of the once-prosperous business, but the flimsy barrier had been sliced open in plenty of places, with one whole section of it knocked flat. Crickets chirped in loud profusion outside the fence, but once Liam and Sean stepped over the fallen chain link, all animal noises ceased.

Liam smelled the stench right after that. Even a human would notice it, but to a Shifter the smell was like a body blow. Liam felt his lips curl back, his teeth elongate into fangs.

He tried to suppress his killing instinct, but it wasn't easy. Dylan seemed to think he and Sean would come out here and solve the problem in cool detachment. But Dylan hadn't seen the Shifter woman's body, hadn't found her children. Liam wanted to savage, no offers of mercy. So did Sean, probably even more than Liam did.

Without a word, the brothers separated, Sean unstrapping the sword from his back. Liam moved noiselessly through the shadows of the warehouse and stepped through a door that gaped open to the night.

The stench made him gag. Liam's cat's eyes adjusted to the dark, and he walked forward, scanning each sable shadow.

Before Liam had made it halfway across the warehouse floor, the feral stepped forward to meet him. He didn't look as wild as Liam had thought he would. He was dressed in jeans and a T-shirt, sweat-soaked in the humid Texas night. Except for being caked with dirt, not wearing a Collar, and his oppressive BO, he looked like any other Shifter from Shiftertown. Of course his neck was so black with filth, Liam wouldn't have been able to see a Collar if he had one.

"Don't you take baths, man?" Liam asked.

The Shifter snarled, his face elongating into something between human and wolf. A Lupine. Bloody wonderful.

"There's good soap nowadays," Liam went on. "Makes you sweet as a garden. You should try it. That is, if you're not busy killing wee ones like the bastard you are."

The Lupine grated, "Traitor. Collared pet."

"No, lad. Survivor. We don't go around murdering anymore, didn't you hear? Especially not the cubs, and damn you don't know how much I want to kill you for that."

"I wanted the woman. Not her spawn by another Shifter."

"Those days are over, lick-brain." Liam took the Collar out of his pocket, feeling the strength of the steel, the bite of magic that wound through it. "I'm offering you this chance because my father makes me play by the rules, no matter what. Me, I'd rather kill you." He stepped forward. "One size fits all. Come on, take it like a man."

"I'm not a man. Neither are you. Are you too weak to fight me, Feline?"

"No," Liam said. "But you have two choices. Face me, or face the Guardian."

The other Shifter tensed. "The Guardian isn't here."

"Yes, he is." Sean stepped out of the shadows behind the Shifter. He drew the broadsword, its blade ringing in the still air.

The Shifter swung to Sean. He inhaled sharply, then whirled back to Liam and did the sniff-test again.

"I only smelled . . ." The Shifter broke off, his light blue wolf eyes fixed on Liam.

Liam held out the Collar, still offering. "You take the Collar, I might resist killing you. Maybe you didn't understand what you were doing. I have about two brain cells that believe that. You refuse . . . Well, let's just say our Sean is even more pissed at you than I am."

Liam felt the air contract as the man shifted all the way. He didn't bother taking off his clothes; he let them fray as his wolf's body split the fabric. Sean waited, and Liam wondered if the Lupine understood how much Sean was holding back. The brothers' instructions were to kill the feral only as a last resort.

The wolf shook off the remains of the clothes, his eyes filled with rage. Liam didn't move. "Come on, lad. Shiftertown pretty much wants you dead without quarter. Dylan convinced me to give you a chance. Don't throw that away."

The wolf snarled. He rose on his hind legs, returning to human form. Now he was naked, not a pretty sight.

"I smell it on you." His nostrils flared in contempt. "A human. You scent-marked a human woman." How the Shifter could smell anything beyond his own stink, Liam didn't know, but his blood ran cold. "Abomination," the Shifter hissed.

"You know big words, do you?" Liam asked. "Let me give you some short ones: *Take the fucking Collar.*"

With a crackle of bones, the Shifter morphed back into a wolf. Liam braced himself for the attack, but the wolf abruptly whirled and sprinted in the other direction.

Sean was there, his sword biting into the Shifter's side. The wolf didn't slow. He howled, leapt out of the warehouse, and ran off into the night.

"Shit." Sean brought the sword up again. "Idiot!"

He could have meant Liam, the Shifter, or himself. Liam balled his fists as fear poured through him. "Bloody hell, he's going to track her."

"What are you talking about?"

"Kim. He smelled her on me."

"He's been wounded by the Guardian's sword. He won't get far. We'll ride after him and finish it."

"Not wounded enough." The feral had seemed unusually strong—he must have been to kill a Shifter female guarding her cubs. Shifter females didn't go down easily, and one protecting her precious young would fight twice as hard. Liam could taste the feral's adrenaline spike in the air, a more vicious tang than it should have had. Something was wrong with him that sharply ramped up Liam's fear.

Liam started swiftly out of the warehouse, running by the time he hit the weed-infested parking lot.

"Liam." Sean sprinted after him. "If he makes it, he'll track the scent back to Shiftertown first, and Dad will make short work of him."

"Not if he's as good as I think he is. He'll track both my scent and hers. Kim took that double-scent home with her."

He started the bike, and as soon as Sean leapt on he roared away. Sean might be right, and the feral Shifter might go nowhere near Kim, but Liam couldn't take that chance.

Liam raced the bike back down the highway to the city, then north on the freeway. He dove off and angled west, through the main city, circling fine homes that clung to the hillside above the river. The night was hot and dank, but the air rushing past the bike felt chilled.

He thought of the red dot on the computer map that indicated Kim's house. To him, the red dot was a target, an announcement of her vulnerability. He needed to warn her, protect her, *hold her, taste her . . .*

If it wasn't too late.

CHAPTER FIVE

A muffled tinkle of broken glass trickled from the kitchen downstairs. At first Kim rolled over in bed, not paying attention. This was a safe neighborhood, never any break-ins.

When hinges of the kitchen door squeaked, she sat up straight.

Kim hadn't been asleep. She'd been staring at the dark ceiling for the last hour, absorbed in thoughts of Liam. How his warm, friendly voice tickled her ear, how the corners of his eyes crinkled when he smiled, how nice his butt looked in those tight jeans. Now her heart pounded, adrenaline pumping as she heard someone moving around her kitchen.

Should she trust her martial arts classes? In her baby-doll nightie?

Screw that. The magic numbers were 911.

Kim lifted her cell phone from the nightstand, thumb reaching for the numbers. She smelled a sudden sour odor, and then the phone flew across the room and shattered against the wall.

Before she could scream, strong hands lifted her by the neck. Kim found herself staring into white-blue eyes in a hard male face that had half changed to a wolfish form. Lips lifted from pointed canines, and the breath that washed over her smelled like rotten meat. Kim fought frantically as the half-shifted man's hands cut off her air, claws raking hot pain. He was going to kill her. Through her dimming vision she realized that this Shifter wore no Collar.

Then suddenly she was free. Kim crashed back into the bed, gasping for breath, as the Shifter was ripped from her. She dragged her hair out of her face in time to see a wildcat slam the Shifter to her bedroom floor. Snarling filled the room, not angry doggy snarling, but the real thing, wild animals in red-hot fury.

Sean Morrissey stood inside Kim's bedroom doorway, holding a broadsword that gleamed with light of its own. Sean's eyes were midnight dark and full of rage. His gaze fixed on the fight in the middle of the floor, but he didn't rush to interfere. He watched, waiting.

The creatures upended Kim's dresser and nightstand and shoved her bed across the room like it was a cardboard box. Sean didn't *do* anything, just stood there with the sword ready. Kim heard herself shouting, but her words were lost in the animal screams as the two creatures fought.

The wildcat—ears back, canines extended—snapped its jaw across the wolf's throat. The wolf yelped once. Its paws scrabbled hard against the wildcat's body, drawing blood, before the wolf's head lolled to the side and it fell to the carpet, lifeless. The wildcat sat back, sides heaving, watching the corpse as though expecting it to get up again.

Kim fought the urge to laugh hysterically. *Excuse me but there's a deceased wolf and a wildcat in my bedroom!* She wasn't certain what kind of wildcat it was—tawny like a cougar, muscled like a leopard, with a hint of stripe like a tiger. It also had the huge jaws and massive paws of a male lion. But the cat didn't look weird, like a mishmash. It was lithe, beautiful, powerful.

Sean finally moved. The wildcat backed off as Sean raised the sword, then drove its point into the dead wolf's chest. The wolf shimmered, became the half-shifted man who'd attacked Kim, then slowly disintegrated to ash. At the same time, the wildcat rose on its hind feet and flowed back into the form of a very naked Liam Morrissey.

Mmm, he looks good, the back of Kim's mind said. Rippling muscles, smooth skin, wiry dark hair spreading across his chest. Tight abdomen, massive thighs, huge . . . *Oh, man.*

As soon as air poured back into Kim's lungs, screams hurtled out of her mouth. She tried to stop them, but hysterical reaction grabbed her and wrung her in its grip.

Liam's big body was next to her on the bed, his hand covering her mouth. "Hush, now, love. It's over."

Delayed shock. Understandable. I'll be all right.

Liam's hand was warm, somehow comforting, even though he was trying to keep her quiet. After a moment he gave her an inquiring look, and she nodded, indicating she'd finished screaming. Liam lifted his hand away, and Kim dragged in a deep breath, inhaling his heady male scent.

"Liam, man, get yourself dressed," Sean said. "You'll scare the woman."

"No, it's all right." Kim closed her eyes, felt Liam's bare arms and legs encircling hers. Nope, didn't bother her at all. She opened her eyes again and looked at Liam. "What the *hell* just happened?"

"We killed him," Liam said. "We had no choice. The bastard would have killed you."

"Is that what happens to Shifters? They dissolve into dust, like vampires on TV?"

Sean didn't answer, standing stoically with the sword still pointed at the floor.

"No." Liam eased himself away from Kim. She wanted to reach for him again, have him enclose her back into that so very nice, naked embrace. "Only the ones Sean runs through with that sword. Sean is our Guardian."

Sean's eyes narrowed. "Liam."

"What's a Guardian?" More nonverbal cues flew between the brothers, not telepathy, but body language so subtle she couldn't catch it all, let alone understand it.

"A protector," Liam said. "Of Shiftertown, in this case."

"I didn't see a Collar on the Shifter." Kim shivered suddenly, violently. "I was going to die, wasn't I?"

"He would have killed you. He was feral. That means he was dangerous, to you, to me, to our families. He'd already killed a Shifter female and her children."

Kim gaped. "Wait, I heard about the Shifter woman dying. I thought she and her kids were killed in a car accident on a back highway in Hill Country. Weren't they?"

"No, lass." Liam looked so sad. Sean stood apart, incongruous in jeans and T-shirt with the medieval-looking sword. "She was murdered. Sean and me, we put her body in her car and pushed it into that ditch and set it alight."

"Why?" Kim got off the bed. She realized all she wore was a short, silky baby-doll, and she grabbed for the robe she'd tossed to a chair. "Why not report the crime and have the Shifter brought in?"

"Because it's our responsibility." Liam's gaze took in her body as she hastily shrugged on the robe, but his voice rang with anger. Sean gave a nod of agreement.

"No, it isn't," Kim said. "Shifters live in the human world now—that means human law prevails. You signed the agreement. The Shifter should have been arrested and tried like anyone else, not killed vigilante-style by you and Sean."

She ran out of breath. The two men weren't listening to her but looking at each other, still talking without talking. The weight of the Shifter's death pressed on the room.

Finally Sean shook his head and slid his sword into a leather sheath. "You're effing crazy, Liam, you know? You do what you have to, I'm reporting in to Dad."

"Do that. Take my bike."

"What, you think I'd be hitching a ride with a sword strapped to my back? I'll see you at home."

With a final scowl, Sean turned and left the room, carrying the sword by its sheathed blade. Kim heard him on the stairs, and then the back door slammed beneath them, shaking the house.

"Come on." Liam got up, still naked and unembarrassed about it. "Get dressed and go downstairs. I'll cook you some dinner—you look peaky."

"The Shifter—he's . . ." Kim swallowed. "All over my carpet." Gray dust coated the rug she'd bought at an antique store out in Fredericksburg. "Ew."

Liam enfolded her in his arms and kissed her neck, his warmth like a blanket on her cold skin. "I'll take care of this, love. Go on downstairs and wait for me."

Kim didn't want to. She wanted to stay here for a while and run her hands along Liam's broad, strong shoulders. His body was solid and reassuring, and so was his smile. She could stand here in his arms all damned night.

Liam kissed her neck again. "You'll be all right. Go on, now."

Kim was never sure how she made herself back away, grab her clothes, and scoot across the hall to her guest bedroom to change. As she made her way downstairs, she strained to hear what Liam did in her bedroom, but all was silent.

Liam found his clothes where he'd thrown them off in Kim's kitchen and slid them on. His adrenaline was still high, his heart pumping hard and fast. He wanted to run, hunt, grab Kim and have unbridled sex with her. Containing himself wasn't easy, but his body running so hot would continue to stave off the pain that was coming. And then he'd pay. Damn, would he pay.

Kim hunched on a sofa on the other side of the breakfast bar. She had no kitchen table and chairs; instead, a couple of stools stood at the counter, and she'd filled the rest of the room with a couch and two comfortable-looking chairs.

Her loose hair straggled over the blouse she'd put on, her blue eyes enormous as she watched Liam dress. He'd cleaned himself up in her bathroom after he'd vacuumed what was left of the feral Shifter from the rug. The bugger wouldn't come out all the way out, though.

"You'll have to send that carpet out for cleaning," he said.

Kim whitened. "Oh, God."

"I'll do it for you. It's my fault the shite came here at all."

"Why do you keep saying it's your fault? Not everything is your responsibility. You live in the human world now."

She was trying to hold on to what she knew, what she'd been told. Humans liked to comfort themselves like that.

"It's my responsibility because I let you come to Shiftertown. The feral smelled your scent on me and decided to hurt me by hurting you. That way, even if he died, he'd know I'd be grieving. It's the feral way—take vengeance on your enemy even while they're killing you." Liam shook his head as he moved to the refrigerator. "I've never seen a Shifter move that fast, or be able to track that quickly. There was something wrong with him."

That bothered him more than he cared to admit. Ferals, ironically, were weaker than Shifters with Collars, because Collared Shifters were well fed, well rested, and had plenty of time to exercise. But this feral had been fast and had brushed off Sean's first sword thrust as though it were an insect bite.

Kim shivered. "Are there any more of them out there?"

Liam didn't know, and that bothered him more than he cared to let on, but he made his tone reassuring. "Shouldn't be. We keep track of the ferals pretty well." Or so Fergus claimed. The refrigerator's shelves were bare except for a few containers of yogurt and a rubber-banded bunch of greens. "You have no food, woman."

"It's in the freezer."

That compartment revealed stacks of boxed frozen meals, all with "Lite" or "Low-calorie" written on them. "This isn't food," Liam said. "It's a travesty."

"I have to watch my weight."

Liam remembered how Kim had looked in her wisp of a nightie—lovely breasts, sweet waist, and thighs he wanted to lick. "I don't mind watching it for you, love. There's nothing wrong with your body."

She went a deep shade of red, and Liam slammed the freezer door. "I can't cook you up my famous mile-high pancakes with this crap. Come on. I'll take you out for some real food."

"I can't go anywhere. My back door is broken."

Two small panes had been smashed, the lock ripped out. "I'll take care of that."

Liam unhooked his cell phone and made some calls. Voices on the other end promised to come and replace the glass and fix the lock in half an hour. *"Does the human woman have any beer?"*

"Bring your own," Liam growled and clicked off the phone.

Kim had a stunned look on her face. "What are you doing?"

"I keep telling you, sweetheart, it's my fault the bastard attacked you. I have friends who will take care of things, as a favor to me."

"Shifter friends."

"What other kind? Come on, we'll leave them to it."

Liam somehow convinced her to walk out of the house

and open the garage, but he took the car keys from Kim's shaking hands and drove her back to Shiftertown himself.

Sean was right, Liam was effing crazy, but he had to do this. Kim needed protecting, but then, so did the Shifters. Liam would have to combine the two needs. Dylan would be livid, but Liam also had the feeling that Dylan would understand. Fergus, now . . . Well, Liam would deal with Fergus when he had to.

"This is where you work," Kim said, as Liam parked behind the bar in the tiny space reserved for him.

"Well spotted, love. They do a mean chicken-fried steak."

Kim's eyes flared with sudden hunger. Did she starve herself, the little sweetheart? She had a man, she'd said. Why didn't the idiot take care of her?

The bar was full when they walked in. Shifters predominated the crowd, with a handful of humans who'd either become friends with Shifters, had come in to gawk, or were Shifter groupies. Most patrons hovered at the long wraparound bar, but Liam guided Kim to an empty booth and sat her down.

Liam's heart was thumping, his adrenaline still high. He'd have to endure the agony sooner or later, but he hoped it held off long enough for him to enjoy his meal.

"Two chicken-fried steaks, Annie, and a mess of chips."

The tall, svelte Shifter woman who'd come to wait on them rolled her eyes. "We call them french fries over here, Liam. I tell you all the time. Not chips."

"I don't see anyone French in this bar," Liam said, continuing the usual banter between himself and Annie.

"The new cook is Cajun. Close enough."

"And we'll need something to drink," Liam said. "What will you have, Kim?"

"White wine?"

White wine. She was precious. "You don't want to drink the wine here. Bring me a pint of plain, Annie."

"Guinness," Annie said, noting it on her pad. "For you, miss?"

"A Tecate," Kim said. She glared at Liam. "With a lime, please."

"You got it." Annie whisked away, her tight barmaid shorts clinging to her trim behind. Every male in the bar turned to watch her pass, but once she'd gone their gazes swiveled back to Kim.

"Why is everyone staring at me?" Kim whispered. "I'm not the only human here."

But she was the only one scent-marked. Every Shifter, male and female, had caught what Liam had done. Nostrils widened, eyes flickered in acknowledgment. Kim belonged to Liam, and anyone who bothered her would answer to Liam. Message sent and received.

"I'm looking after you, and they know it."

"Why did you want to come here? We passed two IHOPs on the way."

"It's safer."

Kim glanced around. "For you or for me?"

"For both of us."

He quieted as Annie set down one sweating bottle of Guinness and one of Tecate, lime firmly wedged into the opening.

"Are you going to explain why you didn't call the police on that Shifter?" Kim shoved her lime entirely into the liquid and lifted the bottle to drink. Her tongue came out and touched the bottle's opening before her lips closed around it.

Goddess help me, it's hot in here.

Liam clenched his beer bottle, but the cold bite on his palm did nothing to calm him. "What do you think would happen if your human police found out he was on the loose?" he asked. "Shifters would be hunted, and the hunters not too worried about whether they brought down a Collared Shifter or a feral. Just so long as they got one."

"All right, I can see that. With one Shifter already on trial, people would freak if another one went crazy." Kim leaned forward, letting Liam see that this blouse didn't stay fastened any better than the last one had. "Do you think *he* killed the girl Brian is supposed to have murdered?"

"I wish it could be that easy. We weren't aware of him until a few nights ago, when he killed the Shifter woman. He wasn't around before that. Brian's girlfriend died months ago."

"How do you know he wasn't here?" She wrinkled her nose. "Of course, you'd have remembered smelling him."

Liam acknowledged that with a laugh.

"What did you mean by 'Collared Shifters'?" Kim went on. "Sounds like collard greens. Before tonight, I thought all Shifters wore Collars. It's the law."

This was getting complicated. Liam sifted through what was safe to tell her. Hell, none of this was safe. "Not all Shifters took the Collar. Your human government knows that, but they keep it to themselves."

Kim's slim fingers toyed with her beer bottle, but she didn't drink again. She watched him with intelligent eyes. Beautiful eyes. *Damn, it's been way too long . . .*

"You make it sound like wearing the Collar is a choice."

"It is, love," Liam said. "It's a choice we were given twenty years ago, and we made it. Most of us. Some Shifters chose to remain wild."

"You mean free."

"Hunted. Dying. Pushed out. We might have survived maybe five more years if we hadn't taken the Collars."

"Are you saying you chose subjugation to save yourselves?"

Liam shrugged, pretending to agree. "Our lines were dying out. We weren't fertile, and children that managed to get born often didn't last their first year. Now look at us."

Kim moved her gaze from him to the filled room. At the bar Jordie Ross stood with his four sons, all tall and bulky, talking and laughing loudly. Their mother had survived their births—she was sitting in a booth on the other side of the room with a couple of friends.

Another Shifter woman held her hand on her swelling belly while her husband kept a protective arm around her. She was prudently drinking bottled water, leaning back against her husband.

"Liam." A tall figure cut his vision. "Nice human you've got there."

Liam looked up and scowled. "Ellison. Get lost, man. I'm trying to convince her that Shifters are civilized."

The tall man laughed. As usual, Ellison wore a black button-up shirt and jeans, cowboy boots, and big hat. He loved Texas, had adopted the state when his Shifter clan relocated from Colorado. Some of his clan missed the cool air of the Rockies, but Ellison Rowe embraced Texas Hill Country, even with its humidity, mosquitoes, bad traffic, and state congressmen.

"Don't believe him." Ellison thunked into the booth next to Liam and smiled at Kim. "Liam doesn't have a civilized bone in his body." Even Ellison's grin was wolfish.

"I'm sure she's comforted, hearing that from a Lupine."

"Lupine?" Kim wrinkled her brow. "I heard you say that before."

"Means I'm a wolf, baby," Ellison said. "Not a pussycat."

Kim's eyes took on a touch of fear. Liam reached across and touched her hand. "It's all right. He's a good wolf."

"Don't tell her that. I'm the Big, *Bad* Wolf."

"Like the feral Shifter," Kim said softly.

Ellison instantly lost his grin. "What?"

Liam shot Kim a warning look. "A rogue. I took care of it."

"He was a wolf? *Damn*. I'm sorry, Liam."

"I said I took care of it."

Ellison frowned, his big body folding in on itself, his sunny nature dimming.

"Two chicken-fried steaks, extra gravy," Annie said, depositing the food in front of them. "And a mess of fries. Anything else you need?"

"Bring me a beer, honey." Ellison glanced at Kim's and Liam's bottles. "A good old-fashioned American beer, nothing Irish, Mexican, or German."

"We got some strawberry blonde ale in the back," Annie said. "Made right here in Austin."

She swished away before Ellison could protest. "Aw, I *hate* microbrew. Yuppie beer."

"Then I won't invite you to the annual microbrew tasting party," Kim said, as Liam munched a crispy, hot chip. They were *chips*, damn it. What asshole came up with *french fries?* "Brewers from around the county set up booths and give free tastings all day long. You have to be invited, but I'm allowed to bring guests."

Ellison's face fell. "Well, maybe it's not so bad. Some of these brews are downright good."

Liam laughed at him, but his heart warmed. Kim was no wilting flower. She was scared, angry, uncertain, and unhappy, but she wasn't going to hunch in on herself and cry.

Good. She needed to be strong to take Shifters. She'd have to take the lot of them, now, because she wouldn't be going home tonight.

CHAPTER SIX

Kim ate hungrily. Getting attacked and watching her attacker die did that to a girl.

This was all so weird. The cowboy sitting next to Liam, sipping his pale beer while watching Liam put away his chicken-fried steak, made jokes, but his eyes were wary, watchful—going from dark blue to light and back again as he and Liam talked.

Ellison seemed very upset that the feral had been a wolf Shifter. Why? Because Liam and Sean, who'd killed him, were big cats? Kim didn't understand what difference that made. A Shifter was a Shifter. Wasn't he?

Kim sensed that she'd stumbled upon something with layers and layers of complexity. She'd been so confident she could help Brian, striking a blow for Shifter rights at the same time, but now she wondered at her ego. The more she'd learned about Shifters today, the more she realized how very little she knew.

Ellison eventually moved off to talk to others, taking his

microbrew with him. Kim wiped her mouth with the extra napkins Annie had brought. "Thank you. I guess I needed the food."

"A good meal with a good friend is one of the joys of life," Liam said, sounding like he meant it. "Even if it's in a Shifter bar."

Kim's chest felt suddenly hollow. She yearned for this kind of simplicity, but her life was chaotic and stressful and so damned busy. How long had it been since she and her girlfriends had met for a meal, to talk and catch up? To laugh and wallow in memories of friendship? Too long. One of them had moved out of state since the last time the group had met, and the others were caught up in their own lives. Kim hadn't talked to most of her friends for more than a minute in months. Silas was the only exception and that was only because of his interest in Brian's case for his documentary. But even his e-mails were brief.

She put down her fork. "I really should get back home. Your friends have probably repaired my door by now, and I have to work tomorrow."

"You're working on a Sunday?"

"I'll work at home, but I have a lot to do. Cases to prepare, appeals to file. Brian's only one of my responsibilities."

Liam piled his silverware on his plate, pushed his plate and hers aside, and clasped Kim's hands. His movements were jerky, and his skin was hot. "You need to come home with me first."

"Why?" Not that, with his hands warm on hers and his sexy blue eyes gazing at her, she wanted to argue much.

"Sean will have told Dad what happened, but Dad will want to hear your side of the story."

"My side of the story? I don't have a side. I saw what you saw."

"This is a Shifter problem. Dad needs all the information he can get."

Kim let herself squeeze his hands in return. "All right, but not for long. I really have work to do."

"Dance first?"

"Sorry?"

The jukebox was going full blast, some country music tune Ellison had keyed in. "I need to work off some energy. Are you too much of a city girl that you can't do a Texas two-step?"

"You're Irish," she said as he pulled her up. "Don't you— you know, jig?"

Liam laughed, a sound so warm that everyone around them who heard it smiled. His eyes crinkled, and his laugh drove out the lingering horror of the wolf Shifter's attack.

Something should bother Kim about what had happened— something more than dead Shifter wolf and Sean with his sword and Liam being a snarling wildcat, that is. She needed time to sit, think, let her adrenaline shut down while her brain took over.

Liam didn't want to let her shut down. He pulled her out of the booth and to the middle of the floor. Other couples were already dancing—very close—but they were Shifters, so Kim couldn't tell the difference between couples who were lovers and those who were friends. Shifters liked to touch.

Liam pulled Kim into an embrace, his feet finding the rhythm of the dance. Kim knew the steps, but she hadn't danced in a long time, and she moved stiffly.

Liam ran his hand along the curve of her waist. "Relax, darling. I'll take care of you."

Kim's eyes were so blue, Liam thought. If he were into poetry, he'd say *blue like an Irish sea.* But he hadn't seen Ireland in such a long time that he couldn't be sure if the waters around it were still so pure blue they would break your heart.

Kim set his already pounding heart to racing. Her lips were red, full, luscious. Liam didn't kiss—when he bedded women he was too busy to do any kissing, and besides, he and the female were usually in animal form. But touching Kim's lips with his suddenly seemed like a good idea.

His libido was getting ahead of his brains. This woman wasn't, and could never be, for Liam. She was here temporarily, dragged into Shifter troubles she didn't understand. She didn't understand how deeply she was in them, either. When she figured it out, she'd sure as hell not be in the mood for any kissing.

His libido told his brains to shut the hell up. Her scent was exciting, sweet. She looked up at him and smiled, and her small hands moved to his waist.

Warm supple woman slid against his body, and Liam's blood flowed toward his groin. He imagined her under him, hips lifting as he slid into her. Her blue eyes would close, her round breasts would press his chest, and her legs would rise to twine his waist.

Gods, he needed sex. After a fight he always ran in his cat form to get it out of his system, before he paid the price. He hadn't had the chance to run tonight, so his body urged him to do an even better thing, take this woman home and love her.

If he'd been doing what Sean suggested, having a good night's shag with a Shifter woman every night, Liam wouldn't be sweating now, fighting his urges and his Collar. He'd never, ever had urges to be with a human woman.

Then again, he'd never met Kim.

Liam pulled her closer, hands moving to her hips. *I'm the Shifter who doesn't need anyone, who puts the good of Shiftertown before everything else.*

Right.

Kim laughed. "I forgot how much I liked to dance," she said over the music.

"Doesn't your man ever take you out on the town?"

"Abel? We go to fancy dinners, usually with a group of lawyers he's trying to impress. No dancing."

"His name is Abel, is it?"

"Yeah, Abel Kane. Can you believe his parents named him that?"

"He could change it. I hear humans do that." As though a name were a mutable thing. Humans were crazy.

"He says people remember it," Kim said. "I guess he's right."

"But he doesn't dance."

Kim laughed. Apparently thinking of this boyfriend dancing was hilarious. "No, he doesn't dance. I didn't know Shifters did, either."

"We do a lot of things." Liam twirled her once, pulled her against him again, and then the song drew to a close.

Couples dispersed. Jordie Ross kissed his wife on her upturned lips, stroking his fingers over her throat. The fond look she gave Jordie as she walked back to her girlfriends stabbed through Liam's heart. His own parents had looked at each other like that once. So had Kenny and Sinead. Mates for life, they'd thought.

Liam kept hold of Kim's hand. "Time to go."

Kim's wariness returned as he led her out of the bar. "Go where?" she asked.

"Home."

"You mean your home." And his father. Would Liam's dad be elderly and kind, with the same blue eyes as his son and a warm smile, or a rigid patriarch who terrified every person who crossed the threshold?

Liam nodded silently, his eyes giving nothing away. His sudden quietness made Kim nervous, but then she thought about her own house waiting for her, how large and lonely it was.

The place had never warmed up again since Mark's death, no matter how hard she and her parents had tried. There'd been a hole in every Christmas celebration, every Easter dinner, every Halloween night's trek through the neighborhood. The family had gone through the rituals each year, realizing that rituals were unfulfilling when someone you loved was missing from them, but they'd been unable to do anything else. Kim had tried to liven up the house with remodeling a few years ago, having a party to celebrate, but while the house looked more modern, it was still empty.

Kim thought about Shiftertown, how alive it was, how these people had been forced to reside here but had made it bearable with the closeness of family and friends.

"I'd like to see where you live," she decided. "Even if I have to be interrogated by your father."

"He won't interrogate you." Liam's smile returned. "Like Ellison said, we're pussycats."

Kim wasn't sure what to make of that, but she followed him through the crowd that had gathered outside the doors and in the parking lot. They were mostly Shifters, laughing and talking and waiting for a chance to ooze into the packed interior.

The night had cooled, the humidity lessening. Overhead, stars poked through the lights of the city against vast blackness that stretched to eternity.

"What a nice night," Kim said. "Do you live far? Can we walk?"

How weird that she wanted to. In this city of cars, walking was what you did along Lake Austin or in Zilker Park or on Sixth Street on Saturday night. You didn't walk to actually get somewhere.

"It's not far," Liam said, "but we'll drive. It will be safer to leave your car inside Shiftertown than out here."

He had a point—this was a bad part of town. Liam drove again, and Kim was content to look out the window. This late, no kids lingered on the lawns, but the houses glowed with light. People sat out on lit porches to talk or simply watch the night.

Liam pulled the car into an old-fashioned driveway—two strips of concrete with grass in the middle—about two blocks from where Brian's mother lived. Liam got out of the car and came around to open the door for her.

Kim looked up in surprise as Liam helped her out and shut the door, a courtesy she wasn't used to. In her world, a woman had to pretend she didn't want or need little courtesies from men. If she wanted a man's job, she had to act like a man. Be even stronger than a man, actually, and more ruthless. Kim knuckled down and played the game, and she was surprised at how much Liam's gentlemanly gestures pleased her.

Liam's house was a bungalow, like Sandra's, two stories with square brick pillars on the porch. One corner of the porch held a picnic bench and a table, the other, a porch swing.

"I've always wanted a porch swing," Kim said. "Stupid, but I was never allowed to have one. Homeowner's association didn't approve."

"You're welcome to lounge on our porch swing anytime you want."

"Anyone ever tell you you're a sweetie, Liam? Isn't it a little late for a visit, though? Will your father be up still?"

Liam's smile answered her. "We're night people."

"Like vampires? Hell, I've had too much beer."

"No. Not like vampires." Liam opened the front door and ushered her into his house. "Vampires are different."

Kim wasn't certain what to make of his answer. Was he teasing? But heck, Shifters existed. Why not vampires?

She'd definitely had too much beer.

The front door led straight into the living room, which was dominated by a big box of a television. The couch and chairs had been grouped around it, with folding TV trays for end tables. The tables were littered with soda cans, beer bottles, bowls holding crumbs of corn chips, and stacks of videotapes and DVDs. It looked as though they'd had a movie night. The floors were polished wood with mismatched rugs and runners on them, unlike Kim's cool tile floors with plush hand-woven carpets.

As Liam led Kim inside, Sean and another man came down the stairs to her left, and a young, lanky Morrissey bounded out of the kitchen that opened beyond the living room.

"Is that her?" the young man asked.

The oldest man moved past him and held out his hand to Kim. "I'm Dylan."

Liam's father. He didn't look any older than forty, but like Sandra, his eyes held the weight of years. Those eyes assessed her, much as Liam's had, but without the warm interest. His grip was strong, not overpowering, but it let Kim know he *could* overpower her anytime he wanted to.

Kim decided that if she'd met Dylan instead of Liam, she'd have hightailed it out of Shiftertown and never looked back. No wonder Liam was the one Brian said everyone approached. You had to be brave to look into Dylan's eyes and not quail.

Sean stepped off the stairs. "Connor, why didn't you clean up this crap? I told you Kim was coming."

"I'm doing it." The young man started gathering the jetsam into his big hands.

"My nephew, Connor," Liam said. "Our brother Kenny's son."

The brother who'd died. Kim watched the long-limbed Connor shoulder his way into the kitchen, trying to carry everything at once.

Liam gestured for Kim to sit down. A couch, which had seen years of bouncing children and men's booted feet, sagged when she sat on it. Connor reappeared and handed Kim a cold soft drink. Kim wasn't in the mood for one, but she thanked him, opened the can, and took a sip. No reason not to be polite.

Liam sat down next to her, close, as he had at Sandra's.

Shifters really didn't understand personal space. Or if they did, they didn't care.

Sean stood ill at ease, his hands in his pockets. He wore a frown, as though he didn't like having Kim there, but not because he didn't like Kim. Dylan watched also, but with a quietness that the younger men of the family didn't have. He was closer to the predator than any of them.

And here I am, the gazelle.

To calm her nerves, Kim looked around at the décor, which was mostly bachelor clutter. "Hey, I have a suitcase just like that." She pointed at a black bag with metallic studs that stood next to the TV set. "Wait a minute, that *is* my bag." She glared at Liam, who didn't look the slightest bit guilt-stricken. "Gee, I wonder how it got here."

"Remember my friends who went to fix your back door? They brought it."

Kim set her can carefully on a TV tray. "Want to tell me why? Or do you have a fetish about stealing other people's luggage?"

It was Dylan who answered. "Because you're staying here, Kim. Liam knew you'd want your things."

"What do you mean, staying here? Spending the night? I haven't had *that* much to drink."

Liam slid his arm around her, strong, holding her there. "You need to stay."

"The Shifter wolf is dead. You and Sean killed him. I'm safe now." Finally the thing niggling at her broke through the fog in her brain. "Liam, *how* were you able to kill him? Your Collar should have stopped you from fighting, even against another Shifter. Right?"

Liam said nothing. She felt Sean standing above her, Connor's awkward uneasiness, and Dylan's strong silence.

"Liam?"

Liam's eyes were blue, hard, holding her gaze. "I'm sorry, love. That's why we can't let you go."

CHAPTER SEVEN

S he took it well. Liam had to give her that.

No screaming, no outraged swearing, no gibbering in terror. Kim simply looked at him, her eyes unreadable.

"Why not?" she asked steadily. "If I can prove that Brian had nothing to do with the murder, it won't matter whether his Collar can malfunction. I have no reason to share the information far and wide."

"You should let someone else take over Brian's defense," Dylan said.

Now the anger came. "Oh, no, no, no. This case is going to make my career. Besides, I'm your best hope of springing him."

Dylan's eyes were hard. "Brian understands the need to protect the Shifters."

Kim struggled from Liam's embrace and sprang to her feet. "Are you saying you'd let him go down? Make him pretend *his* Collar malfunctioned to keep everyone from knowing the Collars don't work at all?"

"This isn't about the Collars," Liam said. "And anyway, the Collars do work."

"You're crazy. If Brian's found guilty, he gets the death sentence for Shifters. Do you know what that means?"

"He won't die at the hands of the human government," Dylan said. "If he's convicted, we'll take care that he doesn't face an executioner."

"What, you'll send Sean to turn him to dust?"

Sean looked away, unable to meet her eyes.

"No, not Sean." Liam stood up beside her. "It's not his job."

Kim gave him an uncomprehending look; then her eyes widened. "You mean it's *yours?* Oh, Jesus effing Christ, Liam."

"It's a Shifter problem," Dylan said in his quiet voice.

"And now *I'm* a Shifter problem? You can't take my word that I won't tell anyone? Liam, you saved my life tonight. I owe you."

"It's not up to us," Sean broke in. "We don't make the law."

"The oldest excuse in the book. Aren't you the leader around here, Dylan? Can't you make, you know, an executive decision?"

Dylan shook his head. "These are clan matters and Shifter secrets. Only Fergus can override the law."

"Who the hell is Fergus?"

"The leader of the South Texas clan," Liam answered. "Dad thinks you should have a hearing with him. I don't agree."

"Why not? Maybe this Fergus will see reason."

"Fergus? Reason?" Liam wanted to laugh. He thought about the big man with the long black braid, the thugs he surrounded himself with. Fergus hadn't been happy when Kim managed to get Brian a jury trial. He'd wanted Brian to plead guilty and be done, the human prodding into Shifter business over. Liam still didn't understand why Fergus was so ready to wash his hands of Brian, but Brian had been ready to obey.

Until Kim had persuaded Brian to fight. Of course she had. Kim was a fighter. Fergus had been livid when he learned Brian had a competent defense attorney.

"He's dangerous, Kim," Liam said, his voice sharp with worry. "All Shifters are dangerous, Fergus especially so. You shouldn't have come to see me at all."

"I owe it to my client to try to help him get free."

"And now you know too damned much."

"Keep it quiet, Liam," Dylan growled. "I can contain this, but not if the neighbors hear you . . ."

Kim looked wildly out the window to the house next door. "What? What happens if the neighbors hear?"

"They might go to Fergus," Sean said. "We might not be able to stop them. We're your best protection."

"You can't keep me here." She had good lung power for such a small woman.

"We can and we will," Dylan said, eyes glittering. "We protect the clan."

Connor looked distressed. "Stop it, Grandda'. You're scaring her. She's going to think we're all crazy."

She'd not be far from wrong, Liam thought. Kim quivered with rage and fear, and Liam felt the overwhelming need to put his arms around her and soothe her. She needed to be held in the same way he and Sean had held Sandra, calming her nerves, easing her worry.

Holding Kim would calm Liam as well. His adrenaline was wearing off—he could tell by the dull buzzing in his head. Very soon now, he'd start to pay the price for killing the feral Shifter. Sean didn't look as bad, but then Sean hadn't fought; he'd only dispatched the feral's soul.

"Keeping you here is the safest thing," Liam said to Kim. "If Fergus thinks we have you under control, he won't send anyone to make sure you are."

Kim's anger would have knocked a weaker man sideways.

She'd started to trust Liam, and now she felt betrayed. "Under control?"

"Kim, love, when I said I'd protect you, I meant it. That means from everyone, my own father or my clan leader if necessary. If you go home tonight, Fergus will send Shifters after you. I'd have to stay with you, bodyguard you day and night." Liam ran a finger along her chin. "Not that I'd find that a bad thing."

Kim stared at him without softening. He wished he could make her understand that she'd put herself in danger the minute she'd taken Brian's case. Dylan and Fergus had argued long and hard when Kim had sent word she wanted to talk to Liam, and now Kim was in greater peril than ever.

Someone banged on the front door, and Liam caught a scent of Lupine overlaid with a large dose of Oscar de la Renta.

Sean rolled his eyes. "Perfect. She's all we're needing."

"Your door's locked," a woman's voice called through the wood.

"Let her in, Sean," Dylan said, resigned.

"About time." A tall woman dressed head to toe in black walked in when Sean opened the door. She wore tight pants and a sleeveless silk shirt and had folded her blonde hair into an intricate French braid. Silver high-heeled sandals studded with rhinestones completed her outfit. "Why'd you lock the door? You never lock it." She fixed white-blue eyes on Kim. "Who's this human woman, and why are you all yelling?"

The newcomer was lithe, with athletic grace, the kind of female Kim had despised when struggling with teen self-esteem. This Shifter lady could be a model for a fashion doll, except that she exuded personality with a capital P. Even her Collar gleamed.

Liam, Sean, and Connor viewed her with irritation. Dylan looked downright uncomfortable and avoided her gaze. *Interesting.*

The woman put a long-fingered hand on one hip. "I'm getting into bed when I hear my big cat neighbors trying to calm down a shouting woman. What am I supposed to think?" She pinned Kim with her predatory stare. "What are you doing to them, honey?"

Kim looked the woman up and down, pretending she wasn't unnerved. *"That's* what you wear to bed?"

"Depends on who's in it with me." The woman's gaze slid sideways to Dylan, who pretended not to notice. "Who is she?"

"None of your business, Glory," Connor tried.

Of all of them, Connor seemed to be the most oblivious to her overt sexuality. But then, if this Glory had something going on with Dylan, his grandfather, Connor would probably think her impossibly old. Even if she looked thirty at most. Damn, Shifters had good genes.

Glory sniffed the air, nostrils flaring. "Liam's scent-marked her. I never knew your tastes ran to humans, Liam."

Liam slid an arm around Kim's waist, and Kim wished it didn't feel so good there. "I'm protecting her from nosy Shifters."

"Sure you are." Glory's light blue gaze moved up and down Kim with too much perception. "But who protects you from *her?*"

Liam's grip tightened. "Good night, Glory."

Glory smiled a knowing smile, her lipstick coral pink. "All right, I won't pry." She gave Kim another assessing look. "Big cats are sensational, sweetie. I keep some extra-large condoms handy if you need them." She spun on the toes of her shiny shoes and sauntered out, black-clad hips swaying.

"I can see why you worry about your neighbors," Kim said as Sean closed the door again. "She's really something."

"Glory's a Lupine," Connor said. "She's always giving us grief. Why she wants to live in a big cat neighborhood, I don't know."

"She doesn't have a choice, does she?" Liam looked out the window, probably making sure that Glory went back to her own house and stayed there. "I'm taking Kim up to my room—alone. We need to have a chat."

"To your room?" Kim stared. "Why?" She wished she weren't so intrigued at the thought. She needed to be afraid of these men, to flee them, to not let them keep her here.

Then she thought of the feral Shifter in her bedroom and her big empty house with the dusty Shifter remains on her carpet. Contrasted with this bright, warm house, her own place suddenly had too many ghosts.

"You'll sleep up in my room," Liam was saying. "It's the cleanest. I even do hospital corners." He picked up Kim's bag, then put his arm around her waist again. He liked doing that, as though she naturally belonged in his embrace.

"Wait a minute. You expect me to stay overnight in a house with four single men?"

Sean grinned. "We're perfect gentlemen, Kim. Everyone knows that. Don't let us worry you."

"I'm not worried about my reputation, I'm worried about the state of the bathrooms."

Liam laughed softly, his warm breath tickling her ear. "They did a cleanup when I told them you were coming. And if they didn't, they'll be doing it now, *won't they?* This way, love."

L iam took her to a roomy upstairs hall with three bedrooms and bath and a stair that led to an attic. Kim had to admit everything looked nice. Polished wood, freshly painted walls, clean carpets. But the house was definitely missing feminine touches, which made it a little sad and incomplete.

Liam led her into a large bedroom with only one picture on the wall, a travel poster of a green vista in Ireland.

"Interesting neighbors you have," Kim said. "Do she

and your dad have something going on? I noticed a lot of tension there."

Liam closed the door and dumped Kim's bag on the floor. "She and Dad have an on-again, off-again affair. When they get along, it's a beautiful thing."

"And when they don't?"

"We head for the hills. Right now they're in neutral."

"That was neutral? I see what you mean about heading for the hills. She's a wolf Shifter, Connor said, but your dad is a big cat like you?"

"Not exactly a match that would have happened before we took the Collar. But they care about each other. Deep down inside."

Must be *very* deep down inside. "I'll take your word for it."

Liam laughed his warm, throaty laugh. "I'm skeptical too, love, but it works for them. Come here." He sat on the bed, putting his back against the headboard, and patted the mattress beside him.

"On the bed. Of course." Kim put her hands on her hips. "If kidnapping and arguing don't work, try seduction."

"No seduction." How Liam could claim that while looking at her with those sinful baby blues, she didn't know.

Why did *no seduction* sound so disappointing? Maybe because Kim had felt a tingle of attraction for him since the moment she'd met him? As she'd talked to him throughout the day, she'd been lulled by his deep voice with its Irish lilt, softened by the warm blue of his eyes. Even him turning into a wildcat and killing a wolf on her bedroom floor hadn't quite brought her to her senses.

Kim gave up and sat down beside him, stretching her legs out next to his. His hard thigh warmed hers.

"What did Glory mean when she said you 'scent-marked' me? That sounds disturbing." Kim didn't smell anything different about herself, but then she wasn't a Shifter.

"Protection, love. Shifters know their families and

friends faster by scent first, then sight. I made sure that when they smell you now they smell me and know to leave you alone."

"I don't remember you spraying me or anything." She wrinkled her nose.

"When I hugged you outside Sandra's house, I let my scent twine with yours."

"Oh." She'd remembered that hug all day, his body hard and strong against hers, his arms so comforting. She'd thought it part of the Shifter's strange need to touch. "But I went home and took a shower."

Liam gave her the smile that made his eyes sparkle. "It's more than smell—the scent-mark is a little bit magic as well. It fades with time if you never see the Shifter again, but for now, everyone in Shiftertown knows I'm taking care of you."

Kim was uncertain how to feel about that. She didn't like being "protected," but then again, having Liam charge in to save her from the feral had been a good thing. She'd also noted how the Shifters at the bar had sized her up. Without Liam's mark, would she have been fair game? Unnerving thought.

Liam had fallen silent, as though lost in thought. His big body took most of the bed, leaving Kim only a tiny portion. She wondered what it would be like to sleep in this small bed with him. A woman would have to cuddle up to him, maybe spoon against his back. Her arm would snake around his waist, and she'd want to tickle his belly button.

"Do Shifters have belly buttons?" she asked.

Liam's preoccupied look dissolved into a smile. "You're a treasure, lass. The gods sent you to us, I think."

"It just occurred to me."

Liam eased his T-shirt upward. His jeans rode low on his waist, baring his flat stomach and the indentation of his navel.

"I'm human in every way when I'm in this form," he

said. "It's not only our appearance that changes. It's everything. Bones, muscles, organs. It's hellacious painful when we first do it."

"How old were you when you shifted the first time?" Kim couldn't drag her gaze from his abdomen. She wanted to taste his belly button and slide her tongue down from there to his low-riding waistband.

"I was about five as humans count years. I was still a cub. I remember thinking I was dying."

"It must have been weird to suddenly be a wildcat—whatever kind of cat you are."

"It's called a Fae-cat. But you've got it the other way 'round, love. I lived as a wildcat for five years before I shifted to human. Standing up on two feet and having eyes that couldn't see so well in the dark—it scared the bejesus out of me."

"You were *born* a cat?"

"My parents were both full-blood Feline Shifters, so yes. When there's a mix—wolf and cat Shifter, or wolf and bear, say—then you're born a human babe. You shift to whatever is the dominant gene when you're about five or six."

Interesting. None of her research had told her any of this, which made her realize just how little humans knew about Shifters. "What is a Fae-cat, exactly? I couldn't decide if you were mountain lion or leopard or what."

"It's hard to explain to a non-Shifter. We're a unique breed, left over from times before humans populated the earth. The Fae made us. They bred in the strengths of all members of the big cat family, at least the big cats of ancient times, the ancestors of wildcats that exist now. We're fast like cheetahs, can see in the dark like leopards, have the power of lions, the cunning of tigers. That's why we call ourselves Felines, not a specific breed. The Lupines are wolves, but not exactly like any wolves you'd find in the wild."

"In other words, the best of the entire species."

"You could say that."

"So, if you can crossbreed, like you said, then your dad and your next-door neighbor could produce children. In theory."

"In theory, though cross-species fertility is not as high as fertility within a species. Dad's only about two hundred, so he can still father cubs. Glory won't tell her age, but she's still in the fertile range."

"Dylan is two hundred years old?" Kim asked in amazement. "He doesn't look much into his forties. How old are you?"

"I was born in 1898, as humans count years. Sean came along in 1900."

Holy shit. "You look damn good for a centenarian. What about Connor? Don't tell me he's eighty-two."

"He's twenty. Born right after we took the Collar. His mum died of bringing him in, poor lass."

Kim's thought of Connor downstairs, with his good-natured smile and his worry about them frightening her. "Oh, Liam, I'm sorry."

Liam shrugged, a shrug that meant he'd resigned himself to it. "It happened often enough when we lived outside of humankind. It's one of the reasons the clan leaders decided to take the Collar. We were a dying people."

"She was married to the brother you lost, wasn't she? Kenny? That sucks. Poor Connor."

"Aye. A feral got Kenny ten years ago. We've looked after Connor, but it's not the same for him."

Kim leaned against Liam's strong arm, suddenly wanting to comfort him. "And I thought I had it bad growing up. But I was always cared for, never had to worry. Even when my parents passed away, they'd taken care of me to the end. I was already working, but they'd left me the house and plenty of money. I never wanted for anything."

The corner of his mouth quirked up. "Poor little rich girl."

"It let me do work I believed in. I don't have to take cases based on how much they pay."

"No, you're free to help hapless Shifters."

Kim sat up. "You all sound like you don't take this seriously, like you don't want me to get Brian free. Brian's mother is barely holding it together. You and Sean had to do the comforting sandwich with her, remember?"

"Aye." Liam went silent. His T-shirt had slid down again, covering his honed body. Damn.

"Believe me, when I'm defending someone, I make certain he gets a fair trial," Kim said. "It's a right we all have that can get lost if we're not careful. And besides, I think Brian's innocent. I seem to be the only one who does."

"Kim." Liam cut through her diatribe. "Brian *is* innocent. He couldn't have killed that girl. But to prove it, you might reveal secrets that could destroy all Shifters, everywhere."

"Secrets like the fact that the Collars don't work? Or that some Shifters don't even wear them?"

Liam gazed into the distance. "It's not quite that simple."

"Then explain to me what's going on." She softened her tone. "Believe me, I'll do what I can to get Brian exonerated, but bringing down your family isn't what I had in mind."

"I'm glad to hear that," Liam said mildly.

"So how *is* it possible that you killed that Shifter?" Kim asked. "The Collars really don't work?"

"Oh, they work, love." His eyes were clouded. "They work."

"May I look?"

Liam nodded. Kim knelt back on her heels to examine the thin black and silver chain around his throat. She lifted his hair at the back of his neck, wishing it wasn't all warm and silky and distracting.

The chain had no clasp and was fused to his skin, the links snug but not tight. A Celtic knot rested at the base of his throat. When Liam had been in his wildcat form in her bedroom, she'd seen the glint of the Collar against his fur.

"How did it not strangle you when you shifted?"

"When the Collar goes on, it becomes a part of the Shifter. Don't ask me to explain the technology or the magic, because I don't understand it myself. The Collar allows us to change to our animal forms—because if we were denied that we'd die. Our animal form is part of us, with us at all times. So the chain adapts to it."

Kim ran her fingers around the Collar, feeling the cool contrast of the silver with his hot skin, the bump of the Celtic knot. "What do you mean by 'the magic'? It's triggered by your adrenal system, isn't it? To shock you or tranquilize you when your chemical balance changes, right?"

Liam chuckled. "You saw me shift from cat to man, and the wolf die away to dust under Sean's sword, and you still don't believe in magic?"

"Not really. There's an explanation for even the most bizarre things."

"Remind me to take you to Ireland someday. I'll show you magic. An Irishman made these chains, an old man who was permeated with magic himself."

"A leprechaun?"

Liam laid his head back and laughed. Kim's hand was still on his neck, and catching his head in her palm felt intimate and warm.

"No, sweetheart, no little men in green with shamrocks. The man who made the first Collars was half Fae. Your government—and others in the world where Shifters are allowed to live—agreed that the old mage could supply the chains that keep us weak."

"You keep talking about *Fae*. What's Fae?"

"Sometimes called Fair Folk or fairies, but they're not cute little people with wings. The Fae are ancient and arrogant beings who once regarded the earth as theirs. Terrifying, they are. They made Shifters to be their pets, their hunting beasts, but we weren't having any of that."

Kim wasn't certain how much of this she bought, and she couldn't tell if he believed it himself or was having her on. "You said the man who made the chains *was* half Fae. Do you mean he's dead now?"

"He is. But he passed the knowledge to his son. The son stays hidden away in Ireland and sends the Collars as they're needed."

"How was it that you could fight and kill the feral Shifter then? Or do the Collars work only if you try to attack humans?"

"No, like you said, the Collars are keyed to our adrenal systems. Doesn't matter who we're violent toward. But some of us have found ways to . . . delay . . . the system. It's painful, but it can be done."

Liam met her gaze calmly, but something raged behind his eyes. He'd changed since he'd come into this room, but she couldn't put her finger on how. "You've learned how to override yours, you mean," she said.

Liam shrugged again, but his shoulders remained hunched. There it was—the key. Instead of Liam the strong and protective, he'd withdrawn into himself. He'd talked with her and smiled at her, but his thoughts were far away.

"I have," he said. "I only override it when necessary."

"Like tonight." Kim touched his chest, feeling his heart beating too rapidly beneath her fingers. "And that hurt you?"

"It did, love. That's why I'm sitting quietly on this bed and leaving your beautiful self alone. My entire body is brutal raw with pain."

CHAPTER EIGHT

L iam hadn't lied; he hurt like hell.

Kim's eyes went wide with shock. "But we were dancing half an hour ago."

"I can hold it off for a long time, especially if the excitement of the kill is high." He let his gaze drift over her delicious little body. "And dancing with you—let's just say I wasn't letting anything stop me from enjoying that."

She looked worried. "And you're in pain now?"

"Excruciating." Agony bloomed behind Liam's eyes and in every nerve ending, every muscle. His spine felt as if someone had twisted it with a giant pair of pliers. The punishment didn't even spare his smallest toes.

"Liam, I'm sorry. I didn't know."

"A man doesn't like to admit when he's hurting. It shames us."

"Can't you do anything for it? Would ibuprofen help? I have some in my purse."

He wanted to laugh. Ibuprofen wouldn't make a dent.

"Nothing to be done but wait it out. Having you sit here with me is nice."

Kim watched him in concern for a few more moments, then snuggled down against him. Liam smiled as he gathered her close, reflecting on the ironies of life. On the one hand, the pain was driving him crazy. On the other, Kim would likely never have draped herself over him if he hadn't admitted his suffering.

"What about Sean?" she asked. "Is he in pain too?"

"Probably a little, but he didn't make the kill. He only cleaned up after."

Kim smoothed his T-shirt over his abdomen. "Why would you do this to yourself? I mean all Shifters. Live with the possibility of this hurting?"

"We had to." Liam stopped, talking becoming too much of an effort. The pain would recede, probably by tomorrow morning, but he'd have horror to go through first. It wasn't so bad this time, maybe because he'd been fighting to protect Kim. He'd acted on instinct when he realized she was in danger, not even worrying about the price he'd pay.

"You make me want to kiss you," Kim said.

His heart beat faster. "What a sweetheart you are. But I don't kiss."

She lifted her head. "What are you talking about? You've kissed me plenty today."

On her hair, her neck. Liam moved as his cock started to harden with memory, even through his pain. "I don't kiss like humans do, on the lips. I don't see the point."

"You mean Shifters don't kiss at all?" Kim's eyes narrowed. "Wait a minute, I saw a Shifter kiss his wife in the bar. That was his wife, wasn't it?"

"You mean Jordie? Yes, she was his mate. I didn't say all Shifters don't kiss. I said *I* don't. When I'm with a Shifter woman we have other things on our minds."

"You mean you hump her without intimacies? Figures.

Tragic that someone who looks as good as you isn't interested in the woman's pleasure."

The pain receded the slightest bit. "What shite are you talking? There's plenty of pleasure when I'm with a woman. On both sides."

"Huh. You don't even take the time to kiss her."

"Since you're not a Shifter woman, you wouldn't understand. It's fast and furious, no time for much else."

Kim shook her head, her curls tickling through his shirt. "You have no idea what you're missing, Liam."

"I've never been with a human." Liam liked her face close to his, her scent filling his whole body. "You're right, I don't know."

"All right, then. Hold still."

Kim knelt beside him. Her jeans tightened against her thighs, and her blouse gaped open, giving him a glimpse of soft breast swelling above lace.

Her scent was driving him crazy. Liam had used protective marking before, but he'd never smelled such a heady mixture as he did now—his scent and Kim's blended in almost equal parts. As though they belonged together.

Kim's hesitant fingertips brushed his cheek, her caress so different from her forthright manner and sassy speech. "Am I hurting you?"

She was worried about him, the sweetheart. "The pain's backing off."

"That's good."

She came close, closer. The warmth of her skin, the scent of it, made Liam's hard-on throb, his lust start to break through the excruciating pain. Kim's lashes swept down as she touched her mouth to his upper lip.

Something shook in Liam's core, and the hurting began to lose the battle. Liam moved his lips in response, clumsily catching her mouth with his.

The satin-smooth slide of Kim's lips took his breath away. He *had* kissed in human form before, but they'd been quick, affectionate pecks with friends or female members of the family. He'd never experienced the full sensations of a slow, hot kiss, lips moving and exploring. He cupped Kim's neck, encouraging her to continue, and nearly jumped off the bed when she thrust her tongue into his mouth.

Kim jerked away. "What? Did I hurt you?"

"No." Liam laced his fingers behind her neck, under her warm hair. "You surprised me, is all. Is that your way of kissing? I like it."

"My way? I think it's everybody's way. Don't tell me Shifters don't French kiss."

"I'm Irish."

Her smile was gorgeous. "Well, well, something I know that the all-powerful Shifter-man doesn't."

"Let's try it again. I'm a quick learner."

Kim cupped his face. "I shouldn't be doing this."

"You should. It's helping me." *Stay with me.*

"I can't get involved with you, and besides, you're trying to keep me prisoner in your house. Not that you'll succeed, by the way."

"It's for your own safety, love. I'm responsible for what happens to you."

"I do feel safer here." It cost her to admit that, Liam could see. "If I were alone in my house right now, I'd be scared. Being attacked by that feral—it was so fast. I always thought I could defend myself, and I suddenly realized I couldn't."

Liam kneaded her neck. "Here you don't have to worry." He tugged her closer. "Let's try the French way again."

Kim wanted to resist—Liam saw hesitation in her eyes. She wanted to say no, to pull away, to walk out. He also sensed her wanting. She craved to be touched, and she thought he was harmless, sitting here in so much pain it made his teeth ache. Never mind that she was mostly right.

Kim closed her eyes before their lips met again. Was this required for a kiss? Liam kept his eyes open, liking to watch the way her lashes curled against her skin, how one lock of her hair slid over her cheek.

She put her tongue inside his mouth again. Liam caught it, licking, lapping, playing. He tilted his head so he could better fit their mouths together.

Damn, this was good. Humans had something going with this kissing, even if they gave it a French name, like the fries he insisted on calling chips. Liam's erection was getting massive now. He wasn't sure whether he'd be embarrassed if the tip peeped above the waistband, or whether he'd be pleased to show her how much he wanted her.

Playing catch-me with Kim's tongue, Liam slid his hands to her thighs, wishing she still wore the skirt from this morning. If so, he could inch his way under the hem, latch his fingers over the tops of her stockings, unhook the garters, peel the stockings down . . .

Kim eased back, her eyes half closed. "Liam, you're going to kiss my lips raw."

Liam smiled. "You say that like it's a bad thing."

"I thought you were hurt."

"I'm feeling so much better." Liam dug his fingers into the denim covering her thighs, his strength returning. He could roll her over onto the bed, press her down into the mattress, have her teach him some more about human kissing.

He touched her lips again. "You're a sweet, beautiful thing, do you know that?"

"For a human?"

"For an anything, love."

He kissed her one more time, then made himself push away and sit up. This was getting dangerous. His strength was growing and with it, rampaging lust.

Kim looked at him in confusion, her lips swollen and red, her eyes dark, pupils wide. "What's the matter? I thought you wanted more lessons."

"Afraid not, sweetheart. I have to get out of here before you regret it."

She smiled a little. "I don't regret a little kissing."

It would be so much more if he didn't leave. Goddess, she was delectable. "You'll be safe here tonight, I promise you. No one, not even Fergus himself, will get through Dad, me, and Sean. Even Connor's a good fighter, young as he is. They like you, and we've taken you in. You'll be protected like you were one of the pride."

She looked surprised, then thoughtful, as though she hadn't considered it that way. "I admit I'm afraid to go back home right now. But I can stay only until morning. All right?"

Liam didn't answer as he stood. He knew damn well she could see his erection—how could she miss a thing of that size pushing at her? If she asked him to, he'd unbutton and unzip to let her see him, or touch him, or take him in her mouth.

Bloody hell, he had to get out of here.

Kim wet her lips. Liam put his hands on his hips, his pulse thumping so hard his fingers hurt. Her mouth was lush and red, lips plump, making him want to bite them.

"I should sleep now," she said, sounding as though she had to make herself acknowledge it. "I have a lot to do tomorrow."

Sleep. In his bed, her head on his pillow, her body damp and warm. Maybe wearing that little wisp of a silk thing she'd been in when he'd rescued her tonight.

"See you at breakfast then," he made himself say.

"What do Shifters eat for breakfast?"

"Wheaties. Or I can fix you my pancakes, like I promised."

Didn't she look mouthwatering, sitting cross-legged on the bed, her blouse half unbuttoned, her nipples hard enough to press through her bra and the white fabric? He could push her back onto the pillows, close his mouth on one taut point through the shirt.

Kim picked up a pillow and hugged it to her chest, cutting off the beautiful view. "Good night, Liam."

"I won't be sleeping much, that's for certain. Not thinking about you down here in my bed."

"Down here? Where will you be?"

He pointed at the ceiling. "Connor's got the whole attic floor. Plenty of room for me to bunk down with him. Want me to knock on the floor, let you know when I'm there?"

Kim got off the bed, still hugging the pillow. "What I want is to sleep and forget about this awful night. Then get up and go home. I don't mind staying here tonight because I'm scared, but tomorrow, when I'm done being afraid, I'm going home."

She wouldn't be going home. Liam wouldn't argue with her right now, though. No point in it.

He smiled at her, forced himself to turn his back on her compact body and pretty eyes and leave the room.

He had to stand in the hallway a long time after he closed the door, waiting for his fierce hard-on to go down. He needed to talk to Dylan, but he couldn't face his father with an erection that could stop a train.

Seeing the light go off under the door behind him and hearing the squeak of his bedsprings as Kim climbed into his bed didn't help deflate him at all.

An hour later, Glory opened her back door to admit a moody Dylan Morrissey.

Glory had never met a Shifter who turned her on faster than Dylan could. So what if he was a Feline? Glory's friends didn't approve, but they could eat their hearts out. Dylan was tall, broad-shouldered, and temperamental, with the best ass she'd ever seen on any male, Shifter or human.

Glory let Dylan pace, happy he'd responded to the veiled invitation she'd thrown out when she'd talked to the human girl. Dylan didn't always respond to hints; he did what he pleased. *Damned alpha male.*

"You're giving me motion sickness," she said after a time. "What have you decided to do about the little human? Let Fergus kill her?"

"I don't know what I'm going to do about her." Dylan finally stopped and rested his broad fists on her kitchen counter. "Liam just spent an hour talking me out of taking her to Fergus, which means I disobey Fergus's direct orders. *Fuck.*"

If only.

Glory knew damn well Liam hadn't talked Dylan out of anything. If Dylan thought the girl should go to Fergus, nothing Liam could do would stop Dylan from taking her there.

"Why do you think Liam's right?" she asked.

Dylan's hard blue eyes sparked with anger, though he flicked his gaze away before his dominant rage could fix on her.

"What makes you think I agree with him?"

"Because if you didn't, you'd have her ass in your truck and be hauling her down to San Antonio instead of standing in my kitchen with me."

Dylan slammed his fists into the counter. "I know that. But Liam . . ." He straightened up and shook his head. Glory glanced quickly at the counter, but Dylan hadn't dented it. This time.

"But Liam what?" she asked.

"He cares about her." Dylan ran his hands through his hair, mussing it in a sexy way. "I've never seen him like this. I thought he wanted to protect her because Liam always protects the weak. But it's more than that. Let's say I'm surprised he's letting her sleep alone tonight."

"You think he'll claim her?" Glory started brewing coffee to cover her nervousness, not to mention her rampaging horniness. "She's human."

Dylan leaned his backside against the counter and folded his arms. "You know how high the ratio of males to females is in Shiftertown. It's doubtful Liam will ever mate with another Shifter."

Glory poured fragrant ground coffee into her coffeemaker and closed the lid. "You'd let him take a human as mate?"

"Never in the old days, but those days are gone." He

looked exhausted, Dylan who'd lived so long and seen so much. "She seems robust, and she's not afraid of us."

Glory snorted. "If she's not afraid of you, it's because she doesn't know any better. Though I agree, she's got spunk." She admired the way the human girl had said what she'd really thought, though Glory would never admit it. In Glory's experience, most humans she encountered either avoided eye contact with her, pretended contempt, or simply ran away.

"Another reason I don't think Liam will claim a Shifter woman is because he thinks too much about the good of the clan," Dylan was saying. "He pushes potential mates on other Shifters rather than claiming them himself. I asked him why, once. He said that Shifters lower in the hierarchy have more time to breed and raise a family, and that's what Shifters need most. Cubs, not testosterone contests."

"How self-sacrificing of him."

"I also think he's never come across a female who stirs him. For sex, yes. As a mate, no. But this one . . ."

"This one he's not likely to charitably pass down to the next mate-seeking Shifter. She's human; she needs his protection. And Liam is a protector at heart." Glory smiled. "Like his dad."

Dylan finally looked straight at her. He'd been sliding his gaze from hers, trying not to pin her with his angry uncertainty, trying not to demand submission. What a sweetie. He must know that if he wanted Glory to go down on her knees, she'd happily oblige.

"It's my job," Dylan answered irritably.

"No, it's you. You're one big protecting hunk of male. The only reason Fergus leads your clan and not you is because he's a ruthless bastard. You don't challenge him, because you fear he'll retaliate on the innocent, Connor in particular."

Dylan's expression went harder still, and it was all Glory could do to stay upright in her high-heeled shoes. His eyes were tinged with red, a sign that he was ready to lose it.

"You only met Fergus the once," Dylan said, tight-lipped.

"Once was enough. I never want to see him again. People respect you, Dylan. They fear Fergus. There's a difference."

She started to turn away, but a steel-strong hand clamped her arm. "What are you trying to do, Glory? Sow insurrection in my clan?"

Glory looked at him in surprise. "Insurrection? Are you kidding? What for?"

Dylan's grip softened, but Glory saw he had to make himself ease off. "Then why are you so interested in me challenging Fergus?"

"Because you're a better man than he is. I've always thought that, and I'm not the only one."

Dylan closed his eyes. He clenched his jaw, a muscle twitching. "The clan's survival is more important than me confronting Fergus."

"I know." Glory dared to step closer to him, now that his awful gaze was shielded. "If we start challenging and fighting one another like we did before the Collar, we'll be dead within a few short years."

"I'm glad you understand."

"See, sometimes I listen when you talk."

Dylan opened his eyes then, the red gone, the beautiful blue so deep it made her heart ache.

"Glory," he said softly.

"Yes?"

"Shut it."

Dylan wove his fingers through her hair, loosening it until it spilled over his hands, and he covered her mouth with his.

Glory rose into the kiss, excitement pumping through her. No one could screw like Dylan could. And Dylan surpassed even himself when he was pissed off and warring with his dominant instincts.

She decided not to fight too hard when Dylan lifted her and deposited her on the counter. She wrapped her legs around his hips, unbuttoned his pants, and leaned back to enjoy herself.

CHAPTER NINE

Liam was wrenched out of sleep the next morning by Kim banging on the attic door and shouting his name. His instincts had him on his feet and wrenching open the door before his brain even knew he was awake.

He found Kim in the hall, her eyes blazing, in a big black T-shirt with a Guinness logo on it. Kim had obviously slept in the rumpled T-shirt, which she must have found in Liam's dresser drawer. Liam knew she'd be warm and very naked beneath it, and then he realized he was naked himself, prepared to shift.

One part of him was shifting already. "Gods, Kim, why are you out here yelling like a banshee?"

Kim held up a small bit of satin fabric, her eyes wide with fury. "Who packed this? It was a *man*, wasn't it?"

"Probably. Why?"

She shook the red satin patch. "This is a *thong*. Have you ever worn a thong? Do you know how it feels to have a string up your ass all day?"

Liam sensed the rest of his family listening: Connor sitting up in bed behind him, Sean in the hall below, Dylan behind him in the same clothes he'd worn last night, which meant he'd slept next door.

"What's wrong with a thong?" Liam asked her. "I bet it's sexy on you." He pictured it, and immediately clamped down on his imagination. *Gods.*

"Oh, right," Kim said. "I'm standing in a courtroom, trying to think on my feet while the prosecution is laughing its butt off at me, but that's all right—*at least my underwear is sexy.*"

Liam leaned on his arm, trying hard not to laugh. He heard Dylan retreat, quietly, into his bedroom. Sean, too, departed, chuckling. Connor folded his arms around his knees, watching this female display in puzzlement.

"Why do you have them, then?" Liam asked.

"Friends buy them for me, all right?" Kim snapped.

"And you hang on to them?"

"I don't want to hurt their feelings. They think they're doing me a favor."

Liam let his grin break through. "They think it's a favor to let you . . . how did you put it . . . wear a string up your ass all day?"

Kim rolled her eyes. "Never *mind*. I'm taking a shower and going home. You got rid of the feral Shifter, so it's not like he's coming back. I'll be perfectly safe."

Liam felt Connor's tension behind him, his troubled worry. Liam relaxed his stance to try to convey to Connor that everything was under control. *Right*. "Kim, love, I'll make you breakfast, and you write out a list of what you need. I'll send someone 'round to retrieve it all for you. Someone female this time. How will that be with you?"

Kim planted her fists on her hips. She shouldn't have done that; the movement thrust out her breasts and let the T-shirt outline her nipples. "Are you still insisting that you won't let me leave?"

"Not yet. It's not safe."

"It's perfectly safe. The feral Shifter is dead, and you had the lock on my door fixed. Make your damn pancakes if you want to, and then I'm leaving. I won't tell *anyone* what happened last night or repeat what you told me about the Collars. I know how to keep a secret, all right? And you can just get over it."

She stomped back down the stairs and slammed her own door so hard the sturdy walls rattled. Liam sensed her beneath the boards at his feet—her rage; her frustration; her warm, pliant body filling out his shirt. Her closed door would be no barrier to him if he chose to charge in and confront her.

Connor was watching Liam with concern. "What are you going to do?"

He meant, was Liam going to subdue her, and would he hurt Kim doing it? Connor was young, still uncomfortable with his own instincts, not yet certain where he fit in the clan and pride hierarchies. Things were more difficult for him than they had been for Liam or Sean, because Connor had grown up a captive Shifter, and boundaries were fuzzier now than they'd been in the wild. Connor didn't yet understand when you showed dominance and when you tolerated, and *what* you tolerated. Plus, he'd been raised by mateless males and had never seen an example of an intimate relationship.

Not that anything Liam had with Kim was going to be straightforward. Educational, maybe. Straightforward, no.

Liam tamped down his own instincts, dousing the pheromones that were putting Connor on edge. "What am I going to do?" He shrugged and headed for the attic bathroom. "What she asked me to. I'm going to make her pancakes."

Kim descended to the kitchen, showered but still irritated. Liam's friends had packed not only the underwear she never wore, but also her shortest skirts and lowest-cut tops, a garter belt, and a bunch of stockings. Nothing remotely comfortable, not even shorts and sandals for surviving Austin in the summer.

She paused at the kitchen doorway, surprise cutting through her annoyance. Liam in a tight T-shirt and jeans, spatula in hand, glared at a griddle full of pancakes. Behind him in the narrow kitchen, Sean scrubbed dishes in the sink.

Every woman's dream—two gorgeous men in the kitchen, cooking and cleaning.

Dylan sat at the table, tipping his chair back on two legs while he watched a sports report on a television that had to be twenty years old. Connor sat next to him, flipping through a car magazine. The air was somewhat tense, as though words had been cut off when they'd heard her coming.

Something else wasn't right about this domestic picture, apart from tall, muscular men working in the kitchen to fix her breakfast. Kim realized that Connor didn't have his nose in the Internet or a video game or a cell phone. Nor did he have an iPod glued to his ears.

Were those more technologies forbidden to Shifters? Or could the Morrisseys simply not afford them? She knew that Liam had a job, which he seemed to take casually. What about Sean and Dylan? Did they work? They seemed in no hurry to rush to an office. Abel was always out of bed as soon as the alarm went off, through the shower and into his suit and tie in fifteen minutes. *"Come on, honey, we're going to be late."* No time for pancakes, coffee, or a chat, never mind a morning cuddle.

Liam took a plate from the stack next to him and flipped pancakes onto it. "These are done. You're supposed to have the table ready, Connor." Liam smiled at Kim, but something in him seemed subdued, the sparkle that had been in his eyes earlier that morning gone. What was going on?

Connor hauled his tall form out of the chair and shuffled to the kitchen. When his body filled out, he'd be as muscular as his two uncles and Dylan. He looked unfinished right now, like a young horse, all arms and legs. But he was handsome enough, probably already drove girls crazy.

"I'll help," Kim offered. She took the bottles of syrup Connor had snatched out of the cupboard and carried them to the table.

Dylan rose. "Sit down, Kim. You're a guest."

Kim opened her mouth to say, *No, guests are allowed to leave,* but she shut it again. There was plenty of time to argue, and besides, the pancakes smelled terrific.

In any case, she had no intention of arguing with them. She'd simply get into her car and leave.

The pancakes tasted as good as they smelled, tangy, sweet, and laced with cinnamon. Damn Liam for being so gorgeous and skilled at cooking too.

"Did you sleep well, Kim?" Connor asked her around a mouthful.

Kim had fallen into a heavy sleep and dreamed about two things—being attacked by feral Shifters and kissing Liam. Both experiences had been intense.

"Sort of."

"Liam didn't," Connor said. "He thrashed all night. The springs on my extra bed squeak something awful. Drove me mad."

"I wasn't used to the bed," Liam said, sitting down next to Kim with his pancakes.

For a man who'd slept restlessly, especially after claiming to be in excruciating pain, Liam looked damn good. His face was freshly shaved, his hair still damp from his shower. She smelled soap and shaving cream on him, which sent her imagination into the shower with him, his body dripping wet and soapy.

Dylan, on the other hand, looked extremely pissed about something. He glowered as he ate, hunkering over his plate. Sean went through his pancakes quickly, without speaking, and returned to the kitchen for more dish scrubbing.

"Do you always make Sean do the dishes?" Kim asked. "Seems unfair."

"We take it in turns," Liam answered. "It's Sean's day to do the washing up."

"Mine tomorrow," Connor said glumly. "I swear I'm taking a mate as soon as I'm of age, so I don't have to do it anymore."

Kim ate her last mouthful of pancakes and wished for more. Screw eating light; these were *good*. "That's going to be your offer, Connor? 'Marry me so you can clean up after me, my two uncles, and my grandfather'? I'm sure every woman would jump at that."

At the sink, Sean laughed. Liam smiled, but distractedly. Connor frowned as if she'd given him something new to think about, but even his enthusiasm was dampened.

The four Morrisseys were certainly wound up this morning. The worst tension was between Liam and Dylan—and Kim gave herself three guesses what they'd been fighting about.

Kim set down her fork. "Let's keep this simple. I'm going to go upstairs, get my stuff, and leave. I'll call you and let you know what's going on with Brian's case—keep you in the loop. I promise. And I won't reveal anything I learned about feral Shifters, Collars, or your werewolf neighbor in glittery shoes."

Dylan looked up from his meal, his eyes dark but tinged with red. Despite his handsomeness, he was damn scary, and Kim again realized why humans sought out Liam instead of his father.

Liam shot Dylan an angry glance, but when Liam spoke to Kim his voice was gentle. "You need to stay a little longer, love. A few more days at least."

"No." Kim wiped her mouth and put down her napkin. "I have a job and a life. Tomorrow is Monday and I have to be at my office, where I work to earn my living. Remember Brian and his case? You do want me to get him free, right?"

"You'll go to your office," Liam said. "I'll go with you."

"Oh, right. A Shifter walking the halls at Lowell, Grant, and Steinhurst. I don't think so."

"It's that or you don't go at all."

Kim shoved back her chair and stood up. "Listen, Liam, I didn't ask to be dragged into your problems. I didn't ask for that—*thing*—to attack me. I'm real sorry I found out about the Collars, but all I want to do is get Brian released and back home to his mother. You don't seem to remember that I'm on your side."

Liam had gotten to his feet with her. Connor watched, worried, and Sean turned from the sink, scrub brush dripping.

"It's not up to me, Kim," Liam said.

"You're damn right it's not up to you. It's up to *me.*" What was the matter with them? "Y'all are *Shifters.* You could be arrested for kidnapping me or holding me hostage—hell, for even talking to me sharply. They'll do to you what they're doing to Brian. A sham of a trial and an execution."

Dylan finally spoke. "We weren't planning on telling anyone. Or letting you tell anyone."

Kim's heart beat faster. Yep, Dylan was the scariest one in this room, all right. Her powers of argument died under his red-tinged stare. The feral Shifter who'd attacked her now seemed like a puppy dog compared to Dylan.

Liam's voice went hard. "Dad, you promised this was mine to handle."

"Aye, but you're not handling it," Dylan answered. "You know what you have to do."

"Let me do it then. In my own time."

"No, you need to do it *now.* It's the only way."

Kim backed up a step. "Do what now?"

Liam wouldn't look at her, while Dylan glared and Sean turned away. Connor had his mouth open, clearly not knowing what they were talking about, either.

"Do what now?" Kim repeated.

If she ran for the door, would she make it? How fast

could Dylan, Liam, and Sean move? Liam didn't look ready to spring, and neither did Dylan, who sat loosely, but these men weren't human.

What was the matter with her? Yesterday, she'd been nervous about coming to Shiftertown and talking to a Shifter who wasn't behind bars. Then Liam had looked at her with those Irish blue eyes, and she'd melted. She'd even slept in their house without putting up much fuss. She'd done everything on their terms, and Kim never did anything on anyone's terms but her own.

Now she was reminded of how dangerous Shifters were. She'd blithely walked into their lives, and she knew they wouldn't let her blithely walk out again.

Kim balled her fists. "Liam, please reverse the scent-marking. I don't do the dominant-submissive thing."

"Kim."

Oh, damn, even him saying her name made her want to flow to his lap and put her arms around him.

"What?" she growled.

"The scent-marking is for protection, not subjugation. Besides, you're less submissive than the highest alpha female I've ever met."

"Oh, sure. You're telling me that Glory is submissive?"

Dylan rumbled, "She's not an alpha. She's fairly far down in her pack."

The surprise of that stopped Kim's speech for a moment. But only a moment. "That explains why she puts up with you. But not me. I'm out of here. I'm sorry, Liam, but you're going to have to trust me."

Liam stepped around her to cut off her retreat. No, she wouldn't have made it to the door. His hands went to her shoulders, and she found herself pinned against the nearest wall.

"And you're going to have to trust me," he said.

This wasn't fair. He smelled too good. His blue eyes held the hint of red that Dylan's did, but she sensed that Liam was holding himself way, way back.

For one giddy moment she wondered what it would be like if he let loose. Would he press her to the wall, cover her with the weight of his body? Watching him lean around the bedroom door frame this morning, stark naked, had made her breasts ache and her thighs grow damp.

I have lost my mind.

The moment hovered, Liam towering over her, Kim's knees wanting to bend. She could slide down Liam's body and press her face to the front of his jeans. Wouldn't that be nice?

"Ow!" Connor shouted. He folded over, arms around his stomach.

"You all right, Connor?" Kim asked worriedly.

"No. Crap." He moaned in sudden pain.

"What's wrong? Are you sick? Geez, Liam, what did you put in the pancakes?"

A plate shattered on the kitchen floor. "Shite," Sean whispered, and at the same time his eyes flooded with pain.

Liam shoved Kim from him. "Kim, get away from us. Now."

All four Morrisseys started growling, eyes changing. Connor moaned pathetically.

Kim didn't know enough about Shifters to know what the hell was the matter with them. Were they shifting? Or sick? Sean slid to the kitchen floor at the same time Liam fell to his knees. Dylan got out of his chair and tried to go to Connor, but he collapsed before he made it to his grandson.

Liam raised his head, lips peeling back from fangs. "Go!" he shouted at her. "Run!"

Kim didn't waste time arguing. She fled through the kitchen, wrenched open the back door, and ran outside into hot, humid Austin air.

She could leap into her car, roar the hell out of Shifter-town, go home, and change all the locks. Move. Quit her job, never see Shifters again. They could keep her clothes; she didn't like most of what they'd packed anyway.

When she reached the bottom of the porch steps, Connor

started screaming. The anguish of it made Kim stop, turn back. Connor was the youngest, the weakest of them, and whatever was happening hurt him most of all.

Kim ran back up the steps and into the house. Connor's keening split the air. Dylan and Liam were both crawling toward him, and she realized that they were trying to touch him, these people who comforted each other with bodily contact.

"Liam, what can I do?"

Liam cranked his head around and looked up at Kim. His eyes were bright red. "No, Kim. Get out."

"I can't leave you like this. How do I help you?"

Liam couldn't or wouldn't answer. He managed to reach Connor, who screamed even louder when Liam touched him.

Damn it. Kim didn't know enough about Shifters—she who'd thought she'd researched everything about them. This could be anything from their Collars going wrong to some kind of weird virus.

"Hang on. I'll be right back."

She had no idea if Liam heard or understood. Kim ran out through the kitchen again and headed down the dirt path to the house next door. She banged on the back door, cupping her hands to peer through the window.

"Glory?"

She heard nothing, and for a few seconds she feared that Glory, too, writhed on the floor, moaning. Maybe everyone in Shiftertown did. *Shit.*

Glory wrenched open the door, as tall and stunning as she'd been the night before. She wore a hot-pink halter top that clasped her throat and hid her Collar, skintight black leather pants, and pink spike-heeled pumps. *Not an alpha, my ass.*

Glory was breathing hard, as if she'd been working out, but there wasn't a drop of perspiration on her face, not a hair out of place. "What?"

"There's something wrong with them. Something Shifter-wrong. You have to help them."

Glory jerked her gaze to the Morrissey house. "With Dylan?"

"With all of them. I don't know what's happening."

Without a word Glory stepped past her and hurried down the porch stairs. Kim had to jog to keep up with the woman's long stride, and this with Glory wearing mile-high shoes.

Glory shoved open the back door of the Morrissey house as though she belonged there. She stopped short, and Kim nearly ran into her. Liam had his arms around Connor now, but Connor still keened with his heartbreaking wail.

"What's wrong with them?" Kim shouted.

"I don't know. I've never seen this before."

Fat lot of help that was. Glory strode to Dylan, who had his eyes closed, his now elongated teeth cutting his lips. Glory grabbed his shoulder. "Dylan!"

She had to shake him and yell at him before Dylan finally looked up, his eyes now yellow swimming with red. He rasped a word Kim couldn't understand, but Glory nodded. She turned back to Kim with a grim look.

"They're being Summoned," she said.

"Summoned? What the hell does that mean?"

"It means their clan leader is calling them. He's put a compulsory spell on them—they'll be like this until they reach him and he lifts it."

A spell? "I thought you said you'd never seen this before."

"I haven't. Summonings happen only about once every two hundred years, because clan leaders who use them indiscriminately don't stay clan leaders long. Shifters don't like being coerced. Fergus must want you bad."

"What, he couldn't use the phone like everyone else?"

"He did use the phone. Yesterday. He commanded Dylan to turn you over to him, and Dylan refused. So Fergus did this."

From Glory's expression, she fully blamed Kim. Glory's shirt might hide her Collar, and Dylan might claim she wasn't high in her pack, but she was still a Shifter, still strong, still deadly.

"You have to get them to San Antonio," Glory said.

"San Antonio?"

"That's where Fergus is. You have to get them to Fergus—they can't drive like this."

"To this Fergus who's demanding that I be 'turned over' to him, whatever the hell that means? Why can't you take them?"

Glory snorted. "Respond to a Summoning from another clan leader? I'm Lupine. I walk into a gathering of Felines, they'll take my head off before I can speak."

"What about *my* head?"

"You'll have to risk it. Fergus will expect you to come with them anyway. Come on, help me get them into your car."

"They won't fit in my car."

"Make them fit." Glory grabbed Dylan under the armpits and hauled him to his feet. The big man could barely stand, but he leaned heavily on Glory and let her drag him across the kitchen. "There's no other choice."

Glory kicked open the kitchen door. It banged against the wall and began to drift shut, small flakes of plaster floating from the ceiling.

Liam snaked one clawed hand around Kim's ankle. "No," he rasped. "Run."

The pain in his eyes broke her heart. Liam was right; she *should* run. She should leave the Shifters to their fate and emigrate to Australia. Kim was coldly terrified at the thought of facing this Fergus, the man who could render four powerful Shifters helpless from seventy-five miles away. But Liam's anguish kept her with him.

"Kim," Glory shouted. "Come *on*."

Kim leaned over Liam. "We have to go, Liam. It's the only way, Glory says."

Liam tried to speak, but his words came out as unintelligible grunts.

Glory charged back inside and grabbed Sean. Kim finally persuaded Liam off the floor, and Liam hauled Connor to his feet. Somehow, the three of them got out the door and to Kim's two-door Mustang.

Sean had already folded himself into the tiny backseat, while Dylan leaned heavily on the car. Dylan seemed the least debilitated, but he was older, probably stronger. Glory took charge of Connor, and Dylan helped her slide Connor into the back next to Sean. Dylan himself cramped in beside his grandson, leaving the front seat for Liam to collapse into.

"What the hell?" A male Texan voice reached Kim. The big Lupine she'd met the night before, Ellison, came running at them from across the street. "Glory, what's going on?"

"Summoning," Glory said tersely.

"Holy shit."

"Kim's taking them to Fergus."

"Aw, man." Ellison's light blue eyes filled with distress. "And I can't go with you, damn it. Liam's got my cell number. You call me and keep me posted, all right?"

"Sure." Kim numbly got into the car.

"Wait." Ellison dashed into the Morrissey house, then out again, carrying Sean's big sword in its leather sheath. "Take this, in case."

There was no room for it in the packed car. Kim opened the trunk and Ellison dropped it inside.

As Kim slammed her door and started the car, Ellison stepped close to Glory and put both arms around her. She leaned into him, not in a sexual way, Kim realized, but for comfort, like Sandra had with Sean and Liam yesterday.

Kim pulled out of the driveway, her fingers cold and shaking despite the July heat, and headed out of Shiftertown.

CHAPTER TEN

They'd better be grateful for this. Kim sped down the I-35 as fast as she dared, cursing under her breath at the crawling traffic. It was Sunday—shouldn't all these people be in church or something? But no, they were meandering along the freeway between Austin and San Antonio, clogging the ramps, driving slowly in the left lanes, cutting her off . . .

She drove as swiftly as she was able, though she didn't dare risk being pulled over for speeding. She imagined herself trying to explain to the nice police officer why she had four half-crazed Shifters stuffed into her car and a big sword in the trunk.

Connor's moans had turned to whimpers. Kim had no idea how this Fergus had caused their state from so far away, but she wanted to scream at him. Liam was the strongest man she'd ever met, and to see him hunched up in the seat next to her, rocking in pain, made her furious.

"It's not much farther." She had no idea if Liam could hear her, and he didn't respond.

The freeway had never seemed so long. Signboards with German-sounding names slid by: New Braunfels, Gruene, the ever-popular Schlitterbahn water park, which Kim had loved as a kid.

When they reached the northern outskirts of San Antonio, Liam at last took his hands from his face. "This exit."

Kim dove for the off-ramp, which took her to a freeway that looped around the city. "Then where?"

Liam flicked his fingers at the road, which she took to mean, "Keep going." Dylan sat up behind her. In the rearview mirror, Kim saw him draw Connor to him, cradling the boy against his chest. Sean had his eyes closed, but Kim couldn't tell whether he slept.

When they'd reached the southwestern edge of town, Liam gestured for Kim to take another exit. He directed her down a road that became a highway, running west out of town again.

"There's a Shiftertown out here?" Kim asked, as they left the city limits behind.

Liam didn't answer. Sean was sitting up now, leaning against the window. Their breathing had calmed, no longer tortured rasping, but they still looked gray and drawn.

About twenty-five miles later, Dylan leaned forward between the seats, long arm pointing out a side road that wasn't signposted. "There."

They'd left Hill Country behind and had reached the deserts of south Texas. The land was flat and dry, grasses clumped and yellow instead of soft green. On the left side of the road, behind barbed wire, a few cows grazed.

No barbed wire lined the right side of the road, the land open and flowing to the white-blue horizon. The humidity had dropped considerably, Kim's sweat was quickly evaporating in the dry air.

"It's coming up," Liam said. He sounded almost normal, and his fangs had receded.

Two wooden fence posts with no fence and no gate

marked a dirt road that reached a pale finger across the land. Kim turned down it, silently cursing the ruts that banged her car's underbody. Maybe she could charge this Fergus for the damage.

A cluster of houses lay about three miles down this joke of a road, and a hand-painted sign read: WELCOME TO SHIFTERTOWN! POPULATION: FIFTY-TWO SHIFTERS, TWENTY HORSES, FIVE DOGS, AND FIFTEEN CATS.

The houses were long, low adobes with tiny windows, probably ranch houses left over from earlier in the twentieth century. Like the houses in Austin, these had been fixed up and painted, but instead of having yards, they were grouped around a somewhat sad playground where no kids played. Pickups were parked haphazardly in the dirt around the houses.

A steel pole corral that surrounded open stalls with corrugated steel roofs sat at one end of the street. A dozen desultory horses moved between pens and corral, paying no attention to the car hurtling toward them in a cloud of dust.

One of the town's five dogs lounged at the front door of the house in front of which Liam told Kim to park. The house was no bigger than the others and had a green-painted door flanked by two windows to either side of it. The dog got up, stretched, and wandered toward them, tail wagging.

"Are you sure this is right?" Kim asked, as she got out and yanked the seat forward to release the others.

"Very sure," Liam said.

The four men had returned to almost normal, except for the tension. Connor leaned against the car once he'd gotten out of it, his face still tight.

"Why did he Summon Connor?" Kim asked Liam in a low voice. "If he wants me, why didn't he just get you and your dad to bring me down? Or can't he pinpoint who he wants?"

"No, the spell can be very specific. Fergus decided who he'd cast it on."

Kim looked at Connor, who had walked away to retch into a stand of tall grasses. "What kind of asshole is this guy? Connor doesn't have anything to do with me."

The Liam who looked at her was no longer the affable, sexy man she'd met yesterday. The Liam next to her sparked with contained fury and would have scared the shit out of her if she'd walked into the bar's office and seen him like this behind the desk. She realized that Liam had showed her the "nice" Shifter, the one humans could talk to. The one she could sit with on a bed and kiss.

No, wait, she could kiss him even now. She'd taste his fury and let him know she shared it, while he ran his hands over her body.

How would sex with Liam be when he was like this? Raw and wild. Against the wall or on the hood of the car— all-out, good-time sex. *That's what I'm talking about.*

Liam opened the door of the house and walked in. The inside didn't impress Kim. People obviously lived here, but they just as obviously didn't much care about cleaning up the place.

Liam strode through the cluttered living room and kitchen littered with dirty dishes, and opened a door. Cool air poured up stone stairs beyond. Cellar? Storm shelter? A place like that could house snakes, scorpions, black widows . . .

"In there?" she asked. She thought she could face a hostile Shifter, but spiders? Not so much.

Liam passed her without a word. Thank God for the Shifter custom of the male entering a place first. If there were spiders down there, Liam could stomp on them before she went down.

Dylan nodded at Sean, who'd retrieved his sword from her trunk, indicating he should enter after Liam. Then Dylan, then Connor.

Kim hesitated at the top of the steps, still thinking about spiders—and Fergus. She could run, make it to her car, and hightail it back to Austin. No one was behind her; she could get a good head start.

Connor looked back at her, the light from the kitchen glinting on the fear in his eyes. He was terrified and, from the greenish cast to his face, still nauseated from the Summoning. Would the bully Fergus try to hurt Connor if Kim ran for it? Probably.

"Bastard," she growled, and started after Connor. She couldn't do that to the kid.

Connor flashed Kim a nervous grin and kept going. Kim picked her way along, feeling out of her depth and refusing to touch the stone walls.

The Morrissey men waited for them in a tiled corridor that was completely incongruous with the house above. The walls were polished wood and, to Kim's astonishment, filled with paintings and beautiful photographs. Real paintings by real artists that museums paid major money for, photographs by people like Ansel Adams. Spanish-style, carved wooden doors with small square windows lined the corridor between the priceless artwork.

What the hell kind of place was this?

Liam led the way to the end of the hall and opened a door to a cavernous room. Dylan went in first this time, then Liam, then Sean, then Connor. Kim, in most need of protection, entered last.

The room was huge, meant to hold several hundred people. The walls were paneled with warm wood, the purple-red hue speaking of exotic Oriental forests. The ceiling was arched like a cathedral, the arches intricately carved and marching toward an enormous fireplace at the end. Money and artistry had gone into shaping the chamber, which was far larger than any of the houses above it.

The room was also filled with Shifters.

There must have been a hundred of them, each as physically honed as Liam, Dylan, and Sean. The sign outside said that only fifty-two Shifters lived in this Shiftertown, so these must have driven in for the occasion. Every single one was male.

The crowd parted as Dylan led the way forward, past the looming arches, through the sea of Shifters, to the center of the room. Four men waited for them there: a big guy with a long black braid and a leather motorcycle vest, surrounded by three equally thuglike men.

"Let me guess," Kim whispered to Liam. "That's Fergus."

Liam nodded grimly. Fergus turned hard blue eyes to Kim and gave her the Shifter once-over.

"This is her?" he asked. His accent was more Southern than Texan, and his tone said he'd expected her to be more formidable.

Liam set his mouth, and Dylan became their spokesman. "This is Kim Fraser, the defense attorney for Brian Smith."

All eyes on Kim. Nostrils flared as the Shifters took in Kim's scent and the fact that Liam had marked her. Every single Shifter in here wore a Collar, but it dawned on Kim that the Collars might not make a damn bit of difference if she tried to run or fight. These were dangerous men, watching for now because they chose to.

"Crap," she said under her breath. "And me without my pepper spray."

"We like pepper spray," Liam answered.

"Figures."

Fergus pinned her with a blue stare, then looked at Sean and held out his hand.

Sean unstrapped the sword on his back and took it to him. Fergus didn't say thank you; he just grabbed the sword from Sean and passed it to one of his underlings. As he turned, strands of braided leather swung across his hip from a handle hooked to his belt.

"Is that a cat-o'-nine-tails?" Kim asked Liam.

"Most like."

"Why, in case he loses his own?"

Liam's sudden smile burst over his face. Connor laughed openly.

"Shut it," Dylan hissed.

Fergus's attention riveted to Kim. "Come here, woman."

Kim remained where she was, not about to trot obediently to him. Liam stood beside her, his body solid and warm, making her feel suddenly safe.

"I *said,* come here."

Kim lifted her chin. "Do the words 'screw you' mean anything to you?"

Fergus's eyes glittered as the Shifters muttered to each other. Fergus's three henchmen folded their arms and glared. One had a shaved head and a neck covered in tattoos, one had a sandy blond ponytail, and the third had short black hair. He looked ex-military, although Shifters weren't allowed to join the military.

"Bring her to me," Fergus said curtly to Liam.

Liam didn't move. The room was silent, the tension ramping high. Fergus's eyes changed from blue to white-gray.

Kim didn't know what all Fergus could do—another Summoning to make Liam drag her across the room to him? Kim felt like a sapling in a tall forest; Shifter males were mostly over six feet tall, and she was five feet high in flats. And where were all the women Shifters? Baking cookies?

"You know you can't kill me," Kim said in her brisk courtroom voice. "There's already one Shifter in jail because of a human's death, and even though *I'm* convinced he didn't do it, plenty of people think he did. If I disappear or turn up dead, you'll have your county sheriff and possibly the feds all over you."

Fergus just stared at her, then turned to Liam. "Does she ever shut up?"

"Not that I've noticed."

"Not a point in her favor."

"I don't know," Liam said with a faint smile. "I kind of like it."

Fergus's lip curled. *"Bring her to me."*

"Sorry, Fergus," Liam said. "I'll be leaving that choice up to her."

The room held its collective breath. Kim didn't have to be an expert in nonverbal cues to see that Fergus's whole stance now said, *Obey me or suffer.* Liam's stance said, *No way in hell,* but Kim noticed he wouldn't meet Fergus's eyes.

"I'm not going to hurt the woman," Fergus said, tight-lipped.

"No?" Kim broke in. "Why am I not reassured?"

"He's telling the truth." Liam's voice warmed her ear, his voice so tight she realized how much he must be holding himself back.

"Could have fooled me."

Liam turned Kim to face him. He touched her cheek, his eyes wary but with a sparkle of excitement deep within them. "He doesn't want to hurt you, love," he said softly. "That was never his intention. When Fergus called Dad last night, he ordered us to bring you down here so he could claim you as his mate."

Kim's blue eyes went wide, shining with anger, fear, and astonishment. "You've *got* to be kidding me."

Liam smoothed a lock of her hair, trying to soothe her with his Shifter touch. "Don't worry, love. I'm not going to let him."

It struck him suddenly that he'd been waiting for something like this. Maybe all his life. He'd told himself he'd passed up potential mates to give other Shifter males a chance at happiness, but he realized now that he'd simply not found a woman he wanted to be with. Easy to be altruistic when he wasn't making much of a sacrifice.

But when this sassy human female had walked into his office yesterday, with her blouse buttons straining, her short gray skirt smooth over her sweet rump, when she'd started laying out a heated, well-reasoned argument why he should help her before Liam could even speak, his well-ordered world had overturned. She'd managed to touch something that Liam had always kept protected. Maybe she'd touched it because he hadn't kept his guard up, hadn't expected a human to reach what no Shifter had ever reached.

Last night, when Dylan had broken the news that Fergus expected Liam to bring Kim to him so Fergus could claim her as mate, Liam had flat-out refused. Dylan had argued, not understanding. What was the fate of one human against the good of all Shifters? Fergus could control Kim, and that would be the end of the matter.

Liam had nearly punched his father in the face, something he'd never in his life dreamed of doing. Kim would go to Fergus over his dead body, he'd said. Dylan had regarded Liam first in amazement, then comprehension, even sympathy. He'd stopped arguing, told Liam he agreed to disobey Fergus, then walked out of the house.

Mate. Mine. Protect.

Liam wanted to hold Kim and not let her go. He wanted to kiss her, screw her, make her pancakes the next morning. The instincts that hadn't manifested in a hundred years of living suddenly rose and raged.

"Why would he want me to be his *mate?*" Kim was asking. "Whatever that means. He's never met me before today."

Goddess, how could a male *not* want her? But she had a point.

"He wants to control you," Liam said. "Because you're right. It would cause him major problems if he killed you. But if you're his mate, you're subject to him and clan law. And no longer a threat to Shifters."

"And if I refuse?"

Fergus wasn't going to let her refuse. Liam wasn't certain how Fergus planned to subdue Kim—drugs, spells, terror—but the man wanted Kim under his thumb.

Fergus also likely wanted to see how far Liam would

go to protect her. Once Fergus knew what Liam felt for Kim, the better he could manipulate Liam and the rest of his family. Either way, Kim would be watched, controlled.

"You won't have to," Liam told Kim.

Fergus gave them a narrow stare. "Does this mean you make the Challenge for her?"

Liam sensed Dylan and Sean move in behind him, their instinct to protect manifesting, no matter how bloody stupid they thought Liam was being. Liam wished Connor would get the hell out of here. Connor was a kid, a cub, and he wasn't ready yet for this kind of confrontation. Liam didn't think Fergus would take that into consideration when he started meting out punishment.

Liam slid his hand into Kim's, looked Fergus straight in the eye, and reached for a Texas phrase that would make Ellison proud.

"Damn straight."

CHAPTER ELEVEN

Fergus's gaze locked with Liam's, and Liam felt a surge of triumph.

"Dylan," Fergus snapped.

Dylan answered in a calm voice. "My son is not yet mated. It's his right."

Don't defend me, Dad. Walk away. This isn't your fight.

Dylan remained in place. Liam hadn't really thought he'd be wise and disappear. Dylan would never desert his offspring, even if it meant his death.

"Ex*cuse* me," Kim burst out. Heads swiveled to her, a hundred pairs of Shifter eyes pinning her, but she didn't flinch. "I don't like all this talk about *mating*, thank you very much—especially when it involves me."

Liam wanted to laugh out loud. She was a treasure. Shifter instincts were starting to blot out his human reason, making him yearn for Fergus's blood under his claws and then Kim in his arms.

Sex with Kim would be glorious, even if he had to stay

in human form for it. He'd gotten a taste of her last night, her sweet mouth, her kisses, her touch on his body. He wanted to lie on top of her, practicing more human kissing as he slid inside her and made her his.

Fergus's own pheromones rolled off him, thick and strong, polluting the air. Smelling them, Liam realized Fergus didn't plan to make Kim mate in name only. He wanted Kim, wanted a furious fuck. Liam would die before he let that happen.

"Silence her," Fergus growled at Liam.

Sean stepped to Kim's other side. Even without the sword, he stood like a warrior, ready to fight. "Liam has made the Challenge," Sean said. "Nothing we can do but see how it plays out."

"Screw that." Kim tried to twist out of Liam's hold, but Liam wasn't about to let her go. "Connor," she said over her shoulder. "Can you find something for me to stand on? A chair or something?"

Her question jolted Connor out of his frozen terror. Good for Kim.

The Shifters parted to let Connor leave the room. Liam hoped it would take him hours to locate a chair, or that he'd think better of returning at all, but Connor came back almost at once with a stepstool.

"Good enough." Kim told him to put it on the floor in front of her, and Liam released her long enough to let her climb on it. He kept his arms around her as she straightened up, both to steady her and to keep her in his protective hold.

"That's better," Kim said. The stool let her stand half a head taller than Liam, and now she could look across the crowd of Shifters.

"There doesn't need to be any violence over this," she said. "What y'all don't understand is that I can be the best *friend* you've got. You have a Shifter in jail, and the world howling for his blood. If I can prove he didn't kill his human girlfriend, think what terrific PR that would be for all of you. Shifters are viewed with suspicion and hostility. If I show the world that Brian was wronged, make him a sympathetic figure, even a hero, imagine what an amazing step forward that would be. They might let you integrate more, let your kids go to schools that aren't held in abandoned warehouses."

Silence. Not one expression changed.

"Hey, maybe they'd even let us have cable," a Shifter in the back drawled. The room rumbled with male laughter.

"I'm serious. I'm good at my job. I can do this if you help me."

Fergus's mouth drew to a thin line. "Liam, shut her up."

Liam wasn't about to. Kim had Fergus baffled, and he liked that.

"You act like you don't want Brian released." Kim went on. "He didn't kill Michelle. Why should he be executed for it? Why would you let him be?"

Fergus drew the cat-o'-nine-tails from his belt. "Liam."

"He's going to whip me?" Kim asked Liam in amazement.

Liam lifted Kim off the stool. "Time to stop talking, love. Fergus, if we're doing this Challenge, let's get on with it, man."

"Not until I teach the bitch some manners."

Connor stormed forward despite Sean's attempts to restrain him. The young man's face was red, his large hands in fists. "Leave her alone! She's not doing anything to you. She's just talking. How can that hurt you, you bastard?"

"Connor, shut it," Dylan said fiercely.

Fergus's gaze chilled the air as it rested on Connor. "Come here, boy."

"He's a cub," Dylan tried. "He doesn't understand."

Connor wiped his eyes. "I understand, Grandda'." He glared at Fergus, though he dropped his gaze almost immediately. "I meant it too."

Fergus was livid. Cords stood out on his neck, and his eyes burned with the intensity of a feral's.

Liam knew full well how Fergus had envisioned this cozy scenario: Liam and family would scurry down to San Antonio, hand Kim over in abject apology, then hurry away again, letting Fergus do whatever the hell he wanted.

Instead all four Morrisseys had defied him—twice. The first time by refusing to respond to his verbal summons, yesterday. Now, in Fergus's own lair, Kim had lectured him, Liam had made the Challenge, and Connor had broken the rule of a cub not confronting an alpha before he was of age.

Cubs could get away with a lot on account of their youth—Goddess knew Liam had been a pain in the ass during puberty—but flouting Fergus in front of the whole clan could not go unpunished. Connor was too young to fight for dominance, so he'd have to be swatted, as a lion might bat aside a cub who'd gotten too rambunctious.

"Come here," Fergus repeated.

The magic in the command propelled Connor toward him. Sean started after him, but Liam shook his head. "No, Sean, let me."

Sean opened his mouth to argue, then nodded, his eyes bleak. He turned away, unhappy, but knowing why he had to stand down.

"Let you what?" Kim asked Liam.

Her eyes were wide in her white face. She was afraid and angry, and so damn beautiful she made his heart ache.

Liam cupped her face in his hands. "Kim, my love, stay here with Sean and Dylan. Don't even think about coming after me, and please, *stay quiet.*"

Kim's lips parted as though she wanted to protest. Then she closed her mouth and nodded. *Good girl.* Liam turned from her and swiftly followed Connor.

Liam was the same height as Fergus. He and the big man looked at each other eye to eye, Liam without flinching.

"If you do this," Fergus said in vicious fury, "then when I answer your mate Challenge, I'll wipe the floor with you."

Gods, what an arrogant bastard. "Just get on with it."

Connor's eyes held tears, but his head was up, though he couldn't meet Fergus's gaze or even Liam's. "No, Liam. Leave it."

"It's my right, nephew," Liam said quietly.

Two of the thugs, the one with the shaved head and the black-haired one, divested Connor of his shirt. Connor couldn't meet their eyes either.

Liam stripped off his own shirt and dropped it on the floor. The thugs ignored him. They turned Connor around and bent him forward at the waist, exposing his young, unblemished back.

Fergus raised his cat-o'-nine-tails. With a grunt, he brought it down. Before it could strike Connor, Liam leaned over his nephew and took the blow directly across his own back.

"What the hell?" Kim shrieked. "What is he doing?" Horror filled her as Fergus, eyes fixed, mouth curled in vicious enjoyment, struck again. The sound of the leather swished through the silence, followed by the slap against Liam's skin.

Dylan moved toward them, grim-faced, tugging off his shirt to reveal a back as broad and muscular as Liam's. When he reached Connor and Liam, he leaned over Connor as well, father and son enclosing the boy in a protective Shifter embrace. Fergus continued to ply the whip as though he didn't notice, lips pulling back from teeth that had become fangs.

Kim started forward, but Sean stepped in front of her, blocking her way. "Stay here. Let it finish."

Sean's eyes held anguish, but she saw he wasn't about to try to stop Fergus. She also sensed that if Sean hadn't felt the need to keep Kim bottled up here, he'd have joined the human shield around Connor.

"This is insane," she said, heart in her throat. Barbaric, uncivilized.

But they're Shifters, a voice whispered in her head. *Isn't that why they're forced to wear the Collars, to keep their barbarism under control?*

The Collar wasn't doing jack to keep Fergus from beating Liam and Dylan to bloody pulp. The leather straps opened Liam's flesh, and blood dribbled to the floor. Liam was taking the brunt of it, only some of the blows hitting Dylan, as though Fergus's aim was to debilitate Liam only. Nothing reached Connor, enclosed in a Shifter wall.

The other Shifters watched without comment, no murmuring, no growling, neither egging Fergus on nor trying to stop him. The beating went on and on, as though Fergus was taking out years of welled-up aggression on the Morrisseys.

"Why don't you do something?" Kim asked Sean, tears in her eyes.

"It's the Shifter way." Sean's mouth was set in a grim line.

"It's a fucked-up way."

Kim waited until Sean again turned to watch, then darted around him and ran through the pack. Short height could be an advantage—the tall Shifters weren't used to dealing with one small, athletic female slithering through their grasps.

She reached Fergus. "Stop this!"

Fergus gave Liam two more vicious blows, then trained his awful gaze on Kim. He was far more frightening than Dylan, his eyes red with rage, a tinge of madness in them. She was looking at a man who would do absolutely anything, no matter how ruthless, to get what he wanted. No holds barred.

Liam jerked his head up. "Sean, take her out of here."

Sean was already behind Kim. Kim spun away and put herself right under Fergus's nose. Fergus snarled. His face had half changed, his lips peeling back from his red, angry mouth. She thought of the Lupine who'd tried to kill her, and realized that Fergus wasn't too far removed from that un-Collared Shifter's vicious rage.

"I'm not Shifter," Kim said. "I'm not afraid of you."

Big fat lie. The man was terrifying, and Kim had no doubt he could kill her fast. But Kim couldn't stand by and watch him beat on Liam, whose back was now coated with blood.

Fergus went for her, whip raised. Liam lunged at him with a fighting snarl. The sound filled the room, loud and inhuman.

Fergus's eyes glittered, not in fear, but in glee. A second later, Dylan was next to Liam, his skin glistening with sweat and blood.

"No, Liam. It's not your right."

"Let him," Fergus said.

"*No.*" Dylan's voice was hard.

As Kim watched, tiny sparks raced around Liam's Collar and into his flesh. Liam flinched as his muscles registered the shock, but he never took his eyes from Fergus.

So the Collars did work. Liam was in a deadly rage, his adrenal system signaling he was ready to fight and kill. The Collar was trying to stop him, to once again torture him from the inside out.

"Liam," she whispered. "Please don't."

Her words seemed to penetrate the haze of fury in Liam's brain. Liam broke the gaze lock with Fergus, turned his head, and looked down at Kim.

"I claim her as mate," he growled.

To Kim's surprise, Fergus's angry look receded until he almost smirked. He spread his arms, the ends of the cat-o'-nine-tails fluttering. "I hereby release my claim. I wouldn't want the bitch in my house, anyway, with my cubs. I wish you joy of her."

The Shifters let out their collective breaths, stances relaxing. *What the hell?* "Liam . . ."

Liam seized Kim's arm, his hand slick with blood. "I claim her before the clan, as is my right."

Fergus's eyes glinted. "The clan recognizes your claim."

"He changed his mind quick," Kim said. "Fastest one-night stand I ever had."

Liam laughed, the sound rumbling. Fergus looked triumphant, as if he'd won, his eyes glittering in a way Kim didn't like.

He wasn't giving in. He was planning something.

Fergus gave the rest of the room a flat stare. "Everybody out."

The Shifters started to leave, their voices growing louder as they wound down. Kim wondered how many truly supported Fergus and how many had been compelled here like Liam and his family. Glory had said Shifters didn't like clan leaders who used the Summons so maybe Fergus had simply bullied them into showing up.

Fergus stepped past the Morrisseys, followed by his thugs, the only ones who hadn't relaxed. His bodyguards, Kim realized. Fergus was the clan leader, the ultimate alpha, or whatever. But if he had such power over the clan, why did he worry so much that he'd lose it?

Dylan pulled his shirt back on, wincing when the fabric touched his raw back. Liam took his T-shirt from Sean and balled it in his hands, his back a bloody mess.

Liam had rushed to protect Connor from dire hurt, and Dylan had rushed to protect both his son and grandson. Kim understood love like that, the same that had reared up and kicked her when she hadn't been able to save her brother all those years ago.

She took Liam's T-shirt from his hands, giving him a watery smile as she shook it out and folded it.

The only one not pleased was Connor. When the last of the Shifters had left the room, Connor launched himself at Liam.

"Why did you do that? I could have taken it. I didn't ask you to stand in for me."

Tears of rage and frustration streamed from Connor's eyes as he beat on Liam's chest.

Liam grabbed his fists, his voice incredibly gentle. "Connor, lad, stop that now."

Connor jerked away from him. He started to strike at Dylan, then probably realizing that was a bad idea, rounded on Sean. Sean responded by wrapping his arms around Connor and pulling him close.

Liam moved behind Connor and stroked the young man's hair. "The punishment wasn't for you, Con. Fergus was pissed at me for not groveling enough. He couldn't come up with a legitimate reason to have me beaten, so he picked on you. It wasn't your transgression, lad, it was mine."

Kim saw Connor relax, the young man leaning into Sean. "Why'd you let him? Grandda', why didn't *you* fight him?"

"Not the time and place," Dylan said. "Come on, we have to go."

He turned and left the room without waiting for them, his boots clicking on the tiles of the hall. Connor finally unwound his arms from Sean and went after Dylan, wiping his eyes, and the other three followed.

"You are going to explain what the hell just happened, aren't you?" Kim asked, as she started up the stairs ahead of Liam. After the elegant surroundings in the basement, the stairs were dingy and musty. She thought about spiders again.

Liam ruffled her hair. "Kim, who likes everything nice and neat. What a woman."

He caressed her neck under her hair. He might have just gotten skin whipped off his back, but his touch still raised goose bumps on Kim's flesh. It was the touch of a man desiring a woman, nothing less.

Damn if she didn't want to turn around right there and jump his bones. Never mind that his father, brother, and nephew were only a few steps ahead of them. Kim wanted to kiss Liam as she had last night, maybe have him lift her so she could wrap her legs around his waist.

Liam kissed the corner of her mouth. "Come on, love. Let's go out to the sunshine."

Kim kissed him back, which did not dampen her fires; then she made herself turn and follow Sean up. They clattered through the silent house, then out the front door.

The Shifters were waiting for them, all of them, arranged in a semicircle between them and Kim's car. Kim's heart started to pound.

"Aren't they going to let us leave?"

"Not yet," Dylan said.

Doors around the group of houses were opening, and female Shifters emerged. With kids. Happy to be released from whatever confinement had been imposed on them, the kids raced to the playground, making the sad patch of grass suddenly come alive. The entire dog population joined them, tails waving.

Fergus had clipped his cat-o'-nine back to his belt, and now stood with arms folded, talking to some of the male Shifters. Kim almost fell over with shock when a woman moved through the crowd and slid her arm around Fergus's waist. She wasn't some wimpy thing, either—she was tall, strong, muscular, with a hard but beautiful face. Like Glory, though not as flamboyantly dressed.

"Who is that?" Kim asked Liam.

"His mate," Liam said. "Andrea."

"Wait, wait, wait." Kim waved her hands. "He was going on about taking *me* as his mate. Why, if he already has one?"

"Clan leaders can mate with more than one woman, and Fergus has two already. Selfish, because there aren't many females to go around, but it's true that mixed offspring have a better chance of surviving."

"Oh, for God's sake." Kim rounded on Liam. "Can *you* have more than one mate? Do you have three wives tucked away in Shiftertowns around the state?"

Liam burst out laughing, and Sean followed suit. Their

laughter held a note of tension, as if they were happy they had something to laugh about. Liam put his arm around Kim. "I couldn't handle more than you, love. And I hope you can handle me."

His smile gave the double entendre impact. Kim flushed. "We need to talk."

"Not yet." Liam walked Kim out to the semicircle of Shifters. He didn't retrieve his shirt; his back had to be killing him under the burning sun.

Fergus faced them as they approached, Andrea letting go of him but remaining only inches from his side.

"Why would she want him?" Kim whispered. "Especially when he has another?"

"Because he is the most powerful man in the clan. Only Dad comes close to him for dominance. And I should have mentioned that Shifters have terrific hearing."

"Thanks."

"Liam." Fergus's voice rolled across those of the other Shifters and the kids playing. "Stand here."

Liam stopped in front of Fergus and turned Kim to face him. He brushed a finger over Kim's cheek, then held up her left hand in his right, twining their fingers.

Without waiting for everyone to quiet down, Fergus said, "Under the light of the sun, I recognize this mating."

He spoke in a monotone, the words rapid, as though he wanted to get this over with. He was ready to move on to the next thing, and Kim wondered what that next thing was.

Liam smiled at Kim. The other Shifters started clapping and cheering, and Connor threw his arms around Kim and gave her a breath-stealing hug.

"Thank you, Kim."

Before Kim could ask, "For what?" Connor was leaping away, whooping and yelling with the others. Fergus twined his arm around Andrea's waist and walked away with her.

Kim never knew where it came from, but all of a sudden beer foam showered the air. Sean shook a bottle and sprayed it over them, laughing hysterically. He'd gotten his sword back, she saw, the hilt protruding over his shoulder.

"Just what I wanted, beer in my hair," Kim said.

Liam rubbed his thumb across her chin. "We'll have time to wash it out later." He leaned down and pressed dry, warm lips to her mouth. "Is this kiss up to your standards? I'm still learning."

He smiled, but his skin was hot under her fingertips, his chest still sweating. "Are you all right?" Kim asked. "I saw the Collar shock you."

"I'll live." Another light kiss, Liam's hand stealing to her waist. "I'm thinking of another ache right now."

The stiff thing pressing her abdomen left no doubt about what he meant. "Your back's a mess," she said.

"So we'll be washing that along with your hair."

Liam kissed her again. Around them, the Shifters partied, a complete change from the cold resentment in the basement. They could have been at a block party, friends and neighbors coming together to celebrate. Dylan struck up conversation with some of the Shifter men, and Sean had been lured away by a couple of females. Sean and the ladies were flirting pretty fiercely, although Shifters liked to touch a lot, so maybe they were discussing movies or something while hands ran along arms and shoulders and backs.

Questions swam in Kim's brain—she'd thought she'd researched everything about Shifters, but she realized she'd only learned what they'd let humans learn. There was too much she didn't know, too many nuances she needed to understand. She hadn't argued about this "mating" with Liam because she saw that it let Liam walk away from Fergus, and Fergus stop trying to beat up on Connor and Dylan. And she definitely hadn't wanted to do any kind of mating with Fergus.

She'd smile and laugh with them, go along with their pretense that everything was all right, but once they got back to Austin, she and Liam were going to have a long talk.

A shadow fell over her, and Kim looked up to see Fergus looming next to them. "You accept the mating?" he asked Liam.

He asked *Liam,* not Kim. Asshole.

Liam's expression remained cool. "I do."

"You know what it means, then?" Fergus kept his voice soft, turning away from the other Shifters. "You are responsible for everything she does. She steps a toe out of line, it's you who pays. Your father won't interfere; he knows the rules."

Kim's anger flared. "You—"

She found Liam's fingers over her lips. "Not now," he said. "I know what it means, Fergus. You forgo the claim forever, then?"

"I do, but I have a condition."

"Why does that not surprise me?" Kim muttered behind Liam's fingers.

"Brian goes down," Fergus said. "You, woman, will let him, and Liam, you'll make sure she does it. He pleads guilty and takes the punishment. Those are my terms."

Without waiting for their answer, he turned from them and walked away.

CHAPTER TWELVE

Liam knew that Kim didn't understand. He held her hand as she drove, and sensed the confusion pouring off her. He'd explain everything to her soon, but right now he just wanted to have her pull the car over so he could drag her off and sex her.

He burned with it. When a Shifter claimed a mate, the urge to procreate released. He'd always known that in theory but never realized it would be this much of a flood. It was all he could do to stop at holding Kim's hand. He wanted to slide his fingers under the waistband of her jeans, lean over and press kisses to her neck, unbutton her blouse and dip his hand inside.

The little sweetheart hadn't let him get into the car until she'd dragged a towel and a first-aid kit out of her trunk, demanded a bottle of clean water from one of the Shifters, and doctored Liam's back. She'd rinsed and dried the wounds, then applied antiseptic, which had stung a little.

Liam had tried to tell her he'd heal quickly, but she

only clenched her teeth and doctored him anyway. He also couldn't tell her, with Sean and Connor hovering, that her touch fired his longing to open his pants and have a go with her right there.

The others must have sensed his craving, because the teasing had begun.

"So does a mate's touch really heal, Liam?" Sean had asked.

"I don't think he's going to last until we get home." Connor snickered beside him.

"You'll live, son," Dylan had said, clapping Liam on the shoulder. "It's worth it."

Kim hadn't known what the hell they were talking about, but from her blush, she'd suspected.

He squeezed Kim's thigh now, and she responded with a smile, albeit a nervous one. Not disgust, not, "Keep your hands off me, Shifter." Kim liked him. Would she like him after she fully understood what was happening?

"Damnation," Connor said from the backseat.

Liam looked over his shoulder. Connor's nose was buried in a magazine Kim had grabbed for him at the convenience store where they'd stopped for gas. Though Kim had offered to pay for gas, magazine, and cold sodas, Dylan had silently fished out some cash and pressed it into her hand.

It was a sports magazine, because the only thing Connor liked better than cars was sports, football in particular. Not American football with pigskin and pads, but *real* football, what Americans called soccer. Connor had never been to a true football game, in a stadium overflowing with raving crowds that made American fans look like a pack of knitting grannies. Connor watched it on telly when he could and avidly followed the Republic of Ireland national football team in the sports news.

"Ireland is playing today," Connor mourned. "Tonight for them, but today over here."

"Never on a major network," Sean said. "That would be a bloody miracle."

"Sportz 3." Connor lifted the magazine sideways, studying the grid of sports offerings for the week. "Satellite channel. Game starts in an hour." He sounded glum.

"Never mind, Con," Dylan said. He leaned against the window and closed his eyes. "It's a human game, anyway."

Dylan had never understood Connor's obsession with sports. But then Dylan had grown up two centuries ago, far from human society, while Connor had spent his entire young life immersed in it. Connor was what Shifters were trying to create by taking the Collar, a generation comfortable with human culture. Maybe in a few generations, the Collars could become a thing of the past, forgotten, Shifters fully integrated into human society.

Dylan wanted that. But it didn't mean he understood Connor's addiction.

"Ellison has a friend in Shiftertown North," Sean said. "He can sometimes get satellite channels. Maybe we can get you up there to see it."

"In an hour?" Connor shook his head. "And I've seen that jury-rigged TV. You have to turn off all the lights, tilt your head sideways, and squint. If he's lucky and can get a signal at all."

"There's bound to be a recording somewhere," Sean said. "Me and Liam will look around for it."

Connor threw down the magazine. "Stop babying me, Sean. I'll not see it, and you know it. It's not like the local DVD stores have a huge section on Irish football."

"Or you can watch it at my house," Kim said.

All four Shifters stopped and stared at her. "I have every satellite channel known to man," Kim went on. "Plus a new flat-screen. No beer, though. Sorry."

Connor shoved himself between the seats, eyes alight. "Are you serious? You'd let me watch your telly at your house?"

"Sure, why not?"

Dylan answered. "Because your neighbors might object to you with a houseful of Shifters. Police might be called."

"It's not against the law for a human to invite over Shifters. Unusual, maybe. And anyway, we'll go in through the garage and no one will see us."

"'Twould be an imposition we can't ask," Dylan said, his tone holding finality.

Connor made a frustrated noise. Liam sympathized with his frustration but for a different reason. He'd pictured taking Kim to Shiftertown and locking them both in his bedroom for three days. But he understood that Kim was offering this hospitality to try to make up for Fergus dragging Connor into this mess—a mess she thought she'd caused.

Kim didn't know that the mess with Fergus was ongoing, that the incident today was a drop in the vast ocean of their struggle with the clan leader. Fergus had gotten what he'd wanted—control of Kim and how she managed Brian's case. Or so Fergus believed. Kim hadn't said anything after Fergus had given her his "terms." She'd scowled but kept her lips pressed together, which Liam didn't think boded well. Fergus seriously underestimated Kim if he thought she'd simply fall into line.

However, in theory, now Fergus could threaten Liam and the rest of the Morrisseys if Kim didn't cooperate. Plus Fergus's capitulation had made him look generous to the rest of the clan—he'd been unwilling to stand between a Shifter and his true mate. Wasn't that noble of him?

"But trying to hold me prisoner in Shiftertown *isn't* an imposition?" Kim demanded. "I'm driving the car, and we're going to my house so Connor can watch Irish football."

Connor hooted with joy and kissed Kim's cheek. "I love you, Kim. I'm so glad Liam claimed you."

Kim looked startled but said nothing. Connor thumped

happily back in his seat, and Dylan made a "Whatever" gesture.

Of course, Liam thought as the Austin exits started to glide by, Kim's house also had a bedroom.

An hour later, Kim had four Shifters in her living room avidly watching guys in shorts running across a soccer field in rainy Ireland.

I could grow to like this game, Kim thought. No helmets or padding, just tight-fitting shirts, enticing glimpses of chest hair, and socks and shorts that emphasized muscular legs.

Not that the Shifters gave a damn what the men looked like. Not five minutes into the game, they were shouting and cheering, cursing or high-fiving. At least Sean and Connor were. Dylan watched with interest if not enthusiasm, and Liam restlessly left the room and followed Kim to the kitchen.

"You made them very happy." Liam leaned on the counter while Kim looked at her mostly empty refrigerator. She wasn't equipped to entertain men, that was certain. No beer, no chips, or whatever men chowed down on when they watched sports. She was pretty sure Abel watched sports, but she'd never caught him doing it.

"They won't be happy when they get hungry."

"They won't care." Liam slid his arms around her from behind. "Now, about that shower?"

"*Liam.* Your dad's in the living room."

"And likely to stay while the game's going. Your bathroom's upstairs, if I remember." He kissed her neck under her hair.

"It's true I'd like to take a look at your back again."

"Just my back?" Liam nuzzled her cheek. "Damn, woman, have mercy on a poor Shifter."

He licked her neck, his tongue hot and wet. Kim closed

her eyes, a shiver traveling from her breastbone to the cleft between her legs.

He wanted sex, and she knew it. Wanted it, craved it, and wasn't ashamed of it. Kim couldn't lie to herself. She wanted Liam back, with her whole body.

The crowd on TV roared, and Sean, Connor, and even Dylan were on their feet, shouting. Through the open door to the living room, Kim saw Sean and Connor slam together in a joyful hug.

Liam nipped Kim's ear. "Let's go upstairs."

"You can't be real. There's sports on TV, and you want to go off with a woman instead."

He slanted her a hot smile. "What you call soccer isn't my thing. Now if it had been *Gaelic* football . . ." He laughed. Kim had no idea what the difference was, but she liked the sound of his laughter.

Liam took Kim's hand and led her to the staircase. As they ascended, the others continued to relive the glory moment of the goal.

Kim's main bathroom was huge—when she'd gone through her redecorating frenzy, she'd combined a hall bathroom with the master bath for one giant bathroom fest. She had a two-person tub in the middle, a large stone-tiled shower on one end, and a gigantic vanity on the other.

"You put a refrigerator and a TV in here, and you'd never have to leave," Liam said.

"Funny. Get your shirt off."

Liam skimmed his T-shirt over his head faster than she could blink. His chest rose with his quick breath, strong bone and muscle under tight, smooth skin. Dark hair curled across his chest to his abdomen. His Collar gleamed, the black and silver links moving with his skin. It might be a symbol of his captivity, but Liam standing with bare torso, jeans riding low on his hips, and the chain around his neck was sexier than any male model could ever hope to be.

Kim wanted to touch every one of his muscles, trace

them from shoulders to spine, pausing at his backside to spend a little time there.

The stripes Fergus had laid on Liam's back had already closed, though the bruises remained. In a couple of days, Kim guessed, no one would be able to tell he'd been beaten.

She gently touched the closing wounds. "How is this possible?"

"I told you, we heal fast." Liam gave her a smile. "That's not what's hurting me, love."

"What is?"

His pants came off a little slower than his shirt but only because he had to unzip them. His underwear followed in a flash, and then Kim found six feet, six inches of aroused male Shifter in her arms.

"*You* hurt me," Liam whispered. His skin was hot and satin smooth under her touch, glistening with sweat. "I need you, Kim. It's killing me."

"What's the matter with you?" she asked, worried.

"Mating instinct. It makes me want to fuck or die."

"You smooth-talker, you."

"I can't help it. I claimed you as mate, and my body wants to complete the process."

No kidding. Kim curved into his embrace, not unhappy to flow against his body. He might call it "mating instinct," but Kim called it desire, one so strong there wasn't a cure but to give in to it.

Liam kissed her forehead and dropped kisses in her hair. Kim let her hands rove his shoulders and then his back, down to his fine, firm buttocks.

"You feel good," she murmured.

"You feel good touching me. Your hands are so cool."

She went on stroking his buttocks, the muscles as strong as she thought they'd be. "You have a nice ass."

"So do you." Large hands clasped it.

"I shouldn't be doing this."

"Most natural thing in the world, mating. The Earth goddess and Earth father joining to make the seasons continue. We're a part of that."

She couldn't help laughing. "You know, I think that's the best pick-up line I've ever heard."

Liam licked the side of her neck. "Is it working?"

"Conflict of interest. I could compromise the case."

Liam kissed her, fingers loosening her blouse. He didn't answer, and she remembered Fergus's parting words, that Kim was to drop Brian's defense and leave the poor guy to take the fall.

The fall for what?

Kim had expected Liam to tell Fergus to stuff his terms, but Liam hadn't protested. Did Liam join Fergus in wanting to throw Brian to the wolves?

"Liam, we need to talk about this."

Talk was obviously not on Liam's agenda. He kept up the scalding kisses, hands stroking. Her body became pliant, the space between her legs moist and needy.

His hardness pressed her abdomen, the feel of it making her nipples tight. She slid her hand down before she could stop herself and closed it around his penis.

Damn. He was frigging enormous. The shaft pressed her palm, moving a little with his pulse. His skin was hot, and she'd never felt a man's need so obviously before.

Not a man. A Shifter.

What women speculated about Shifter men was obviously true. They *were* bigger. And stiffer and hotter. Kim rubbed her thumb over his tip, feeling it slick and needy.

"Why are you doing this to me?" she asked.

Liam didn't appear to hear her. His eyes flicked to slits, cat's eyes, and he growled low in his throat.

"Don't you dare turn into something while I'm holding you." Kim squeezed his shaft, and Liam let out a soft groan. "That would be just too weird."

"Humans." Liam nipped her ear. "Teach me more about kissing." His tongue moved to her mouth, slid briefly between her lips.

Liam might not know how to kiss with finesse, but he did it with fervor. He licked her mouth from corner to corner, hands roving her back. Downstairs, Sean and Connor gave another whoop of victory, and Kim wanted to echo it up here. Liam's teeth scraped her mouth, his kiss clumsy, but his hands were skilled.

He loosened her blouse and brushed the tops of her breasts with callused fingers. Her lacy bra parted.

"Let me see you."

Kim let go of Liam long enough to pull her blouse open, to let her bra fall to the floor. Liam's gaze roved her, his cheeks flushed, eyes dark.

Abel had never looked at Kim like this, as though she were some Greek goddess. Liam cupped her breast almost reverently and slid his thumb across the areola. The nipple rose and tightened, and Liam leaned down and tugged it lightly with his teeth.

"You are so beautiful," he whispered into her skin.

Abel had never said that, either. "For a human?"

"For an anything."

"I don't disgust you, then?"

Liam laughed softly. "Stand still and take a compliment, love. Your body is made for loving." He moved his hand down her abdomen and unbuttoned her jeans. "I like that your hips are so curved." The zipper went down, the jeans slid past her butt, cool air touched her thighs.

"Fat-assed, you mean."

"I'm not meaning that, and you know it." Liam's hands eased her jeans to her ankles. "So you wore the thong, then."

His big hand found her bare butt cheek, betraying the truth of the statement. He softly kneaded, and Kim shivered. Here she was, in nothing but a thong in the middle of her bathroom, pressed against the hottest man she'd ever seen in her life.

Liam kissed his way down her neck and licked up between her breasts, and Kim's thoughts ceased being coherent. Liam bit her lip, then her cheek, strong hand moving to her nape and holding her there.

The thought tapped on her brain that even with the Collar, Liam was three times as strong as any man she'd ever been with. He could toss Abel across a room without working up a sweat. He could rip away her clothes in a heartbeat.

As though he read her thoughts, Liam hooked his fingers around the elastic of the thong and twisted it until it broke. His fingers found the moisture between her thighs, and she gasped, arching into his hand.

Liam eased back from the long kiss, both of them breathing faster. He softened his grip on her neck, caressing a little as though in apology.

"I don't want to hurt you." His eyes were still the cat's, narrow, slitted, light blue.

"I'm pretty tough."

"You're such a little bit of a thing." Liam's voice went soft with wonder. "You're so small, so fragile." The caresses on her neck changed to a light touch. "Goddess, what if I hurt you?"

Kim smiled a hot smile. "I've never heard a guy call me 'a little bit of a thing.' Usually it's, 'Are you sure you want to eat that, Kim? You know you're watching your weight.' "

"Screw them."

Kim touched her forehead to Liam's, looking into his scary eyes without flinching. "I'd rather screw you."

Another growl came from his throat. "I don't know if I can hold back. I've never done this before."

"A virgin Shifter? What do you know?"

"I meant not with a human woman." Liam furrowed her hair with strong fingers. "Especially one so soft."

Kim wriggled against his body. "We have to do this," she said. "I predict that we'll implode if we don't."

Another cheer erupted from downstairs, followed by prolonged shouting. Kim had to wonder which room was more charged, her living room or this one.

Liam's growl changed to an animalistic snarl, and he pulled Kim down with him to the bathroom floor. She found herself on top of him, straddling him, her fluffy white rug cushioning her knees.

Liam held her hips. "Do this, Kim. I don't trust myself."

Kim hardly trusted *her*self. She leaned forward and kissed his lips, at the same time shifting her hips so that his tip rested against her opening. "You're a hell of a man, Liam Morrissey. I only met you yesterday, and today you're sexing me on my bathroom rug."

Liam didn't answer, his face tight. Kim leaned forward a little more, then slid back onto him.

Oh, dear God in heaven. She closed her eyes, her head going back as a groan left her mouth. Liam was big, but she was so wet that she slid smoothly onto him, her body happy to accommodate him. But the feeling . . . She groaned again, she who never made noise when she had sex. She prided herself on being discreet, even delicate. She realized now she'd never wanted to make noise, never had reason to.

Liam's hard face softened, his eyes changing back to the deep blue she'd already come to love. He made a raw noise as his warm hands moved to her breasts, rough fingertips catching on her nipples.

"I never knew humans could be so beautiful," he said.

Kim smiled, her heart warming as it beat faster. *He* was the beautiful one. And skilled. She'd teased him about being a "virgin," but Liam obviously knew exactly what he was doing.

Kim felt the loops of her white rug on her knees, the fiery heat where they joined, Liam's soothing hands. He smelled of sweat and sex and himself. His chest shone with perspiration, the black curls damp across hard pectorals. His jaw was dark with unshaved whiskers, which glistened as he rocked his head back, eyes closing in ecstasy.

Kim leaned down and kissed him, tasting male musk and the cold soft drink he'd drunk in the car. He slid his hands to her waist, letting his hips rise and rise again, pressing himself ever deeper inside her. Kim's head lolled back, and she let sound come out unchecked, drowned out by the television and shouting downstairs.

Liam half sat up, helping her ride him. Their lips met, parted. His eyes remained dark blue, although once or twice they flickered to the cat's until he forced them dark again. He was holding back with effort, Kim sensed through her haze of pleasure. She wondered what Liam *not* holding back would be like. Delightful thought.

Sweat trickled down her skin. Liam gripped her waist and rose into her with strong thrusts, sending rivers of pleasure through her body.

"Liam."

Liam growled. His eyes moved to white, then snapped back to human blue. He pulled her down to kiss him. Their mouths locked together, and he rolled with her, putting her on her back on the sweat-soaked rug.

Could anything be better than this? Lying naked on the bathroom floor with a gorgeous, hard-bodied Shifter on top of her?

Kim lifted her hips to meet his thrusts. They were both panting, both groaning, Liam's face flushed, eyes half closed. The muscles in his arms and shoulders played as he made love to her, and the mirror across the room showed his fine buttocks tightening.

Kim's orgasm, when it came, was nothing like she'd ever experienced. The world went away except for the incredible feeling that pierced her where they joined. Nothing mattered, nothing existed, only the two of them, their sweating bodies sealed together and the madness ripping through them.

Kim's throat ached, but Liam was quiet as he thrust the final few times.

"Feel my seed, Kim," he whispered. "Take it, love."

Liquid scalded into her, the semen of a Shifter. Liam's mouth covered hers as his hips worked.

It occurred to Kim that it had gone pretty quiet downstairs when Liam finally collapsed on top of her, panting as though he'd never find his breath again.

CHAPTER THIRTEEN

So this was happiness.

Big-smile-on-his-face, heart-swelling happiness.

Liam rolled over on the rug again, gathering Kim on top of him. Kim kissed him, her lips soft and warm. Liam had never known such happiness was possible. This was his lady, his mate, the female he'd protect with his life.

Way down at the bottom of his mind lay fear—he'd seen what had happened to his father and then his brother when they'd lost their mates. Dylan had gone off on his own for a year. Kenny had folded up into himself, not speaking to or looking at anyone for weeks.

Liam understood their pain now. He'd hurt like hell if he lost Kim. And he'd only known her since yesterday. Right now their happiness was fresh, fragile. Imagine the hurt after years of being together, of learning each other, body and mind. To lose that . . .

Liam held her close. She was lush and curvaceous, her

sweet breasts pressing his chest. Any man who'd told her she wasn't perfect as she was deserved to be shredded.

Kim looked down at him with a smile. "That was . . . Wow."

"*Wow?* This is the articulate lawyer talking?"

"Wow about sums it up."

He stroked Kim's hair and kissed her lips. "I'm catching on to this kissing."

"I think you need more practice."

"You keep on teaching me, love."

Kim licked his mouth. When she did it again, he caught her tongue with his. He pulled her down for the kiss, lacing his fingers through her hair. He could enjoy these lessons, even when their mouths were raw from lovemaking. He'd make sure he kissed her—real kisses—for the rest of his life.

Something burbled on the other side of the room.

"Oh, hell." Kim jerked up.

Liam let her go with reluctance. His reward was watching her crawl to her pants, her backside enticing him as she went. Kim yanked her cell phone out of her pocket and sat up, and now he got to watch her firm, creamy breasts tipped with dark nipples. Liam propped himself on his elbow and enjoyed himself.

"Yeah?" she said into the phone.

A man answered, loud enough for Liam to hear him across the room. "Hi, honey. How are you?"

Kim squeezed her eyes shut. "Abel."

"Did you want something?" he asked.

Her eyes popped open again. "What are you talking about? You called me."

The voice changed to one of tired patience. "Last night, when you called, you sounded like you wanted something. What was it?"

"It's not important now."

"Well, I'm going to be tied up all day, all this week, actually, but maybe next Friday I can come over."

Maybe? With this woman waiting for him? The man was a thrice-damned idiot.

"Abel." Kim gazed into the distance, folding her legs under her. "I won't be free Friday. In fact . . . Abel, we need to break up."

"Fine." The line hummed quietly while her words processed. "What did you say?"

"I said I'm breaking up with you."

"Why?" Abel sounded baffled. Not hurt, not angry, just puzzled.

Kim made an impatient noise. "If you have to ask why, then that's why."

"Kim, honey, you're not making sense."

"Don't *Kim, honey* me. I met someone. I didn't mean to, but it happened. You and I weren't going anywhere, so I figured, what the hell?"

"Oh." Again, puzzlement instead of anger. "Is it someone in the firm?"

"No. Like I said, someone I just met."

"Right. Well, I guess I'll see you around."

"Yeah, I guess so."

Abel clicked off. Kim sat staring, every muscle tense, and then she flung the phone across the room. It landed on the tiles and spun until it hit the big bathtub.

"Two years of my life I wasted on him, and all he can say is 'See you around'?"

Liam rolled over and braced himself on both elbows. "He sounds a bit of a fool."

"More than a bit." Kim pressed her hand to her forehead. "Do you know *why* I went out with him? I just now realized it. Because he would go out with me. No other reason. No compatibility. Convenience, for both of us. I'm pathetic."

Liam held out his hand. "You weren't pathetic, love. Lonely. There's a difference." He wriggled his fingers. "Come here."

Kim walked to him, no more crawling, until she stood over him. This was the best view of all. Liam roamed his gaze up her tight, petite legs to the slick tuft of hair between them, over her cute navel, her round breasts and bare neck, ending at her beautiful face.

"You're mated now," he said, as Kim knelt on the floor next to him. "You've no more need to be lonely. You have me."

"You and your ego."

"You make me laugh, love. You have me and my father and Sean and Connor. Ellison and Glory. All the Shifters."

"Even Fergus?"

Liam grimaced. "Him too. He's bent out of shape about Brian, and I don't know why, but usually he's a fair leader. Mostly."

"Fair? He tried to *whip* Connor for talking back to him!"

"I know, and it might be hard to understand, but Connor did wrong. He's a cub. He doesn't have a place yet, and attacking the clan leader needs punishment. Connor knew that. Any other time, he might have been let off with a warning, but in the middle of a moot, when our family was already in disgrace—Fergus couldn't let it go."

"So he whipped you and your father instead."

"Any member of a pride has the right to take a punishment for any other, but it has to be voluntary. Dad and I could take the lash; Connor never has. And I wasn't wrong about Fergus wanting to punish me instead. Connor gave him the excuse."

"This is one of those Shifter things I don't understand, isn't it?"

Liam let himself grin. "You'll get used to it. You'll get used to all things Shifter."

"No, I won't." Kim pulled her knees to her chin, shaping her body into delectable curves and shadows. "We can't date right now, Liam. Not until after the case is over and Brian is free. Then, I won't lie, I wouldn't mind getting to know you—much better. What we did today will have to be a one-off."

Liam laced his fingers through hers. "We're not *dating*, love. We're bonded for life."

Kim gently disengaged her fingers and scooted a few inches away. Liam let her go; this was new to her, and he had to ease her in a bit at a time. "That's what it means for Shifters to be mated."

"That's not the human way," she said. "I'd only be bound to you if I married you. Signed a piece of paper saying so."

"Shifters aren't allowed to get marriage licenses. Not under the current laws."

"I know. I'm sorry."

"Fergus pronounced us mated, in the Shifter way, under the light of the sun. In a few days, my dad will pronounce it so under the light of the full moon. Then it's you and me together forever. Because you're human, I'll seek a Fae to bond us as well, increasing your lifespan to match mine." He grinned at her. "Think of how many cases you can defend that way."

"The Fae can increase lifespan?" Kim's eyes widened. "Why isn't everyone out to find a Fae and stay youthful?"

"Because the Fae are bloody elusive to humans, and it only works if the human is bonded to a Shifter. That happens rarely, for obvious reasons, and only the Shifter can seek out the Fae. The Fae have certain obligations to Shifters, as much as they hate it, and this is one favor they grant us if we ask for it. Your natural lifespan will lengthen to match mine. When I grow old and die, so will you."

"Great, what if you get hit by a bus?"

"I said *natural* lifespan. It would be like a human relationship but longer."

Kim half smiled, shaking her head as though she thought he was talking nonsense. "That's not how it works."

She still didn't understand. She would in time, though; Kim wasn't stupid. And then—she'd kill him.

"It is working, love. Anyway, you've taken my seed. What will you say to the wee one that comes if you haven't bound yourself to me? It'll be embarrassed."

"Wee one? Oh, you mean if I have a baby. Don't worry about that. I take contraceptives."

"Contraceptives?"

"You know, birth control. I don't know if Shifters have that."

"I know what it is, Kim." Humans bred like rabbits, and they were always looking for ways to keep babies from coming. So few Shifter babies were conceived and so few survived that Shifters wouldn't dream of preventing them. Shifter women knew how dangerous it was to give birth, and yet they sought it with everything they had.

"I was taking it because I was going out with Abel," Kim said in reasonable tones. "It would look bad if he and I had a child together. No, let's be honest—it would be a hell of a complication if we'd had a child together."

"And if you had one with me?"

"You're a Shifter."

Liam lay back on his elbows, eyes narrowing. "This makes a difference?"

"Please don't be offended. If I had a half-Shifter baby, that would be the end of my career. I researched this when I took up Brian's case, because he was dating a human. There haven't been many hybrids since you took the Collar, but the woman in question gets shunned by human society every time. In fact, my theory about Michelle's death is that her ex-boyfriend killed her because she'd betrayed him with Brian, a Shifter. I imagine that made him crazy." Kim sighed. "Proving it is a bitch, though."

Liam heaved himself to his feet and stalked to the medicine cabinet over her pristine pedestal sink. He opened it and started pulling out bottles.

"What are you doing?" Kim asked.

"Looking for your birth control pills. I want to flush them."

"I don't take pills. I get injections from my doctor."

"Then stop."

"Excuse me?" Kim stood and planted her hands on her naked hips. "How is this your business?"

"Everything you do is my business."

"Liam, if you want someone to breed little Shifters with you, you have plenty of Shifter women drooling over you. I saw the waitress at the bar—what's her name?—Annie. She'd have gone to bed with you in a heartbeat."

"And she has."

"Oh." Did Liam dare hope that was jealousy in her eyes? "Did you throw away *her* contraceptives?"

"She's Lupine. I told you that the chances of conception in those cases are low, remember?"

"How lucky for you."

"You say *lucky* like you'd never want a child."

"I do want one." Kim threw him an exasperated look. "I like kids. But not right now."

"And not with a Shifter."

"If I decided to pick a Shifter, it would be you." Kim smiled her beautiful smile. "Maybe later, when I have a solid career, and if you're still available . . ."

Liam moved across the floor and had her in his arms before she could turn away. "Understand me, Kim. We are *mated*. That means I go to no other female unless I lose you to death, and even then it will feel like betrayal. I protect you, I take care of you, I bind myself to you, and you alone."

Her face lost color. "That's your custom?"

"It's not custom. It's Shifter law. It's magic that runs deep inside us. This mating brings you into my pride. Even Fergus can't touch you without going through me. That was the point of me claiming you."

Kim squirmed away, and Liam let her go.

"It was necessary," he explained. "If I hadn't made the Challenge, Fergus would have taken you as mate whether you liked it or not."

"How could he?" Kim asked. "I'm not bound by Shifter law."

"He could because we're animals. We look like humans and you put Collars on us, but we're born animals and only learn to become human later. The leader of the clan can claim whatever unmated female he wants, and we have to step back and let him unless we want to Challenge. It's his right. But Fergus is hellaciously strong, and most in the clan don't want to fight him, so he takes the mates he wants."

"But I'm not Shifter . . ."

"Do you think Fergus gives a damn about that? He wants to control you, needs to control what you tell the humans about us."

"Wait a minute." A look of horror moved over Kim's face. "Are you telling me that if I hadn't agreed to do this mating thing with you, Fergus might have taken me off and raped me?"

"Very likely."

"But he'd go down for that. A human court would crucify him."

"Would they? Or would they say it was your own fault for hanging out with Shifters? You just said that having a child with me would ruin your career, that you think Michelle died for associating with a Shifter. Shifter-whore is the term."

Her face went white, and she sat down hard on the edge of the tub. "Shit."

Liam came to her, crouched in front of her. "Don't be afraid, love. I'll never let Fergus hurt you. Ever. The mate claim overrides clan hierarchy. He can beat up on me, but never you. Even if he kills me, you'll still be protected by my family, my pride."

"But why would Fergus still want to kill you?" Kim asked in confusion. "He seemed to back off all of a sudden, like he didn't care about the mate thing anymore."

"Because he knew he'd won. He got me to promise to control you, for the good of all Shifters. If he'd pursued it further, for nothing but self-satisfaction, the clan wouldn't have approved, and even though he's leader, he can't afford to lose the clan's respect. Besides, Dad was there. Fergus has never been one hundred percent certain he's dominant to Dad, and he didn't want to put that to the test, especially not in front of the whole clan."

"So why doesn't your dad fight him, then? It's obvious none of you like him."

"To tell you the truth, love, I'm not sure," Liam said, troubled. "Dad won't talk about it. Maybe he knows he *isn't* dominant to Fergus, and if Dad were killed, he couldn't protect the rest of us from him. But I don't know. He's never said and gets pissed off when anyone brings it up."

Kim frowned, rubbing her arms. "But when Fergus came at me with the whip and you almost attacked him, Dylan stopped you, said it wasn't your 'right.' What did he mean? I thought you were *supposed* to fight."

Liam remembered the surge of adrenaline rising white hot, searing him like a brand on flesh, when he'd seen Fergus focus on Kim. Only Dylan's harsh voice had stopped him from making a fatal move, or this day would have ended differently.

"Because at that moment, I wanted to kill him. The Fae-cat in me wanted to go after Fergus in a clan dominance fight, to take him down for good. The mate Challenge isn't to the death—at least, not anymore—but fighting for clan leadership usually is, unless the clan leader surrenders before the fight. Dad stopped me from making it a clan dominance issue, thank the Goddess."

"Why? It seems like you could have saved him a step." She let out her breath. "Not that I want to see you in a fight to the death. I'm happy he stopped you too."

"Shifter politics." Liam tried to sound offhand, but something subtle had changed during the moot today, and he wasn't yet certain what. "Only Dad, as pride leader, has the right to fight for clan dominance. If I want to take out Fergus,

I first have to take out Dad, and I won't be doing that anytime soon."

Kim gave him a faint smile. "Because you know he could kick your ass?"

Liam laughed. "No, because he's my dad, and I love him." Another laugh. "And yeah, he could probably kick my ass."

Kim hugged her chest. "I thought I researched Shifter law down to the last degree. I don't remember any of this."

"Because it's not written law. It's passed down through the generations, and it's based on instinct and what you call custom." Liam laid his hands on her shoulders. "It's complicated even for us. I'm going to protect you, Kim. Believe that."

She looked up at him with anguished eyes. "Liam, I can't be your mate. I only came to Shiftertown to get help building my defense for Brian. I'm fine with you keeping Fergus off my back, but I can't move into your house to become a Shifter baby-making machine. You're crazy if you believe I'll agree to that."

He traced circles on her shoulders. "I'd never believe you'd do anything you don't really want to, Kim Fraser."

Kim broke his hold, got to her feet, and reached for her clothes. "You got that right." She pulled on her jeans in short jerks. "Now if you'll take your family and go home, I *really* have a lot of work to do. I'm seriously behind."

"All right."

She stopped and stared at him. "You agree? Just like that?"

"Just like that, love."

"Stop calling me 'love.' "

Liam chuckled. "Now that, I can't do."

He watched Kim's breasts softly bounce as she scrabbled for the rest of her clothes. He wouldn't push her now—she was human, this was sudden, and it would take her time to get used to him. But Kim was *his*. His mate, his lover.

All mine.

She finished dressing and hurried out of the bathroom. Liam followed, not bothering with his clothes. He paused on the landing to watch her hips sway as she ran lightly down the stairs.

As angry and confused and hurt as she was—and as likely to make his life hell—Kim glowed with beauty. Her body was covered with Liam's scent, filled with their lovemaking. Beautiful, beautiful Kim.

Liam went down the stairs after Kim. Below him, she stopped abruptly, noting that the TV was dark, the living room quiet. Sean and Connor looked at her with innocent faces.

Connor grinned. "Everything all right up there? I thought the ceiling might come crashing in."

Kim flushed. "Where's Dylan?"

"Gone," Sean said. "Took the bus back to Shiftertown. Dad does his own thing."

"I see," she said, clearly flustered. "I can call a taxi for the rest of you."

Sean shook his head. "No need. Dad said he'd be back to fetch us."

Connor lost his smile. "Aren't you coming home with us, Kim?"

Poor cub. He liked Kim, was ecstatic about the mating, and probably assumed Kim would instantly become one of them. Connor had much to learn about females.

"Now that Liam says Fergus is no longer a threat, I'm going to stay in my own home," Kim said. "I didn't mind helping out today, and thank you for the pancakes, but I'm kind of tired and have a lot of work to do."

Liam shifted. His Fae-cat didn't wait for him to ready himself, and for the first time in his life, the shift didn't hurt. He leapt off the bottom step, the stairs creaking under his weight, and he tackled Kim. His big, sheathed paws sent her to the ground, and he landed on top of her, balancing so he wouldn't crush her.

In this form he could truly smell her, and she was better than the best field of blossoms. She combined her scent and his in exact proportion, the sign of a perfect mate.

Kim tried to squirm out from under him. "Liam, what are you doing? Someone get this big cat off me."

Liam didn't mind her wriggling while his brother and nephew laughed at them. He swiped her face from chin to forehead with his large tongue, shifting back to human form as she turned her head and cried, "Eeewwww."

Incredibly, Liam did leave with his family, and Kim found herself alone in the house. She'd expected Liam to stay on his overprotective kick and insist she come back with them to Shiftertown for the night. Or maybe move his whole family to her house so they could watch satellite TV, she wasn't sure.

But Liam had gone back upstairs, put on his clothes, and herded Connor and Sean out through the garage just as Dylan pulled a big pickup into her driveway. As the others piled in, Liam slid his arms around Kim and kissed her.

"You rest now," he said, smoothing her hair. "We'll talk later."

Kim's lips tingled and she wanted more, but she made herself step back. "I'm going to work in the morning. I'm not dropping the case, whatever Fergus might think."

"I know." Liam lifted her hand and kissed her palm. "You wouldn't be yourself if you dropped it. But as you like to say, we need to talk."

Kim suddenly, inconsistently, didn't want him to leave. "Tomorrow?"

"Tomorrow."

Liam brushed another warm kiss to her lips and walked out. Kim resisted the urge to rush after him, to tell him to come back, to beg him to stay.

What was the matter with her? Liam and his family

had imprisoned her in Shiftertown, and then she'd driven them a hundred or so miles to the middle of nowhere so she could endure the abuse of Fergus the Irish biker thug.

Then why did her heart ache as the pickup backed away, all four Morrissey men squished into the cab? Liam must have brainwashed her with his fine blue eyes and incredible smile, not to mention intense, mind-blowing sex.

As Kim closed the door, the emptiness of the house pressed on her. The TV was dark and quiet, no male voices raised in jubilation. She stood in the middle of the living room and felt the silence.

Kim went through the rest of the afternoon on automatic. She showered, trying not to gaze at the rug where she'd ridden Liam so ecstatically. The tactile memory of his body on hers, of every finger press, every kiss, every slide of skin on skin was imprinted on her. Kim had never had sex like that in her life.

In a half daze she drove down the hill to her local grocery store. She found herself putting things in her cart that wouldn't have occurred to her a few days ago—steaks, ground beef, potato chips, and Guinness stout. *Why?* she wondered as she paid without meeting the cashier's eyes. *It's not like I'm going to invite them over again.* But just in case . . .

Kim took the food home and crammed everything into the refrigerator. She fixed herself a salad that she picked at, and then she opened her briefcase and laptop and flipped listlessly through files.

She needed to get her head around all this—Brian, the Collars, Fergus, this mating thing. She reread a note from her friend Silas asking Kim whether she could get him an interview with the Shifter leaders. Silas was a good, even-handed journalist who didn't shrink from bald truth but didn't make something out of nothing either. Two days ago, she'd have eagerly set up an interview for him. Given what she knew now, she wasn't so sure it was a good idea, or if Liam would even agree to talk to him.

On the other hand, everything that had happened today helped Kim look at Brian's case from a new angle. Had Brian intended to make Michelle his mate? If so, wouldn't he have been as protective of her as Liam was of Kim? If Brian had decided to "claim" Michelle, that might mean he'd never dream of hurting her. Wouldn't he have done everything in his power to keep her safe?

Michelle's ex-boyfriend, on the other hand, might go ballistic. Brian, a Shifter, would be hard to kill, but not Michelle. And if Brian could get blamed for Michelle's death, so much the better.

Then again, why hadn't Brian been there to protect his girlfriend from her killer? Where had he been and what had he been doing to keep him from Michelle at the critical moment?

Kim sighed and rubbed her temples. She was getting nowhere.

After an hour or so of trying to think and failing, Kim went to bed. Mistake. She should have been exhausted after rolling on the bathroom floor with Liam, but instead she was wide awake, her pulse speeding as their lovemaking played over and over in her mind.

She'd never, ever felt like this before. Kim should be sated after that incredible sex, but she wanted more of Liam. And more.

"What is the matter with me?"

She sat up and snapped on the light. Three seconds later, her phone rang.

Kim picked it up, her heart pounding as Liam's rich Irish tones rolled over her. "Kim. You all right?"

Kim wanted to sigh with happiness. "I'm fine. Why wouldn't I be?"

"I wanted to make sure."

"I am fine." She lay back down on the pillows, feeling warm and content. "Really. Really, really fine."

"Good." He sounded as though it was the best news he'd heard all day.

Kim hesitated. "How's Connor doing?"

"Still not happy with me, but he'll be all right. Letting him watch Irish football has made you his superhero."

"I'm glad he's okay."

"I'm glad you're glad."

Kim wondered if Liam was in bed talking to her, if he was stretched, naked, on top of the bed she'd slept in last night. Her heart beat faster.

"I'm going to my office tomorrow." She said it firmly.

"I know you are. I wouldn't expect you to do anything else." Liam's voice softened. "Good night, love. You call me anytime you need me, all right?"

He meant it—his sincerity came through loud and clear. All she had to do was say, *Liam, I need you,* and he'd be there. So different from Abel and his *I'm busy, honey, I'll call you later.*

"Good night, Liam." Kim made herself click the phone off and set it on the nightstand, but it was a long time before she snapped off the light.

Outside Kim's big house, Liam tucked away his phone and kissed his fingers to her bedroom window. He faded into the shadows against the wall and settled in to guard her for the rest of the night.

CHAPTER FOURTEEN

The next morning Kim raced her car into her parking space at Lowell, Grant, and Steinhurst, half an hour late.

Late. On a Monday. Missing the Monday morning meeting. Kim scrambled out of her car, snatched up her briefcase, rushed for the front door, and stopped in dismay.

Liam leaned against the Harley he'd parked at the curb in front of the firm's walkway, smiling his wicked smile.

"Morning, love," he said.

"What are you doing here?" Kim demanded.

"Looking after you. Like I should."

July sunshine gleamed on Liam's dark hair and flat black sunglasses. With his black T-shirt and jeans, Collar around his neck, his jaw working as he chewed a piece of gum, he looked nothing less than a dangerous Shifter male. Which he was.

She made an exasperated noise. "Liam, I cannot bring a *Shifter* to work with me."

Liam lifted his sunglasses, blue eyes dancing. "I don't see any signs: 'No Shifters Allowed.' 'Shifters Must Keep Off the Grass.' 'Absolutely No Territory Marking Anywhere.'"

"Very funny. Go home."

"No." He lowered the sunglasses and took her elbow. "If you work here, I stay with you. I'm your guard dog. You won't even know I'm here."

"Because no one will notice a six-foot-six Shifter in my office."

"I'm staying, Kim. Or you're coming home with me. Your choice."

She jerked from his grasp. "You're a pushy pain in my ass."

"I'm not taking a chance that Fergus will leave you alone. He can't touch you anymore, but that doesn't mean he won't order other Shifters to make trouble for you. Some of Fergus's lackeys are . . . Let's just say they're fanatically devoted to him."

"You all are crazy, you know that?"

Liam shrugged. "Hey, you're the Shifter lover, which means you're crazier than we are. Come on."

Liam opened the heavy glass door and, Shifterfashion, entered the building first. Once he determined that the polished granite and marble foyer was harmless, he nodded for Kim to come inside.

Kim knew of nothing that could make him leave, short of having him arrested, and even then the police would have to break out the tranquilizer guns. She also knew that, deep down inside, she didn't want him to leave. Kim didn't trust Fergus either, and Liam's presence made her feel safe. Embarrassed, awkward, and confused, but safe.

As they moved through the plush halls, lawyers looked up through open doors or stepped into the hall in astonishment. Liam nodded at the head of the firm who'd stopped short in his doorway. "Top o' the morning to you."

Kim scuttled into her office suite where the secretary,

Jeanne, who worked for Kim and two other lawyers, typed on a computer keyboard. Jeanne looked up, gawked, and lost her place. "Who the hell . . . ?"

Liam smiled. "Top o' the mornin' to you."

"It's all right," Kim said in a hard voice. "He's helping me on the Shifter case."

Jeanne looked as though she'd melt through her chair. "Can I get you coffee?" she offered Liam in an eager tone.

"Coffee would be grand," he said.

Kim grabbed Liam's arm, shoved him into her cluttered office, and slammed the door behind them. She pointed at the leather couch wedged between two bookcases.

"If you're staying—*sit.*"

Liam grinned, removed his sunglasses, stretched out full length on the couch, and folded his arms behind his head. He looked good enough to eat.

Kim slapped her briefcase to her desk and popped it open. "What is this 'top o' the morning' crap?"

"It's how people expect the Irish to talk. That and 'faith and begorra!' I'll throw those in later."

"You are so full of shit."

Liam chuckled and closed his eyes. He looked prepared to lounge there the rest of the day, reminding her every second of their thorough sexing in her bathroom. She'd dreamed about it all night, the main reason she'd been late. When he'd rolled her over and driven into her, his warm weight on top of her, she'd never felt more connected or intimate with a man in her life. She'd felt . . . complete.

Forget the goopy, romantic stuff. The sex had been damn fantastic.

Kim had to stop thinking about it. She had to be professional and do her job. She had other cases to prepare for, a load of witness statements and evidence reports to go through. Brian's defense to figure out, the private investigator's weekend reports to read.

Once she won Brian's case, she'd be finished with Shifters.

Fergus's wishes would be a moot point, Liam wouldn't need to guard her anymore, and he'd go back to Shiftertown and leave her alone. For good.

Why did the world suddenly go colorless at that thought?

Kim dumped files back into her briefcase. "I need to talk to Brian. I assume you want to come with me? We'll take my car—I'm not riding to the county jail on the back of your motorcycle."

Liam didn't move. "You're not going to see Brian."

"I need to. I want to ask him about Michelle again, whether he planned to mate with her, whether he already did. If Brian thought of her as his mate, he'd never have hurt her, right? He'd come over all protective, defend her rather than attack her."

"You might be right about that, but you're still not going to see him."

Kim clicked the briefcase shut. "Why not? He's in jail. He's not going anywhere."

Liam finally came off the couch. "You're not going because Fergus told you to drop the case."

He was a tall, solid wall, blocking her way to the door. "We've discussed this. I say screw Fergus."

"I wouldn't. I hear it's not good."

Kim didn't laugh. "So you agree with him?"

"I didn't say that." Liam rested his hands on her shoulders. She'd never get by him, and she knew it. At the same time, she knew he wouldn't hurt her. He'd prevent her from leaving, but not by hurting.

"Then what are you saying?" she asked.

"That Fergus won't trust me to keep you off the case. I was the one who talked him into letting you come to Shiftertown in the first place. So he'll have sent his own men to watch you, to stop you. I'm here to keep them from tangling with you. If you go to the jail, there will be tangling."

Kim made a noise of exasperation. "Explain how I'm

supposed to defend a man I'm not allowed to talk to. I need to ask him questions, important questions."

"Ask him some other way."

Kim tried to dart around him. Liam put one arm out and hauled her back against him.

"Liam."

He closed both arms around her and pulled her close. "Do this my way, love. Don't mess with Fergus more than you have to. He'll make you regret it."

Kim wanted to succumb to the wonderful, protected feeling of having his arms around her. Even her parents hadn't been this protective of her. After Mark had died, they'd wavered between being overly paranoid about her safety to backing way off when they realized they were smothering her.

They'd gone on like that until they'd died. She'd found herself alternately on a choke chain or floundering during her parents' "you don't even have to check in with us" moods.

Liam's protection was like a soft blanket, not a leash, but the tether was there nonetheless.

"I can't work like this," Kim said.

"We'll find a way." Liam kissed the crown of her head.

The warm touch of his lips electrified the memories of their lovemaking, reminding her that her throat was still scratchy from all the screaming. She couldn't help putting her hand on his waistband and sliding her fingers downward, her pulse speeding when she found that he was hard and hot behind his zipper.

Liam laughed. "Vixen." He tilted her head back and kissed her.

Liam was still learning how to kiss. Which meant he experimented and explored, his tongue sliding all over hers while he gripped her buttocks with one firm hand. He tasted like the gum he'd been chewing, minty fresh.

If anyone came in, they'd see his sun-browned hand

planted against her gray business skirt, Kim letting a Shifter put his tongue down her throat. And they wouldn't know the half of it.

"Stop," she whispered. "Don't do this to me."

A gentle kiss to her forehead. "I'd never hurt you, Kim."

"It's not pain I'm worried about." Kim rested her head against his chest. His skin was hot through the shirt, his heart pounding at breakneck speed. "It's me."

"You're not making sense."

"I know what I mean. You are seriously damaging my mental health."

Liam broke away, but he was smiling. "You mean I make you spare."

"If that means crazy, then yes. That too."

There was a soft knock on the door, and Jeanne poked her head in. She carried in a tray of coffee, in real mugs, not Styrofoam cups. Kim turned from Liam, hoping she looked nonchalant.

Jeanne set the coffee on the polished side table. "Abel is looking for you."

"Abel?" For one crazy moment, Kim couldn't remember who he was. Ah, yes, buttoned-up, executive exboyfriend. The man who looked incredibly boring next to Liam. "What does he want?"

"To ask you about the judge you had on that indecent exposure case. He's got a similar case before the same judge."

"Oh." Business. Tips on what swayed a judge or pissed him off. Kim had won the case, because the man they'd arrested had had erectile dysfunction, verified by a doctor, when the witness had sworn the defendant had been quite, um, pointed. "Set up a meeting with Abel," Kim finished. "I'm busy until tomorrow."

"He's here now."

Before Kim could answer, Abel Kane pushed around the door and strode into the office. Kim had always thought him good-looking—tall, blond, well-dressed—but he was a lightweight compared to Liam. And there was no comparison at all in the sex department.

"Can't this wait?" Kim asked him.

Abel was looking at Liam in curiosity. "Kind of in a rush."

Liar. He couldn't be paid to care about indecent-exposure cases; he'd used the excuse to come in here and eyeball Liam.

"Why?" Kim asked in an annoyed voice. "Client can't keep his pants on?"

Abel ignored her attempt at humor. "So the Collars really do fit all Shifters. What neck size would you say he has?"

"He can hear you, Abel."

Liam gave Abel his slow smile. "Top o' the morning to you."

"Will you stop that?" Kim snapped.

"Is he Irish?" Abel said in surprise. "I didn't know Shifters could be Irish."

"The Shifters in my family go back generations in Ireland," Liam said. "We had a castle on a hill and everything."

Abel continued to assess Liam like a scientist examining an interesting specimen. "Type up a report on him," Abel said to Kim. "It would be useful if we ever have to defend another Shifter."

"Abel, will you please stop talking about him like he's not in the room?"

"What's eating you, Kim? Is it the new guy you met or your time of the month?"

What an idiot. Abel hadn't connected Kim "meeting someone" with the extremely virile Shifter standing in her office. Abel couldn't imagine for one second that she'd dump him for a *Shifter.*

Liam's grin died. He'd been taking Abel for what he really was, a self-centered moron, but Liam's eyes narrowed at Abel's last statement. The predatory thing Liam did so well came out, proving that up until now, he'd been a wolf watching the sheep frolic.

"The lady said she's busy." Liam's voice held a hint of growl.

Without moving, Liam gained the attention of everyone in the room, plus Jeanne listening outside the door. A sheen of perspiration glistened on Abel's forehead.

"Right. I'll call you later, Kim. About that judge."

Abel couldn't turn around to walk out. Liam wouldn't let him. And yet, Liam did nothing but stand there, not moving, not touching the man. He hadn't even let his pupils go slitted.

Abel had to back to the door, one step at a time, before he finally turned and fled. He ran into Jeanne, who was plastered solidly against the crack in the door. They tangled a moment; then Abel fled and Jeanne slammed the door, leaving Kim and Liam alone again.

CHAPTER FIFTEEN

Kim took Liam out for lunch. Liam enjoyed riding in her small car, watching her gray businesslike skirt riding up her thighs. As he'd guessed, she wore stockings with lacy tops, held in place by garters. Thinking about skimming off the skirt and looking at her in only the garter belt and stockings didn't do his rising erection any favors.

What deflated his arousal was being turned away by the first restaurant they reached. The hostess took one look at Liam's Collar and got the manager.

Kim stormed away, furious, but Liam didn't know why she was surprised. Shifters hadn't been welcomed in most places for twenty years.

The next two restaurants wouldn't let them in, either. They ended up at a greasy spoon close to the north Austin Shiftertown, where the owners had figured out that Shifters paid for the food and didn't cause trouble, unlike the gang kids that roamed the nearby neighborhoods.

"How can you stand it?" Kim fumed as she dumped sugar into her coffee. "I never realized how blatant it was."

Liam blew on his coffee to cool it before he sipped. "Bans against Shifters? If you never witnessed it firsthand, I'm guessing you frequent places Shifters don't even bother trying to go to. But it doesn't much matter to me where I go. I don't really want to eat at a place where they don't serve Shifters."

"Stop being so blasé. They treat you like animals."

"We *are* animals."

"Be serious."

"Kim, sweetheart, I've lived a hundred years under various and sometimes nasty conditions. This life isn't so bad. There are certain people I keep out of my bar too. I'd ban Lupines altogether, except Ellison and Glory would try to wipe the floor with my butt."

"Be serious," she repeated.

"What for?" Liam looked straight into her blue eyes, trying to calm her rage. He liked her anger, though, because it meant she cared. "The way people treat Shifters can be amusing."

"Discrimination is never funny."

"You're a righteous woman, Kim. I like that."

"How can you just *sit* there?"

"I usually sit when I'm drinking coffee. Or I lean against something. If I lie on my back, it goes down the wrong way." Kim started to rage, and Liam reached over and took her hand. "I'm sorry, love. I'm glad you care so much. It's sweet. But I'm not bothered."

"How can you not be bothered to have people walk all over you? Abel acted like you were behind a viewing wall in a zoo."

"Because they don't walk all over me." He glanced around, but they were relatively alone in their corner of the restaurant. "We don't ever let them. Do you understand?"

"Not really."

Liam lifted his coffee again. "Neither does Fergus. That's why he chose the Shiftertown out in the desert. He can't stand for anyone to bruise his ego."

Kim sat in silence, running her finger around the rim of her cup. She spoke carefully, as though she had to choose each word. "What you mean is, you don't get upset when they won't let you into restaurants or forbid you having cable, because those things aren't important to you."

"Now, you're catching on."

"And Abel doesn't bother you because you don't value his opinion."

"Not really. On the other hand, he says anything nasty like that to you again, I'll crush him."

Kim had a sudden vision of a lion lying on a veldt in complete relaxation, swatting an obnoxious fly with his tail. The fly had Abel's head. The same lion would have cubs climbing all over him, which he'd turn and greet with a lick.

"It's like we live in a different world from you," Kim said. "And we don't even know it."

"Something like that."

The look she gave him was stunned. "I've been feeling sorry for you."

"Don't worry about that, love." He grinned. "If last night was a pity fuck, I'm all for them."

She turned bright red. "It wasn't. And don't talk about sex while I'm trying to get my head straight."

"I was thinking about doing more than talking about it."

"Stop." She pressed her palms flat on the table. "When you do that, I can't think."

"I'm glad. Thinking, it's an overrated activity."

"Liam, where does Fergus get all his money?"

Liam managed to look blank. "Does Fergus have money?"

"You know he does. There's that underground complex

for one, and all that artwork for another. It didn't spring there overnight."

"Shifters live a long time, and some are good with money."

"But Shifters aren't supposed to have much money."

"No." Liam took a calming sip of coffee. Trust Kim to pry at their most basic secrets, leaving Liam to have to think of ways of explaining. He didn't want to lie, not to the woman he'd chosen as mate, but at the same time she wanted to rip the lid off everything they desperately needed to keep protected.

"How do you think we live, sweetheart?" he asked her, keeping his voice down. "We're only allowed low-wage jobs, and yet we're expected to feed our families, pay the rent. You don't think I live on what I make as a part-time bar manager, do you?"

"I did notice you had a casual attitude about going to work. As in, you never go."

"But I have the job. So the human committees can mark down on their sheets that I have employment and be happy that they've done well by me."

"So you do have money?"

"Now then, Kim, a man would think you didn't want him for his looks and his fine personality."

Kim flushed again. "You obviously don't want me prying, but you expect me to be your mate—for life—without explaining what's really going on with you."

Liam laid his hand lightly over hers. "I was teasing. Let's just say my family is provided for. As will be my mate and my offspring."

"Offspring. Now we're back in dangerous territory."

"I thought all women would want to know that their mate can take care of the cubs. But all right." Liam withdrew his hands. "Let's talk about Brian."

Kim looked surprised at the change of subject. "All

right, let's talk about why Fergus doesn't want me to save him. Why he wants Brian to plead guilty."

"I wish I knew, love. Brian's no threat to Fergus, nowhere near challenging for leadership. Fergus has helped Brian and his family in the past. They aren't close, but not enemies."

"Maybe Brian pissed him off somehow."

"If he did, I never heard about it. I would have heard." It bothered him that he knew little of what had gone on between Brian and Fergus. Liam had always thought he had his finger firmly on the pulse of Shiftertown. He knew everyone, and they knew him. If a Shifter were in trouble, someone would tell him or Sean. That was the way it worked. In Brian's case, it hadn't.

Kim said, "When I first came to see you, you told me you didn't know much about Brian."

"I was trying to put you off. A human poking around in Shiftertown is dangerous."

"But you took me to see his mother."

"I liked you." That liking was growing into something far deeper, perilously deeper. The joy that flashed through him every time he saw Kim's beautiful eyes and sassy smile grew stronger each day. The thought should dismay him, yet it didn't.

Mating could start off as nothing more than a drive to reproduce, and some Shifters never moved beyond that. But others, like his father and mother, his brother Kenny and mate Sinead, had developed a relationship that went beyond mating, even beyond love. It was a bond humans couldn't understand, and Liam felt it forging between himself and Kim.

It was a heady feeling, and one he feared would turn into worse pain than any he'd ever experienced. The Collar's torture would be nothing compared to Kim breaking his heart.

Kim frowned at her coffee. "I can't believe that now

that I have good questions to ask Brian, you won't let me near him. You're not making my job easy." She looked up, an idea lighting her eyes. "But wait a sec, I can't believe Fergus wouldn't let Brian's *mother* talk to him."

"Possibly. Clan rules are one thing; maternal ties are another. Sacred, you could say."

"The same way Fergus can't mess with me if I'm your mate."

Liam nodded. "He can't unless I let him."

"*Let him?* What's all this 'let' shit? Shifters don't understand the term 'feminism,' do they?"

"I wouldn't say that, love. Shifter females are no pushovers. But realize that Shifters have lived in small groups for thousands of years, the males protecting the females and the cubs. It's instinctive for us. This is the first time we've dwelled in close communities—we still had the clans, but we rarely saw others in our clan. It's taking us a little bit of time to adjust."

She watched him in curiosity, one finger still rubbing the rim of her cup. Liam thought about her sweeping the same finger over his cock and instantly got hard again.

"Where did you live before?" she asked. "I mean in Ireland, before you came to Shiftertown? You told Abel you had a castle."

"A castle. That we did."

"With battlements and everything?"

"It was mostly a ruin by the time we moved in, but we fixed it up and made it livable."

"What did the Irish think of you? This was before Shifters came out, right?"

"Oh, they had all kinds of explanations for us. The ones inclined to believe in ghost stories thought we were the Fae, and that wasn't far off. Lucky for them, Shifters are ten times kinder than the Fae. Others thought we were former IRA come to hide out. The more skeptical just said we were crazy. But everyone knew we kept the village protected, so no one tried to drive us out."

Kim was watching him now, a bit like her office colleagues had, but Liam didn't mind so much being subjected to her blue-eyed scrutiny. "Why did you come to Austin if you had a fine castle in Ireland, and everyone loved you?"

Liam shrugged. "Once the traitorous bastard Shifter in England sold his story and demonstrated that he could shape-shift, Ireland got a little dangerous for us. People who needed money started taking bounties on Shifters, dead or alive. Kenny's mate, Sinead, was pregnant, and we couldn't risk her getting hunted. We heard that in this country, Shifters were being herded into camps rather than exterminated, but allowed to live in safety. So we packed up, and here we are."

"But Sinead—Connor's mom—died anyway."

"That she did." The sadness of her death had never gone away. "But if we'd stayed in Ireland, we'd likely have lost Connor too. He came early and was so weak. He needed quiet and medical care. Here, me and Dad, Sean and Kenny, we were able to look after him without having to worry about fighting off villagers with pitchforks."

"Are you saying that you took the Collar to save him?"

"Pretty much."

"And then a feral Shifter killed Kenny." Kim's eyes flashed with rage. "Bastard."

Liam's heart warmed at her anger. She understood. "May hell rot all feral Shifters."

"Ferals are the ones who refused the Collar, right? Why do they kill other Shifters?"

Liam's deep anger stirred. "Because in their eyes, we betrayed them. Instead of waiting to get slaughtered or watching our children die, we chose to sacrifice our freedom and band together. What infuriates them most is that we now live with other species of Shifters—which, to ferals, is even worse than letting humans believe they tell us what to do."

"Safety in numbers?"

"And strength." Liam smiled. "When we buried our cross-species hatred, we got stronger. We helped each other instead of fighting. Shifters were scattered and dying out. Now we're growing in number again. And growing stronger."

"Are you telling me that Shiftertowns aren't so much places of captivity as they are fortresses? No matter what humans think they are?"

"I'd say sanctuaries, but you're not far from wrong." He lost his smile. "Do you understand now why Fergus doesn't want a human learning all our secrets?"

Kim glanced around, but still, no one had come to sit near them. The coffee shop was pretty much deserted, the lunch crowd not yet surging through Austin's streets. "Then why are you telling me?"

A nonchalant shrug. "You're my mate. I tell you everything."

"Sure you do. You're saying that you live in Shiftertowns for your own ends and that you don't care about the things humans keep you from having—like cable and new cars and high paying jobs. I sort of understand that. But the Collars are still cruel."

"They are. Invented by a half-Fae with no love for Shifters. The truth is Shifters weren't all that violent in the wild. We used to hunt animals to eat—now we get our meat from the supermarket. But then, same with humans. We fight among ourselves for dominance or to protect the pride, but no indiscriminate slaughter."

"This from a man who killed a Shifter in my bedroom and was about to battle his clan leader yesterday morning."

He shrugged. "Extenuating circumstances."

"And you are supposed to hate other Shifter species?"

"We've learned to suppress our prejudices for the health of us all. Mostly. I count Ellison my friend, but I can still call him dog breath."

Kim's eyes sparkled. "What does he call you?"

"Cat shit."

She burst into nervous laughter. "I thought it would be 'Hairball.'"

"Glory calls us that sometimes. That or 'Cock-sucking Feline Irish bastards'."

Her brows rose. "And your father sleeps with this woman?"

The relationship between Glory and Dylan was unexplainable. "I'm glad to see him take an interest," Liam said. "I give him a break. He lost his mate."

"Your mom."

"Yes." Liam didn't fight his memories of his mother anymore. He had for a long time, not wanting to examine the hole in his heart. Dylan's taking off for a year had, in retrospect, been a good thing, even though at the time Liam had been furious with his father. But he realized now that Dylan had needed room to grieve, and Sean, Liam, and Kenny had needed to figure out how to live without a guiding hand.

"She was a fine woman," Liam said softly. "Beautiful, with green eyes and red hair. The wildcat she turned into was amazing—graceful and deadly—you didn't mess with her. She and Dad loved each other so much, it got embarrassing sometimes. You'd walk into a room, and they'd be kissing, with their hands all over each other. Imagine. At their age."

"I have a hard time thinking of your dad as old. Yes, I know you told me he's like two hundred. Do all Shifters age so well?"

"If they don't die young, yes."

"Do many die young?"

She was asking painful questions again. "They do. Or at least they did."

"Another reason you took the Collar."

Three people sat down in the booth behind them, humans, who must have been used to Shifters, because they didn't look too nervous. Liam changed the subject. "I should talk to Sandra on my own."

"Want me to drive you? Before I head back to my office?"

"Not now. After you get off work tonight." Liam pushed aside his coffee cup and stood, reaching to help her to her feet. "And after we stop by your house and get the things you want."

"You expect me to spend the night with you again?"

Kim said it a little too loudly. The diners in the next booth looked around, startled, curious, knowing.

"I meant at your house," Kim amended. "I don't need to stay there. I have my own house."

"But my nephew will be heartbroken if you don't come."

She gave him her annoyed look. "We'll talk about it later." She spun on her high heels and marched to the door, her sexy ass moving provocatively.

Liam took money from his pocket and dropped it on the table, thinking he could watch Kim's fine backside all day and never get tired of it. And after the day was done, he could lie next to her and her fine backside all night. He'd not get tired of that, either.

K im decided she'd never have let Liam win the argument of her returning with him to Shiftertown that evening if she hadn't spied the shaved-headed Shifter from San Antonio sitting at a bus stop outside her house. He wore a turtleneck to cover his Collar—in this heat, what an idiot—but she recognized him and knew he wasn't waiting for any bus.

The thought of Liam leaving her alone in the house while Fergus's Thug Number One lurked outside made her cold with worry. Ironic, Kim thought as she drove through the city, heading back toward Shiftertown, that she felt safer in a house full of Shifters with a crazed woman next door than in her own neighborhood. Everything about her life since she'd met Liam was upside down.

Shiftertown was as lively as ever as she followed Liam on his bike through it. Kids were being called in from playing to have dinner. Kim smelled barbeques firing up and burgers on the grill. Men and women alike looked up as Kim's Mustang rolled past. Liam, ahead of her, sexy on his Harley, lifted his hand in greeting time and again.

Liam's yard was quiet, no barbeque going here. Kim wondered whose turn it was to cook and hoped the men inside hadn't decided it was hers. But something seemed wrong; the door was shut too tightly, the windows too dark.

Liam sensed it too, stepping silently in front of her as they went up the porch steps. He opened the door to reveal Dylan and Sean in the living room, facing each other in livid anger, their eyes feral white. Connor huddled in the kitchen, as far away from the other two as he could get and still be downstairs.

Liam's voice was very quiet as he asked, "What's the trouble, Sean?"

Sean swung from Dylan, his body so tight with rage Kim wondered that he didn't flow into his wildcat form. Claws extended from his fingers as he grabbed a paper from the table and shoved it in Liam's face.

"*That's* the trouble."

It was a printed e-mail. Kim rose on tiptoe to read it with Liam.

After the mate-bonding at the full moon, it has been decided by clan council that Dylan Morrissey shall step down as leader of the East Austin Shiftertown and another Feline of the council's choosing be put into his place. Authorized by Fergus Leary, leader of the South Texas Feline clan.

CHAPTER SIXTEEN

Kim had never seen Liam less than completely self-assured, never at a loss for words. Not her Irish Shifter with his gift of blarney.

Now Liam stared at the paper while his face flooded with color and his eyes changed to white-blue.

"I told Dad"—Sean's voice was strained—"that he needs to confront Fergus and get it over with. Dad refused."

Kim folded chilled fingers into her palms, deciding for once to keep silent. She remembered Liam telling her that he didn't know why Dylan never fought Fergus for dominance, but that he thought it was so the Shifters could live in peace.

"Son of a bitch," Liam said. "Dad, why?"

Dylan's voice was tight, his hands clenched. His fingers had changed to claws, and blood smeared his fists. "Leave it alone, Liam."

"I can't. Fergus wants you to step down? To put one of his lackeys in your place? Our lives won't be worth shite if that happens. He's undercutting your position in your own pride, not to mention the clan."

"I said, leave it alone!"

Liam didn't flinch. "Dad, this is a blatant smack in the face, an invitation to challenge him."

Dylan's eyes were red with rage, but Kim saw anguish behind the animal fury. "Don't you think I know that? But I won't. Not now."

"Why the hell not?"

"I have my fucking reasons!" Dylan roared.

If he'd directed that anger at Kim, she knew she'd run like hell. Liam stood his ground, his own hands showing claws. "If you think you're giving in for the good of Shiftertown, you're crazy. This will be his first step to drive us out of here. He'll make sure we end up in a Shiftertown far from here, where we're clanless and at the bottom of the pile. Kim will have to abandon Brian, and Brian will go down for the murder."

Kim noted Liam's big assumption—that if the Morrisseys had to go, she'd go with them—but she decided this was not the time to bring it up.

Dylan's eyes were bleak. "I know."

Liam's claws shredded the paper, which fell to the floor. "I can't go after Fergus myself. You know that."

"Yes," Dylan said quietly. "I do."

"Then why . . ."

His words trailed off as the back door banged open and hot wind flooded past them. Glory charged in, dressed in hot pink with silver sandals, her finger- and toenails painted in matching pink. "Dylan, what the hell is going on?"

Dylan gave her a weary look. "Glory. Not now."

"Fergus wants Grandda' to step down from leading Shiftertown," Connor babbled from the kitchen.

Glory's mouth opened in shock. "What? We won't stand for that. The asshole."

"You said it," Kim agreed.

The males in the room, except Connor, ignored both women. Sean met Dylan's gaze, his face quiet. "I'll do it. I'll fight Fergus."

A chorus of shouting drowned him out. Liam huffed a bitter laugh. "What, Sean, you'll kill me, then Dad, then go after Fergus?"

"No." Sean's face was white. "I'll just kill the gobshite. I can shoot him, can't I, and then stick him with the sword. Fergus is dust, no more problem."

"And then by Shifter law I'll have to take you out," Liam said in a hard voice. "Bad plan."

"What does it matter?" Sean asked.

The others fell silent, and Kim couldn't contain herself. "Are you all crazy? Why would you let Sean even think of that?"

"Stay out of this, Kim," Dylan said without looking at her.

"No, Kim has a point." Glory folded her arms, her perfect breasts straining against her pink shirt. "Sean, why should you sacrifice yourself?"

"To keep the peace," Sean said in a tired voice. "I would be the logical choice to be the assassin and pay the price. Because I'm mateless." Sean shot Liam a hard look, and Liam, surprisingly, dropped his gaze.

Glory said, "Listen to the human girl. If anyone should pay for this, it's Fergus himself. Let *him* be the sacrifice."

"Good idea," Connor echoed.

Dylan let his voice roar through. "There will be no argument. We do what Fergus says."

Kim opened her mouth to protest, and so did Glory, but suddenly Glory shut hers, as though she understood something. Dylan was staring hard at Liam, those nonverbal cues flying between them. Dylan's eyes were feral white, Liam's not much better.

Liam dropped his gaze and turned. Dylan gave him a look of almost disappointment, then swung away and slammed himself out the back door. Glory took a deep breath, but to Kim's surprise, she didn't follow Dylan.

"I really don't understand," Kim said into the silence. "Why would your dad stand back and let Fergus win?"

Liam shot her a quick look. He was worried. "I don't know."

"Because Dylan isn't ready to die," Glory said. "He's not that old, and he's completely virile. Besides, he has me."

Her smug statement broke the tension a little. Connor even gave a nervous laugh. "Sure, that would be worth living for," he said.

"You're a cub, youngling," Glory said. "You'll learn."

Liam remained silent, the smiling, damn-your-eyes man Kim had come to know fading into a bleak, angry Shifter. When he looked like this he was scary as hell, but Kim walked to him and ducked under his arm. The others had backed off, and for the first time since she'd met this group, they were giving another Shifter space.

Kim sensed that Liam didn't need space right now; he needed touch, reassurance. She melded to his side, and Liam finally looked down at her, the feral white-blue of his eyes darkening to human blue once again.

"We'll fix this somehow," Kim dared to say. "Without anyone dying or Sean shooting Fergus in the back. Although I wouldn't mind doing that—after I give him a piece of my mind."

"Don't you dare," Liam said, lips flat. "Or I'll chain you up in the basement."

"Are there spiders down there?"

"Possibly."

Kim lifted her hand. "All right, I'll try to be sensible. I see that I need to speed up my campaign to free Brian, and I have a few ideas about that."

Liam's gaze flickered, as though suspicious about her ideas, but his fangs and claws had retreated.

Glory snorted. "The little kitten has teeth, Liam. Watch that when she goes down on you."

Connor laughed out loud. Liam gave Kim a little smile. "I'm willing to risk it."

Glory stepped past them. "Excuse me. I think Dylan's had time to cool from killing rage to an even simmer. Time for me to go be a good little lapdog."

"I don't even want to know about that," Connor said in disgust, as Glory sashayed out.

Connor came to Kim and put his arms around her in a smothering hug. "I'm glad you're Liam's mate, Kim, and I'm glad you came home. The full-moon blessing tomorrow night is going to be some party. Me and Sean have invited everyone."

Kim remembered Liam saying something about his father pronouncing his blessing under the moon, but she hadn't paid much attention. "Party?"

"Mate blessings don't happen very often, so all of Shiftertown will want to see it," Liam said. "Don't worry, we dress casual."

"Oh, thanks." All of Shiftertown, coming to stare at her. Then again, it might be a good time to put some of her ideas in motion. If Silas was dying to learn about Shifters, she could give him a glimpse, and he could help Kim's cause at the same time. "Do you mind if I invite a friend?"

Liam's eyes narrowed. "Friend?"

"Someone I know who's helped me out in the past. Is this blessing something humans can witness?"

Liam gave her a nod. "Sure. It won't make Fergus happy, but screw him."

"That's what I keep saying." She smiled up at Liam. She knew she couldn't ease all his tension, but she could tell how far she'd made him relax. "I need to make a few phone calls. Mind?"

Liam released her. "Is this human all right about Shifters?"

"Yes, he likes them."

"He?"

Kim laughed at Liam's sudden, possessive stare. "Don't worry. He's just a friend. I've known him for a long time."

Liam's gaze softened a little, but Kim made a mental note to warn Silas not to touch her, not even casually.

"You make your calls," Liam said, his voice gentling. He'd climbed down a long way from the ready-to-kill Shifter, but he was still tense. "Myself, I'm going to go visit Sandra again. I'd like to figure out why Fergus is pulling out all the stops to keep Brian from going to trial."

Liam found Sandra in her backyard, alone. She'd wheeled her shallow charcoal-burning grill to the middle of the grass and started a fire in it. As Liam approached, he heard her chanting a prayer to the Earth goddess at the same time she tossed fragments of paper into the fire.

Liam approached silently. He meant to give her privacy to pray, but when he saw what she burned, he stepped forward and grabbed them out of her hands.

Sandra jerked around with a sharp intake of breath. Her wildcat fangs extended, her eyes going white.

Liam looked at the photos Sandra had been trying to burn. One showed Brian grinning at the camera with his arm around his mom, a bottle of beer dangling from his hand. Another showed Brian and his friends at a lake. Then Brian and a human girl, probably the murder victim, Michelle.

"It's not desperate enough for this yet," Liam said.

"Don't stop me. I need to make sure he gets to the Summerland."

"Brian's not going anywhere near the Summerland." Liam put his arm around Sandra's shoulder, trying to let his warmth comfort her. "That's why I've come, to ask for your help in springing him."

Sandra looked up at him with dead eyes. "There's nothing I can do."

"That's not true. Now come on, let's go in and have something cold to drink. It's too bloody hot out here to be doing any straight thinking."

Sandra let Liam take her into the house, where he fetched her a cold beer. He opened a bottle himself and sank down onto her couch to drink it. He'd sat here a couple days ago, he remembered, massaging Kim's feet. She had lovely feet, tiny in his big hands.

Liam tucked the photos of Brian into his pocket, knowing that if he let Sandra have them, she'd go back to burning them after he'd gone. An image of the loved one, sacrificed to fire, was the best way to make sure the loved one's passage into the afterlife was peaceful.

Sandra drank the beer but made no sign of enjoying it. "What do you want, Liam?"

"I want to know about this human girl, Michelle. Did Brian intend to make her his mate?"

Sandra regarded him in surprise. "I don't know."

"Because he would never have killed her if he did, and you know it. I hadn't thought of it before, because taking a human female for mate wasn't something I'd ever considered. But Kim, she's damn smart."

Sandra eyed him sharply. "I heard that you claimed her."

"That I did. Don't worry, it was sanctioned by Fergus himself. He insisted on it, actually, though I intended to make the bond anyway."

"Sun and moon?"

"Under the sun, so far. The moon is at its fullest tomorrow night, and Dad will bless us then. Come over. It will be a grand party."

"And Kim, she's fine with you claiming her?"

Liam thought of Kim's confusion, her outrage. He grinned. "Maybe 'fine' is going a bit far, but she'll get used to it. I'll make sure of that." He took a sip of beer and saw Sandra actually smile.

He got Sandra to let him have a look in Brian's room.

Brian wasn't a cub anymore—he'd come of age and found his place in the hierarchy, but he had continued to live here to help out his mother. The custom of human kids moving out as soon as they turned eighteen had always struck Liam as odd. Shifters lived together in family groups for generations.

Sandra had lost her mate long before she and Brian had moved to Shiftertown. Only Brian and she lived in this house, and before Brian's arrest, Sandra had been hopeful that Brian would soon claim a mate and fill the house with little ones. Now her eyes were devoid of any hope as she led Liam upstairs.

Brian occupied two rooms on the second floor—he'd used one as a bedroom, the other as an office. An old computer stood on his desk, jury-rigged to a couple other boxes as though he was trying to set up a network. Liam wasn't a computer whiz by any means, though he could navigate the Internet fairly well. But he didn't know enough to understand whether Brian was trying to make his computer do something illegal or simply work better.

Sandra turned away after she let Liam in, as though she couldn't bear to enter Brian's rooms. That was fine with Liam. He went through Brian's desk thoroughly while he waited for the computer to boot up, but he didn't find anything useful. Old receipts for gas, cardboard coasters, souvenirs from various attractions around Austin, and old raffle-type tickets.

The computer, it turned out, didn't have the helpful screen full of icons to click on. A list of files scrolled by when Liam hit the Enter key, and then the cursor sat at the bottom of the screen, blinking at him.

"Shite." He'd have to have Sean take a look. Sean knew far more about computers than Liam did, more than Shifters were allowed to know.

The rest of Brian's living room—his video and DVD collection, his books, his magazines—told Liam nothing except that, like Connor, Brian had an obsession with cars. Cars were a sickness among younger Shifters. Liam couldn't see the attraction; it wasn't as though they were Harleys.

Liam took a quick look through Brian's bedroom, but came up with even less. If Brian had secrets, he didn't hide them in the house he shared with his mother. Liam did find a few pictures of Michelle tossed carelessly into the drawer of the nightstand. She'd been a pretty girl, with honey-blonde hair and a sweet smile, her skin tanned from the Texas sun. Photos of her and Brian together told Liam she didn't mind at all that he was Shifter.

"Did you put these in here?" he called to Sandra.

"No," she said when she looked. "Brian kept them there. The police took away about half of them when they searched."

Liam was surprised they'd left any. But maybe they'd taken enough to show the jury what a pretty, helpless innocent Brian had corrupted.

"Can I have this one?" He held up a photo of Michelle with both arms around Brian.

"Sure."

She was trying to make herself stop caring. Liam recognized the signs, having seen them in both his father and Kenny when they lost their mates. Pretending that they'd let go, that their beloved's things were just things, of no importance.

"Will you ask Brian about her?" Liam asked as he pocketed the photos. "Find out whether he was going to claim her? It's important."

Sandra shook her head. "I'll not be visiting him again."

"Don't give up yet."

Vehemence entered her eyes, making her come alive. "I can't visit him. *He* won't let me."

"Who?" Liam's eyes narrowed. "Fergus?"

"Yes, Fergus. I've been told to stay away, to let Brian go."

Liam went to her and rubbed her shoulders. "Sandra,

you can't do that. He's your son, your cub. He needs you now more than ever."

"Tell that to Fergus. I had orders."

"Well, here's me overriding those orders."

Sandra laughed, an unhealthy sound. "You can't."

"I'm using my prerogative of second in command of this Shiftertown." *For now,* he thought silently. "I say go see Brian, and let me deal with Fergus."

"I can't let you do that. He can kill you."

"He already wants to kill me for so very many reasons. You're the only one who can do this for us, love. Fergus won't let me near Brian, and he won't let Kim talk to him anymore, but stopping a mother from seeing her cub—that one he won't be able to justify. I'm betting he knows that."

Sandra looked tired. "I can't stand up to him, Liam."

"You won't have to. He's not here, and his lieutenants won't interfere with a mother's rights." Liam gave her an encouraging smile. "Even Fergus's thugs have mothers who wouldn't let them hear the end of it if they kept you from your cub."

Sandra relaxed a little. "You are full of shit, Liam."

"Try it. They won't hurt you, not around so many humans. You want to see Brian, don't you?"

"Will you come with me?"

"I can't." Liam rubbed her shoulders again, wishing he could tell her that everything would be fine and mean it. "They'll waffle about stopping you, but they won't let me anywhere near the jail. But you go on. Have a good talk with him, and tell me everything he says."

Kim hung up her cell phone as Liam walked in the back door. A strange sensation flashed through her, and it took her a minute to recognize it—she was glad to see him.

She hadn't been so happy to see someone enter a room in a long, long time, not since her parents had passed. Friends were fine, and Abel was— All right, so whenever Abel had walked in, her first reaction usually had been impatience and irritation.

Seeing Liam made her heart beat faster and not simply because of lust. She went warm as he smiled at her and leaned down to kiss her cheek.

"Where is everyone?" he asked.

"Your dad, still next door with Glory. Connor went out to hook up with some friends, he said. Ellison came over, and he and Sean took off."

"Oh, did he? Leaving you alone and unprotected?" He played with the hair at the back of her neck.

"Not with every single one of your neighbors outside staring at the house. Maybe you noticed them?"

"Wondering what I'm doing in here with the human woman." Liam massaged her neck, leaning down to nip the shell of her ear. "What would you like me to do?"

Kim's body grew pliant. "Liam, about this friend I want to invite . . ."

"What about him? He wasn't your lover, was he?"

"No. Really, he's just a friend. I've known him since college. I didn't want to say this in front of all the others, but Silas is a journalist. A very good one. He wants to do some pieces on Shifters and make a documentary. Kind of show how they're mistreated, that kind of angle."

Liam straightened up, eyes wary. "Let another human uncover Shifter secrets?"

"No, I mean show Shifter life in its reality—the kids playing in the yards, like that Michael in his pool I saw the first day I was here. He's cute, and he'd have great appeal. Humans can watch Shifter moms planting gardens, dads coming home from their working-class jobs. Teenagers like Connor playing soccer or holding hands with their girlfriends. Let people see how peaceful you are, how *normal*."

"Is that all? You know Fergus would never let that happen."

"That's why I'm asking you." Kim smiled up at him, trying to look impossibly sweet.

Liam's gaze softened. "You're a crafty lass, Kim. You want these stories to switch public opinion to Brian's side, don't you now?"

"It couldn't hurt."

Liam laughed softly and kissed the top of her head. "And you know if I say yes, I won't tell Fergus."

"Something like that. Or your father?"

"Or my father, who would feel obligated to pass on the information. Bring this Silas to the party and let me meet him. No cameras, no notebooks. Strictly off the record until I get to know him."

"Of course. He's fair, Liam, which is why I thought of him."

"But if I don't like him . . ."

"I tell him no. Promise."

"All right then." Liam leaned down, resumed nibbling her earlobe. "But enough talking. I'm thinking about the fact that we're alone in this house."

"Having someone in the house didn't stop you yesterday," she pointed out in a shaky voice.

"That was mating frenzy. Today I want to take it slow. To give you everything I want, in my own time." Liam ran his fingers down her spine, trailing fire. "I want to see if you're wearing garters under that sexy skirt."

Kim leaned against the kitchen counter and slid her skirt up a few inches. "I am."

Liam's warm hands covered her thighs, his thumbs hooking into the tops of her stockings. "That's my girl."

CHAPTER SEVENTEEN

Kim found herself seated on the counter with Liam standing between her legs. Liam's warm lips played on hers while he slid his hands to the insides of her thighs. "Could this be a thong?" he murmured, touching it. "The thing you said you couldn't be wearing?"

"Could be."

"Did you wear it for me, Kim?"

"Yes."

Liam nuzzled her cheek. "I like that." He licked where he nuzzled. "It's easy to move aside."

"That's the point of it."

"You're wet for me," he said.

"I am." Kim drew her hand along his zipper. "You're ready too, I see. Either that or you shoved a baseball bat down there."

"I'm thinking that would be painful."

"I'm thinking you're in pain now," Kim whispered in his ear. "I would be, if I had something that big in my pants."

"Want to find out what it's like?"

"I wouldn't mind."

She'd never done it leaning back on a counter, her skirt up, her panties shoved aside, and her lover letting his jeans drop around his ankles. But then, she'd never had a lover like Liam, a large, raw-muscled Irishman with beautiful eyes.

She found herself with her legs locked around him, his hands cradling her head while she felt the burn of them joining. His lips were all over her, face, throat, hair, mouth.

"You feel so good, Kim. You feel so fucking good."

Kim didn't answer. She sensed desperation in him, the need to bury himself in sex and forget the strange argument he'd had with his dad as well as Fergus's ultimatum. Liam seemed the most unnerved of all of them, even Dylan.

The untamed joy of what they did made Kim want to shout out loud, and so did the danger that someone could walk in and catch them. Her partners had always practiced safe sex—not only in the sense of using condoms, but in ensuring the lights were out, the doors locked, and the windows shaded, so no one would ever know what they were doing.

Liam wanted Kim and didn't care who knew. He'd broadcast the fact far and wide, proudly. Instead of being embarrassed, Kim's heart swelled with joy.

Another part of her did too. She rocked her hips, loving the sensation of him deep inside her.

"Liam," she groaned. "I want you to do dirty things to me."

"Happy to, love," he said, his face against hers. "You name them, I'll do them."

She moved faster, and he did, and she did again. "I'm loving *this* right now."

"I love what you make me feel," he whispered.

Kim tried to think of something sexy to say, but words fled her brain. "Just shut up and do me."

Liam laughed. He rocked into her swiftly, until they were both breathless with it. Liam held her tightly as he came, his seed scalding, his mouth hard on hers. His kisses were still unpracticed, but Kim didn't care. She caught his tongue, his lips, his teeth with hers, kissing him back with joyous abandon.

Liam smiled into her mouth, and Kim laughed with him. Sex didn't get better than this.

Her heart beat wildly when she thought that maybe it did—with Liam. The idea triggered her orgasm. She gyrated against him, unsure how much noise she was making and not really caring.

When she wound down, Liam backed out of her, still hard, pulled up his pants, and carried her to the sagging living room sofa. He collapsed onto it, Kim on top of him, both of them panting.

"Oh, man, that was good." Kim lay against his shoulder trying to get her breath. Laughter didn't help.

Liam ran his fingers through her hair. "Not what I had in mind, but not bad."

"What do you mean, not *bad?*"

Liam regarded her with half-closed predator's eyes. "I told you, I wanted to take it slow. Love you like you deserve. Not screwing you quick-time on a kitchen counter."

Kim kissed the tip of his nose. "I didn't mind. Not at all. Maybe you noticed?"

"I want to give you so much." Liam's hold tightened into a hard embrace. "So much, Kim. Everything I once had, everything I lost. I want it back—for you."

She heard Liam's heart beating rapidly beneath her ear, and her own heart squeezed. His declarations scared her. She could dismiss his words as those of a man happy he'd just gotten into a woman's pants, words that would evaporate as soon as he was sated. Except the throbbing of his heart was from more than physical exertion. His voice held uncertainty, a longing he feared he couldn't fulfill.

Kim ran her fingers along the hard plane of his chest. "You don't need to do anything for me."

"Don't be daft, woman. I take care of you now. I want to do everything for you."

She shook her head. "I take care of myself. I have a decent job and a nice house. That's more than a lot of people have."

"Before we took the Collar, a man took his mate home to his family and sequestered her. He did everything for her, hunted for her, kept her warm and fed and comfortable, pampered her in every way."

"Really? I guess you hadn't ever heard of women's rights."

"Not in the nineteenth century, love." Liam smiled. "Not *sequestered* as in kept in prison. Sequestered as in protected from all others. Female Shifters have always been in short supply, and we had to keep them from being stolen by other Shifters. The mate bond is sacrosanct, but when times were bad, other males stopped caring about sacrosanct." He cradled Kim closer. "So I have to fight my instincts not to lock you somewhere safe and beat off everyone from even looking at you."

Kim had never considered herself a precious object before. Certainly Abel had never treated her as more than a convenience, and men she'd dated earlier in life hadn't been much better. Her relationships had been the "friends with benefits" kind. No true, undying love, no *I want to take care of you and protect you for the rest of our lives.*

Kim had spent enough time taking care of herself that having someone want to relieve her of the burden felt strange, though nice. She wasn't going to let Liam do it, but the feeling was still nice.

Liam swung her into his arms and rolled to his feet at the same time. Kim found herself against his chest with her head on his shoulder, Liam striding toward the stairs.

"What are you doing?" she asked.

"Taking you upstairs where we belong. I'm tired of fighting my instincts."

A pleasant shiver went through her. "What does that mean?"

His eyes were white-blue when he looked down at her, his

pupils changing. "I'm going to love you all night, my *mate*. On a bed. I'm going to love you until we can't stand up."

If Abel had said that, Kim would have rolled her eyes or thought about what unsatisfying work that would be. When Liam said it, her whole body came alive.

To tease him, she said, "I really should look at my case files."

The look Liam gave her was savage. "Screw your case files."

Kim laughed. Liam growled and sprinted up the last of the stairs, slammed into the bedroom and tossed her on the bed. As her clothes came off, then his, Kim gave in. For one night of her life, she was going to enjoy making wild, crazy love with a man who promised to make it unforgettable, no matter what might come in the morning.

I t was Sean's turn to cook breakfast, and Liam grabbed a plateful of pancakes from him as the sun poured through the eastern windows. "Kim will be down in a minute."

Sean sent him an annoyed look with bloodshot eyes. "I'm thinking of soundproofing your room."

"The sounds of loving bother you that much, do they?" Liam asked him.

"It does when you're shouting all night."

Connor grinned from his place at the table. "I had to wear headphones with the music cranked up. It barely drowned you out."

"You gobshites are just jealous. Where's Dad?"

Sean slammed the spatula to the counter. "Where do you think?"

Next door. With Glory. Good. "Do you begrudge your old dad getting some?" Liam asked Sean in a light voice. "A grateful son you are."

"Sean's pissed because *he's* not getting any," Connor said. "I don't mind because I'm still too young and innocent to know what it all means."

"Bullshit," Sean growled.

Connor laughed at him. Liam clapped Sean on the shoulder and turned away with his breakfast. "You'll find a mate some-day, Sean. Then we'll make fun of the noise from *your* room."

Sean gave him a dark look and went back to his bat-ter. His bad mood was about more than Liam keeping him awake. Sean had been ready to lay down his life for them yesterday, and that hadn't been an easy thing for him to do.

Liam started to sit down, then felt the unmistakable pres-ence of Kim coming down the stairs. Smelled her as well, all fresh from her shower. She wore a casual skirt and sleeveless shirt, her legs bare, feet in strappy, high-heeled sandals.

"Are those pancakes?" she asked. "I'm starving."

Liam drew her into his arms. He'd woken with her in his arms not an hour ago, and hadn't that been the best feeling in the world? Liam nuzzled her cheek, then kissed her lips.

Kim smiled up at him. "Pancakes are that good, are they?"

"Sean's almost as good a cook as me. Come and sit."

Connor got out of his chair as Kim approached, and Liam gave him a nod. Kim looked startled as Connor wrapped his lanky arms around her, ending his sloppy hug with a kiss on the cheek.

"Good morning, Kim," he said as he released her.

"Good morning to you too. I—" Her speech cut off as Sean stepped up and gave her a more practiced hug, tight squeeze, a rub on the back, a kiss to her hair.

"You like blueberry, Kim?" Sean asked, as he released her and turned back to the stove.

"Sure. Blueberry. Great."

Liam caressed the back of Kim's neck and led her to her place at the table. "Sleep well, did you?"

"No." Kim plopped down, reached for the pitcher of juice in the middle of the table. "But you know that. Sean, Connor, are you trying to comfort me for having to spend the night with Liam?"

Connor hooted with laughter. Even Sean broke out of

his sour mood to grin. "Are you in need of comfort, Kim?" Sean asked. "Is he that bad?"

"Shut it," Liam growled, but he was too full of afterglow to care about their teasing. "They're acknowledging you as my mate, love. Welcoming you to the family."

"I forgot. Shifters like to hug. A lot."

Liam ran his hand up Kim's arm, her silken skin a joy beneath his fingertips. "Is there something wrong with that? Touching and hugging is a good thing."

"It's unusual," Kim said. "For humans, I mean."

"Touching is reassurance, keeping the bonds between family intact. It's more than love; it's necessary."

"Humans do it too," Sean said from the stove. "Except they get embarrassed. So they invent strange rituals, like giving flowers and candy to ladies. Human men punch each other when they like each other. I've seen them do it."

"Sean has made a study of humans and their behavior," Liam said. "It gives him something to do."

Kim gave Sean a look of respect. "Well, if you can figure out human behavior, more power to you. Even humans can't figure it out."

"But I'm outside looking in," Sean said. "It's different."

"So are Shifters to humans." Kim accepted her plate of pancakes and dug in. "I know you all don't want to talk about this, but I don't want to hear any more discussion about you giving in to Fergus. He's just trying to sow dissention. I've been thinking it over, and I think what y'all really need is a good lawyer, and one just happens to be eating pancakes with you. I'm going to dig into Shifter law and see if Fergus really can tell your dad to step down, or try to find some loophole to keep him from succeeding. So I'll need to know what rules and customs or whatever aren't written down. I need to know *everything*."

With his mate so near, with her scent and his all over her, Liam didn't much care about Fergus, Brian, and the screwed-up mess they'd gotten the rest of Shiftertown into.

"That's fine, Kim. I won't stop you trying. Just don't be getting your hopes up, love."

Kim finished the last of her pancakes and got to her feet. "It beats letting Fergus win."

"He won't," Liam said, watching her hips sway as she took her plate to the sink. "I won't let him."

Sean gave him a dark look. "I still think my way is best." He didn't mean it like he had yesterday, Liam could tell, because Sean's tension had eased a long way. But Sean was still angry.

"We need you as the Guardian, Sean," Liam said softly. "Connor's not yet ready to take up the sword."

"No-ho," Connor said, from deep in his car magazine. "Don't you dare die on me, Sean."

Kim looked confused again. Liam gestured her out to the back porch and followed her down the steps to the fenceless backyard and the Austin summer sunshine. It would be another hot one, but later tonight, the cool moon would cover the yard in silver light.

"I have to go to work," Kim said.

"I know."

"You'll try to come with me, won't you?"

"I will be coming with you. I'm not letting you out of my sight, not with Fergus's thugs wandering about and Fergus mad as hell at the Morrisseys. He's not above making an example of disobedient clan members."

"I'm going to fix this, Liam."

Liam just gave her a nod. "Even so—not out of my sight, love."

"What's with Sean?" she asked, glancing back at the house.

It took Kim a while to voice questions, Liam noticed. Must be the lawyer in her, thinking carefully before she pried out the information she wanted.

Liam rubbed his hair, not liking to think about it. "Sean has always blamed himself for Kenny's death. I blame myself, because I was stupidly obeying orders when I should have been protecting them both. But Sean was right there beside Kenny. Sean fought and survived, but he couldn't save Kenny. It eats at him, it does."

Kim gave him a skeptical look. "Oh, please. I know damn well Sean didn't simply stand aside and watch Kenny get killed. He must have fought."

"As the Guardian, his first duty is to the sword, and he couldn't risk letting the feral get it. Kenny knew that. He was fighting to protect the Guardian and the sword."

Kim gave him a wide-eyed stare. "You mean that piece of metal was more important than your brother?"

"No, that's not what I'm saying. But the Guardian has a huge responsibility to the whole clan. He has to survive to keep the sword free in case he needs to use it on one of us. Kenny knew what he was doing."

He could tell Kim didn't really understand, but her look softened. "That doesn't make it any easier, does it?"

"No."

Kim slid her arms around his waist. "Liam, I'm so sorry."

He felt her sorrow. Liam melted into her, tears tracking down his face for the brother he'd lost. Being a Shifter was all about sacrifice, and the fact that Kim understood that untwisted something inside him that had been knotted for a decade.

Kim worked through the day in her office, catching up on phone calls and paperwork, preparing for the court case she was determined to have for Brian. The private investigator she'd hired told Kim he'd discovered evidence that Michelle's ex-boyfriend had burned with plenty of resentment when Michelle had started seeing Brian. Threats had been made, and friends of the ex-boyfriend had been worried. Good. Kim told him to keep searching that angle.

Kim also pulled up every single piece of information

she had on Shifter law and went over it again. She'd find something to stop Fergus trying to defeat the Morrisseys, no matter how long it took. The human government didn't usually interfere with Shifter hierarchy, mostly because they didn't understand it. But Kim would find some way to solve this, and Liam would figure out why Fergus wanted Brian executed.

Working with Liam stretched out on her office couch unnerved Kim, especially when he spent the whole time watching her. He didn't demand her attention or interrupt; he just . . . watched.

He reminded Kim of lions on the African veldt, sitting under the shade of whatever those trees were, watching herds of gazelles. Maybe the lions wouldn't be hungry right then, but they'd watch. Heads up, ears pricked, alert. Still. Waiting.

By five-thirty, the gazelle in her was ready to go home.

Kim didn't bother trying to go to her own house. She drove with Liam straight back to Shiftertown, feeling a strange kind of relief to do so.

When Kim and Liam arrived at the Morrissey house, Sean had a big charcoal-burning barbeque going in the backyard, and beer and ice overflowed from several coolers. A dozen Shifters lounged on the porch and through the yard, talking to Sean and Dylan. Connor kicked a soccer ball around with a few other young men his age, while two teenaged females stood back and assessed them.

Kim's journalist friend Silas pulled up shortly after. He was tall and very thin, with a prominent Adam's apple.

"What is this party for?" Silas asked when Kim presented him to Liam. Kim had warned Silas that only Liam knew what he was really doing there, and he promised to be discreet.

"It's a blessing under the moon, that it is," Liam answered him. He flashed his teeth in a grin. "It's after being a very interestin' ritual."

Kim rolled her eyes at the exaggerated Irish-isms, but at least he'd quit saying, "Top o' the morning."

"You sound like a cartoon leprechaun," she said to him, after they'd introduced Silas around and left him talking animatedly to Annie from the bar.

"Whist, it's my feelings you'll be hurting."

"Shut it, Liam."

His brows shot up, and he laughed. "You're learning, darling." His laughter was warm, reminding her of him loving her all night, and even now he gave her a look of undisguised hunger. "I haven't touched you in too long."

Pleasant shivers ran through her. She agreed. It had been too long since any intimate touching. Hours.

"I'm already wishing the ritual over and everyone gone home," Liam said in her ear.

"We should probably eat first. Be social."

"Aye." Liam slid his hands to her backside and scooped her against him for a kiss. "But I hope this doesn't take all night."

They strolled back to the barbeque as more Shifters joined the throng. Everyone Kim had met in Shiftertown was there—the wolf Ellison, Glory, Annie, Sandra, the women on the porches she'd passed the first day, little Michael who'd been proud of his plastic pool.

Kim stiffened when she saw Fergus's two thugs—the shaved-headed, tattooed guy and military guy with sunglasses. But Sean handed them plates of charred burgers with buns, unsurprised.

"They aren't going to fight anyone, are they?" Kim asked as she took her burger from Sean. The two men had moved off to eat, and she noted the other Shifters gave them a wide berth. "Or bring out a cat-o'-nine-tails and start whaling on people?"

"They're here to observe the ritual," Sean told her. "Stand-ins for Fergus. And they'll be on their best behavior."

"I could have put Silas off if I'd known they'd be here."

Liam shook his head. "They won't disrupt the ritual. Fergus wants this mating done, and he wants to make sure Dad relinquishes power tomorrow."

Kim nodded glumly. She hadn't yet found a law that Fergus was bending by asking Dylan to vacate his post, but she would. She'd leave no stone unturned.

She chewed the burger Sean handed her, which was very good, especially with the gooey cheese melted on it. Her diet had gone to hell, but she couldn't bring herself to care.

Ellison came out of the crowd in his big black Stetson and cowboy boots. He high-fived Liam, and then the two men shared a tight bear hug.

"Kim!" Ellison boomed, his arms opened wide, and before Kim could duck away, Ellison swept off his hat and spun her off her feet. Liam rescued Kim's plate of half-eaten burger as Ellison swung Kim around. "Congratulations, woman." Ellison set Kim down and gave her abdomen a gentle pat. "When's it due?"

"What the hell are you talking about?"

Ellison looked shocked. "Liam, haven't you touched her yet? What's the matter with you? You're already sunblessed. Are you waiting for Christmas?"

"We've done it, trust me." Liam handed Kim back her meal. "It will be soon."

Kim's face went hot. "Not that it's any of your business."

"Not my business? Hon, it's every Shifter's business whether a Shifter male can do the job. We have to be good at making babies, so we practice a lot." He balled his fists and thrust his hips in a parody of sex.

"Ignore him, Kim. Lupines are disgusting."

"Thank you," Glory said. She stepped past Ellison, tall and sleek in skintight black pants and silk top, every blonde hair in place. "Fucking Felines."

"Gobshite Lupines," Liam said cheerfully.

Dylan approached. "Kim."

Kim watched him in trepidation, but Dylan folded his arms around her and squeezed her in a very tight hug. She sensed something different in his hug than she had in the others'. Not happy exuberance—relief. Dylan held her close, and she smelled the damp cotton of his shirt and his shaving soap. But Dylan's hold wasn't in any way sexual. He held her as he'd cradle a child, as he might soothe Connor.

Dylan held Kim a long time, and his eyes were wet when he pulled away. He wiped them, unashamed, then turned and wrapped his arms around Liam.

Father and son stood still in the embrace, while Kim took her burger back from Ellison. To stem the tears that insisted on filling her eyes, she reflected that she needed to eat fast, before more people wanted to greet her with hugs.

Kim noticed that Glory didn't try to hug her—the woman sauntered away to get food with Dylan when Dylan finally released Liam. Kim wondered whether Glory was showing her disapproval for Liam taking a human mate, or whether the woman didn't feel like she was close enough to the family to join the hug-fest. Glory and Dylan might be hard at it, but sex did not necessarily mean intimacy, Kim knew from experience. The woman was a puzzle.

It took a while for the summer night to darken, but Liam and Dylan seemed in no hurry. Liam introduced Kim to all present, holding her hand or with his arm around her waist as they strolled from group to group. Kim met Lupines and other Felines, and bears.

The bear Shifters fascinated her, large-boned men and women who sported long manes of hair. Many of the bear-men were bearded, and both men and women obviously liked tattoos. They, too, welcomed Kim with hugs, though they were less intimate than the family's hugs. Not all of them looked happy that Liam was bringing a human into their midst, but they were cordial.

By the time Liam walked Kim back to the center of the

yard, the night was dark and mercifully cooler. The moon rose rapidly, and as it reached its zenith, the crowd grew quiet.

Liam's neighbors silently formed two concentric circles, putting Liam, Kim, and Dylan in the middle of the inner one. The smaller, inner circle contained Liam's immediate family and friends, along with Fergus's two henchmen. The outer circle held the rest of Shiftertown.

Cool moonlight filtered through the trees, touching Kim's face as Liam turned her toward him. As he had when they'd stood before Fergus in the San Antonio Shiftertown, Liam held his left hand up, palm out, and pressed it to Kim's right one. He twined his fingers through hers and met her gaze with steady eyes.

Dylan closed both his hands around theirs and began chanting something in a language Kim didn't recognize. Irish—Gaelic? Or some kind of Shifter language? The circles of Shifters answered, chanting in slow rhythm. The Shifters began circling around them, the first circle moving clockwise, the second one counterclockwise. They stepped in deliberate, slow movements, an ancient-looking dance that was simple and powerful.

Dylan finally stopped chanting. "By the light of the moon," he said in a loud, grave voice, "I recognize this mating."

Ellison howled. Soon all the wolves joined in, followed by wildcat roars and the loud growling of the bears. Liam drew Kim against him and buried her in a kiss.

"Thank you, love," he grated. "Thank you."

In the San Antonio Shiftertown, the Shifters had gone nuts with beer and an impromptu party, but that had been nothing compared to the revelry that exploded here. Shifters grabbed one another, hugging, laughing, dancing around like maniacs. Beer flowed, kids ran around shrieking, couples kissed. More than one shed clothes and Shifted, and soon the yard was filled with wildcats, wolves, and bears.

Kim looked around for Silas, wondering what he'd make of all this. The tall man stood with Annie, a bottle of beer in his hand. Annie and he were the same height, and Annie had draped her arm around his shoulders.

"Great party, Kim." Silas grinned. He looked happy, not angry or scared. Good.

Glory approached, looking a little more relaxed. "Annie," she said. "Caught a human? Liam's starting a trend."

Annie pressed herself closer to Silas. "He's all right."

"He's my friend," Kim said. "I invited him."

"I know." Glory stepped away from Dylan and actually enfolded Kim in a well-perfumed hug. "They need you, honey. Be good to them."

Connor came hurtling toward her, followed closely by Sean, and Kim backed up against Liam. "More hugging? I'm going to be bruised all over."

"They're happy," Liam said in her ear. "We haven't had a joining in a long time. In our family, we thought we'd not have another for many years. If ever."

Kim's reply was cut off by first Connor, then Sean embracing her, then Connor again. "I have an aunt," Connor shouted. "I have an aunt, and I'll have a cousin soon."

"Something you want to tell me, Kim?" Silas said, grinning.

"Go along with it," Kim told him. "They like babies. They like even the possibility of babies, no matter how remote. They've had a hard time with infant mortality."

She'd piqued his interest. Again, good. Liam talked conversationally to Silas about the low ratio of females to males and the fact that it used to be sadly common for Shifter women to die in childbirth. "But it's getting better," Liam finished. "That's one thing taking the Collar gave us, a bit of peace in which to take care of our families."

Silas looked curiously at Liam's Collar. "What are those made of? I heard that they have magic in them, but that's just a story, isn't it?"

Liam's eyes were clear and innocent. "Don't you believe in magic?"

"Shifters aren't magic," Silas said, smiling to acknowledge Liam's teasing. "You have some genetic quirk that allows you to shift to animal form, right? An ancient ancestor that we knew nothing about until Shifters were discovered."

"It's genetics partly, yes," Liam answered. "We were bred long ago to be playthings and hunters. Until our breeders discovered that hunters bite." He smiled, showing all his teeth.

"You were bred deliberately?" Silas asked. "I hadn't heard that."

"Aye. And our creators used magic to do it. What other explanation is there for us?"

"Genetic manipulation?" Silas shrugged. "Could ancient cultures do that?"

Kim wondered how much Liam would explain, but Liam kept talking. "The Fae could. That's the Fair Folk of Celtic and Gaelic legend, I'm meaning. Their magic made us, but our strength kept us alive when the Fae started disappearing from the world. Shifters were good at survival; Fae were good at running away. So which of us was stronger?"

The Shifters around them smiled and nodded.

Silas looked interested. "So the story that magic is in your Collars . . . ?"

"Is true," Liam answered. "Not that humans believe it, but it doesn't matter, does it? All they know is that the Collars keep us tame. That's why you can stand so close to Annie without her eating you. Yet."

"The night's young," Annie purred.

Silas grinned. "Are you trying to terrify the human and make him run away?"

"Now, would we do that?" Annie asked him.

Liam's teeth were getting a little pointed. "How about a demonstration of what the Collars do? Would that put you at your ease?"

The Shifters looked uncomfortable. Kim knew Liam

brought this up for Silas's benefit, the perfect opportunity to prove that the Collars worked, to show that Brian couldn't possibly have murdered a human. But the Shifters, including Dylan, started frowning.

"I read that the Collars send deep pain along the nervous system," Silas said, not noticing. "I couldn't ask you to show me that."

"But humans want to know everything about Shifters, don't they?" Liam continued, his voice silky. "The good, the bad, the underbelly."

A wolf loped up to them and threw himself on his back at Kim's feet, squirming happily.

"Underbelly," she repeated nervously. "Ha."

"Very funny, Ellison," Liam said. "Get on with you, now."

"That's Ellison?" Silas asked in surprise.

The wolf rolled to his feet, gave them a roguish look, and loped off again.

"In his glory." Liam turned back to Silas. "You're right, lad. The Collars are bloody painful. That's why none of us are violent, including the notorious Brian sitting in his jail cell. And no, none of us want to show you that."

"Speak for yourself, Liam." Glory put her hands on her hips, her skintight outfit stretching in interesting ways. "The human isn't going to believe the Collars work until he sees it for himself. You want a demo, I'll give you one."

She fixed her gaze on Silas, her eyes going Shifter white. Her face didn't change, but the wild wolf she was shone out through the sex kitten she pretended to be. Annie and Liam moved to protect Silas, and as they did, Glory spun, caught Kim in a headlock, and started to strangle her.

CHAPTER EIGHTEEN

So this was what it was like to die. No thought of martial arts, just Kim clawing at Glory's hands. She flashed back to the feral Shifter trying to kill her in her bedroom, her fear spiking.

Kim had no breath. Her vision went dark, her lungs burned, and her heart pumped frantically, desperate for oxygen. Dimly, she heard Liam roar.

Sparks flew out into the night, Glory's Collar going off. Air poured back into Kim's lungs, and she sat down hard as Glory flung her aside to face the wildcat leaping at them.

Liam.

Glory half changed, trying to meet the attack, but her Collar kept sparking, her body jerking with pain.

Dylan knocked into Liam's side, shifting as he went. Liam's clothes ripped as the wildcat burst out of them. Then the two were rolling over each other with savage intensity, snarling, raking claws, biting. Their Collars triggered, muscles and fur shuddering with the shocks, but they didn't stop.

"Mate," Glory rasped. Her hands were at her neck, the Collar stark black against her white throat. "Stupid. I attacked his mate. He couldn't help it. He had to defend . . ."

The rest of the Shifters moved back to give the fighting wildcats room. Sean watched, white-faced, looking poised to run back into the house.

"Stop them," Kim shouted at him.

He answered, tight-lipped. "I can't. I'm the Guardian."

"So *guard* something!"

Connor shrieked. Shifters jumped, turned his way. Connor balled his fists. "No," he yelled. "*No!*"

Sean grabbed for him, but Connor shook him off and leapt for the two snarling wildcats. He'd half changed to a gangly young wildcat when his Collar went off in mid-leap. His scream echoed through the clearing.

"Connor," Kim shouted.

Glory dragged herself up and ran to him. Still Sean hung back, watching, waiting.

Connor's Collar kept sparking, and he keened as he had when Fergus had done the Summoning. He shifted back to human, his clothes in shreds.

Glory pulled him into her arms. "Kim, help me," she called.

One of the wildcats rolled away from the other and landed against a tree. Its limbs distorted, and Liam emerged, naked, dirt and long, bloody scratches streaking his body. The other cat became Dylan, lying flat on his back in the mud, panting.

"Kim!" Glory yelled.

Glory was rocking Connor on her lap. Kim went to them and dropped to her knees behind Connor, feeling ineffectual.

"He needs your touch," Glory said. "You're family now."

Kim put her hands on Connor's bare back. "It's all right, Con."

"He needs more than that. Goddess, how do you humans survive?"

Because being human is all about personal space?
Shifters' personal space was different. Kim had thought
she understood—Shifters liked to touch, the same way cats
rubbed against other cats they knew and liked.

But she realized now that there was more to it. The
Shifters' need to touch wasn't simply for affection; it was
comfort and reassurance. And maybe release from pain?
Kim remembered how Sean and Liam had held Sandra
between them to calm her the first day Kim had come to
Shiftertown. Kim had thought that the three were being
sexual, but she knew now that there hadn't been anything
sexual about their group huddle.

Kim slid her arms around Connor and leaned onto his
back. "It's all right, sweetie," she said. "They've stopped."

Glory had Connor's head on her shoulder, her arm around
him. Connor had stopped his horrible keening, but he shivered violently.

He really was young, Kim had realized when he'd shifted.
As a wildcat, Connor was underdeveloped, little more than a
cub, never mind he was twenty in human years and attending
college. The gulf between his world and Kim's gaped wide.

Gulf. Oh, hell, *Silas.*

Kim looked up. Silas remained with Annie, who'd taken
a protective stance in front of him. Silas's eyes were wide,
but the man had seen the worst areas of Iraq and Afghani-
stan. Two Shifter-cats battling it out shouldn't faze him.
She hoped.

"Why didn't your Collars work?" he asked into the silence.

Dylan still lay on his back with his eyes closed, his face
ashen. Liam answered, "They did. This is pain you're looking at, lad. Dad was teaching me a bit of a lesson, is all."

Liam's answer was evasive, but he wasn't lying about
the pain. He looked awful, and so did Dylan.

Ellison had shifted back to human form but hadn't
resumed his clothes. He went to Liam, helped him to his
feet, put an arm around him. Sean stepped to Liam's other

side, wrapped his arm around Liam's shoulder, nuzzled his cheek.

"Go to him, Kim," Glory said. "I've got Connor."

"What about Dylan?" Dylan lay alone, breathing hard, his body white and gleaming with sweat.

"Leave Dylan be. Liam's your mate. He needs you."

Kim gave Connor one last hug and unfolded to her feet. She never could decide whether Glory was a complete bitch or a complicated woman. Glory's tongue was sharp, but she looked up at Kim with such anguish in her eyes that Kim suddenly wanted to hug *her*.

She resisted and went to Liam.

Ellison relinquished his place at Liam's side to Kim. Kim kept her eyes averted from Ellison's very naked body, but Ellison didn't seem to notice or care.

"We need to get him to the house, away from everyone," Sean said from Liam's other side.

Kim nodded. She and Sean helped Liam walk, step by shaky step, to the back porch, and inside the quiet Morrissey house. It was dark, no one having been inside since sunset, but neither she nor Sean bothered to turn on the light.

"Get me to the couch," Liam said. "I'll be all right."

Kim and Sean lowered him gently. Kim took Liam's hand between hers, and Sean started to sit down next to him.

"Stop fussing like old biddies," Liam growled. "It's not that bad. You need to make sure Connor's all right."

"What about your dad?" Kim asked.

"Glory will see to him." Liam reached for her. "Poor Kim. We've given you a fright."

"Now you're patronizing *me*." Kim climbed to her feet and glared at both of them. "That was some serious shit out there, wasn't it?"

"It's over now."

"You can barely talk, Liam. So be quiet. And *you*." Kim pointed at Sean. "You just stood there. Like you did in San Antonio when Fergus went crazy with his whip. You stood there and let them fight each other, let Connor rush in and get hurt. I thought you were supposed to be the big Guardian of the clan. Doesn't that mean you're supposed to protect them?"

"Kim," Liam said. "Don't."

"It's all right, Liam," Sean answered. "She doesn't understand."

"So make me understand."

Sean looked at her a few moments, then lifted the sword from where it rested beside the couch. He drew it from its sheath and held the sword toward her in both hands, letting Kim see the interwoven Celtic designs etched into the hilt and blade. The workmanship was amazing, the lines featherlight, every single one part of the intricate pattern.

"It's Shifter forged and Fae spelled. Very old, not meant for fighting."

"For what, then?"

"The Guardian doesn't guard the clan," Sean said softly. "I'm the Guardian of the Gate. The Gate to the afterworld."

Kim dragged her gaze from the sword to look into Sean's quiet eyes. "You've lost me."

"It used to be that the Guardian was for his pride only. But now that we've taken the Collar, I'm responsible for every Shifter in this Shiftertown. When a Shifter dies or is without hope of survival, I bring the sword. The sword frees the soul, allowing it to enter the Summerland. The Guardian makes sure the souls aren't stranded, which makes them vulnerable to be enslaved again by the Fae. I save them from that."

Kim tried to understand, to make her very practical mind believe. "So, when you stand there, watching a fight . . ."

"I'm waiting to see if the sword is needed. If I join in, and I'm hurt or killed, there's no one else who can wield the sword. When I die, a new Guardian arises. Usually from the same family, but it's complicated."

"Are you telling me that if Dylan had hurt Liam enough tonight, you'd have stuck Liam with the sword? Turned him to dust like you did with that Shifter in my bedroom?"

"He would have, love," Liam said. "He'd have done what he needed to do."

"Aye, I'd have sent him to dust," Sean agreed. "Just like I did with our Kenny." Sean sheathed the sword, turned on his heel, and walked out of the house, clutching the sword in a tight hand.

"Oh," Kim said into the quiet. "Now I feel like a complete idiot. What a thing to remind him of. I'm sorry, I shouldn't have said anything. I was just so angry at him for not helping you."

"It's an old hurt. My fault for not explaining about it."

Liam looked exhausted, lines etched into his tired face. Kim sat down next him, kissed his hand. "You're not all right. You told me how strong your dad was, and the Collar really punished you out there."

"It's not so bad," Liam said, his voice nearly a whisper. "Yet. Can you help me up to bed, Kim? I'm thinking I'll be spending the rest of my mate-bonding night there. Not what I really had in mind, but eventually, I'm going to feel better." He smiled. "And I'll want you next to me."

He tried to speak lightly, but Kim saw the pain in his eyes, remembered how it had clouded him the night he'd saved her from the feral Shifter. She kissed his lips, softly, trying not to hurt him, then put her arm around him and helped him to his feet.

Dylan had never screwed like *this* before. The sofa springs dug into Glory's back, and Dylan's weight pinned her wonderfully. He drove into her hard, harder, never mind the angry scratches and bruises that covered his body. His face was set, his eyes almost feral.

She'd feared that he'd be enraged with her, and he *was* angry, but it was anger Glory didn't understand. Instead of berating her when he stormed in her back door, he'd grabbed her and started sexing her before they even reached the sofa.

His clothes had already been gone, and she helped him tear off her own clothes before clasping him in her arms. Now Dylan pumped into her until Glory screamed with joy, not caring if everyone in Shiftertown was still outside to hear.

She was under no illusion that Dylan loved her. Dylan still loved his mate and resented himself for what he did with Glory. Dylan tried to be kind, but Glory knew that he considered himself betraying the woman who'd borne his children. His need for Glory angered him. Whenever the anger finally overrode his desires, he'd refuse to see Glory for months.

Glory held on to him, feeling him slip away from her again. Damn it, why couldn't he make up his mind? He was tearing her apart.

She felt his seed as he groaned with it, and she hoped against hope that *this* time, she'd conceive. Dylan might consider taking her as mate if she had a cub. It was more difficult to produce a baby cross-species, but it could be done, and Glory would love bearing Dylan's child.

Glory squeezed him inside her and held him close. Dylan collapsed on her, breath ragged.

The sounds of the revelry outside filtered into the house. The Shifters were enjoying themselves again. The fight was over, nothing had changed, and there was a mating ritual to celebrate. Perfect excuse to party all night.

Dylan disentangled himself from Glory and sat up, breathing hard. He ran his hands through his sweaty hair.

She loved his hair. He kept it fairly short, and it was going gray at the temples, which complemented the fine lines around his eyes. If this man could be hers . . .

"I won't ask if you're all right," Glory said. Her lips were swollen, and she winced as her tongue found a cut. "You wouldn't be here if you weren't."

Dylan didn't answer. He sat back, still catching his breath. Glory got up and went to the kitchen, gratified that when she came back with a wet towel his gaze was fixed on her naked body.

She sat next to him and started dabbing blood from his face.

"Thank you," Dylan said. "Are *you* all right?"

Now she worried. Dylan never reverted to politeness unless things were truly bad. "My Collar gave me only one burst. It went away fast." A lie, but Glory knew that Dylan's hurting when it came would be far greater than hers. Staving off the consequences of the Collar brought worse hurt than going along with it.

"I'm sorry, Dylan," she said. "I didn't realize Liam would react so strongly. I thought my Collar would stop me, and he'd laugh at me for being foolish."

Dylan looked away. "I didn't think he'd react like that, either."

"And then you leapt in to save me. My hero."

Dylan shot her a look. Glory went back to dabbing his wounds. "It's over now," she said. "You wrestled, you stopped the fight. I'm sorry about Connor."

"Connor needs to learn to back off until he's fully grown." Dylan paused. "And I didn't stop the fight. Liam did."

"Liam backed down. I saw him."

"No." Dylan's words were flat. "Liam stopped the fight, because he was winning it."

Glory froze, and the cloth dripped water on her bare thighs. "Goddess, are you sure?"

"Very sure, love. Liam stopped before he could hurt me. If this had happened before the Collar, he'd have killed me." Dylan closed his eyes and rested his head on the back of the sofa.

"What are you going to do to him?"

Dylan gave a mirthless laugh. "I'm not going to do anything to him. I can't. He's my son, and he's mated now. It's up to him." He opened his eyes. "If you say anything, tell *anyone*, I'll . . ."

She liked that he didn't finish the sentence. When a Shifter said, "I'll kill you," he meant it. Dylan wouldn't say it casually. "Like I would. I keep your secrets, Dylan."

Dylan's look softened, and he closed his eyes again. "Thank you. I know you do. The Collar's going to pay me back now. You might want to go out to the party. This won't be pretty."

"I'm not leaving you."

Dylan reached out and took her hand. Glory twined her fingers through his, her heart thumping. Dylan's body shuddered as the pain started to flow. A tear slid from his tightly closed eyes.

"Thank you," he whispered.

"It's bad," Liam said. As though all the agony in the world was twisting his body to one fine point.

"What can I do?" Kim knelt on his bed next to him.

"You being here with me is good." Liam broke off as a spasm rocked him. *"Damn."*

Kim put her arms around him. Liam loved that she instinctively knew he needed her warmth and closeness. Nothing else would get him through this.

"That was one hell of a fight," Kim said. "Why did you have it?"

"Glory attacked my mate. The beast inside me had to stop her." He grimaced as another wave rocketed through him.

"Her Collar activated right away. She knew she wouldn't be able to hurt me."

"Sure, my brain reasons that now. But at the time, the feral Shifter in me wanted nothing more than to protect you."

"And your father tried to protect Glory. Is that it?"

"That's it in one, love." Liam tried to smile, though the muscles of his mouth didn't want to move. "The big liar. I knew Dad cared about her more than he let on."

"That's a good thing, isn't it? Even though you two had to tear each other up to learn it?"

Liam looked into her honest eyes and felt something break inside him. He knew what had happened in the fight, something far more significant than learning that his father liked Glory more than he admitted.

Dylan had felt it too. Liam had seen what was in his father's eyes when they pulled apart.

Defeat.

The wildcat inside Liam wanted to roar his triumph. The pride was *his*. Liam was mated, powerful, and he'd just bested the only one in Shiftertown stronger than himself.

"Crap," he whispered. "Goddess help me."

Kim kneaded his shoulders. "Does it hurt?"

She thought he meant the Collar. The Collar was nothing compared to the grief that now twisted him, warring with the fierce joy of his victory. It was nothing to the heartbreak of what he'd seen in his father.

Fear. Dylan feared him.

"Kim. I've just screwed everything all to hell." Liam pulled her down on top of him, held her close, and explained in a low, rapid voice what had happened.

L iam's descent to breakfast the next morning was difficult for three reasons. First because he was sore as hell—from the fight with his father and the Collar's payback, then from sex with Kim, as gentle as it had been. Second, because Kim lay snuggled and cute in his bed, sound asleep. Third, because he'd have to face Dylan.

In the space of a few seconds last night, Liam's entire life had changed. He didn't know what to do about it, or even how he felt about it. The turmoil of emotions and thoughts nauseated him.

He descended the stairs, scrubbing his hand through his wet hair. He'd showered twice, once last night with Kim while she washed his cuts, which had led to water all over the bathroom floor. There was something about bathrooms and Kim. The second time was this morning after he'd left the bed.

Dylan leaned on his elbows on the breakfast bar, drinking coffee and reading a newspaper. Morning sunlight winked on his Collar.

"Did Fergus oust you yet?" Liam asked, as he headed for the coffeepot. They didn't have a coffeemaker, not because it was forbidden to Shifters, but because they'd never taken to anything but coffee brewed right in the pot.

"Haven't heard from him. I'm sure he'll be along."

Liam poured coffee. "Where have Sean and Connor got to?"

"I sent them off."

"Why?"

"So we could talk."

Liam took a sip and grimaced. "Sean must have made this." Sean, terrific at the griddle, lousy at the brew-up.

"Fergus has to know."

"That Sean made the damned coffee?"

"Liam."

"Shit."

Both men fell silent. Liam cradled his cup while Dylan pretended to read the newspaper. Liam had never heard Dylan come in last night; Glory must have been comforting him the way Kim had comforted Liam.

"Do you want me to leave?" Dylan asked without looking up.

"No, you're fine. I don't mind you reading the paper." Liam stopped pretending. "You mean for good, don't you? Why should you?"

"My own father died before we found out whether I could best him. Defeated males had two choices back then—be killed or cast out."

"I know."

Dylan turned a page. "I knew in my heart it would happen to me sooner or later. I didn't think it would be last night."

"We never finished the fight."

"Good thing." Dylan finally looked up at him. The man

was much too calm. His eyes were watchful, but other than that, he rested against the counter, the cuts on his face already healing. "If it had been obvious that you'd bested me, Fergus would be up here demanding to fight you, to establish his dominance."

"Did you tell anyone?"

"Glory."

"You trust her then?"

Dylan gave him a thin smile. "I might have to move in with the woman. I thought it only fair that she knew why."

"Damn it, Dad. You don't have to move out. We're not feral anymore. We don't have to disembowel each other to make a point."

"No, we're too civilized for disemboweling," Dylan said in a dry voice. "The choice is yours, Liam. I don't mind going."

"No." Liam slammed his cup to the counter and it broke. Hot coffee spilled on his hands and spattered on his thighs. "I don't want you going. Why the hell should you? You belong here."

Dylan left his newspaper, caught Liam's shoulders in his big hands. "It's natural, son. It happens."

"Blow that."

Dylan pulled him close. Liam resisted the hug, wanting to push him away. All his life he'd felt protected and confident because Dylan and his strength was there. Even when Dylan had disappeared to grieve, his protection had permeated the walls of their castle, and Liam had known Dylan would return. He'd never doubted.

When they'd come to America, a land they'd never seen, and during the torture of taking the Collar, Dylan had been there. Dylan was the anchor in the madness of Liam's life, in the chaos of the world.

Last night, the moment Liam's wildcat had known he could destroy Dylan anytime he wanted to, that world had changed. Gone was the ground beneath Liam's feet, the tie to sanity. The abyss howled at him, and now he'd have to face it alone.

Liam jerked away. He and Dylan were the same height; he could look his father straight in the eye. "Don't tell Fergus. Not yet. I don't want him coming after you."

Dylan nodded, and Liam tamped down his anger with difficulty. Primal rage made him want Fergus in front of him, right now. Liam would make the man eat his fucking whip.

"Is this the true reason you never would fight Fergus?" Liam asked. "Because you knew once you'd bested him, I'd be compelled to best you?"

Dylan waited a silent moment, then nodded.

The enormity of the knowledge was enough to make Liam sick. He had always thought Dylan held back from challenging Fergus to keep the peace in Shiftertown, because living life and raising the children were more important than fights for dominance. Liam had agreed, believed it with all his heart. Now Dylan was confessing that part of the reason he'd kept himself from fighting Fergus was simple fear.

When a clan leader died, usually the second in line stepped into his place without fuss, unless a Shifter close to the second knew that he could vie for leadership. Other Shifters down the line might fight among themselves to move up a place or two, and a series of fights could happen until the pecking order settled again. Typically the hierarchy didn't change, but sometimes a young Shifter grew more dominant or an older Shifter weakened and moved down. Dylan had realized that Liam's natural dominance would emerge the instant Fergus was gone, that Liam wouldn't have been able to stop himself from challenging his father.

"Shite, Dad."

"Fergus will have to know sometime," Dylan said.

"We wait. We'll tell him on our own terms, when *we're* ready."

Dylan nodded once. "Agreed."

Liam loved his father so damn much, and now his

instincts were telling him to push Dylan out, take over his power. The Collars might keep Shifters from being violent, but they didn't take away the fiery urge to dominate.

Dylan knew it too. His instincts must have been telling him to cut and run, get out while the going was good. By the white lines around his mouth, Liam knew he was resisting the urge with difficulty.

"Damn it," Liam said. "Why didn't you warn me this was coming?"

"I hoped it wouldn't happen for a few more years, that we'd both have time to prepare. But claiming a mate triggered something in you. You're the oldest son. Don't tell me you didn't know that one day you'd take over the family."

"I didn't think it would be now, and I didn't think it would hurt so much."

Dylan smiled. "Your mother would be proud of you for showing compassion. For not throwing me out with your bare hands."

"Mum was too damn good for us."

"I know that."

Liam met his gaze and said something that would have gotten him knocked across the room before today. "She'd want you to be with Glory. She'd want you to be happy."

"Don't push it, Liam."

Liam wanted to laugh, but he was wound up too tight. His dad might have switched places with him in the hierarchy, but that didn't mean the man was a wimp.

Liam grabbed Dylan in a bear hug, then released him abruptly and left the house.

Even in the embrace, Liam's instincts had kicked in, urging him to remind his father who now ran the pride. Liam needed some distance from his father to get used to his new position, to learn to control himself.

He looked back and saw Kim peering down at him from his bedroom window, but even that couldn't make him stay.

CHAPTER NINETEEN

Kim found Liam in a sorry excuse for a park on the far side of Shiftertown. He sat on a low brick wall next to the only trees in the somewhat bare strip of land, hands braced on the top of the wall.

The park had one swing set for kids, no picnic tables, and bald patches where grass should grow. The city had tacked the park onto Shiftertown as an afterthought, then forgotten about it. The Shifters didn't use it much, from what she'd seen, seeming to prefer the common greens behind their houses.

Kim approached Liam slowly but determinedly, wondering if he'd stand up and walk away. He didn't. Liam didn't look at her, either, as she sat down next to him and stretched out her bare legs. The summer warmth felt good on them, though she knew the day soon would turn excruciatingly hot.

"Is this your place?" she asked him.

He glanced at her. "Mmm?"

"The place you go when you want to think. My place is a

coffeehouse on the river that sits right on the water. You can suck down a latte and watch the river go by. It's soothing."

Liam looked into the distance. "I'm thinking they wouldn't be letting Shifters in."

"Maybe not. But this is your place, isn't it?"

"No, it was a convenient spot to sit my sorry ass down."

Kim let it go. She wasn't sure she should have followed Liam, but what she'd overheard of his conversation with Dylan confused and bothered her. She didn't understand fully what Liam had explained about him knowing he was now dominant to Dylan, but she sensed the tension, the violence simmering below the surface. A person didn't have to be a Shifter to feel it.

She argued with herself that maybe Liam wanted to be alone, but something inside told her she shouldn't leave him by himself. His shoulders were tight, arms knotted, his mouth a rigid line. As usual, Liam kept his words light, almost careless, but the darkness in his eyes spoke volumes.

Kim sat in silence with him. Birds chattered in the trees, but otherwise, the park was quiet. No kids came to swing, and no cars turned down the quiet street beyond it. She heard faint sounds of the city on the other side of the derelict block beyond Shiftertown, Austinites heading to the city to make money or play politics. Here in Shiftertown, power that humans didn't understand ebbed and flowed in ways they'd never realize.

"Are you all right?" she ventured. "I mean from having your Collar go off and . . . well, everything."

"You're referring to the exuberant and athletic sex we had later?" A ghost of a smile touched Liam's mouth. "That's why I had to sit down."

Kim covered his hand, feeling the tension in it. "Liam, last night was my fault. I was the one who wanted to bring Silas here. There never would have been a Collar demonstration if I hadn't."

Liam touched her fingers to his lips. "Don't fret yourself,

sweetheart. I agreed to invite Silas. It's my fault for encouraging his questions about the Collars. I didn't anticipate Glory jumping in, damn the lass, or that Conner would get hurt or that anything very dramatic would happen. My thought was that I'd grab for Silas, let my Collar spark, and have everyone laugh at me."

"Laugh at you in pain?"

"I've been in pain before, and I've gotten over it."

"Liam . . ."

"What's between me and Dad would have happened sooner or later, love, and maybe it was best the fight occurred with you and Connor and your journalist watching so avidly. You all gave me the strength to break it off. If me and Dad had been alone, it might have turned deadly before I could shut down my instincts." He smiled, a little shaky. "So maybe I should be thanking you instead."

Kim caressed his fingers with her thumb. "Don't make me feel worse, damn it." She sighed. "And on top of it all, I have to go to work."

"I know."

"Come with me?"

"No fear I'd let you go alone, darling. Not with you flagrantly disobeying Fergus every second."

"I thought you wanted me to keep helping Brian."

"I do. I was referring to your lack of stealth. I know why you're such a good defender. You're so honest it glows from you. When you say the man didn't do it, everyone wants to believe he didn't do it."

"I wish it were that simple. Every *i* has to be dotted and every *t* crossed. You miss one, the case goes the other way."

"Sandra is visiting Brian this morning, and she's going to ask if he was ready to take Michelle as mate. Sandra's grateful to you for believing in him."

"Really?" Kim asked. "Her looks of hatred are false impressions, are they?"

"She's afraid. Fergus has put fear into her, and she doesn't know why. All she knows is that she's been told to sacrifice her son." He shook his head. "For a mother to lose her child—I can only imagine how it feels. If it's anything like losing a brother . . ."

"Then it's pretty shitty."

Liam ran a hand through Kim's hair. "It would be like losing you."

Her pulse sped. "Not the same thing at all. We barely know each other."

"We know a lot about each other. I know you have a little mole on the inside of your right thigh."

"I wasn't talking about sex."

"Neither was I." Liam turned and straddled the wall, pulling her between his thighs. "*Mating* doesn't mean going at it until we have a litter of cubs. It means a bond that no one breaks. Ever."

"It's not a marriage humans would recognize or sanction," Kim pointed out.

"Damn, woman, will you stop shoving everything into your legal terms? I'm not talking about the bits of paper humans love so much. It's a bond inside us, stretching between us. Nothing can sever it, not human law or my family, or bloody Fergus. Are you telling me you don't feel it?"

His eyes held anger, fear, hope, and something raw—all fighting inside him.

Did Kim feel the bond? Of course she did. This man was compelling and mesmerizing, with his blue eyes and lilting voice, not to mention his hot body. But it was more than his sexiness and his strength.

Liam dominated any room he walked into without saying a word. Every Shifter Kim met was drawn to Liam, every Shifter hero-worshipped him, even if they might not admit it. Anyone who had troubles went to him. Even the kids did, like little Michael in his pool. Michael had called out to Liam, had been excited to tell Liam of his achievements. He'd wanted Liam's approval.

Kim remembered Liam's words to the boy—"you look after your brother, now." Kim realized now he'd not been making an offhand remark. Liam, who had lost a brother, knew the importance of taking care of those you loved.

Liam took care of everyone in Shiftertown, even more than Dylan did. Kim had always sensed that, and she knew that Dylan had too, and had let it happen. Not because Dylan feared losing to Liam, but because Dylan loved him.

"I wish I'd never come here," she said.

Liam stroked her bare leg, his fingers sliding beneath the hem of her skirt. "Why is that, love? Me, I'm glad you walked into my bar."

"Because you've messed up my mind. I was independent, didn't worry about anyone but myself. When I went home at the end of the day, I could do whatever I wanted. Hang out with friends, watch TV, be alone, whatever. And now I'm worried about you—and Sean, and Connor, and your father, and Brian and Sandra, and every other Shifter in this damned Shiftertown. Even Glory." She glared at him. "Stop making me care. It's annoying."

Liam's fingers moved farther under the skirt. "Then you do care?" His eyes held heat. "I'm not dreaming that?"

"Of course I care. Who could help caring about you? But we're still not married."

"No," he said softly. "Not in the marriage license kind of way. You're my *mate,* Kim. I have you and no other." Liam rubbed the small of her back, his body warmer than the Texas sunshine. "Will you have me, and no other?"

Kim's heart pounded. *Forsaking all others, as long as you both shall live.* "There is no other for me."

"Maybe not now. But what if some human male, some high-powered lawyer in your firm, decides to make you his wife? His prize? So you can flash your beautiful legs at his parties and draw people to his side?"

Kim shook with nervous laughter. "His *prize?* Thanks a

lot. Besides, I don't like high-powered lawyers. They take credit for cases I win."

"Good."

"I liked you when I met you, Liam, but what I feel now, it's gone far beyond like." Kim leaned against his chest as his seeking fingers found the elastic of her underwear. "But you're asking me for commitment."

"I don't need to ask. The mate-bond does it for us."

"Maybe it does for Shifters. Not for humans."

"Shifter-human pairings happen sometimes. We'd never have survived all these centuries if the gene pool had remained pure. Inbreeding makes for weakness. Mongrels survive."

"*Mongrels*. You sweet talker."

"I think we're doing too much of the talking."

The leg band of her panties moved aside, and strong fingers touched the moisture between her legs.

Kim glanced around. "We're outside."

"Are we?" He sounded amazed.

Kim didn't object to sex, and in college she'd once done it in a car, but that had been late at night in a deserted parking lot. This was broad daylight in the middle of thriving Shiftertown.

Liam leaned down and pressed an openmouthed kiss to her throat, making Kim's body hotter. She was wet, she was naughty, and she loved it.

Liam drew his tongue up her chin and kissed her mouth. His kissing skills had certainly progressed. He knew how to part her lips, how to stroke his tongue inside her, how to make her mouth tingle.

"This is bad," she whispered.

"No. It's good."

"I want to unbutton your pants right here on the street," she said. "I'd call that bad."

"Our notions of bad and good are the exact opposite, then."

Kim gave in and popped the button of his jeans. His cock was hard behind his underwear, the tip reaching past the waistband. Kim slid her fingers inside the elastic and grasped the full shaft.

Liam groaned. "You've got the touch, love."

Kim slid her thumb over the crown, and Liam's fingers moved between her legs. She'd never thought she could get turned on sitting on a wall, but Liam also had the touch. More than the touch. She found herself rocking back, closing her eyes.

"Liam."

"I'm right here, baby."

He was, all eleven inches of him. Not that she'd measured, but she could guess. She ran her hand along Liam's penis, gripping it all the way down. He moved his hips, face softening in pleasure.

"Love, you don't know what you do to me."

"I have a pretty good idea. I make you stiff and hard, and when I touch you, you want to screw me."

His eyes were slits. "You're close."

"You mean you *don't* want to screw me?"

"I mean I want to screw you all the time, whether you're touching me or not. I want to lift your pretty skirt and do you right now."

Excitement spiked through her. "Right here on the wall?" she asked in an innocent voice.

"Right here on the wall."

Liam half stood, and she lost her hold of him. The next thing she knew, his jeans were around his thighs, her underwear was gone, he was sitting on the wall again, and he'd pulled her down to straddle him. Her skirt hid their mutual bareness, but only just.

She opened her mouth to admonish him, but he kissed her. The wicked look in his eyes both excited her and made her want to laugh.

She'd never gone out with a man as in-your-face as Liam.

He was a Shifter, restricted and shunned, but he was better
at doing whatever he damn well pleased than anyone she'd
ever met.

Right now, he was doing her on a wall in the middle of
a park. In broad daylight. As he went deep, he pulled her
close and kissed her.

Words flew through Kim's mind, then dissolved. This
wasn't about words. It was feeling, pure, basic, raw feeling.

Liam was opening her like he never had before. The sun
on her thighs excited her as much as his hardness inside
her, a hardness that stretched and widened her. This was
free and wild and strange. Sweat rolled in a bead between
her breasts, and he leaned forward and licked it away.

His breath came fast, and so did hers. Liam's fingers were
hard points on her thighs, then her back, her buttocks, her face.
He pressed into her, fast, faster, his mouth twisting in pleasure.

Kim's head dropped back. She bit back her scream, not
wanting people to come rushing out to see what was going
on. Liam licked between her breasts again, his breath
scalding. "I'm coming," he whispered into her skin.

So was she. White-hot waves of excitement poured
through her, blotting out everything but the feeling of Liam
joined to her.

He took her face between his hands. His eyes had gone
Shifter, the predator wanting her. Then he gave a strangled
groan and shot everything he had into her.

Shaking and sweaty, Kim clasped him to her breasts
and kissed his hair. *I love you, Liam,* she wanted to whisper, but she kissed his hair again and rested her cheek on
his head.

Liam insisted on accompanying her to work, and Kim
was fine with that today. Having him next to her in her
car, though, his dark sunglasses trained at the world going
by, distracted her.

Kim's body felt warm and supple, aching slightly from having to spread so far for him. Liam caught Kim looking at him, and he reached over and laid his hand on her thigh. He didn't have to say a word. Kim felt the connection between them, the warmth that wouldn't go away.

Kim earned a few stares when they walked in. She was: one, late; two, not in a suit; and three, shadowed by her tall Shifter with menacing eyes.

She was starting to dress like a Shifter woman, she realized as she sat down and sorted through her messages. She never came to work outside of a skirt suit, stockings, and black pumps. She'd changed out of the clothes she'd made love in, but had put on another loose skirt and blouse and high-heeled sandals. Clothing easy to remove.

She sensed that the last thing Liam had wanted to do this morning was leave Shiftertown, but he'd been adamant about not letting her go to work alone. Last night he and his father had switched places in Shifter hierarchy, which meant he could go one-on-one with Fergus now—a fight that might end in Liam's death.

The entire balance of Shifter power in South Texas was at stake. Liam showed how torn he was about this by stretching out on her sofa and catching up on the latest issue of *Angler Today*.

"Will you stop that?" she asked in irritation.

"Stop what? Reading's good for you. You learn things."

"Sitting there like nothing's wrong. I might have made a breakthrough in the case. Your dad might have to leave Shiftertown. Fergus might try to kick your ass into the next county. And you read about fishing. Do Shifters fish?"

"Kim, sweetheart, if I didn't absorb myself in fishing lures, I'd either tear down the building or come over there and screw you senseless on your desk. Maybe both. Is that what you want? I can oblige."

Kim scrubbed her hand through her hair. "Never mind.

You have me on edge. I guess the Shifter pheromone thing really works."

Liam was off the couch and on his feet, the magazine falling to the floor. "And yours are pouring over me, enticing me to come and slide my hands up your skirt."

"You've already done that."

"That was two hours ago. I want to do it again. And again. All day and all night. It burns like fury."

Kim's blood heated. "I can't say I'm turned off by that."

"You're lucky you're not Shifter. You can't feel the mating frenzy like I do. If you were Shifter, we'd have been doing it constantly since San Antonio. To hell with work or family, or eating and sleeping." Tension rippled through his big body.

"You've been feeling that since San Antonio?"

"Hell yes. I want to be inside you every second. Fergus and his demands, your case, and even my father can go to hell."

"Oh." Kim moved closer to him. She was in her office, her very formal, law-firm office in its nice building in downtown Austin, and she wanted nothing more than for Liam to throw everything off the desk and lay her back on it. Or maybe sit her on the edge. Or against the wall. She wasn't particular.

Liam's smile was feral. "Don't play with fire, Kim."

"I think I have a little of this mating frenzy too." Kim pressed her hands to his chest to feel his heart pounding beneath her fingertips. "I want to touch you all the time, have you kiss me, have you *be* with me. I didn't say that, because I was afraid you'd think I was clingy."

"My love, what gobshite wouldn't want you clinging to him?"

"Pretty much everything male."

Liam drew her against him. "Bloody fools can't see what's in front of their own noses. It means you're all mine."

Kim rose to meet his kiss, not caring that her secretary

could pop in any moment, not to mention all the lawyers in the building. But what the hell? She'd already done it outside on a wall, and her colleagues probably thought she was shagging the Shifter in here anyway.

The kiss turned deep. Kim tasted his need, the frenzy inside him, and his conflicted emotions. Likely his heartbreak was fueling his sexual needs, and Kim would be the one fulfilling those needs. She somehow couldn't be sorry about that.

Liam's cell phone buzzed. He kept kissing her a few seconds, then reluctantly reached for the phone. "Damn it." He flipped it open. "What?"

His expression changed, and he turned away, shutting Kim out. She thought the voice she could barely hear was Sean's, and from the stiffening of Liam's body, something had happened.

Her heart froze. Dylan? Or Connor?

Liam snapped the phone shut and turned to her with a grim look. "Michael's mum says he's missing. She can't find him anywhere."

Kim blinked. "Michael? The little kid with the pool?"

"Yes. Dad and Sean are organizing a search."

Kim's blood went cold. "Fergus?"

Liam shook his head. "I don't think so, and neither does Dad. Fergus's head would come off if he tried to hurt a cub, or even use him as a diversion. Fergus has power, but cubs are sacrosanct."

Kim wasn't sure she took Liam's word for it. "Call the police," she said quickly. "They'll do one of those alerts . . ."

Liam shook his head. "Shifters can find him a hell of a lot faster than your police can. We know his scent." Liam slid his phone back into his belt. "I have to be there. His mum and dad . . ."

"Will need you." Kim thought of the way Liam and Sean had done everything to calm Sandra, how the woman had relaxed somewhat under their mutual touch. The parents would be terrified, need reassurance. "Go then. I'll be fine."

More conflict. Liam looked uncertain, and Kim had never seen him uncertain. "Really," she said. "I have a hell of a lot to do here. You know, Brian's butt to save. I'll be fine."

Liam came to her, his hard body against hers the best thing in the world. "You stay in this office, all right? Have someone bring you lunch; don't go out. And after work get into your car and drive straight to my house. No stopping, no lingering. All right?"

Uneasiness stole through her. "Fine. I can do that."

Liam pulled her into an embrace. A Shifter embrace, tight, long, warm, comforting and drawing comfort at the same time. "I hate to leave you."

Kim hated for him to leave her too. When did she get so needy? "I'm fine. Go."

Liam kissed her again, lips lingering on hers. "You call me," he said. "Every hour if you have to."

"It will be all right, Liam."

Liam gave her a hint of a smile. "I wish I could believe that, love." And then he was gone.

Kim tried to concentrate on work but found her attention wandering to Shiftertown. She had much to catch up on, phone calls to return, reports from her investigator on Michelle's ex to go through, letters to compose. But she worried about Michael—had he merely wandered off or had something more sinister happened? Was he exploring some place exciting to small Shifter boys; was there another feral Shifter on the loose?

Liam hadn't been gone an hour before she was on the phone to him. He told her, his voice warm as ever, that he had nothing to report. Apparently, Michael's mother had stepped inside for a minute, when his little brother had come running to the front porch to tell her that Michael

was gone. Early searches had turned up nothing. All Shiftertown was now about to start a serious one.

Kim heard the worry in Liam's voice. This happening, on top of his fight with his father and Fergus's threats,
couldn't be easy on him.

When had she started caring so much? Her fascina-
tion with Shifters, her first attraction to Liam, her growing
physical need for him had blossomed into something much
deeper. It was more than the mating frenzy Liam kept talking about. There was something about Liam that made her
want to be near him, to hold him when he hurt, to laugh
with him when he was happy.

She squeezed her eyes shut. *Damn it all, I've fallen in
love with him. When did I get so stupid?*

Kim tried to return to work. She couldn't bother Liam;
he'd have his hands full. But she couldn't help calling him
back as she ate lunch at her desk. Nothing, Liam reported.

He sounded even grimmer. Kim assured him that she
was all right—no need to worry about her. He told her to
take care, warmth in every word. When Liam said the trite
phrase, he really meant it.

Kim called Liam back at two, but he didn't answer.

Leave him alone, she told herself. *He's busy doing
his job.*

To think she'd once assumed his job was managing
a bar.

By three, Kim couldn't take it anymore. She packed her
briefcase and told Jeanne, her secretary, that she'd work the
rest of the day at home.

Kim hurried out into the parking lot to nearly run into
Abel, who was returning from a day in court. "Kim," he said.

"Hey, Abel. I gotta go. See you tomorrow."

Abel stepped in front of her. He was perspiring, his face
red and shiny above his tight suit coat. He looked furious,
which meant he must have lost his case.

"I heard that you dumped me for a Shifter."

The boy wonder had finally caught on. "That's none of your business. I have to go."

He stepped in front of her again. "Where to? Your Shifter? That stinking animal you dragged in here? You're screwing him, aren't you? You're screwing an animal."

Kim rolled her eyes. "You were always so clueless."

"I'll have you fired. I'll get you disbarred."

"It's not against the law to go out with a Shifter. Or even to go to bed with one. Grow up, Abel."

Kim tried to go around him again, and again, Abel barred her way. After meeting Fergus, Abel frightened Kim about as much as a gnat, but she wondered what he was going to do. Deck her in the parking lot? Great PR for the law firm.

"Would you get out of the way?"

"Were you doing him while you were going out with me? Tell me the truth. You were already screwing him then, weren't you? You were double-dipping."

"Obviously you want me to say yes."

"Shifter-whore," Abel said. "I'll tell everyone I know that you're nothing but a Shifter-whore."

"Abel, you moron . . ."

She broke off as two Shifters materialized on either side of Abel. Fergus's thugs—bald Tattoo Guy and Military Man. Their Collars glinted in the hot sunlight. Military Man wore sunglasses and looked like the Terminator.

"Everything all right, Ms. Fraser?" Tattoo Guy asked.

"Everything's fine. I'm heading to my car."

"We'll walk you there."

Kim's heart started to pound. "No need, I can make it."

Military Man stepped to block Abel, while Tattoo Guy motioned for Kim to go. "Want us to teach him some manners?" Tattoo Guy asked her.

"No, leave him alone," Kim said. "He's just a dickhead."

Tattoo Guy shrugged as if he didn't care one way or another. Abel beat a retreat into the building, and Kim started for her car, which was only a few feet away. The two of them fell into step beside her.

"When Shifters don't wear Collars," Tattoo Guy said, "assholes like that will be wetting themselves to be nice to us."

Sure. Kim quickened her pace, but she reached the car without incident. The two men didn't try to grab her or drag her off; in fact, they acted more as though they were protecting her. Whose side were they on? Military Man opened her car door for her, shutting it again once she was settled. "Drive carefully, now."

"Right," Kim said as she started up.

"Hey, no one messes with our females," Military Man said. "You're Liam's now."

She wasn't sure whether to be reassured or irritated. "Thank you, gentlemen," she said. "I appreciate your help."

She firmly rolled up the windows and backed out of her parking space. The two followed her to Shiftertown on their motorcycles, keeping pace with her, again, protectively.

Kim was halfway to Shiftertown when Tattoo Guy's words struck her. *When Shifters don't wear Collars.* What the hell did that mean? He'd said the words as though it was a real time to come, not wishful thinking.

Kim gripped the steering wheel and kept driving. She'd have to ask Liam whether the man was simply blowing off steam—if Liam would ever answer his damn phone.

CHAPTER TWENTY

Liam walked around the next block of derelict and empty buildings. The brick walls were battered and worn, and rotted boards covered broken-out windows.

A place like this might attract a curious kid who'd decided to head out on his own. Liam remembered how he, Sean, and Kenny had liked to explore the ruins of castles—Ireland was full of them—crumbling stones barely held together of some long-forgotten keep. Did they care that it was dangerous, that they could get trapped, buried, crushed by unexpected rock fall?

Not really. They were Shifters. Tough, dangerous, bold.

"Bloody stupid," Liam said under his breath. No wonder their mum had raised hell with them.

He turned a corner between buildings and heard Michael crying.

The sound came from the warehouse beside him, the wide door covered with planks of old wood. Liam kicked apart the wood, mildewed and rotted, and it broke easily.

The warehouse inside was dim, the concrete floor pitted and covered with dust. A metal door made of new, shining, solid steel, gleamed in the wall to his right. Its handle was wrapped in chains and padlocked. Banging came from behind it, along with two voices—Michael's high-pitched wail and the shouts of a man he didn't recognize.

Liam's nostrils widened as he took the scent of the air. Nothing but terror from Michael and the man behind this door, overlaid by the decay of the building. Even if this was a trick to trap Liam for some reason, it was certain that the prisoners hadn't padlocked themselves into the room from the outside.

Liam wrapped the hem of his shirt around the padlock, let his hand shift to strong Shifter claws, and broke the lock. He swung the door open, backing up quickly when a wave of fetid air poured from the tiny room beyond.

A man rushed out and collapsed on the floor outside his makeshift cell, breathing hard. His hair was tangled and matted, and his clothes were rank. A Lupine, by his eyes and smell, but Liam didn't know him. Michael rushed out behind him, his hands manacled, and Liam gathered the boy up in his arms. Michael clung to him, soaking up all the comfort he could.

"How did you get locked in there?" he asked Michael.

"The bad man brought me."

"What bad man, sweetie?"

"A Feline captured *me*." The man on the floor glared up at him with bloodshot eyes. "Like you."

"Which Feline? Fergus?"

"No. That wasn't his name." The stranger pushed himself to his feet, screwing up his eyes against even the dim light. "Oh, yeah, Brian. That was it."

Liam's blood froze. "Brian."

"That's what he said. Then this morning, some other Feline opens up the door and throws this little guy in with me. I'm glad you came when you did. I was getting hungry, and the Feline said I wasn't allowed to eat."

The Shifter's gaze moved to Michael. The boy wasn't timid, but when those bloodshot Lupine eyes landed on him, he backed away fast until he crouched into a dusty corner. "Something's wrong with him, Liam," Michael whimpered.

The Lupine moved out into the light, and Liam saw clearly that instead of a Collar, a line of blood-blackened bare skin ran around his neck. His Collar had been removed.

"Michael," Liam said. "Run!"

Eyes round with terror, the boy scuttled away. Liam grabbed the Lupine by the shoulder, spinning him around. The Lupine snarled and leapt, and Liam met the attack.

The two fell to the ground, Liam's hands becoming claws. They fought, Liam trying to sever the feral's spine. The feral reared up and brought down a most unlikely weapon—a hypodermic needle. Before Liam could roll aside, the feral plunged the needle into his shoulder.

Liam fought a few more seconds, and then his muscles went slack and he couldn't move at all. He didn't black out, but he prayed hard in the next hours for unconsciousness to come.

At first glance Shiftertown seemed to be in chaos. Shifters roamed everywhere in parties of two and three, calling Michael's name. Shifters on motorcycles and in ratty cars cruised the streets both inside and on the outskirts of Shiftertown, moving slowly and peering into the shadows of every building.

When Kim entered the Morrissey house, she realized that the searching had been organized in almost military fashion. Dylan stood alone in the kitchen, a map of Shiftertown and its environs spread across the table. A careful grid had been drawn on the map. Dylan's cell phone was at his ear, and he marked off squares in the grid as he talked to the person on the other end.

Dylan spotted Kim. "Kim's here," he said into the phone. "And Nate and Spike. Come back to the house and pick up Kim. Nate and Spike will make up another team."

Nate and Spike? Tattoo Guy and Military Man were dismounting their motorcycles at the front curb. Kim briefly wondered which was which.

Dylan hung up his phone, came to Kim, and enfolded her in his arms. *Shifter greeting. They're tense; I bet they need a lot of reassurance right now.*

Kim returned the hug, squeezing Dylan hard before releasing him. "Were you talking to Liam? Where is he?"

Dylan shook his head. "Sean. Liam hasn't checked in."

"He doesn't answer his cell phone, either."

"Cell phone service isn't the most reliable around here. He'll find a way to call when he has something to report. Sean's on his way."

"I want to help."

"You will." Dylan turned back to his map. "I want you and Sean to make up a team. Sean's the strongest, next to Liam, and I don't want to worry about you on top of everything else."

"Liam told me what happened," she said in a low voice. "About you and him, and the fight."

Dylan turned from the map again. He didn't look conquered. He was as tall and formidable as ever, only the touch of gray at his temples betraying that he was older than his sons. He radiated strength, competence, and decisiveness—everything you'd want in a general.

"It's irrelevant right now," Dylan said.

Meaning they'd talk about it once Michael was found. "I just wondered what was going to happen."

"That's up to Liam." Dylan looked past her, and she realized that Nate and Spike were approaching the front door.

Kim shut up, and Dylan invited the two inside. The hostility they'd exhibited to Dylan in San Antonio was absent as the three bent over the map. Nate turned out to be the military guy, and the shaved-headed, tattooed man was Spike.

The two Shifters left with their orders, and Dylan took another phone call. Sean approached through the backyard, and Kim went out to meet him.

"Where's Connor?" she asked.

"Searching with Glory and Ellison. Dad's putting you with me."

Sean looked grim, flat black sunglasses hiding his eyes, his sword hilt protruding over his shoulder. Kim knew without being told that his greatest fear was that he'd have to use the sword on Michael when and if they found him.

"Have you heard from Liam?" she asked him.

"No."

"That doesn't worry you?"

"It does. But Liam's one of the strongest in the clan, and if he's out of communication, it's for a good reason."

His words made sense, and so had Dylan's. But Kim shivered, some feeling in her gut bothering her. "We should find him."

"We should find Michael."

Kim nodded. Michael's mother must be going through hell. Kim remembered how her own mother had sobbed uncontrollably when she'd been told that Mark was dead. Mark had lingered in the hospital all night, giving them hope he'd survive, but in the end, he hadn't. Michael's mother must be living through that same hell of hope.

Kim nodded. Find Michael. That was top priority.

"I t's easy," the feral Shifter said. "Go with it."

Liam gritted his teeth against profound pain. "Easy for who? Who the hell are you, anyway?"

"I was called Justin."

"Yeah? What are you called now?"

"Human names have no meaning for us anymore."

"Oh, for the gods' sake." Liam lay flat on his back on the cement floor, his limbs on fire. He felt the beast in him snarling and raging, but his body hurt so much it could snarl and rage all it wanted to. Lying still was a good thing.

Heat pressed on the warehouse, and Liam felt the tingle of an approaching storm. He sensed clouds building, the electricity that fused the air miles away.

"Where is the boy?" Liam asked.

"Still here." The Lupine smiled. "I'm saving him for you, like I was told."

Liam then sensed Michael in the alley outside. The Lupine must have chased after him and tethered him. Liam tasted the boy's fear on the wind, arousing both Liam's protective nature and his innate instinct that the male offspring of another male had to be eliminated. The two feelings warred in him, escalating his confusion.

"And why haven't you rid yourself of me as I lay here helpless?" Liam asked.

"I know my place in the hierarchy. You will lead us to greatness."

"You've lost it, mate."

"You're the leader. I smell it on you. You defeated the only one greater than you, and now no Shifter can best you. I'm weak, but you will make me strong."

"Shite." Liam's neck felt like fire and at the same time, strangely light. Justin peeling away Liam's Collar had been the worst agony Liam had ever felt in his life. He'd screamed as the metal had unfused from his skin, his mind clouding with nothing but pain. When the fog cleared he'd found himself flat on his back, unable to move.

"The pain will go away," Justin said. "And then you'll be free."

"Terrific."

"Shifters are strong, my master. Stronger than any human

will ever be. Why should we be slaves to them? When they put Collars on us, they only made us stronger."

Liam felt weak as a flea. "How did you figure that?"

"You feel it, don't you? The instincts you suppressed for so long, the strength you lost when the Collar was put on you. I bet at first you didn't have the strength to make it through a day without vomiting. We've learned how to live even with the oppression of the Collars. So when they come off, the instincts pour back, your strength comes back—twenty years worth of it in one go."

"Bloody hell."

Liam knew Justin was right, as crazy as the man sounded. His strength was slowly returning to his limbs, whatever drug he'd been given starting to wear off. Liam's sense of smell and hearing seemed sharper than ever, and the growing storm pounded at his brain.

The heightened scent ability was a little unfortunate, since Justin hadn't bathed in a long, long time. Justin didn't seem to mind, but then ferals had different ideas about cleanliness. To hell with that. Even if Liam were now feral, he was still taking showers.

Liam worked to mask his raw fear, and raw fear covered the killing instinct rising inside him. All his protectiveness was quickly ebbing. Michael was not his offspring. He should kill the cub while he could. Liam fought the urge with difficulty.

I am so screwed.

Liam thought of Kim, how terrified she'd be if she could know the thoughts that whirled through his brain.

Mate. Mine.

Liam wanted her—on her back, on her hands and knees, he didn't care. He wanted her here so he could bury himself inside her. Over and over again until she and her sassy mouth knew who had mastered her.

No, I'd never hurt her.

Kim would give him children, his brain ground on

remorselessly. As many as Liam wanted. Birth control be damned. He'd find some way to counteract it and never allow her to take it again. He'd lock her in the attic room of his house until she obeyed. It was big up there—Connor could take Liam's room. And Liam would move into the master suite after he killed Dylan.

Oh, father god, help me.

Dylan should die. He was defeated, Liam now leader of the pride. Justin had known that without being told. Dylan should be driven out where he'd face death alone—or he could be given the dignity of letting Liam break his neck.

Glory would mourn him. But Glory was a be-damned Lupine, and who cared how much she howled? If she loved Dylan so much, she could join him.

Liam rolled over and pressed his face to the floor. *This isn't me. These aren't my thoughts.*

It's inside you. It's what's right. Give in to it.

"No!" he shouted.

Justin laughed. "I went through that too. It's much more fun to go with it."

Liam hated Justin's laugh. He hated the male for doing this to him. Liam's Collar lay on the floor about ten feet away. It was nothing but a piece of silver and black chain with a Celtic knot on it, a harmless bit of metal. Without it, Liam was free.

Liam climbed to his feet. Pain still gripped him, but it was starting to recede. He fixed his gaze on Justin.

Justin grinned. "You see? You're getting stronger. I'll show you how the Collars work, and we can go back to Shiftertown and start freeing Shifters. You're stronger than this Fergus, now. I can feel it. It won't take you long to kill him."

Liam growled. Justin backed up some more and let out a growl of his own.

Weak, mewling bastard who's made me want to kill my own father and make a slave of my mate.

Justin growled again, this one defensive. A growl of fear.

Wherever he'd come from, Justin must have been fairly far down in his hierarchy. He smelled wrong, weak, evil.

Liam followed Justin's advice and let the feral beast come. All the thoughts that had been spinning in his head focused into one specific thought, and Justin was its target.

Liam leapt, and Justin started to scream.

CHAPTER TWENTY-ONE

Sean took Kim to the east side of Shiftertown, speaking little but tight with tension. Dylan remained behind, saying it was his job to keep coordinating the search.

"These streets are a maze," Kim said anxiously as they turned down yet another block.

"We can't search as well in a car."

"No kidding."

The roads were narrow and potholed, and blind alleys ran behind buildings like a maze without end. This part of Austin had been more or less abandoned when the Shifters moved in nearby. Kim had been a kid at the time, but she remembered her father saying that thriving businesses had moved out of the area and left it to Shifters and the homeless.

Not many homeless were around, which was odd. It was true that in the summer, vagrants left southern cities, like migrating birds, to find the cooler climes of the north. Even so, many stayed, panhandling from prosperous businessmen and politicians in downtown Austin. None lingered out here. Was that because they thought the pickings wouldn't be good or because they feared Shifters?

Whatever menace they felt, Kim picked it up as well. The humid air bristled with electricity, a prelude to a storm. She glanced at the horizon and saw that dark clouds were indeed building, thunderheads ominous. Austin didn't get many tornadoes, but some came through on occasion, and those clouds looked ready to play. All the more reason they needed to find Liam and Michael.

"I hope we find Michael before Nate and Spike do," Kim said. "I know they're helping, but I don't trust them. And I can't believe his name is Spike."

"He was a *Buffy* fan."

Kim had a surreal vision of Tattoo Guy eating popcorn and cheering on Buffy and her pals, and wanted to laugh in nervous hysteria.

Sean, Shifter-fashion, would not let Kim walk ahead of him. He turned down yet another alley, shadows gathering in it from the storm and the coming night, and stopped so abruptly that Kim ran into his back.

"What?" she demanded.

"Call Dad."

"Mind telling me why?" Kim pulled out her cell phone as she tried to peer around him.

"We've found Michael." Sean walked slowly into the alley.

Kim's phone read "no service." Damn wireless providers. Perfect when you were in the middle of a teeming city where there were plenty of other ways to communicate, useless out where you needed them the most.

She *could* walk back down the long alleys behind the crumbling buildings until she found a good spot. Alone. Without Sean and his mean sword to protect her.

Kim ducked into the alley behind Sean. If they'd found Michael, they could grab him and hightail it out of here.

Sean slipped his sword out of its sheath without breaking stride. *Oh, no. Please, no.*

Kim raced after him, her sandals pattering on the broken asphalt. She reached the small body stretched out on the pavement the same time Sean did and went down on her knees beside him.

"Michael." Kim lifted him, breathing a sigh of relief to find him warm, his small heart beating. "Oh, thank God."

Michael whimpered, and Kim held him close. The boy's eyes were tightly closed, as though he'd withdrawn far into himself. Kim cradled him, rocked him, pressed her cheek to his hair. One of his hands was manacled, the chain stretching to a ring in the brick wall.

"You're all right, sweetheart," she said. "I have you. Sean, can you get the chain off him?"

Sean didn't sheathe the sword. "Something's dead."

"What?"

Sean's nostrils flared, and his eyes went white. Gripping his sword, he kicked the rest of the rotten boards free from the open doorway and ducked into the shadows of the building. A second later, Kim heard him exclaim violently.

Kim stood up. Michael clung to her, whispering, "The bad man. The bad man."

"What bad man, Michael?"

He didn't answer. The tether let her carry him just inside the shaded doorway. A wide warehouse floor opened out in front of her, an empty room a couple of stories high. Texas dust coated the floor and hung in the air.

Sean stood over a body sprawled in the middle of the floor. The man was large and naked, with shreds of clothes around him. Kim couldn't see his face, and fear stabbed through her.

"Liam?" she asked, heart in her throat. *Please, please, no.*

"No," Sean said. "I've never seen him before. But he's Shifter, and he's dead."

Sean solemnly raised the sword, point down, the hilt

between both hands. He whispered words Kim couldn't catch as he brought the blade down into the Shifter's chest. Air around the fallen man seemed to shimmer. Then, as had the Shifter who'd attacked Kim in her bedroom, its body crumbled to dust.

"He was feral." Liam's rich voice rolled out of the shadows. Sean straightened and turned, and Liam himself walked toward them from the back of the warehouse. Kim went slack with relief. "He told me Fergus and Brian were experimenting on him," Liam went on. "They found a way to remove his Collar. That's what Brian was doing the night his girlfriend was killed, and that's why he couldn't tell anyone where he'd really been."

Kim put Michael down on the cool pavement, smoothed his hair, and reassured him she'd be right back. The boy lay down and curled into a ball, and Kim hurried inside. "Liam."

Sean put a large hand on Kim's shoulder and yanked her back. Kim collided with Sean's chest, and his hard hand kept her pinned.

"What are you doing? Let go of me."

Sean didn't release her. Liam kept walking toward them. He was shirtless, and angry scratches bled across his chest. But he didn't move as if he was hurt; he walked slowly, like a lion stalking its prey, every step deliberate, focused.

"Don't touch her," Liam said clearly to Sean.

Kim tried to start forward again, but Sean's iron grip held her back. "No," he said in her ear.

Liam stopped. "I said, *get your fucking hands off her.*"

Kim went ice-cold. Sean let go of Kim's shoulder, but he didn't step away. "Let her take Michael home."

"Better idea. You run like hell and leave Kim and the boy to me."

Kim's heart pounded. "Liam, what is the matter with you?"

Liam walked into the light. His eyes were fixed, glittering, wrong. Around his throat was an angry red line where his Collar had been.

"He's feral," Sean said grimly.

"Oh, God."

Kim's heart pounded. No wonder Fergus wanted Brian dead; no wonder he'd told Brian to plead guilty and face the consequences. Fergus couldn't risk that Brian wouldn't tell a courtroom about their experiments on the Collars. *Shit.*

The Liam who stood before them was nothing like the Liam Kim knew. His warm smile, his loving blue eyes, the compassion that usually radiated from him—all had been wiped away. This man had hatred in his eyes, primal rage, the need to kill. He'd killed the feral in there and left Michael chained.

"Liam," she whispered.

The Lupine who'd invaded Kim's bedroom had terrified her. Having Liam's white-blue gaze trained on her now was ten times scarier. No other Shifter was powerful enough to stop him, and Liam knew it.

"Run away, Sean Morrissey," he said. "Or I'll kill you too."

"I have to stay. I'm the Guardian." Sean went on in a low voice, "I already sent one of my brother's souls to eternity, Liam. Please, please don't make me have to do it to you."

"You stood back and let him die."

Kim gasped. "Liam."

Sean flushed. "How the hell would you know? You weren't even there."

"I know you, Sean."

Sean's rage crackled, and the storm outside answered with a rumble. "Fuck you. Kenny died while you played good little deputy to a man you loathe."

"And Fergus will pay for that."

"Stop it!" Kim put herself between the two Shifters— not a reassuring place to be. "I know you're not thinking clearly right now, Liam, but fighting Sean isn't going to help. Kenny died, and I'm sorry, but you two killing each other won't bring him back. Do you think that's what he would have wanted, you remembering him by blaming each other?"

Liam's gaze swiveled to her. Being pinned with that stare had to be one of the most frightening things that had ever happened to her.

She'd had sex with this man, watched him while he slept, held him when he hurt. Somewhere inside that walking menace was the Liam who mourned his dead brother, who teased Kim and worried about the missing Michael, who grieved that he'd hurt his father.

Please don't let that all be a sham. Please let that man still be in there.

Please let me reach him.

"Don't leave me," she said to him. "I love you."

Liam didn't move, didn't betray any emotion. "It's not love. You're my mate. We have the mate bond."

She put her hands on her hips. "I'm not a Shifter, thank you very much. I have emotions, not instincts, not mate-bonds. If I say I love you, that's what I mean. At least, I love Liam."

"Emotions are instincts. You dress them up and write songs about them, but that's what they are."

"Oh, way to romance a girl. I liked you better with the Collar."

"Of course you did. Because you could control me."

"Like anyone could ever control *you*, Liam Morrissey. The man who does whatever he pleases, Collar be damned."

Sean leaned down to her. "Do me a favor and run like hell instead of provoking him."

Liam roared. "I *said*, don't touch her!"

Michael started crying. Sean backed off. Kim headed for Michael, and found Liam blocking her way. She hadn't seen him move, but suddenly there he was, right in front of her.

"Michael's hurt and scared," Kim said to him. *Right there with you, kid.* "Let me take him home. His mother is worried."

"Sean, get the boy out of here. Before I give in to my instincts and kill him, and you."

Kim folded her arms, trying a glare. "What, you mean you haven't given in to your instincts already?"

"No. Sean, *do it.*"

Kim sent Sean a shaky look. "I agree with him. Please get Michael out of here."

"And leave you here with *him?* Are you insane?"

"Liam is right about the mate-bond thing," Kim said. "I don't think he'll hurt me."

"You don't *think* so?" Sean asked. "Not very convincing."

"Stop arguing. Michael has a mother worried sick about him, and he needs to go home. I'll be fine." She glanced at Liam. "I'm pretty sure."

"Kim, I've never seen him like this. He wasn't like this before we took the Collar. This is—something else."

"The instincts are enhanced," said a new voice.

Fergus pushed himself from the wide door frame where he'd been leaning and strolled inside. His own Collar was still intact, thank goodness, but he moved confidently, as though he knew he'd done something clever.

"See, this is why you shouldn't argue," Kim said to Sean. "You lose your window of opportunity to get away."

"Says the woman who never shuts up," Fergus said.

Kim turned what she hoped was a fearless gaze on Fergus. "Just what I need. Another asshole to make my day complete."

"Your mate has a mouth," Fergus said to Liam. "You need to teach her manners. If you don't, I will."

Liam pivoted to face Fergus, his boot heel turning on

the gritty cement floor. Fergus stopped, his body coming alert.

"Then again," Kim said. "I might enjoy this."

The world had gone to hell. The smell of death clogged Liam's nostrils, despite Sean already sending the feral's body to dust. He smelled fear as well. Watery terror from the cub. Fear from his own brother. Fear from Kim, his lover, his pride mate.

Fergus's fear was the strongest of all.

The whole place stank of terror, enough to gag him. If Liam killed all of them, except Kim, he could get rid of the smell.

A little corner of his brain tapped him. *What the hell is the matter with you?* Sean was right—it hadn't been like this before the Collar. They'd lived freely, hunting when they wanted to, going hungry when there was no food to be had. They'd huddled together—three brothers, father, and mother—warming one another, playing together in the good times, sticking together in the bad. Loving each other.

Now Liam hated every Shifter in this room, Fergus especially. He didn't hate Kim, but she drove him the most crazy. He wanted to get her away from the others, to keep her safe. They wanted her—Shifters needed mates, and Sean had never claimed a mate. Sean was a danger.

The cub was a tiny thing, no threat, but it was the offspring of another Shifter. *Kill it,* Liam's senses whispered.

Fergus wanted Liam to kill the cub, then kill Sean. Liam knew it, and he didn't know how he knew it.

Fergus wanted power, Fergus wanted Kim, and most of all, he was afraid of Liam.

Ergo, Fergus should die first.

"The Collars were programmed to suppress everything that makes us who we are," Fergus was saying. "The Fae who made them hated Shifters. And understood them. Removing the Collars will remove that suppression and make us powerful. Unstoppable."

"And crazy as hell," Kim said. "Look at him."

Fergus couldn't look at Liam. His gaze slid sideways, back to Kim. "He senses his mate. He wants to fuck."

"Wipe that disgusting look off your face," Kim said. "I don't even want you *thinking* about us like that."

"Shut up, human. You'll be his slave, and that's all you'll be. He'll screw you until you die pushing out his cubs, and then he'll find another female to give him more. It's what we do."

"I'm sure your mates would be happy to hear that."

"My mates know their place."

"I see," Kim said. "Is this how you plan to take over the world? Repulsive imagery and insults?"

"We're far stronger than humans. Without the Collars, we'll quickly suppress those who suppressed us."

"If your plan is so terrific, why is *your* Collar still on?" Kim asked him.

Fergus gave her a deprecating look. "The leader of the clan couldn't be risked. We first needed to know that removing the Collars wouldn't simply kill us."

"How many did it kill?" Sean asked. The storm outside was building, the pressing humidity cut by an icy breeze.

"One or two."

"Did it make one victim so crazy he went out and killed a Shifter woman and her cubs?" Sean went on.

Fergus's eyes flicked sideways. "There were complications. You took care of him."

"Sure," Kim put in. "After he attacked me in my house."

"He wouldn't have if you hadn't smeared your scent all over Liam," Fergus said in disgust. "It smelled a rival's mate."

That's why the thing was so fast and so good at tracking, Liam thought. *It was a Collared Shifter, made crazy by having its Collar ripped off.*

"I didn't know that feral," Sean was saying. "Or this one. Where did they come from?"

"New Orleans. I offered them something better than hiding out in the bayous."

"Great offer," Kim said. " 'Come to Austin. First we'll make you insane, then we'll kill you.' "

"No," Sean said, voice tight with fury. "He no doubt offered them mates, their pick. Maybe the chance to move up in the hierarchy. My guess is they were low in their packs in the first place. And they were Lupines. If something went wrong—death or madness—they were only bloody Lupines."

"I offered them freedom," Fergus growled.

"Free to be hunted like you were in the past?" Kim asked.

Fergus's face darkened. "Free as we were before humans rounded us up like animals. We had the run of the land. We feared no one. Humans took that away from us. All I'm doing is taking it back."

"We were hungry," Sean said, his voice quiet. "Remember? Winters with no food, watching family die, watching cubs not make it until spring?"

"And if we had humans feeding us, being our slaves, not the other way around, that wouldn't happen."

"Dream on," Kim broke in. "Shifters are strong and hard to kill, but not impossible. I'm sure machine guns would do the trick. Is that what you want to see happen? Your pride mates mowed down by a SWAT team?"

"It won't happen if you're the slaves, you stupid woman. Liam, you might want to consider a different mate. Or at least use her up quick and get rid of her. I knew she was a pain in the ass the minute I laid eyes on her."

"You touch Kim, you die," Liam said clearly.

Everyone stopped talking. Liam walked toward Fergus, his boots loud on the stone floor. Fergus wanted to run— Liam saw that in the man's eyes, his stance, every inch of his body.

Liam wouldn't let him run. Fergus was his inferior; he had to obey Liam, and Fergus knew it, no matter how much he blustered. The instincts Fergus boasted about would force him to acknowledge his own weakness.

Kim had a power that Shifters lacked: the power to see all sides of a situation clearly, no matter how scared she was or how angry. She could argue with conviction, she could find a flaw in the other person's obsession and tap it until he opened his mind and saw what she saw.

Fergus would never see anything clearly. But Liam did. At least, Liam had before Justin had ripped off his Collar and made his brain scramble.

Liam's emotion and instinct warred with his reason, and none of them won. The wind outside grew colder, a bad storm for certain. Liam smelled the icy hail in the clouds, electricity that would fork down on the city at any moment.

One thought stood out from the others: Fergus had to be stopped. If Liam let Fergus go today, he would continue to push to "free" the Shifters, continue his awful experiments, making his victims crazed and violent while he honed the process. Fergus couldn't control his ferals yet, and, Fergus-like, he was trying to make other people clean up his mess. For him, the end always justified the means.

"Kim is right," Liam said, surprised his voice was so calm. "You are an asshole. You'll set Shifter against Shifter. We'll kill each other long before the humans even know there's trouble. We'll each want *our* families to survive, and ours alone. Our gene pool, our pride. The Shiftertowns, the living with other species—you're right, that's artificial."

"Exactly my point," Fergus said. "We get Sean's Collar off him, we get the Guardian—who can stop us?"

"I can." Liam came to a halt in front of Fergus.

He saw Fergus's pupils change to slits, his nostrils widen, his body emanate fear. He was not far shy of wetting himself. He tried to cover it by puffing out his chest with false bravado. "You can't touch me. I'm your clan leader."

"You are weak." Liam's voice was completely flat.

"I outrank you," Fergus said abruptly. "It's me first, then Dylan, then you. You can't beat me."

"Liam fought Dylan and won," Kim said. "Last night."

"What?" Sean stared.

Fergus's face whitened until it was almost green. "You don't know what you're talking about, girl. No one can best Dylan. Only me."

Kim went on. "You've been out of the loop. Liam defeated his dad. Liam isn't happy about it, but he did."

"Shit," Sean whispered.

"That doesn't matter," Fergus tried. "I am still clan leader."

"You are nothing." Liam sounded strange, even to himself. "I have no ties to anyone outside my family. Michael would be easiest to kill. But I think it's more important to kill you."

"Crap." Sean braved Liam's wrath to grab Kim and pull her well out of the way of Liam and Fergus.

Liam fought the urge to take Kim back and rake his claws across Sean's face. He forced himself to let Sean go; Sean was protecting Liam's mate from the enemy. Fergus would use Kim to distract Liam, and Sean was right to get her out of the way. Liam's bloodlust still wanted him to throw Sean down for touching her, the need burning through him.

Deep down, his love for Sean, his brother, boiled up, wanting his attention. It showed him visions of himself and Sean and Kenny, playing together as cubs, wrestling until they fell asleep in a pile in exhaustion. When they were older, talking about the world and speculating on females and what it would be like to be with one. Celebrating when Kenny took a mate, and again when Sinead became pregnant. Sean and Liam holding each other the day Kenny had died, weeping profusely.

Memories of love, frustration, joy, and family were being erased by the adrenaline, the need to fight. Fergus wanted to do this to all Shifters everywhere. He'd destroy them.

Liam fixed on Fergus again. He toed off his boots and peeled away his T-shirt. Fergus watched with a sneer, then smiled and began yanking off his own clothes.

Fergus attacked while Liam was still shifting. Liam rolled out of the way, his limbs crackling and stretching, muscles moving into new positions. Fergus leapt again, and this time, Liam spun out of reach and came to his feet as his wild Fae-cat.

Liam couldn't stop his roar. It came from deep within, the beast finally free. It proclaimed that this place was *his*, not only the warehouse or Shiftertown, but everything for miles: the city, Hill Country, as far as Liam could roam. He was clan leader, and Fergus was nothing. As it should be.

The roar shook the building. Beams shifted, and loose bricks and plaster rained to the floor. Michael started screaming, his screams becoming yowls as he shifted into Feline form. Sean dragged Kim outside, straight into a pouring rain.

Liam closed his mouth, shook out his body, and leapt on the terrified Fergus.

CHAPTER TWENTY-TWO

"Can you get him free?" Kim yelled at Sean, over the frenzy of violence inside the warehouse.

"If he'll hold still." Sean grabbed the chain that had been linked to the wall. Michael continued to snarl and thrash, the manacle cutting into his paw.

"Michael." Kim knelt next to him and reached for him but got scratched for her pains. "Michael, sweetie. It's all right."

Michael knew damn well it wasn't all right. Inside, two enormous wildcats fought for dominance, and they wouldn't stop until one was dead. Their snarls sounded over the thunder that boomed through the alley. The building heaved when the two battling Shifters smashed into a wall.

If Fergus wins, he'll kill the rest of us. Or maybe Fergus would keep Kim alive to be his sex toy, which was not something she wanted to think about. Still less did she want to think about Liam losing, dying, Sean having to send him to dust.

Sean yanked the chain, hook and all, from the wall. Michael yowled, then took off down the alley, the chain dragging behind him.

"He'll run home," Sean said. "You go too, Kim."

"I'm not leaving Liam."

"Kim, damn it, I don't know what's going to happen in there."

"Why don't *you* go? Round up Dylan and everybody to come and stop Fergus."

"With Liam like that? Too dangerous."

"At least you'd be safe. Fergus won't let you live, and Liam keeps thinking you want me for yourself for some reason. He might kill you in his frenzy."

"Oh, and you'll be safe from him, will you? I'm staying, Kim. I'm the Guardian."

He meant he'd have to dispatch the loser with his magic sword, sending his soul into the next world. From Sean's grim look, he feared it would be Liam.

"Then I'm staying too," Kim said. Inside, the two Shifters fought like crazy, foam and blood flying. "I love him."

"Fine then. We'll die together."

Sean marched back into the warehouse. The rain changed to a pelting of pea-sized hail, bouncing on the alley floor.

"Perfect," Kim muttered.

The hail came down so fast it piled on the pavement before it could melt. Kim ducked into the shelter of the building, afraid and angry.

The two Shifters rolled over and over, and Sean stood back like a referee, his sword ready. Weeks ago, Kim wouldn't have been able to tell the fighting wildcats apart, but she knew Liam now. He and Fergus were matched in size, but Liam's cat was thicker with muscle, his coat darker, his eyes a deeper gold. Right now his eyes glittered with hatred, and his teeth were fully extended as he snapped them at Fergus's neck.

Fergus scrambled out of the way, half shifting back to human to do so. Liam followed him, pinning him again. The wildcats clawed and bit. This was worse than the fight between Liam and Dylan, because there'd never been love lost between these two. Rage and hatred burned in the thickly humid air.

Thunder boomed outside, and then a bolt of lightning struck the roof. Kim screamed as bricks came down around her.

She saw Liam turn to her, drawn from the fight. In that moment, Fergus, his hide nothing but bloody strips of skin, pounced on Liam's back. His mouth was open wide, jaws ready to snap Liam's spine in two.

Sean shouted. Kim couldn't hear him over the thunder; she just saw his mouth open. Liam whirled in time, closing his teeth on Fergus's throat. He ripped, and blood sprayed across the floor.

Fergus went down in a heap. Liam stepped back, his fur red with Fergus's blood, and roared his victory. His eyes held fire, joy, and triumph.

Sean walked forward with his sword. Liam stopped him, rising into his human form as he moved, his body covered in scratches and angry bruises. He went to Fergus and nudged him with his foot. The wildcat's body flopped against the floor, blood spilling from a pool beneath it.

Liam turned away, contempt for his fallen enemy in every movement. As soon as his back was turned, Fergus whipped to his feet, bellowing in dying rage as he launched himself at Liam. Kim shrieked.

But Sean was there. He stepped between Fergus and his brother, and caught Fergus's leap on the Guardian's sword.

Fergus's wildcat eyes widened as the sword went through his chest. He'd been dying already, and the blade completed it. The body fell to the ground, silent and still. Chanting in a language Kim didn't know, Sean slowly withdrew the blade. The big cat shimmered, then crumbled to dust.

"You weren't supposed to do that," Liam snarled at Sean. "His final breath should have been mine."

"Yeah, well, I've done it." Sean's stance was defiant. He'd have done anything, the tiny rational part of Liam realized, to keep from having to send a second brother to the Summerland.

Again his love for Sean and the wildcat's jealousy warred within him. "Go," Liam said. "If you don't, I might kill you, and I don't want to lose you too."

"Kim," Sean said.

Liam's white-hot rage rose. "Kim stays with me."

Sean strode for the door, moving fast. "Kim," he said again.

"It's all right. I'll stay."

Her voice was quiet, a cool note amid the heat. Sean gave Kim one last look, then made himself sheathe the sword and duck out into the deluge.

Liam was across the floor, pulling Kim against him before Sean's footsteps faded.

"Kim." He loved saying her name.

"Are you hurt?"

"I don't know, and I don't care." Liam pressed Kim against the brick wall.

He wanted her with an intensity he'd never felt before. She was his mate, his, forever. A dim part of Liam's mind kicked him. *You love her. Don't hurt her.*

"You should get away from me," he said.

"What?"

Liam focused on her eyes. They were beautiful, wide and blue. Like an Irish lake, he'd thought once. He hadn't changed his mind.

"Don't let me hurt you."

Kim touched his face. He flinched, then made himself accept her touch. "I don't want to go," she said. "Besides, it's frigging hailing out there."

"I can't go slow. I can't be *nice.*"

She smiled and laced her arms around his neck. She was shaking, but her eyes were soft. "Sounds like fun."

"Kim."

"Liam." She kissed the tip of his nose. "I don't want to go slow. I need you."

He kissed her. The bricks scraped his arms as he shielded her from the wall. She wrapped her legs around his hips, her skirt riding up her thighs. It was easy to shove aside the elastic of her thong, to find her opening with his cock. She sucked in a breath, eyes widening, as he slid firmly into her.

How could he have ever thought that sex in human form was boring? He was content never to do it as a wildcat again. Kim was hot and wet, so easy to enter. She arched against him, her nipples rubbing him through her thin shirt. Liam shielded her from the wall with his arms, the bricks abrading his already bloody skin.

His adrenaline hadn't cooled from the fight. He *needed* this mating. Liam's heart rocketed, his blood hot.

Kim's sheath clenched him, her body and his fitting together perfectly. His mind went blank. All he felt was Kim, all he smelled was her body and her sex, her breath, her hair. He licked her face. He tasted her neck. He thrust into her, his blood pumping. Outside, lightning crackled, blinding flashes followed by booms of thunder. The hail fell like bullets on the roof, balls of ice bouncing in through the wide door.

"Liam. *Yes.*"

Liam squeezed his eyes shut and leaned his forehead on the wall. He shoved himself into her as though he wanted to crawl inside her and be part of her. His shoulders bunched; his breath burned in his lungs.

Kim shuddered in climax, her feet around his buttocks. The heels of her sandals grated his skin, and he didn't care.

Still holding her with one arm between her and the wall, Liam pounded his fist into the brick. Another lightning strike lit the world, and Liam came.

Sweat poured from him, his body on fire. Kim was screaming, and Liam heard his own voice ring through the warehouse. He was falling. Kim, he had to catch her.

He landed flat on his back, Kim's soft body on top of his. The movement slid him out of her hot sheath, and he groaned with loss.

Kim smiled down at him. "Holy shit. That was . . . *good.*"

Liam wanted to answer her, tell her it was the best he'd ever had, that he loved her. He could only gasp for breath. The pain of his fight, the bewilderment of his flooding instincts, robbed him of his voice.

Kim closed her hand on him, and he groaned again.

"You're still hard. I thought you came."

Liam nodded. "I did." Gritting his teeth, he turned her over to put her beneath him and entered her once more.

Sex had never been like this before. Not free-for-all, no-holding-back, wet and messy sex. Kim laughed with it.

Not to mention having it on a bare cement floor with a naked, half-crazed, hard-bodied Shifter on top of her while a hailstorm raged outside. Another lightning bolt could strike the building and bring it down on top of them, and Kim didn't care.

"I love you, Liam," she shouted.

He opened his eyes. Once beautiful blue, they were now Shifter gray-white.

Kim would be afraid later. Right now, she was as crazed as he was. Was this what he meant by *mating frenzy*?

Liam pumped into her for a few more minutes, then dragged in a breath and filled her with his hot seed. Liam collapsed on top of her, breathing hard, his body roasting. He lingered on her, kissing her face and hair, then rolled off onto his back, still breathing as though he'd just finished a ten-mile run.

They lay still for a long time, Liam's breathing hoarse, Kim too tired to move. Gradually the hailstorm slackened, the time between lightning strikes increasing. Thunder rumbled in the distance, the storm drifting away, following the river.

Liam didn't move, and Kim wondered if he'd dropped off to sleep. She propped her aching body on one arm. "Are you all right?" she asked.

Liam lay face up, eyes open, his breathing rapid. "I don't know."

"The storm's letting up. It's what my mother liked to call a 'wham-bam, thank you, ma'am' storm."

Liam didn't answer, didn't laugh.

"You know what the storm dying off means," Kim continued. "It means that Sean and your dad are going to come looking for us. I bet Connor and Glory will too. And Ellison. He was real worried about you when I saw him earlier. In fact, every Shifter curious about what happened to you will be showing up pretty quick."

Liam raked his sweating hair from his face. "They shouldn't."

"Like that's going to stop them."

"Kim." Liam's face twisted, and he wrapped his arms around his chest. "I need to find my Collar before they get here."

"Is that what you really want?" she asked in a quiet voice.

"Fergus was crazy. He'd have destroyed us."

Kim noticed he hadn't answered the question. "You don't think Shifters can adapt to going without the Collar again?"

"Not like this." Liam's chest expanded with an agonized breath. "We'll kill each other. Gods, Kim, I wanted to kill

Michael. I *needed* to. Even Sean. My own brother. And the feelings haven't gone away. If they come to get us, I'll fight. I'll kill until someone kills me."

"And me?"

He reached for her. "No. You, I just want to fuck."

"I should be flattered, but I have the feeling I wouldn't last very long. You have stamina."

"I'd hurt you. I've already hurt you." He touched her bruised lip.

"You didn't. Don't you get it, Liam? You could have, but you didn't."

"That's no guarantee, love. I want you so damn bad." He kissed her swollen lips and drew back, eyes flicking from white to blue to white again.

Kim touched the red line on his neck. Liam flinched but didn't stop her.

"Or you could go," she said softly. "Run away back to Ireland or something. Live free."

Liam closed his eyes, blotting out the awful look in them. "Not without you. I don't want to live without you." He bowed his head, resting on Kim's shoulder. "But Fergus was right. I'd use you until there was nothing left of you. I'd not be able to stop myself." He raised his head, expression anguished. "Don't you understand? If I'm this way, I can't have you."

Kim rubbed his arms, wishing she could tell him that everything would be all right. *You'll be fine, you'll get used to it, you'll learn to control your instincts.* But she had no idea whether it would be all right. The Lupine who'd attacked her in her bedroom had been the victim of Fergus's experiments, ready to slaughter Kim to torture Liam. She'd seen the way Liam had looked at innocent Michael and at his own brother, as though they were enemies he needed to destroy. She had no idea what kind of crazed being Liam would become.

"I can't tell you to put yourself into captivity again for me," she said. "I don't want you to."

"I hate the Collar. Kim, I hate it so much. It hurts us when we so much as think about the way we used to be. One surge of adrenaline and it's giving us pain. You can't know what that's like. Always living in fear of the pain."

"You're right. I don't know."

"Being free of it . . ." Liam slid his fingers and thumb around the mark where the Collar had been, his wild smile emerging. "It's a joyous thing, love. I can do anything I want, and no one can stop me."

"Not even me?"

"No. That's the trouble."

"Sean said you weren't like this before—before you all took the Collar, I mean."

"Not this out of control. Not with twenty years of need falling on me at once. But it *was* like this too. We were strong and free, and those few who knew about us were in awe of us. Even the Fae acknowledged our strength, that we no longer served their whims. That's what rankles most—the Fae helped to bind us. They've always wanted to bind us." Anger danced in his eyes, lines pulling the sides of his mouth. "We hate them for it."

"What about humans?" Kim made herself ask.

"Human beings are weak, short-lived. No threat." Liam's eyes eased back to the blue she'd fallen in love with. "The one I'm lying on now is so beautiful. And I love her."

"I'll help you escape, Liam. I want you to be free. Don't find the Collar. Please."

Liam closed his eyes again, tight. He shuddered, lips shaking, as though wave after wave of panic ripped through him.

After a long time, he opened his eyes again, and something in them had been defeated. "No, love. They need me here. And I never, ever want to wake up in the morning knowing that I hurt you."

Kim touched his face. The anguish in his voice a moment ago when he'd said he hated the Collar had been real. He hadn't mentioned his loathing before this, but Shifters were strong and could resign themselves to pain, and he'd probably seen no use in voicing his rage to Kim. Having the Collar off, feeling the pain evaporate for the first time in twenty years, must be incredible for him. She wasn't sure how he could even contemplate putting it back on.

"No one would blame you if you went," she said. "Dylan would take over again, like before, and Sean would still be Guardian. They'll look after Connor and everyone else. You know that."

"I'd blame me."

"But free, you could start working on how to liberate the rest of your kind."

Liam kissed her forehead. "No, love. Free I'd be thinking of only myself and how good it felt to be away from all this. I'd start despising them for being weak, find myself a pride of ferals and try to take over. A wonderful Shifter-man I'd be."

"You can't know that. Like you said, all these urges are built up. Maybe in time—"

"And maybe not." His voice went hard, and he rolled off Kim and to his feet. "We find the Collar."

Kim remained on the floor, staring up at his hard body. He was beautiful—firm muscle, broad shoulders, chest dusted with dark hair, now damp with sweat. His skin was covered with scratches from the fight, but they were healing, even the deepest ones only angry red lines. The worst wound was around his neck, where his Collar had been.

As he forced himself to turn from Kim to look for the Collar, Kim knew that Fergus had never understood just how strong Liam was. He'd made the choice to give up his freedom to stay with his family and help them in their captivity. Fergus had sacrificed others in his cause; Liam was sacrificing himself, just as he had when he'd stepped forward and taken the whipping to spare Connor pain.

Kim got reluctantly to her feet, trying to brush off the

worst of the dirt she'd rolled in. Liam was already looking, quick gaze darting everywhere as he skirted the dust
in the corner that had been Fergus. He didn't show much
remorse about killing his clan leader, but Fergus had been
nuts. Also, she knew the man wouldn't have gone meekly
home, promising to stop his experiments: *I'm sorry, Liam,
you're right. I've been a bad Shifter.*

Kim thought about Fergus's mates, and the offspring
Fergus had mentioned. Would they mourn him? Would they
try to exact revenge on Liam or move on with their lives?
What would Liam, as clan leader, do to them? Would all
of those Shifters down in San Antonio accept him without
rancor? This would be interesting to watch—*interesting*
being a euphemism for *scary.*

Behind her, Liam said, "Here it is."

She swung back to find Liam holding the thin silver and
black chain as if it was a poisonous snake. Kim chewed her
lip as he gripped the ends, one plain, one with the Celtic
knot, in his white-knuckled fists.

"Will it work?" she asked. "It's not broken?"

"Once it's on me again, it should. Justin said that Brian's
experiments let him figure out how to unfuse the Collars
from us, not disable the chips inside. He hadn't got that far,
yet." Liam took a long breath. "This will hurt me, Kim.
You should go."

"I'm not going anywhere."

"Maybe I just don't want you seeing me weak and
pathetic, love. A Shifter's got his pride."

"Liam, I've seen you strong, crazed, violent, angry,
happy, sad, and far gone in passion. I love every single one
of those, especially the last one. Did you know your pupils
widen when you come? It's like you want to take all of me
in, forever. It's very sexy."

"Is it, now? Well, this won't be. It wasn't pretty the first
time I put on a Collar, and I don't imagine this will be
much better."

Kim folded her arms. "I'm not leaving. I'm your *mate*, remember? In the traditional human wedding ceremony, we promise to stick together for better or worse. That means not just when everything's pretty, but when it's bad, very bad."

"I'm thinking there's no line in there about watching your Shifter mate take his Collar."

"Not last time I checked, but the idea is the same."

Liam looked down at the Collar, chest rising sharply. "I can't lie to you, Kim. It's a bit easier knowing you're near me." He looked up, his eyes clear, dark blue, full of fear and full of love. "Wish me luck."

"I love you," Kim said.

A hint of his warm, wicked smile touched his mouth. "Love you too, sweetheart."

He studied the Collar a long moment, then took another sharp breath and lifted the chain to his throat.

Liam's muscles tightened as the Collar settled against his neck. Kim had no idea how the thing fastened, but as he touched the bare end to the Celtic knot, she heard a loud click, and then Liam screamed.

Cords stood out on his neck, and his entire body arched backward. He balled his fists and clenched his teeth, fighting the agony.

Kim rushed to him. Shifters comforted and helped each other with touch—maybe she could ease him a little bit if she could hold him. Liam thrashed as spasms racked his body, his screams becoming hoarse cries.

She reached for him. "Liam."

Liam focused on her, his eyes white-blue. "No, Kim. Stay back."

"You need me." Kim grabbed his wrists, but he snapped them away from her.

"I said *stay back.*"

"And I said, you *need* me."

Kim darted between his hands and slid her arms around

his sweating waist. His skin was ice-cold. She rubbed his back, trying to warm him.

"Kim, no."

"You need me," she repeated firmly.

Liam drew breath after shuddering breath. He stood stiffly, body shaking at the same time. Then with a cry of agony, he wrapped his arms around her and buried his face in her neck.

CHAPTER TWENTY-THREE

How long they stood like that—arms locked around each other, Liam rocking in pain—Kim didn't know. She held him while his hot tears dropped to her shoulder, while he kissed her neck and held her as if he'd never let her go.

Kim heard shouting outside. She lifted her head to see that the warehouse had grown darker, the rain still pelting but more softly now, the storm over. Flashlights cut through the gloom, and then the tall forms of Sean and Dylan emerged out of the darkness. Others trailed behind them— Glory, Ellison, Connor, Nate, and Spike.

Dylan played his flashlight on the two of them in the middle of the warehouse, Liam filthy and naked, Kim in rumpled clothes and probably just as filthy.

She called to them, "He put the Collar back on and the pain is tearing him up."

Dylan approached, but the others hung back. Liam managed to lift his head, his eyes filled with incredible pain. "Dad."

Dylan stopped just shy of Liam, eyes troubled. "Do you want me, son?"

"Of course he wants you," Kim said. "You're his dad."

"He's clan leader now," Dylan said. "And pride leader. He can reject me if he wants."

"He won't." Kim shook her head. "He told me once that he wouldn't fight you because he loves you."

"That was before," Dylan said.

"Doesn't matter. People's status might change, but love stays the same."

Dylan opened his mouth to argue, but Connor jerked away from Ellison, who was trying to hold him back. The lanky boy charged past Dylan and threw his arms around both Liam and Kim. "Damn it, we thought Fergus would kill you," he sobbed.

The others tensed, Dylan taking a step back.

Liam looked up at Connor, his eyes wet. Connor held him tighter, and Liam's eyes flicked from feral white to beautiful blue. He wrapped an arm around Connor and pulled him close.

Like water released from a dam, the others flowed to them. Dylan clamped his arms around Liam and Connor, gathering them in. Sean laid down his sword and joined the group hug, followed by Glory, Ellison, and to Kim's astonishment, both of Fergus's thugs.

Kim's eyes filled as Sean leaned his head into Liam's neck. Kim could feel the warmth, the caring, in the huddle, heard the soothing words they whispered to each other. She was squished between Dylan and Liam, Ellison and Connor. She started to giggle. "A Kim sandwich."

Ellison laughed his big, booming Texas laughter. "Sounds good. Let's eat."

"You are so disgusting," Glory said to him. She had her arms firmly around Dylan's waist.

Ellison gave Glory a big kiss on the cheek. "You love it,

darling. I say we all blow this place and go get shit-faced drunk."

"Damn straight," Spike said.

Liam's immediate family remained silent. Kim felt the energy flowing between them, love that had kept them alive and together all these years. And now they wanted her to be part of it.

"Drunk," Liam rasped. "You don't know how good that sounds."

The group began to part, slowly, smiling the unembarrassed smiles of people who'd shared a happy experience. Sean rubbed Liam lightly on the back and moved to pick up first his sword and then Liam's clothes.

Connor gave Liam one last squeeze, then backed off, wiping his eyes. Dylan was the last to leave. He held Liam's arms and looked straight into his eyes.

"Are you all right, Liam?"

"I will be."

"I know you will. You've been moving toward this moment all your life. It's yours now."

Liam put his hands on his father's shoulders. "With you at my back, Dad, there's nothing we can't do."

Dylan relaxed, as though he'd still been waiting for Liam's acceptance. "I'll be there." He pulled Liam down to him and pressed a kiss to Liam's forehead. He finally turned away, eyes full.

Liam reached for Kim's hand. "Are you all right? Did I hurt you, love?"

"I'm resilient." Kim kissed his lips, and Liam crushed her to him in a long, satisfying hug. "Let's go home," she whispered.

"Are you up to the walk?" Sean asked, handing Liam his clothes.

Liam hugged his T-shirt and jeans to his chest and looked around at the assembly, a hint of the old glint in his eye. "Are you telling me that none of you thought to bring wheels?"

"No," Connor said. "As soon as the storm let up, we ran out here."

"What, you were thinking you'd trundle me back in a wheelbarrow, all hurt and bloody? This is the planning of my friends and family."

"I'll run and get my car," Kim said. "There isn't room for everyone, but that's all right. I can take Liam home, at least."

Liam gripped her wrist. "No. Don't go yet."

His eyes were desperate. Kim gave him a reassuring smile and a little hug. "I won't leave you."

Glory swayed forward. She was wearing sturdy boots for once, though they had three-inch heels. "I'll get it." She plucked the keys out of Kim's fingers and gave Kim a big tooth-filled smile. "I'll take good care of it. Promise."

L iam lay in his bed in heavy sleep next to Kim for about four hours after they got home. Then he woke up, threw back the covers, and declared he needed to go to the bar.

"What for?" Kim demanded, not liking the absence of his warmth in the small bed.

"I've taken too many days off. The paperwork in the office must be a mess."

"Liam."

Liam stopped in the act of leaning over for his pants, his delectable backside in full view. "I'm all right, love. Shifters heal fast."

Maybe their bodies did. "Why do you work at the bar at all? You don't seem to live paycheck to paycheck. And how did Fergus afford all that artwork in his basement? How did he even afford that huge basement?"

Liam sat back down, his eyes a mystery. "Shifters live a long time. We accumulate things."

"Like money and Old Masters paintings?"

"Like money and Old Masters paintings. Which Dad thinks should be sold to a museum."

"How are you going to explain where you got them?"

"We won't." Liam reached for his jeans again and pulled them up. "There are dealers who will work with us discreetly."

Kim sat cross-legged against the headboard. "Before I came down here the first time, I thought I knew every little thing about Shifters. I didn't know jack, did I?"

"No." Liam's smile flashed in the harsh lamplight. "I thought I knew all about humans. You taught me so much." He stopped. "I'm going to miss you, love."

Kim's heart skipped a beat, then gave a hard bang. "What do you mean, 'miss me'?"

Liam sank to the bed again, one blue-jeaned leg folded under him. The red gashes on his torso had closed, the heavy bruising already fading. A dark swirl of hair covered his chest and pointed to his navel, the indentation into which she'd slid her finger the night he'd first brought her up to his room.

"I want you to go home," he said. "Go back to living your own life."

She stared. "Hold on. For days you insist I stay here, whether I like it or not. Tonight, after all that's happened, not to mention the incredible sex, you're telling me to *go?*"

"Fergus is dead. His followers have gone home. His threat is removed. No one will be taking off any more Shifter Collars."

"You sound very sure."

"I am sure. I lead the clan now, which means our pride is now first. No other Shifter will dare harm you, whether they approve of you or not. My protection is on you, and no other Shifter can override that."

Kim slid out of bed. She wasn't wearing anything, but at the moment, it didn't seem important. "What about this mate thing? That's all gone now too?"

Liam smiled. "That will never be gone. We've been

mated under the sun and moon, the mating recognized by the clan. We'll always be mated."

"So what does that mean?"

"For Shifters, it means I take no other mate. For humans, it means—nothing. A Shifter mating isn't valid in the human world; it's not marriage. I remember you telling me that."

"I meant, what does it mean to *you?*"

Liam looked away. "It means everything to me."

"Then why are you telling me to leave?"

Liam got to his feet, looked across the bed at her. "Because you can't stay. You've tried to pound it into my brain all this time why you can't. I'm a *Shifter*. I can love you with everything I've got, but I'll ruin you, and you know it. You'll lose your job, your friends, your respectability. I'm from the wrong side of the tracks, darling. Not from your world."

"It's not that simple—Shifters bad, humans good. I know that."

"*You* do. But the rest of the world doesn't. Not yet. Maybe in another twenty years, when people are used to us. Right now, I love you enough not to keep you here."

Suddenly cold, Kim reached for a long T-shirt and dragged it over her head. It was one of Liam's, too big for her and carrying his scent.

"Don't come over all altruistic on me, Liam Morrissey. Like you haven't put me through enough hell already. You made me love you, damn it. *Really* love you. Now you're saying, 'Thanks, Kim, go away'?"

"Do you think this is easy for me?" Liam asked. "When my Collar was off, I wanted nothing more than to lock you away upstairs and never let you go. No matter how much you screamed or begged or told me off, which is more likely what you'd do. I wanted to imprison you here with me. Mine. Forever."

"Your Collar is back on, now," Kim said.

"And that fact cancels everything out? It doesn't. I'm still feral. I always have been, always will be." Liam tapped the Collar around his bruised neck. "This keeps it down so I don't destroy myself, my people, and everyone I love. All Shifters are like me. Wild beasts in captivity. Not domesticated. There's a difference."

Kim folded her arms. "I'm not afraid of you."

"Then you're foolish. You saw me. I was ready to kill a child, my own brother, my father."

"But you didn't."

"Only because Fergus distracted me, love. Thank the Goddess he did, because he drew my fury. If he hadn't been there for me to fight, I would have destroyed everyone I loved."

"So you won't take your Collar off again," Kim said. "End of worry."

"But Fergus was right. We need to be free of the Collars someday. He was in too much of a hurry, but he wasn't wrong."

Kim balled her fists. "Make up your mind. Do you want the Collar on or off?"

"Shifters are getting stronger, love. We were dying off before, which is why we needed to capitulate with the humans and take the Collars. To let us live again, regroup, regain our strength. When we're powerful enough again, we'll rid ourselves of our chains, and be who we are supposed to be."

"And you think I have no place in that world?"

"No." Liam stood with his hands on his hips, his body still, eyes dark.

"You're lying to me," Kim said.

"I'm not."

"I'm not as good as you are at reading body language, but even I can tell you're coming up with excuses for sending me away. You think it's for my own good."

Liam whirled suddenly and punched the headboard. It cracked, wood splintering. "You're maddening, Kim, did you know that? Of course it's for your own good. You have your career, your life, your pretty house, your friends. I want you to have that. Find yourself a normal man, not one who might go crazy on you, not one who has to pretend to be a bar manager while he runs Shiftertown. Go home and be human."

"Just like that?"

"Yes. Go, Kim. Please."

"Doesn't it matter that I love you?" she asked, throat hurting.

"Yes, that matters. It matters a lot." Liam reached across the bed and touched the bruise on her lip. "And it's all the more reason I want you gone. I need to know I can't hurt you, ever again."

Kim stood still under his touch, her heart constricting. She'd broken up with men before, had sometimes done the breaking herself. She recognized Liam's look, the implacable expression of someone who'd made the painful decision to walk away and wouldn't be talked out of it.

"I don't want to go," she said. Kim knew how pathetic she sounded, but she couldn't stop herself.

"It makes me glad that you don't want to." Liam touched her lip once more, then took up his shirt and boots from the floor. "But it's all the more reason you need to."

He gave her another long look, as though he were memorizing her, then turned and walked out. He shut the door behind him, and a few minutes later, the front door's banging shook the house. Kim heard his motorcycle rev, heard its throb as he drove off down the street, the noise dying into the distance.

Kim stood by the bed for a long time, staring at the closed door. Tears choked her throat, but her burning eyes wouldn't shed any.

She heard the others downstairs, talking, their voices

inquiring. Wondering where Liam was off to? Or had he told them he was sending Kim home?

Suddenly she wanted nothing more than to get out of there. Kim dressed with numb fingers, packed what things she'd brought here, and carried them down to her Mustang.

The last thing she saw as she backed out of the Morrissey driveway was Connor standing under the glow of the front porch light, his arms folded, a look of vast sadness on his face.

K im arrived at her office early the next morning, dressed in a conservative gray suit.

"No Shifters today?" her secretary asked innocently.

"No, Jeanne." Kim's voice had gone cold and hard, the take-no-shit defense lawyer returning. "No more Shifters in the office. Sorry."

Jeanne, used to years of Kim's ups and downs, smiled at her. "Too bad. He sure was hot."

Kim had to admit that yes, he sure was. Her gut was so churned up that she didn't know what she was feeling. Loss, pain, sorrow, anger. Liam had thrown her out. That hurt. But hadn't Kim told Liam repeatedly that she couldn't stay? She wasn't certain who provoked the most anger, herself or Liam.

Once at her desk, Kim immediately dove into Brian's case. Arguing with the prosecutor's office helped keep her thoughts from Liam—from the traumatic fight in the warehouse, from the amazing sex afterward.

She worked all day, her businesslike suit and panty hose more confining by the hour. She'd gotten used to loose skirts and sandals far too quickly.

The next day wasn't any better, though the monotony was interrupted by a call from Silas.

"I talked to Liam," Silas told her. "He's agreed to let me interview him for the documentary, and for the feature stories for the newspaper. He's going to show me around Shiftertown himself."

"That's great." It really was great. Trust Liam to begin his rule of Shiftertown by doing what Fergus would have loathed. But Liam wanted the world to stop fearing Shifters, to move toward freedom. Showing the world what Shifters truly were was a first step.

A few weeks later, Kim's hard work and persistence finally paid off. With her tip on the jealous ex-boyfriend angle, her investigator had found out Michelle's ex had been boasting that he'd brought the Shifters to their knees and about his obsessive behavior toward Michelle before her death. He'd started calling her "the fucking Shifter-whore who'd got what she deserved." That was enough for police to reopen the case and bring the guy in again for further questioning. He'd been reluctant to talk about Michelle at all, until the detective revealed evidence of photos on the young man's digital camera of Michelle lying strangled on the floor. A vitriolic confession came pouring out. Michelle had betrayed him—with a *Shifter*. Michelle should die, and the Shifter should be ripped apart. If there were any justice in the world, he'd be given a medal for ridding the world of filth.

After that, it wasn't too difficult for Kim to get the prosecutors to dismiss the case against Brian, who was released to a surge of publicity. Kim walked with him, under the scrutiny of black camera lenses the day he was freed, to where Sandra waited in her old car. Mother and son had a tearful reunion, but Kim could see Brian's grief over Michelle. Sandra had confirmed that Brian had been prepared to take Michelle as his mate, and her loss was hard for him. He'd truly loved her.

After seeing Brian off, Kim returned to her office and went to see her boss.

The head of the firm was a large man with graying hair and pictures of his wife and four children on his desk. "Good work, Kim," he said, a man who rarely praised. "But I doubt we'll be getting any more Shifter cases. People wanted Shifter blood, and we just made the prosecutor's office look stupid."

Kim shrugged, not caring about the damned prosecutor's office right now. "It doesn't matter. I came to tender my resignation."

"What?" His thick brows shot up. "Why? You've just won the biggest case of the year."

"I'm contemplating a business venture of my own. Human advocate and legal liaison to Shifters in the Austin–San Antonio area. Want in?"

Her boss sat there with his mouth open, then moved his nameplate from one side of his desk to the other, which he did when he got nervous. "Are you crazy, Kim? You're a good attorney. One of my best. You're on your way to a terrific career. You throw in with Shifters and you'll be finished."

"Shifter-human law needs to be reevaluated and changed," Kim said. "It will be a challenge, something to live for. You could make your mark as a champion of Shifter rights. You love defending people's rights."

He glanced at the photos on his desk. "But Shifter-haters can be dangerous, and I wouldn't be risking just myself."

Kim nodded, understanding. "Well, I don't have anyone but myself to risk. I'm tired of living an empty life, so I'm going to fill it doing something crazy like helping Shifters wade through the morass of law. Jeanne's agreed to go with me. She's training as a paralegal, and she's excited about getting a chance for more experience."

"She's as crazy as you are."

"Maybe," Kim conceded. "But that's what we want to do. Thanks for taking me on when I was a green law-school graduate."

"No problem," her boss said faintly. "Good luck."

Kim dragged in a breath as she left her boss's office, the words *Good luck* ringing in her head. She knew she'd need it.

Kim spent the next weeks cleaning out her office and finding space to rent for her new office, a tiny one with enough room for herself and Jeanne. The others in the firm agreed with the head, that Kim was crazy. Some admired her; some openly castigated her, Abel in particular.

Kim ignored them and bought office furniture. Jeanne was an enthusiastic partner and even helped take Kim's mind off her sorrows for five minutes now and again.

The first day Kim spent at her new office, Silas e-mailed her some video files for the Shifter documentary he was working on, asking for her feedback.

Kim played the files, her heart aching. There was a lot of footage of Liam smiling his warm smile and speaking in his deep Irish lilt, telling Silas what he wanted the world to know about Shifters. Dylan spoke too, giving the same details but in a different enough way that it didn't sound as though they'd worked it out beforehand. Kim knew they had. She also knew exactly what they had decided to leave out.

There was footage of how the Shifters lived from day to day, shots of Michael playing in his front yard. Michael was photogenic, and his cuteness radiated from the screen. Silas also showed Connor and his friends kicking a soccer ball around the backyards, Connor talking about his love of "football" and what a fan he was of the Irish national team.

Silas didn't show only sparkles and smiles, however. He talked to Shifters about the darker side of their lives—the high death rate of Shifter children, which had started to come down only in the last decade, the low fecundity of the females. He talked about how the different Shifter species didn't get along "in the wild" but had made concessions to live together in harmony. Ellison was particularly eloquent in that segment, looking handsome with his big cowboy hat and wide smile.

A group of Shifters did a Collar "demonstration," which proved that Collars worked well, and Silas showed a meditation by some Shifter parents for children they'd lost.

Kim viewed the files again and again, pausing on Liam's smile, his blue eyes assuring the viewers that Shifters were little different from humans.

She watched the recording far too often. And far too often, she opened her cell phone and looked at Liam's number, wondering if she should tell him all the things she'd decided.

"Call me anytime, love," he'd said, when he'd programmed the number into it weeks ago.

Damn Shifters.

In the cool of late September, Kim came home from her new office on a Friday and spent the weekend packing.

Sunday afternoon, she put everything in her car that she could fit. She'd get help with the rest. She closed the trunk, started the car, and drove back to Shiftertown.

CHAPTER TWENTY-FOUR

Liam knew the car was Kim's without looking up. He crouched in the driveway beside his motorcycle, wrench in hand, completing a few tweaks to his bike.

He'd ridden this motorcycle to the posh neighborhood north of the river every night for the last two months, cutting the engine before he reached the hill above Kim's house. He'd sit there for a long time, the bike silent between his legs, watching her lighted bedroom window. When the light went out, Liam would kiss his fingertips to it, then coast back down the hill and ride home.

The hole in his heart wanted to close in hope as she stopped the Mustang and climbed out. She wore the high-heeled sandals he liked, ones that made her bare legs sexy as hell.

He watched the legs out of the corner of his eye as she strode up the driveway, letting her scent flow over him as she walked past him.

Walked past him?

Liam looked around to see Kim shove a cardboard box at Connor, who'd bounded out of the house.

"Will you carry that in for me?" Kim asked Connor sweetly. "Put it anywhere. I have a couple more in the trunk."

Kim returned to the car, again moving past Liam without speaking to him. She reached through the open passenger window, giving him a view of her nice ass, and pulled out an overnight bag.

"Hello, Sean." Kim smiled as Sean came out of the house behind Connor. "Can you grab the suitcases in my backseat? They're heavy."

She waltzed up the driveway, a determined smile on her face, bag slung over her shoulder.

Liam wiped his hands, stood, and planted himself in her path. "And what would you be doing here?"

"Moving in. Don't worry, I'll pay for my share of the groceries."

Kim started to go around him, and Liam stepped in front of her again. "Why?"

"Don't argue with her, Liam," Connor said, carrying the second box from the trunk. He rubbed Kim's shoulder as he went past her, like a cat to a litter mate. "She's back to stay, where she belongs."

"She belongs with her own kind," Liam said sternly.

"Not anymore," Connor said. "We need her, Liam, you especially. You've been pissed off for weeks. Don't mess this up."

Sean, Liam's dear supportive brother, didn't offer any comment. He silently removed Kim's suitcases from the backseat and carried them inside.

Liam's breath hurt. Gods, Kim was beautiful. Her dark hair looked shinier than ever, her eyes a deeper blue, her full breasts making his hands itch to cup them. If he did that right now, he'd leave greasy handprints on her pretty white shirt, and wouldn't everyone laugh?

"Why, love?" he asked. "Why are you back to tear out my heart?"

She smiled. "It's got nothing to do with you. I want our kid to know its father, and when it first changes into a wild-cat, he or she will need someone who knows what to do standing by."

Liam stopped. "Kid?"

"A little half-Shifter boy or girl. I don't know which; haven't had an ultrasound yet."

"Ultrasound . . ."

Kim laughed in true mirth. "You knocked me up, Liam Morrissey. Now you have to live with the consequences."

Connor came running out of the house, whooped, and punched the air. "Kim's pregnant! Woo-hoo!" He hurtled toward Kim, caught her in a hug and swung her off her feet. "I'm going to be a cousin!"

Connor's shouting drew people outside. Glory emerged first, sauntering down her porch stairs, her tight leopard-print pants startling. Dylan strolled out behind her. He'd moved in with Glory the day after Kim left, further emptying the house.

"Did I hear that right?" Glory called. "You're up the spout?"

Kim drew a breath once Connor finally put her down. "Confirmed by my gynecologist last week."

Liam kept wiping his hands on the rag. "I thought you took contraceptives."

"I was coming up on the end of my dose, and we had a lot of sex, Liam, if you recall. And maybe Shifter sperm are livelier than human's."

"Shite," Liam said around the lump in his throat.

More neighbors emerged onto front porches, and Ellison came around from his backyard, shirtless, his jeans cov-ered with dirt and grass stains. When Ellison understood what was going on, he put his hands on his hips, threw back his head, and howled. Answering howls came from up and down the street.

Great. How long before the news reached the other side of Shiftertown? Five minutes? Two?

"I'm staying, Liam," Kim said. "Whether you like it or not."

"Gods." Liam threw down the oily rag and caught Kim in his arms, damn the stains. He crushed Kim against him, lips finding her hair, her face, her mouth. "I love you, Kim. Don't ever leave me."

"That's the idea."

"I need you."

She rubbed his cheek. "I know."

Liam had driven her away to keep her safe, most of all from himself. But having her in his arms again, smelling her, tasting her, hearing her voice—it broke him, defeated the beast inside him. The feral in him crumpled as surely as Fergus had crumpled under the Guardian's sword.

Liam held her tighter. "You're all mine."

"You betcha."

Liam touched his forehead to hers. "I love you so damn much."

Kim grinned at him. "And I adore you."

Liam gave her a long, heartfelt kiss. She got into it, sliding her arms around him to cup his butt, snaking her fingers into his back pockets. She was a loving, warm, sexy woman. How'd he get so damn lucky?

Liam eased back from the kiss, licking the light bruise he'd already put on her lip. He'd learn how to be gentle with her, tender. And then he'd be wild. The sparkle in her eyes told him she wanted it both ways.

As soon as he raised his head, they were hit by the family. First Connor, still shouting, throwing his arms around both Liam and Kim. Then Sean, laughing, catching Liam in a bear hug, rubbing Kim's shoulders and kissing her cheek.

Dylan, his eyes full, holding Liam hard, then Kim. Kim gasped when Glory flung her arms around her, squeezing her.

"You did good, kid," she said.

And then Ellison, whooping and howling like the Lupine he was, jerking Liam off his feet in a rough embrace. "You virile shit, you. Taking the best woman for yourself."

"Watch it," Glory said.

Ellison draped his arms around Connor and Sean. "This calls for a beer." He started with them for the house, his way of leaving Liam and Kim tactfully alone. Glory followed, after a look at Dylan.

"Seamus," Connor was saying. "Patrick, maybe?"

"What are you talking about?" Ellison asked him.

"Names for the wee one. Eoghan, maybe?"

"Give the kid a break. Who the hell could spell that?"

The house swallowed them. Dylan put his hands on Kim's and Liam's shoulders. "The Goddess bless you both." He kissed Kim's forehead. "Thank you, Kim."

He smiled and walked away. Liam watched him, his heart full.

"Is he thanking me for getting pregnant?" Kim asked. "It wasn't difficult, with all the sex we kept having. You did as much as I did."

Liam pulled her against him again. She belonged there, felt so right fitted to him. "He meant for coming back to us. For keeping us a family."

"That wasn't difficult, either." She gave him a smile. "You're wrong about where I belong, Liam. This is the kind of family I had before my brother died, one of warmth and laughter, of knowing the house was full every night. It's what I've been looking for in the last decade or so, even when I didn't know it." Kim looked up at him, her blue eyes full of love. "I belong right here. With you."

She'd break his heart all right. Or maybe she'd finally heal it. Liam pulled her close, his lips meeting hers.

Damn, kissing the human way was good. How could he have never liked it before?

Because he'd never done it with Kim before.

Kim caught his lower lip between her teeth, and Liam felt the front of his jeans get unbearably tight. He murmured in her ear, "Do you think we can make it upstairs?"

"I'm all for trying." Her gaze turned sultry. "Besides, they're shouting so much, they'll cover up all the noise I plan to make."

Liam squeezed her, growling. "I love you, woman."

"Good to know."

They did make it past the mob and up the stairs. Dylan saw them go, but he only smiled quietly and turned away.

The door closed, the lock locked. Clothes came off, and Liam had Kim naked against him. His heart was whole, his brain clear, and his body melting with desire. Kim's smile put him over the top.

"Love you, Liam," she whispered.

"Always," Liam said brokenly. "I'll love you forever."

They had strong, bed-shaking, wet, and sweaty sex that drowned out even the revelry downstairs.

Liam's brother, nephew, friends, and every member of his clan never let them hear the end of it.

Turn the page for a preview of the next
Shifters Unbound novel by Jennifer Ashley

PRIMAL BONDS

Available now from Berkley Sensation!

CHAPTER ONE

A ndrea Gray had just set the beer bottle in front of her customer when the first of the shots rocketed through the open front door. The bar just outside of the Austin Shiftertown had no windows, but the front door always stood wide open, and now a cascade of gunfire poured through the welcoming entrance.

The next thing Andrea knew, she was on the floor with two hundred and fifty pounds of solid Shifter muscle on top of her. She knew exactly who pinned her, knew the shape and feel of the long body pressing her back and thighs, trapping her with male strength. She struggled but couldn't budge him. Damned Feline.

"Get *off* me, Sean Morrissey."

His voice with its Irish lilt trickled into her ear, swirling heat into her belly. "You stay down when the bullets fly, love."

A ferocious roar sounded as Ronan, the bouncer, ran past, heading outside in his Kodiak bear form. Andrea heard more shots and then the bear's bellow of pain. Bullets splintered the bottles above the bar with a musical sound, and colorful glass and fragrant alcohol rained to the floor. Another roar, this one from a lion, vibrated in the air, and the hail of bullets suddenly ceased. Tires squealed as an engine revved before the sound died off into the distance.

Stunned silence followed, then whimpers, moans, and the angry voice of Andrea's aunt Glory. "Bastards. Human lickbrain assholes."

Shifters started rising, talking, cursing.

"You can get off me now, Sean," Andrea said.

Sean lingered, his warm weight pouring sensations into Andrea's brain—strength, virility, protectiveness—*You're safe with me, love, and you always will be.* Finally he rose to his feet and pulled her up with him; six-feet-five of enigmatic Shifter male, the black-haired, blue-eyed, Collared Feline to whom Andrea owed her freedom.

Sean didn't step away from her, staying right inside her personal space so that the heat of his body surrounded her. "Anyone hurt?" he called. "Everyone all right?"

His voice was strong, but Andrea sensed his worry that he'd have to act as Guardian tonight, which meant driving his sword through the heart of his dying friends to send their bodies to dust and their souls to the afterlife. The Sword of the Guardian leaned against the wall in the back office, where Sean stashed it any night he spent in the bar. Since Andrea had come to work there, he'd spent most nights in the bar, watching her.

She'd also seen in the two weeks she'd lived next door to Sean Morrissey that he hated the thought of using the sword. His primary job was to be called in when there was no longer any hope, and that fact put a dark edge to his entire life. Not many people saw this, but Andrea had noticed.

Andrea was close enough now to Sean to sense his muscles relax as people assured him they were all right. Shifters climbed slowly to their feet, shaken, but there was no one dead or wounded. They'd been lucky.

The floor was littered with glass and splintered wood, the smell of spilled alcohol was sharp, and bullet holes riddled the dark walls. Half the bottles and glasses behind the bar had been destroyed, and the human bartender crawled shakily out from under a table.

A wildcat zoomed in through the front door and stopped by a clump of humans not yet brave enough to get up. Feline Shifters were a cross between breeds: lion, leopard, tiger, jaguar, cheetah—bred centuries ago from the best of each. The Morrissey family had a lot of lion in it, and this wildcat had heavily muscled shoulders, a tawny body, and a black mane. It rose on its hind legs, its head nearly touching the ceiling, before it shifted into the tall form of Liam Morrissey, Sean's older brother.

The human males at his feet looked up in terror. But what did the idiots expect if they hung out in a Shifter bar? Shifter groupies baffled Andrea. They wore imitation Collars and pretended to adore all things Shifter, but whenever Shifters behaved like Shifters, they cringed in fear. *Go home, children.*

"Sean," Liam said over the crowd, eyes holding questions. "No one in here got hit. How's Ronan?"

"He'll live." The anger on Liam's face mirrored Sean's own. "Humans, a carload of them." *Again,* he didn't say.

"Cowards," Glory spat. Eyes white with rage, the platinum blonde helped another Shifter woman to her feet. The Collar around Glory's neck, which she wore like a fashion accessory to her body-hugging gold lamé, emitted half a dozen sparks. "Let me go after them."

"Easy." Liam's voice held such calm authority that Glory backed off in spite of herself, and her Collar went silent. Liam's Collar didn't spark at all, although Andrea felt the waves of anger from him.

One of the Shifter groupies raised his hands. "Hey, man, it had nothing to do with us."

Liam forced a smile, stuffing himself back into his

ostensible role as bar manager. "I know that, lad," he said. "I'm sorry for your trouble. You come back in tomorrow, why don't you? The first round's on me."

His Irish lilt was pronounced, Liam the Shiftertown leader at his most charming, but the humans didn't look comforted. Liam was stark naked, except for his Collar—a large, muscular male, gleaming with sweat, who could kill the men at his feet in one blow if he wanted to. As much as they pretended to want the thrill of that danger, Shifter groupies didn't like it when the danger was real.

Ronan staggered back in, no longer in his bear form. Ronan was even bigger than Liam and Sean, nearly seven feet tall, broad of shoulder and chest, and tight with muscle. His face was sheet white, his shoulder torn and covered with blood.

Andrea shook off Sean's protective hold and went to him. "Damn it, Ronan, what were you doing?"

"My job." The amount of blood flowing down his torso would have had a human on the floor in shock. Ronan merely looked embarrassed.

Sean got to the man's other side. "In the back, lad. Now."

"I'm fine. It's just a bullet. My own fault."

"Shut it." Sean and Andrea towed the bigger man to a door marked "Private," and Sean more or less shoved him into the office beyond.

The office was ordinary—cluttered desk, a couple of chairs, a storage cabinet, shabby sofa, and a small safe in the wall that only the bar's human owner was supposed to know the combination to. Andrea knew good and well that Liam and Sean knew it too.

The Sword of the Guardian leaned against the wall like an upright cross, and threads of its Fae magic floated to Andrea from across the room. Andrea had no idea whether pure Shifters could sense the sword's magic as she, a half-Fae, half-Lupine Shifter could, but she did know that the Shifters in this Shiftertown regarded the sword, and Sean, with uncomfortable awe.

Sean pushed Ronan at a chair. "Sit."

Ronan dropped obediently, and the flimsy chair creaked under his weight. Ronan was an Ursine—a bear Shifter—large and hard-muscled, his short but shaggy black hair always looking uncombed. He didn't have an ounce of fat on him. Andrea wasn't used to Ursines, having never met one before moving to Austin. Only Lupines had lived in her Shiftertown near Colorado Springs. But Ronan had proved to be such a sweetheart he'd quickly overcome her uneasiness.

"I can't stay in here," Ronan protested. "What if they come back?"

"You're not going anywhere, my friend, until we get that bullet out of you." Sean snatched a blanket from the sagging sofa and dropped it over Ronan's lap. Shifters weren't modest as a rule, but maybe Sean thought he needed to protect Andrea from a bear in his naked glory. Ronan, admittedly, was . . . supersized.

"I thought I'd be away from the door maybe a minute." Ronan's deep black eyes filled. "What if someone had gotten hurt? Or killed? It would have been because of me."

"No one got hurt but you, you big softie." Sean's voice took on that gentle note that made Andrea shiver deep inside herself. "You frightened away the bad guys before anything worse could happen."

"If I'd been at my post, I would have blocked the door, and none of the bullets would have gotten inside."

"And then you'd look like a cheese grater," Sean said. "And be dust at the end of my sword. I like you, Ronan. I don't want that."

"Yeah?"

Andrea set down the first-aid kit she'd fetched from the cabinet and perched on the edge of the desk, her hand on Ronan's unhurt shoulder. "I don't want that either."

Ronan relaxed a little under her touch—he needed touch, reassurance, all Shifters did, especially when injured or frightened. Andrea wanted to give Ronan a full hug, but she feared hurting him. She kneaded his back instead, trying to put as much comfort as she could into the caress.

Ronan grinned weakly at her. "Hey, you're not so bad yourself, for a Fae."

"Half Fae."

Anyone else mentioning her Fae blood made Andrea's anger rise, but with Ronan it had turned into friendly teasing. Ronan squeezed her fingers in his pawlike hand.

"This is going to hurt like hell, big guy," Sean said. "So just remind yourself who you'll have to answer to if you turn bear on me and take my head off."

"Aw, I'd never hurt you, Sean. Even if I didn't know Liam would rip my guts out if I did."

"Good lad. Remember now. Andrea, hold the gauze just like that."

Andrea positioned the wad of sterile gauze under the ragged hole in Ronan's shoulder as Sean directed. Sean sprayed some antibacterial around the wound, reached in with the big tweezers he'd dipped in alcohol, and yanked the bullet from Ronan's flesh.

Ronan threw his head back and roared. His face distorted, his mouth and nose lengthening to a muzzle filled with sharp teeth. Blood burst from the wound and coated first the gauze, then the clean towel Sean jammed over it. Ronan's hands extended to razorlike claws, which closed on Sean's wrist.

Sean pressed the towel in place, unworried. "Easy now."

Ronan withdrew his hand, but not before a blue snake of electricity arced around his Collar, biting into his neck. He howled in pain.

Damn it. Andrea leapt to her feet, unable to stand it any longer. She batted the surprised Sean's hands aside and pressed her palm directly to the wound. Folding herself against Ronan, she held her hand flat to his chest.

The threads of healing spiraled in her mind, diving through her fingers into Ronan's skin, swirling until she closed her eyes to fight dizziness. She sensed the threads of Fae magic from the sword across the room drifting toward her, as though drawn by her healing touch.

Ronan's skin knit beneath her fingers, tightening and drying, slowly becoming whole again. After a few minutes, Andrea opened her eyes. Ronan's breath came fast, but it was healthy breathing, and the blood around the wound had dried.

Andrea drew her hand away. Ronan probed his injury, staring at it in amazement. "What the hell did you do to me, Andy-girl?"

"Nothing," Andrea said in a light voice as she stood up. "We stopped the blood, and you heal fast, you big strong Ursine, you."

Ronan looked from Sean to Andrea. Sean shrugged and gave him a small smile, as though he knew what was going on, but Andrea saw the hard flicker in Sean's eyes. Oh, goody, she'd pissed him off.

Ronan gave up. He stretched and worked his shoulder. "Slap a bandage on me, Sean," he said in his usual strong voice. "I need to find my clothes."

Sean silently pressed a fresh wad of gauze to the wound, secured it with sterile tape, and let him go. Ronan kissed the top of Andrea's head, clapped Sean on the shoulders, and banged out of the office, his energy restored.

Andrea busied herself putting things back into the first-aid kit. Sean said absolutely nothing, but when she turned from tucking the kit back into the cabinet, she found him right behind her, again invading her personal space.

It was difficult to breathe while he stood over her, smelling of the night and Guinness and male musk. She had no idea what to make of Sean Morrissey, the Shifter who had mate-claimed her, sight unseen, when she'd needed to relocate to this Shiftertown.

A mate-claim simply meant that a male had marked a female as a potential mate—the couple wouldn't be officially mated until they were blessed under sun and moon by the male's clan leader. All other males had to back off unless the female chose to reject the male's mate-claim.

When Andrea had wanted to move to Austin to live with Glory, her mother's sister, Glory's pack leader had refused to let Andrea in unless she was mate-claimed. The pack leader had the right to disallow any unmated female to enter his pack if he thought that the female would cause dissention or other trouble.

Andrea, a half-Fae illegitimate Lupine, was considered trouble. When Andrea's mother, Dina, had become pregnant by her Fae lover, Dina had been forced from the pack. That same pack now didn't want her half-Fae daughter back. But Andrea had needed to flee the Shiftertown in which she'd been living in Colorado, because a harassing asshole, the Shiftertown leader's son, had tried to mate-claim Andrea for his own. He hadn't taken her answer—*no way in hell*—very well.

Glory had turned to Liam, the Austin Shiftertown leader, as was her right, to appeal her pack leader's decision to keep Andrea out. Apparently the arguments between Glory's pack leader and Liam had been loud and heated. And then Sean had cut the arguments short by claiming Andrea for himself.

Why he'd done it, Andrea couldn't figure out, even though Sean had explained that it had been to keep the peace between species in this Shiftertown. But if that was all it was—a formality to satisfy a stubborn pack leader—why did Sean watch Andrea like he did? He'd not been happy with Liam for hiring her as a waitress, and Sean made sure he was at the bar from open to close every night Andrea worked. Didn't the big Feline have better things to do?

Sean was tall and blue-eyed, and he radiated warmth like a furnace. Andrea loved standing close to him—*How crazy is that? I'm hot for an effing Feline.* She'd thought that after what Jared, the harassing asshole, had done to her, she'd never have interest in males again, but Sean Morrissey made her breath catch. To her surprise, Sean's mate-claim had awakened her instincts and made her come alive. She'd never thought she'd feel alive again.

"What?" she asked, when Sean made no sign of moving.

"Don't play innocent with me, love. What did you just do to Ronan? I watched with my own eyes while that wound closed."

Andrea had learned to be evasive about her gift for her own safety, but she somehow knew Sean wouldn't let her. If she didn't answer, he might try to pry it out of her, maybe by seizing her wrists and backing her against a wall, looking down at her with those blue, blue eyes. Well, a girl could hope.

She made herself turn her back on his intense gaze—not easy—and start straightening the shelves in the cabinet. "It's something I inherited through my Fae side. Of course it's through my Fae side. Where else would I have gotten it?"

"I didn't notice you mentioning that you had healing magic when you arrived. I didn't notice Glory mentioning it either."

"Glory doesn't know," Andrea said without turning around. "I had a hard enough time convincing Glory's pack to let me move in with her, not to mention the pair of Felines who run this Shiftertown. I figured, the less of my Fae part I revealed, the better."

Sean turned her to face him. His eyes had gone white blue, an alpha not happy that a lesser Shifter hadn't bared every inch of her soul to him. As much as Andrea's gaze wanted to slide off to the left, she refused to look away. Sean might be an alpha, but she'd not be a pathetic submissive to his big, bad Feline dominance.

"Why keep such a thing to yourself?" Sean asked. "You could do a hell of a lot of good with a gift like that."

Andrea slid out of Sean's grip and walked away. First, because it proved she could; second, it got her away from his white-hot gaze.

"The gift isn't that strong. It's not like I can cure terminal diseases or anything. I can boost the immune system, heal wounds and abrasions, speed up the healing of broken bones.

I couldn't have magicked the bullet out of Ronan, for instance, but I could relieve his pain and jump-start his recovery."

"And you don't think this is something we should know about?"

When she looked at Sean again, his eyes had returned to that sinful, summer-lake blue, but his stance still said he could turn on her anytime he wanted. If Andrea hadn't been intrigued by Sean the moment she'd laid eyes on him in the Austin bus station, the man would terrify her. Sean Morrissey was different from Liam, who was a charmer, in your face, laughing at the same time he made damn sure you did whatever it was he wanted. Sean was quieter, watching the world, waiting for something, she wasn't certain what.

It had been one hell of a long ride from Colorado to central Texas, but Andrea had had to take the bus, because Shifters weren't allowed on airplanes, nor were they allowed to drive cross-country. Glory had brought Sean with her when she'd picked up Andrea from the station. Tall, hard-bodied, and black-haired, Sean had been dressed in jeans and a button-down shirt, motorcycle boots, and a leather jacket against the February cold. Andrea had assumed him to be Glory's latest conquest until Glory introduced him. Sean had looked down at Andrea, his hard-ass, blue-eyed stare peeling away the layers she'd built between herself and the world.

She remembered thinking, *I wonder if he's black-haired all the way down?*

Sean, being the alpha he was, had sensed her distress and exhaustion and pulled her into his arms, knowing she needed his touch. He'd smelled of leather, maleness, sweat, and cold February air, and Andrea had wanted to curl up in a little ball against him like a wounded cub. "You're all right now," Sean had murmured against her hair. "I'm here to look after you."

Now Sean stood patiently, waiting for her explanation. The damn stubborn Feline would stand there all night until she gave him one.

"I wasn't allowed to talk about it in Colorado," Andrea

said. "The Shiftertown leader gave my stepfather permission to let me use it, but they didn't want me telling people how I healed them. I understand why. Everyone would have freaked if they thought I was using Fae magic on them."

"That's a point," Sean conceded. "But we're not as easily, as you say, *freaked*, around here. You should have told me, or Glory at least."

Andrea put one hand on her hip. "My life as a half-breed illegitimate orphan hasn't exactly been pleasant, you know. I've learned to keep things to myself."

"And you thought we'd treat you the same, did you, love?"

Damn it, why did he insist on calling her *love*? And why did it sizzle fire all the way through her? This was crazy. He was a *Feline*. If Sean Morrissey knew little about her, Andrea knew still less about him.

"Well, you're part of us now." Sean came to her, again stepping into her space, a dominant male wanting to make her aware just what her place was. "You're right that not all Shifters are comfortable with Fae magic, but my brother has to know about your healing gift, and my father. And Glory has a right too."

"Fine," Andrea said, as though it made no difference. "Tell them." She moved to the door, again deliberately turning her back on him. Alphas didn't like that. "We should go help clean up out there. Does the bar get shot up often? I should get hazardous duty pay."

"Andrea."

He was right behind her, his warmth like sunshine on her back. Andrea stopped with her hand on the doorknob. Sean rested his palm on the doorframe above her, his tall body hemming her in. She remembered the feel of him on top of her on the floor, the tactile memory strong.

"Glory says something's been troubling you," Sean said. "Troubling you bad. I want you to tell me about it."

Andrea shivered. Damn Glory, damn Sean, and no, she didn't want to talk about it.

"Not now. Can we go?"

"It's my job to listen to troubles," he said, breath hot in her ear. "Whether I'm your mate yet or not. And you will tell me yours."

Andrea's tongue felt loose, her pent-up emotions suddenly wanting to spill out to this man and his warm voice. She clamped her mouth shut, but Sean stunned her by saying, "Is it about the nightmares?"

She hadn't told anyone about the nightmares, not Glory, not Sean, not anyone, though Glory might have heard her crying out in her sleep. The nightmares had started a week after she'd moved in with Glory, when they'd risen in her head like a many-tentacled monster. She didn't know what they meant or why she was having them; she only knew they scared the hell out of her. "How do you know about my nightmares?"

"Because my bedroom window faces yours, love, and I have good hearing."

The thought of Sean sitting in his bedroom, watching over her while she slept, made her shiver with warmth. "There's nothing to tell. When I wake up, I can't remember anything." Except fear. She had no idea what the images that flashed through her head meant, but they terrified her. "I really don't want to talk about it right now," she said. "All right?"

Sean ran a soothing hand down her arm, stirring more fires. "That's all right, love. You let me know when you're good and ready."

From the feel of the very firm thing lodged against her backside, Sean was good and ready now. One part of him had definitely shifted.

Andrea deliberately leaned on the door and pressed back into him. A jolt of heat shot through her, the fear of the nightmares dissolving. After Jared, Andrea thought she'd be afraid of Sean, turned off, ready to run. Instead, Sean made her feel, for the first time in years . . . playful.

"So, tell me, Guardian," she said, lowering her voice to a purr. "Is that where you carry your sword, or are you just happy to see me?"

WORLD WITHOUT END

STAR TREK®

ADVENTURES

STAR TREK NOVELS

STAR TREK ADVENTURES

WORLD WITHOUT END

STAR TREK®

ADVENTURES

JOE HALDEMAN

TITAN BOOKS

STAR TREK ADVENTURES 12: **WORLD WITHOUT END**
ISBN 1 85286 538 5

Published by
Titan Books Ltd
42-44 Dolben Street
London SE1 0UP

First Titan Edition June 1995
10 9 8 7 6 5 4 3 2 1

British Library Cataloguing-in-Publication Data. A catalogue record
for this book is available from the British Library.

Cover illustration by Alister Pearson.

Printed and bound in Great Britain by Cox and Wyman Ltd, Reading,
Berkshire.

Any sufficiently advanced technology is indistinguishable from magic.
—Arthur C. Clarke

1

Nearing the end of our benchmark survey of Sector 3, we were treated to a rare sight this morning. At 0739, Antares occulted Deneb—the two brightest stars in our sky appearing to come together for an instant, red and blue fires merging.

Most of the crew turned out to watch. It hasn't been an exciting trip.

"Lopike thopis." Lieutenant Martin Larousse was babbling at Mr. Spock in the officers' lounge. "Yopoo poput opan 'opop' opin fropunt—"

"I see," Spock said. "That's not difficult to decipher. You are only putting the sound 'op' in front of each vowel."

"It's not difficult for *you*. But Earth children use it to mystify their playmates, communicate secrets."

"I doubt that a Vulcan child would be mystified."

"Well, we don't have a Vulcan child here to experiment on, do we? . . . Do you believe you've mastered it, from that sample?"

"Of course. If it's consistent throughout your inconsistent language."

"Well then," Larousse rubbed his chin and looked at the ceiling, "try 'uranium hexafluoride.'"

"Opuropanopiopum hopexopaflopuoporopide," Spock said without hesitation. "Allowing for your mispronunciation of 'fluoride.'"

He shook his head. "That's inhuman."

"Precisely." Spock didn't smile. "Vulcan children do use secret languages, but they are codes of gesture and intonation, constantly changing. Otherwise, they would not remain secret for long."

"They never mentioned that when I studied Vulcan." Larousse was the *Enterprise*'s linguist.

"That's not surprising. Vulcan—" Spock and Larousse stood up. "Good afternoon, Captain."

"Good afternoon, gentlemen." Kirk set his cup of tea on their table and pulled a chair over; the three sat down simultaneously.

"Another benchmark down," Kirk said and sighed, or snorted, almost inaudibly. "Exactly where it was supposed to be. As the last one was, and the one before . . . I wish one of them would be a meter or two off. We could use some excitement."

"You don't mean that, Captain," Spock said.

"No, of course not." He smiled without conviction. "But four weeks of this is enough. I'm sure the crew will be glad to move on to something else." If either Spock or Larousse knew differently—the crew seemed happy enough with the uneventful routine—they didn't say so.

"Ten more days, sir?" Larousse said.

"Nine, unless we run into trouble. Then we pick up new orders at Starbase Three." He nodded at Spock.

"We did finally get word. Sealed orders waiting."

"It must be something important," Larousse said.

Kirk sipped his tea. "Not necessarily. Whether orders are sealed is not always a command decision. A clerk can decide."

Uhura's calm voice filtered into the lounge: "All decks. Yellow alert." Kirk set the cup down with a plastic clatter, spilling some. "This is not a drill. All crew to duty stations."

Spock headed for the turbolift, Larousse blotted at the tea on his pants leg, and Kirk slapped the intercom. "Bridge, this is the captain. What's going on?"

"Captain, most of our instruments are completely scrambled—white noise. There's no . . . wait."

"What is it?"

"Everything seems to be, um, functioning normally again."

"Well, maintain alert status." He thumbed the intercom. "Engine room."

"Scott here."

"Scotty, cut the engines. We'll be backtracking at warp factor one. Stand by for either a slow search pattern or fast evasive maneuvering."

"Aye, sir."

Spock was holding the turbolift for him. "You wanted excitement, Captain."

Kirk grunted and watched the doors close. Almost to himself: " 'Speak of the devil and he will appear.' "

"We have a similar saying in Vulcan."

Kirk arched an eyebrow at his friend. "Superstition, Spock?"

"Not at all, Captain. Observation."

From the Captain's Log, Stardate 7503.0:

> We have made a most remarkable discovery. At 7502.931 the Enterprise crossed an extremely strong magnetic field. All of the instruments that weren't heavily shielded were scrambled.
>
> I felt it well within the limits of my discretion to delay our current mission in order to go back and find the source of the magnetic field. It is some sort of a vehicle, the size of a large asteroid (217 kilometers in diameter). There are sentient beings inside.
>
> I've called for a meeting of the science staff, at 1830 hours.

Twenty-five people were crowded into a briefing room designed for half that number. Spock, at the captain's request, had invited all of the science officers and those ensigns with kinds of academic training that might be useful. Scotty brought along three engineers, propulsion systems specialists.

"Ha'e we anyone who disna' know what a 'Bussard ramjet' is?" Several hands went up, Larousse and two life scientists; and one paw: Glak Sön, a short hairy alien from Anacontor, ensign-mathematics.

"It's simple enough: a way that an interstellar ship can gather fuel for a primitive fusion engine. We made a few of them in the twenty-first century, before the space warp was discovered.

"Interstellar space is full of hydrogen—it's spread out very thin, but there's a lot of it. A Bussard ramjet uses a strong magnetic field to suck up this hydrogen, which it fuses for power.

"They are very slow, taking centuries to go from star to star. Of the Bussard ramjets that left our solar system, two were automated probes and three were 'generation ships'—where the original crew knew they would not live to reach their destination; their great-grandchildren would finish the mission.

"The Federation has tracked down two of the generation ships and boosted them on to their destinations at warp speed. One, called *Forty Families,* has been lost for 250 years.

"We hoped we had found *Forty Families,* but it turns out that this ship is far too big. Mr. Spock has the details."

"It is very large, essentially a hollowed-out asteroid some 217 kilometers in diameter. I have prepared two diagrams. Ensign Fitzsimmons?" She turned down the lights and projected the pictures onto the wall.

"The top diagram is simply a picture of the ship. Note the direction in which it travels; it is decelerating. It is moving at only one one-hundredth of the speed of light; its deceleration is at the rate of approximately one millimeter per second per second."

"So it has another ninety-five years before it stops," the hairy mathematician said.

"And forty-seven days," Spock said.

"The inhabitants live inside the sphere, of course. It rotates, to provide them with 'gravity' via centrifugal force."

"They don't even have real artificial gravity?" someone asked. Spock looked in his direction and hesitated, then decided not to bring him to task for putting those two adjectives together.

"No, they don't. That's part of a paradox, which we will discuss in a moment.

"The lower diagram is a cutaway drawing, showing the inside of the sphere. I have charted the population density as derived from biosensor data.

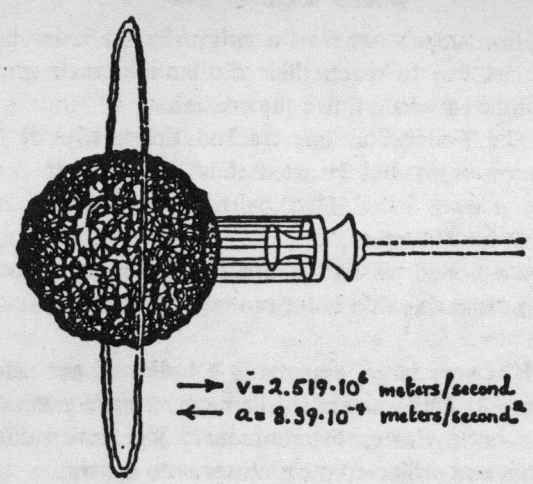

$\rightarrow \bar{v} = 2.519 \cdot 10^6$ meters/second
$\leftarrow a = 8.39 \cdot 10^{-4}$ meters/second^2

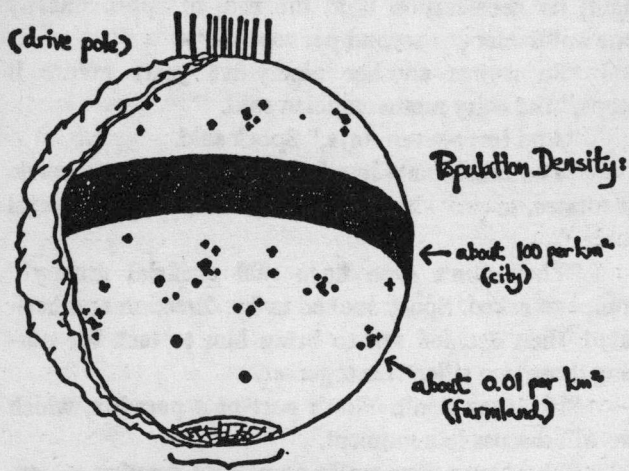

(drive pole)

Population Density:

$\leftarrow$ about 100 per km^2
(city)

$\leftarrow$ about 0.01 per km^2
(farmland)

Pole is about 10 per km^2
with heavy concentration
at the exact center.
Other pole uninhabited.

"There are more than a million individuals inside that small planet. Nine tenths of them are concentrated in a band around the equator. That, of course, is where the 'gravity' is highest, though it is slightly less than one half of what we are used to."

He signaled the ensign and the lights came back up. "We have attempted to communicate with them, to no success. Everything we beam at them is reflected directly back to us." This information caused a murmur of comment.

"It is remarkable, yes. We don't yet know whether the transporter will be effective. We do not wish to beam down an inanimate object until we can follow it immediately with a contact party, so they will not have time to misinterpret our motives."

"Or get ready for us," someone said.

"That was taken into consideration, of course. They *are* a star-faring race, albeit a slow one, and it is conceivable that they might have weapons of considerable violence at their disposal.

"And there is a mystery at work. By neutrino diffraction, we found out what causes our signals to be reflected. The entire globe, under an eighty-meter layer of ordinary rock, is covered with a skin of an impossibly dense metal or alloy. Its atomic weight is apparently on the order of twelve hundred."

He waited for them to quiet down. "Supposedly impossible, yes. Nevertheless, the figure is correct. They seem to be rather more advanced in metallurgy, or physical chemistry, than they are in astronautics.

"The ship's computer has prepared a summary of what we know about this object." He nodded at Fitzsimmons and she started passing out copies of the one-

page report. "Take a minute or two to read it over."
He sat down next to Captain Kirk.

"Serious business," Kirk said, staring at the sheet
of paper, which he had already read.

"It is indeed." Spock couldn't have failed to notice that although Kirk's expression was serious, his
eyes betrayed him: he was looking forward to some
action.

"Very serious," Kirk repeated, staring, smiling.

2

SUMMARY

1. At time of measurement (SD 7502.9576) the object is described by the following parameters:

POSITION:	119.70239^D, 689.4038 psc.; —1.038572^D, —0.9965 psc. w.r.t. Rigel.
HEADING:	37.903^D, 0.0127^D.
VELOCITY:	0.00840l303 c (2,518,651.8 m/sec.)
ACCELERATION:	—0.000839 m/sec^2 (0.0000855 g)
RADIUS:	108,576.3 m.
MASS:	35.527835 teratonnes
RATE OF ROTATION:	0.006578 rad/sec. (once each 15^m 55.12^s)

2. Extrapolating to the past, it appears that the object has been in flight for nearly 3,000 years. Its point of origin is at the center of a tenuous globular shell of gas, which is all that remains of an ancient supernova.

2a. This supernova exploded circa 750 B.C. There is no human record of the event, but it was identified by Vulcan astronomers.

2b. The object (and perhaps others like it) left its system several centuries before the explosion.

3. If the object continues to decelerate at 0.000839 m/sec^2 (and to do so it must soon switch to another mode of propulsion), then it will eventually come to rest about one-eighth of a parsec from here.

3a. At that point they will be two parsecs from the nearest star.

3b. This cannot be the destination they originally planned for. All of their energy must eventually dissipate as waste heat without a nearby star to use as an outside energy source, and they will eventually freeze to death (though this may take centuries or even hundreds of centuries).

4. It may be that they wish to die. In this case, doctrine of self-determination would require that we not interfere.

DISCUSSION

+ The efficiency of a Bussard-type ramjet decreases as its velocity decreases, since less hydrogen is swept up per unit of time. Therefore, the object must soon adopt some other mode of deceleration.

Early human starships of the Bussard type used a "sputter drive" (also called Daedelus System) for the initial acceleration and final deceleration. In this phase the ships were sped up or braked by radiation pressure from the explosion of hydrogen fusion bombs fore and aft.

The large concavity (which appears to be a natural crater) that is antipodal to the Bussard-type generator on this object may be part of such a system.

+ Assuming the transporter will function properly, and a confrontation team is sent into the object, a special communications system must be devised.

Lieutenant Uhura believes she can use the particle generator on Deck Two to create a system using amplitude modulation of neutrinos.

+ The confrontation team will be beamed to the equator, where population density is highest.

3

Captain Kirk headed up the confrontation team, which was top-heavy with officers: Dr. McCoy, Lieutenant Larousse, and the security chief B. "Tuck" Wilson. The only ensign was Moore, also from security.

Wilson was an older man, quiet and formal. He centered a small black box on one of the transporter units. "Ready, sir."

It was a passive one-shot neutrino generator, which Spock had put together to test Uhura's communication system. If it were beamed down successfully, Kirk and the men would follow it.

"All right." Kirk nodded to Scotty. "Energize."

Warble, fade, disappear. Uhura's voice came over the intercom: "It's sending loud and clear, Captain."

"Let's go." The five men stepped up onto the raised dais and took their places.

"This is gonna be weird," McCoy said. "Anybody else want a pill?"

"That trank you were talking about?" Kirk said. "Did you take one?"

"You bet, Jim. It's not really a tranquilizer; just

affects the inner ear. Keep you from getting dizzy inside that spinning beach ball."

"No, thanks. I'd rather live with it." Nobody else took McCoy's offer. "Energize."

The disconcerting limbo of transport seemed to last a split-second longer than usual. What followed wasn't comforting.

Kirk opened his eyes and then shut them quickly, dizzy. He opened them again, and held on to Larousse, who was also holding on to him.

No horizon. A sun overhead, but no sky.

Looking "down" fifty, a hundred kilometers. Or was it "up"?

"We knew it would be disorienting," Wilson said calmly. "I was not truly prepared for the scale of it. Are you all right, Captain?"

"Yes." Kirk gulped and cautiously let go of Larousse's shoulder. He didn't fall.

"They're ignoring us," Larousse said. They had materialized in the middle of what appeared to be a market square, jammed with hundreds of aliens.

The creatures were slightly humanoid. They had the "correct" number of eyes, hands, feet, noses, and mouths. There the resemblance ended. They were covered with short dense fur, and otherwise wore no clothing except necklaces of ribbon, yet displayed no clue of gender. Each had a pair of wings, similar to those of a flying squirrel: continuous leathery membranes that grew out of their sides, from wrist to ankle.

Most of them were about a meter tall, though four or five were as tall as Kirk. They walked around the humans, eyes studying the ground. Every now and then one would give them a sidelong glance, but only for a moment.

They were in the center of the city, as planned. Buildings marched off uphill in every direction; to their left and right, pale green fields met the edges of the city and continued rising into the "sky," dissolving into purplish-gray haze.

The buildings were all between ten and thirty stories high, constructed of pale yellow brick and shiny metal. As the city stretched off into the distance, the buildings tilted in toward them, giving them the uneasy sensation of being in the middle of a city that was collapsing. Most of the farther buildings, whose roofs they could see, had roof gardens; the sides of many were decorated with intricate abstract mosaics of colored stone or ceramic fragments.

Each building had one or several open doors at every floor above the ground, the structures joined to one another by a graceful web of cables. The creatures climbed and glided from cable to cable; there seemed to be more of them in the air than on the ground.

The creatures had a graceful beauty while gliding, but their walk was a clumsy shuffle-and-sway. And by any human standards, they were ugly—not just odd looking, but ugly. Their eyes, bright yellow, twice the size of humans', bulged out and they blinked sideways. The nose was two red holes. The mouth was fixed in a grinning U, the upper lip fixed while the bottom jaw gaped open and shut, exposing rows of tiny sharp teeth. Their heads were elongated almost to a point, and bulged out behind.

Their hair was silky and short, brownish-red, but was missing from various places—elbows, knees, feet, hands, and the points of their heads—and where skin showed it was dead fish-belly white, as were lips and eyelids and the insides of their mouths.

Not pleasant to look at, but it's safe to say that none of the *Enterprise* people was put off by their appearance. Not only did they live in close quarters with Glak Sŏn—who was also short, hairy, and less than beautiful—and the other alien crewmembers, but they would never have drawn a berth aboard the cruiser, had Star Fleet psychologists been able to detect any trace of xenophobia in their profiles.

"This is bizarre," Ensign Moore said.

Kirk nodded vaguely, watching the milling mob for some sign of interest. "Well, here goes."

He turned on the translator. "Uh, hello . . . greetings." No response. He increased the volume. "Greetings from the United Federation of Planets." The circle around them widened; the crowd noise got louder.

"I am Captain James T. Kirk, of the starship . . ."

A few of the aliens closest to them broke and ran —then, suddenly, as if a signal had been given, the whole square dissolved into pandemonium. Creatures running, gliding, screaming; fleeing in every direction away from the humans. In twenty seconds, Kirk and his men were standing in the middle of a deserted square.

"I can tell," McCoy drawled, "that this is the beginning of what is to be a long and fruitful relationship."

Kirk chewed his lower lip, thoughtful. "Well, I guess I can understand their panic. They probably haven't seen anything new in three thousand years." He stepped over to the nearest open stall, three tiers of low tables displaying exotic vegetables and fruits, and picked up a squarish purple thing. Sniffed it, wrinkled his nose, set it back. "But why no response until I used the translator? I didn't say anything particularly unfriendly. Nothing confusing . . . did I?"

"It's hard to say," Larousse said. "Some of the words might have been unfamiliar—'Federation of Planets' might not mean anything to them. But surely they know what a starship is. . . . It probably wasn't the words. We'll have to wait until we can get one to talk to us; back-translate to see whether our meaning is clear."

"Come to think of it," McCoy said, "their behavior might not be so odd. You can stand over an ant-hill all day, and the ants will work around you, more or less ignore you. Poke the hill with a stick and they all go wild, all at once."

"You think they might be members of a group mind, then? A hive consciousness?"

Bones shrugged. "It wouldn't be the first."*

"What should we do, sir?" Lieutenant Wilson said, his eyes scanning the buildings that surrounded them. "We're pretty exposed." A few dozen of the creatures sat suspended in the webs overlooking them, watching. The others had evidently disappeared into or behind buildings.

"Are your phasers set on 'stun'?"

"Yes, sir."

"All right. We'll just wait." Kirk was himself searching anxiously from window to window. Looking for what? White flag? Gun barrel? "I'd rather beam back up than use force, of course, if it comes to that."

"Of course."

---

*The Tholians, for instance; described in "The Tholian Web" in *Star Trek 5* (Bantam Books, New York, 1972), adapted by James Blish from the original *Star Trek* script by Judy Burns and Chet Richards.

The silence was oppressive, frightening. "Larousse, they were certainly talking to each other. What use would a group mind have of language?"

Larousse answered quickly, aware of the need to fill the silence. "Depends on the degree of integration. Your own brain and nervous system comprise a group mind, in a sense, if you consider all the cells as individuals. Certainly they have no need of a language. At the other extreme, human civilization is a kind of slow-acting group mind, integrated mainly through language."

"Semantics," McCoy said. "What about *real* group minds, like termites—they can't use language, can they?"

"That's a common fallacy. Termites don't operate under a group consciousness. They appear to cooperate, but that's only because of a simple set of instinctive responses."

"Might be the same thing, on a small scale."

"No." They were arguing without looking at each other. "There's no overriding guidance, no integration. They push balls of dirt around at random. When two come together, they put a third on top; instinctive response. Then another pile next to it, and so forth. Eventually they'll build a cathedral. To instinct. What was that?"

"Steps," Wilson whispered. He put his hand on the phaser at his belt. "Marching in step."

Kirk flipped open his communicator. "Kirk to *Enterprise,* Scotty, we may have a bit of trouble here. Be prepared to beam us up instantly—when Lieutenant Wilson says 'go.' "

"Aye, sir."

Wilson took the hint; he let go of the phaser and held his communicator ready.

A group of about twenty aliens marched around a corner and into the square. "One thing there's no mistaking," McCoy said, "no matter what planet, what culture . . . police."

All but one of them were armed—some with quarterstaffs, some with coils of rope. The unarmed one, who led the procession, wore three blue ribbons around his neck. The others all wore red-orange-green ones. The leader said something and they stopped marching, spread quickly into a wide semicircle, and began to advance on the men.

"Wait!" Kirk said, and a greatly amplified alien syllable echoed around the square. The police paused, glanced at their leader, and kept coming.

When they were about ten meters away, Kirk said, "Better pull us out."

"Go!" Wilson said.

Nothing happened.

"Scotty!" Kirk said. "Beam us up!"

"Disna' work—energize!" They could hear the warbling of the transporter in the background. "Again! Captain—"

Suddenly the creatures were on them, gliding in low, swinging staffs at their legs, throwing loops of rope. Moore had just enough time to draw his phaser, but it was knocked away before he could fire. Wilson wrenched a staff away from one of them and managed to stay on his feet for a few seconds, returning blows, but like all the others he was clumsy in the low gravity, and he soon joined them on the ground, hopelessly tangled up.

The police fell back in a ragged line—two of them holding their heads as a result of Wilson's handiwork —and the one with three blue ribbons stepped forward and began talking.

It was a mellifluous, lisping language, rising and falling in a pleasant sing-song. Of course it made no more sense than the chirping of a wild bird.

Kirk, whose arms were bound, made pointing motions with his head, toward the translator. It had been knocked out of his hand, and had bounced for several meters along the hard ground. "Hope that thing still works," he said.

McCoy moaned. "It might. It's made of stronger stuff than we are."

Finally the alien appeared to understand. He retrieved the translator, studied it for a moment, and spoke into it. "You need this machine to talk and hear?"

"Yes," Kirk said. "You can understand me now, can't you?"

"Of course. You are speaking the language of magicians, as I have been. It's obvious that you *are* magicians, though I must admit I didn't know that no-caste ones existed. Is that why you don't have wings?"

Kirk hesitated, then plunged ahead. "I don't know what you mean by 'magicians.' I am Captain James T. Kirk of the starship *Enterprise,* and these other—"

"What is this word 'croblentz'?"

" 'Croblentz'?"

"Oh, my God," Larousse said.

"The croblentz enterprise. What is this?"

"They don't have a word for it," Larousse said. "They don't know they're inside a starship."

"Oh, boy."

"If this is a riddle," the alien said, "I don't understand the gain of it."

"Listen," Larousse said, "we came from outside your world. Do you understand?"

After a long pause: "I think I understand. Either you are crazy or you want me to think you are."

"No," Kirk said. "Try to understand. We really are . . . we don't look at all like you, do we?"

"So?"

"We appeared out of nowhere," McCoy said. "Doesn't that strike you as peculiar?"

The alien made an oddly human gesture, spreading his wings slightly in a shrug. "Magicians are always doing things like that."

"I think we'd better arrange to meet a magician," McCoy said to Kirk.

"I'm sure you will, of course," the alien said. "You couldn't be condemned by a ven–Chatalia judge."

"Condemned!" Wilson struggled to a sitting position. "What did we do, to make you attack us like that? All we want is to talk with you."

"Maybe you really are crazy."

"Let me put it as simply as possible," Kirk said. "We live inside a world that is like yours, but smaller. We saw that you were in trouble and came to help."

"More riddles. Theology. Where is this world of yours? Under the ground?"

"In a sense."

"If you dug through in the right place," Larousse said, "you could see it, riding alongside."

He looked at Larousse for a long time, then turned away. "Guards—help these creatures to their feet."

"You *could!*" Larousse insisted.

"I think you said the wrong thing," McCoy said.

"I'm neither a fool nor a blasphemer," the alien said, loudly. "Don't try to trick me." The guards pulled the humans roughly to their feet—they were surprisingly strong—and retied their bonds, so they were hobbled but could walk.

Calming, Larousse said, "I really don't understand. Pretend I'm a newborn babe. Explain why I can't dig through to the outside."

"All right, in case this is some strange magician's test. If you dig down far enough you hit Bottom. There is no 'outside'; Bottom is everywhere. Maybe not at Below. I think you'll find out."

Kirk's communicator was beeping, but he didn't try to talk the alien into untying him. " 'Bottom' must be the metal skin Spock was—"

"Skin?" the alien said. "Metal? What metal is it that nothing can mark or dent? It's the world's end, that's all." They started walking.

"Where are you taking us?"

"To the House of Education and Justice." The translator did a pretty good job on euphemisms. "You'll be interviewed there, interrogated, and wait for the next magician, I suppose."

It looked as if the city was getting back to normal; the square filled up as they were marched out. Curious aliens watched them from above, hanging on to cables by hand or foot. There were very few pedestrians on the ground level; mostly freight traffic. There were wheeled vehicles that whined softly and left a tang of ozone behind, and pedal-powered carts like jinrikishas, and even a few draft animals that resembled small oxen. These were always led by the human-sized aliens.

"Why are some of you so much bigger than the rest?" Larousse said. Into the subsequent silence he added, "Pretend I'm a newborn infant again."

"Would you *stop* speaking gibberish! I would think it beneath a magician's station."

"You'll just have to get used to it," Kirk said. "We aren't magicians and *we did come from outside.*"

"All right, blaspheme. You won't catch me in it, though." They all huddled up against a wall while a wide creaking cart lumbered through, heaped full of pungent flowers.

"Pretending you are new . . . well, maybe you are. I've never seen a new one, let alone a new magician. You certainly haven't grown any hair to speak of." The cart was making too much noise; he stopped talking until it was by. "The tall ones are lan-Chatalia who live in the country. I am a ven-Chatalia, because I live in the city. Or maybe I live in the city because I am *ven.* You magicians live in the center lands, over Below, and are ela-Chatalia."

"You mean magicians look like us?" McCoy said.

"Oh, are you a new one, too?" They started walking again. "The masters of life can take any form, of course. Normally they look like lan-Chatalia, only a little bigger. Different faces. Better wings."

He looked at them carefully. "I would like to know why they made you without wings. There must be some purpose. It seems cruel, to my ignorance."

"I'll have to speak to Mother about that," McCoy muttered.

In less than a kilometer they came to a tall building and entered through what appeared to be an open portal, though their Chatalia used several rods on it that appeared to be keys (which he produced from a natural pocket at his waist).

They were joined by another Chatalia, who was evidently a jailer, and were herded into a lift that looked remarkably like an old-fashioned freight elevator, buttons and all. They went to the top floor.

At the end of a dark corridor was another doorless door, which the jailer unlocked. Inside, there were several low pads, too small to sleep on, a three-legged table, and an odd-looking toilet (just a depression in the floor with a drain and a dripping water hose) and an open bay window that gaped over a hundred meters of empty space and cables.

While they were being untied, Kirk asked, "What keeps us from climbing out of the window and escaping?"

The jailer—he had the same three ribbons as the guards, plus a fourth black one—said something to one of the guards, who said something to the blue-ribboned one.

"Don't make things worse for yourselves," he said. "Direct your games toward me or other nocastes."

"The extra ribbon must be rank," Wilson said. "Is that right?"

"I am losing patience. Wait—guards!" He set down the translator and said something to them. While the humans' hands were still tied, he removed the phasers and other equipment from their belts.

"Leave us a communicator," Kirk said, when the Chatalia picked up the translator again.

"Another nonsense word. Which of those is a 'repabclo'?" He pointed at the pile of equipment. "Why do you need it?"

"So we can stay in touch with the outside."

He said something to a guard, who talked to the jailer and returned the message.

"You do have some property right, even though you are mad. You may keep anything that is not a weapon." He gathered up the phasers. "From the way you used these, they must be weapons, correct?"

"Yes," Kirk said, "and they are very dangerous. You mustn't allow anyone to . . . experiment with them."

Again the shrug. "They will be held for the next magician. These other things—will you bond that they are not weapons?" There were two tricorders, medical and scientific; five communicators, and McCoy's medikit.

"You have my word."

"Very well. Know that if you try to escape, or harm anyone, every one of you will be killed, regardless of caste or family. This is within the law, even for magicians."

"We understand."

"You will be sent for." He followed the jailer out; the guards followed him. They locked the invisible door.

After the elevator sighed away, Kirk stepped over to the door opening and tried to thrust his hand through it. Something stopped him.

"That's strange." He pushed again. "It's something like a pressor field, but not . . ." He put all his weight behind one finger. "Ouch!" He jerked his hand back and the fingertip was bright with blood.

"Let me see that." McCoy wiped the blood off and peered at the wound in the dim light; led Kirk to the window and studied it more closely.

"Looks like crosshatching, tiny squares. Healed already." He poked his own finger at the window, and it was stopped the same way. Pushed hard, and it came back with a drop of blood. He wiped it off and peered at it. "A screen."

"Energy screen?" Wilson asked.

"No, like a window screen. But made of metal, not plastic. Impossibly thin wire."

"Acts like knife blades," Wilson mused. To Larousse: "Lieutenant, won't that sciences tricorder tell you what it's made of?"

"Should." He picked it up and brought it over to the window. "Haven't really used one since Academy —not much use to a linguist."

Kirk was still squinting at his finger. "Just activate the sensor array, channel B, and select the chemistry disc. Set the range on zero and touch it to the screen."

Larousse gave the captain a wry look and did it. "Flashes red. 'Sensor malfunction,' it says. Isn't there an override?"

"Here." Kirk twisted a knob. "Try again."

The video display flashed a confused jumble of letters and numbers—there was no compound or element recorded in its memory that matched the properties of the screen—but one line remained stable:

"ATOMIC (MOLECULAR) WEIGHT 1132.-4963."

It must be the same stuff that surrounds the ship," Larousse said. "The Bottom."

McCoy was staring out the window. "They use draft animals and have metals beyond our science. Live in a starship and think it's the whole universe. I think we'd better call Spock."

"Think he'll make sense out of it?" Wilson said.

"*Vulcan* sense, maybe. Actually, I just want a chance to confuse him."

Captain's Log, Stardate 7504.5

This is being recorded by Science Officer Spock, temporarily in command.

Captain Kirk and his confrontation team are stranded aboard the starship; the transporter only works one-way and cannot return objects from inside the vessel. Several theories have been advanced to explain this phenomenon. The most likely seems to be that the outer surface of the vessel's metal skin (which is invisible, under some eighty meters of rock) is perfectly smooth optically, to within a fraction of the wave length of an electron. How this could be done, we have no clue. But the end result is that the transporter cannot maintain a standing wave guide (the convex surface reflecting its energy divergently); thus, it can deliver anything to within the vessel, but cannot effect an exchange of information (and therefore material objects) from the inside out.

If this theory is correct, we need only breach the structure, opening a small hole anywhere on its surface, for the transporter to work. We are postponing this action, which could be construed as aggression and might possibly harm the vessel's inhabitants.

I have established a rotating shift of security personnel to stand by in the transporter room. They will beam down at the first sign of physical danger. Captain Kirk and his men are currently detained in a prison cell, awaiting interrogation.

A guard keyed open the invisible door and set down a tray with five bowls, then withdrew hastily.

Ensign Moore picked one up and cautiously

sniffed it. He made a face. "Wasn't very hungry, any-how."

"Well, we don't need it," McCoy said, crossing over with the medical tricorder. "They can beam us down field rations. I'm curious, though."

He selected the nutrition disc and put a drop of the stuff by the sensor array. "Wouldn't kill you," he said, "not unless you ate it for a week or so. Arsenic trace." They called up for lunch.

While they were eating the field rations, the guard came back and took their full bowls. He made a wing-rustling shrug and said something in a guttural voice. Moore answered "wooga-wooga," mimicking.

"Seriously," Larousse said, "it sounded like the one who was talking to us spoke a completely different language than the guards use. It was more delicate sounding, and had that peculiar whistle." He demon-strated, a half-musical hiss through the teeth.

"How could that be?" Kirk said, carefully un-zipping a package of peach slices. "Even if they started out with different languages, you'd think that in three thousand years they would've settled down to one."

"There could be some tradition at work, different languages for different activities. Church services were given in Latin for centuries, even though most of the churchgoers couldn't understand a word of it."

"Or different social classes," Wilson said. "The one with the rank-ribbon we weren't supposed to talk to."

Larousse nodded. "That happened on Earth, too. Before the first Russian Revolution, the aristocracy spoke French."

"I'd bet money that it's less complicated," McCoy said. "An alien who listened to a man and a woman speaking English might think they were speaking two different languages—high-pitched gibberish as opposed to low-pitched nonsense. It's probably just individual differences in vocal anatomy."

"I don't think so," Larousse said. "That wouldn't fool a linguist."

Wilson's communicator beeped. He flipped it open and his opposite number up in the transporter room said, "Situation report, sir." They called every twenty minutes, precisely.

"Sit-rep negative." He snapped it shut and smiled. "What language would you call that?"

"Security-ese," McCoy said. "You guys remind me of . . ."

Six guards trooped in through the doorway. They were more impressively armed than before, carrying spears and a sort of slingshot device that propelled needle-sharp arrows. They were followed by the blue-ribboned Chatalia, carrying the translator. "You will come with me now."

They followed him silently. In the elevator he looked at the translator and said to no one in particular, "I have experimented with this machine. It is very dangerous—why was it invented?"

"So that people can talk with other people . . . without knowing their languages," Kirk said.

"That is obvious. But why?"

Kirk looked at Larousse questioningly. The linguist also was puzzled. "I guess we don't really understand your question," he said.

The door opened. "There will be other questions." There was no corridor here; they stepped out into a large room.

All four walls were covered with a continuous

mosaic of polished ceramic tiles, with glittering crystals, maybe jewels, inset here and there. The bright colors clashed in jarring combinations that made no sense to the human eye. The ceiling glowed with a uniform phosphorescence.

Some thirty Chatalia stared at them from three tiers of perches. They sat with feet curled around the perch, wings drooping behind, like furry birds of prey. At the rear of the room, a single one perched above the rest.

A pattern emerged from the confusion: they were arranged by ribbons. All of them had four ribbons, three of which were red-orange-green. In the row closest to them, the fourth ribbon was black. In the tier behind those, it was red. The last tier had silver. The lone Chatalia perched above wore red, orange, green, and gold.

He spoke: "The magicians—" Translator snapped off.

"Hey!" McCoy said. "Don't we get to hear . . ."

The alien looked at him expressionlessly, and turned his back.

"Wonder if it's a court," Wilson muttered.

"I suppose we'll find out," Kirk said. "Some sort of ritual, anyhow."

The last tier was listening attentively to the obvious leader, their heads craned around at an impossible angle. All the others were looking straight ahead, except for the ones they had come in with, who stared at the floor.

When he stopped speaking, the middle (red-ribboned) tier turned around and listened to one of the silver-ribboned ones. He finished, and a red-ribboned spokesman addressed the black-ribboned ones.

"It sounds as if they're all saying the same thing," Larousse said.

"It's a religious ceremony," McCoy said. "We're all going to be sacrificed."

"Come on, Bones," Kirk said. "Try to be serious."

"Who's joking?"

In the final stage of the ritual, the middle Chatalia in the closest row addressed the group that stood on the floor. The translator turned to them and clicked on the machine.

"The chief of police would like to know whether you are ready to begin telling the truth."

"Is that all he said?" Kirk asked.

"All you need to hear."

"Then this is all he needs to hear." Kirk stepped forward to the machine and raised his voice: "We *are* telling the truth." He straightened abruptly, the points of two spears prodding his back.

The Chatalia on the tiers were staring at the floor, ceiling, walls—anywhere but at Kirk.

"Do you want to die?" the blue-ribboned one said, then clicked off the translator and spoke rapidly to the first tier. The guards released Kirk.

When he finished, one of the black-ribboned ones turned to face the next row, and the relaying process was repeated, in reverse.

"How can they ever get anything done?" McCoy said.

"They can't do this all the time," Larousse said. "It must have some ritual significance."

A minute or so later, the chief's reply filtered back.

"The chief reminds you that he is an enforcer of proper behavior, not a philosopher. Since you are magicians, he will temporarily suspend judgment, and wait for one of your own family to assess your sick behavior."

"I think it's time to start lying, Jim," McCoy whispered.

"I think you're right." He addressed the one holding the translator. "You don't seem to fear us much. Why? You know what we can do to you—or you *think* you know."

"Then you admit to being no-caste magicians."

"We admit nothing. We don't have to answer to you. But *you* will answer for much, if we're harmed."

"We've done you no harm." He moved his hands in a complicated pattern, then turned and said something to the gallery.

" 'A committee,' " Bones quoted, " 'is an organism with many heads and no brain.' This is beginning to look less and less alien."

After the procession of query and response:

"The chief will not countenance threats. He reminds you that caste takes precedence over family."

"But we don't *have* any caste."

"Exactly. So you understand, the chief may imprison you or even put you to death, unless a first-caste magician forbids it."

"He wouldn't dare kill us," Kirk said, mildly— and then remembered that his tone of voice didn't necessarily mean anything. "Don't you think there would be reprisals?"

"That's not for me to—"

"Has *any* magician ever been put to death?" Groping.

"This is outside my family's concern. Besides, you first claimed that you weren't magicians. Now you claim that family's protection."

"Wait," McCoy said. "I can make this more clear. Do you know what the word 'amnesia' means?"

"Of course."

He took a deep breath. "Now. Could we be any family other than magician? The way we look?"

"I don't think so," he admitted, "unless you are machines the magicians made for some purpose."

"I'll even admit that possibility," McCoy said slowly. "But look. As far as we know, we did come from outside—that may be blasphemy, but it *is* the truth, as we know it. We don't know anything at all about families, castes . . . isn't it possible that we are magicians with amnesia?"

After a long silence, the alien replied. "And delusions."

"So can we ask that you orient us a little, so we can at least understand what you're talking about?"

"I'll see." He passed the question up, and the answer came back. "You may, but be brief."

"Larousse, you'd better do this," McCoy said.

"All right. Explain families—how many are there, what are they?"

"There are 256 families, some of which have no members. I belong to the interpreter family. Everyone else in this room is a behavior enforcer. Except yourselves: your lack of adornment identifies you as magicians."

"How can a family have no members?"

"If its function ceases, members are not replaced when they die. Within my own memory the last of the *alfgan* herders died. The *alfgan*, of course, had stopped breeding long before."

"The ribbons identify your family?"

"Family and caste."

"And what you do for a living is determined by the family you're born into?"

Pause. "I don't understand."

"For instance, could you be a behavior enforcer, if you wanted to? Could they be interpreters?"

"Of course not. They aren't made—"

Wilson's communicator beeped. He slowly took it off his belt and looked at the captain.

"Report negative," Kirk said.

He flipped it open and the metallic voice said, "Situation report, sir."

"Sit-rep negative," he replied.

The interpreter made a hand-signal and one of the guards enforced Wilson's behavior by laying the point of a spear on his chest.

"Who are you talking about, 'negative first-caste administrator'?"

"What?"

Larousse tried not to smile. "The machine doesn't work perfectly. It doesn't know the word 'sit-rep,' so it translated the one that was closest—'satrap,' which is a kind of first-caste administrator."

"Why was he talking to the little machine?"

"It's in contact with our people outside. Part of our delusion," he added hastily. "They call us every twenty minutes, to make sure we're in no danger. If we didn't answer, they would send help."

"That's remarkable," the interpreter said, then turned around and delivered a speech. Wilson looked a little uncomfortable while they waited for an answer.

The alien gave his guard a sign and withdrew, slowly.

"The judge's opinion is that his interrogation is

becoming unsafe. Our magician comes tomorrow; we will suspend the matter until then."

"Will you continue to answer questions?" Larousse said.

"In your cell?" The alien half-turned as if to ask permission of the judge, then said, "Of course . . . if you will answer some as well."

4

Maintaining standby alert.

Thanks to adroit questioning by Captain Kirk and his team, we have a fairly complete picture of Chatalian society.

Every individual belongs to a family and has a caste level assigned to him. He may only speak to members of his own caste, or those immediately above or below him. Isolation of the individual is further intensified by the fact that each family has its own language (technically, some of these are dialects, rather than separate languages). Thus, a second-class carpenter might be allowed to speak to a second-class baker, but they wouldn't be able to understand one another.

Therefore one of the largest families is the interpreter family. Almost every transaction beyond the level of simple barter requires one of these Chatalla.

The magicians, who are relatively few in number, are exempt from the caste restriction, and may speak to anyone, although they also require interpreters. They evidently have only two castes, first and second, and first-caste individuals are rarely seen. They live in a separate area, an island which resides at the "north" (normally forward) pole of the sphere. Their main function seems to be reproduction, which the informant claims is done by magic.

The population is strictly controlled. When an individual dies, a replacement is delivered, after a time lag of about two years.

The word "child" does not translate. According to the informant, fully grown individuals are delivered by the magicians to the lan-Chatalia, who live in the rural areas surrounding the city. There they are trained, and eventually delivered to their families.

"That's about the craziest social setup I've ever heard of," Uhura said. The Bridge was idle; not much to do until Kirk and his team woke up below.

"It is unorthodox," Spock said, "but there is an admirable logic to it."

"Logic?" Sulu was incredulous. "I can't imagine a less efficient way of running things."

"In this context, efficiency was evidently subordinated to stability—which is sound reasoning, when you consider that a population of a million was to be preserved for hundreds of generations, on a space the size of a small island."

"So you think the original Chatalia were different," Uhura said. "They set up this society as a sort of a huge space ship crew—"

"And then made them forget they were on a space ship?" Sulu said.

"It seems necessarily so," Spock said. "One would conjecture that the actual working crew of the ship is the magician family, of course. The others are kept in ignorance because it would be psychologically painful for them to know they were on a trip they could never live to complete."

"Ignorance is bliss," Sulu said.

"An odd notion." The communicator chimed and Spock answered. "Spock here."

"Mr. Spock, this is Ensign Berry, in Cartography." Her voice was harsh with excitement. "We've found the wreckage of a ship on the planetoid's surface."

They had been mapping the surface in hopes of finding a portal into the planetoid. "What sort of a ship? Please give us a picture."

"It's nothing currently in use." A picture appeared on the main viewscreen, obscured by wavering streaks and sparks from the magnetic field's interference. "By its general lines, it looks Klingon."

"It does indeed. A primitive design, though. Computer."

"Working," the machine said.

"The ship pictured on the bridge viewing screen. Do you have any record of a ship similar in design—specifically, a Klingon vessel?"

"There is no such record. Captured Klingon data do not reveal designs of vessels more than 114 years old. The vessel pictured bears a superficial resemblance to a long-range cruiser of that period, which it could predate by several centuries, if our understanding of Klingon history is accurate."

"Very well. Ensign Berry, did you get any bio-sensor reading for the vessel?"

"Negative, sir. There's too much interference; the signal-to-noise ratio is too small from this range."

"Thank you, Ensign; that will be all for now. . . . Mr. Sulu. Make yourself a detail of three security men and an ethnologist, whoever it is who has the most knowledge of Klingon society. I believe that would be Lieutenant Sydny. And have Mr. Scott give you someone with a background in antique spacecraft—someone besides himself. Draw space suits and beam down into the vessel."

"Aye, sir!" Sulu was halfway to the turbolift.

"And Mr. Sulu."

"Sir?"

"Use utmost caution. Nothing is as it seems."

"Aye, sir." He slipped quickly through the doors.

Spock manipulated the viewer controls to get the highest magnification. "Very curious. I wonder what could have caused that sort of damage." The ship evidently hadn't been holed, but it was bent out of shape; crumpled inward, as if a large hand had closed over it.

"Tractor beams?" Uhura offered.

"Possibly . . . but it would seem that in that case the compression would be more uniform. There's something bothersome . . . of course! It shouldn't be there at all."

"What do you mean, sir?"

He thumbed the intercom control. "Mr. Sulu. Please contact the Bridge." A moment later, Sulu answered.

"Don't transport directly into the ship, not at first. There is an anomaly here. There is no reason for the wreck to remain on the surface. The planetoid is spinning and decelerating, and certainly isn't massive enough to provide sufficient gravity. The wreck should have spun away as soon as it made contact.

"So your first order of business is to find out what

keeps it on the surface. Take the security men and transport alongside. After we have a satisfactory explanation, you can go inside the craft."

"Could it be magnetism?" Uhura said.

"I wouldn't rule anything out, not yet. But I think the force would be insufficient, even if the wreck were made of iron."

"A trap, maybe."

"It seems unlikely." He turned to Chekov, who was manning the weapons station. "Mr. Chekov. If anything happens to Mr. Sulu, be prepared to react with force."

"Aye, sir."

"At my command, fire Phaser Bank One on the narrowest possible setting; pick a target anywhere on the planetoid except the drive system or magnetic field generator. We would like to have the option of repairing the damage."

To Uhura: "Lieutenant, if I am forced to initiate this action, I want the confrontation team beamed up as soon as the planetoid is breached. Will you arrange that?"

"Yes, Mr. Spock." She called up Scotty and linked the transporter room to her board.

Spock stared impassively at the image on the screen.

Sulu hadn't worn a space suit in over two years. It was a claustrophobic feeling, made even stranger by the necessity of equipping the suits with tractor gloves and boots (so the planetoid's rotation wouldn't fling them off). The four of them stepped up to the transporter dias and Sulu gave Scott a "thumbs-up" signal.

The planetoid's surface resembled the surface of the Moon, if you could sweep the Moon free of dust and loose rock. The horizon was less than a kilometer away; stars rose too rapidly over the edge. And the stars were too bright, lurid, because in the absence of any other light their suits automatically amplified star-light to make the surroundings visible.

The Klingon ship lay upside-down, to their right. They moved toward it, walking as if through thick syrup, the tractor boots holding them down.

"So far, no cables or any other support equipment," Sulu said. He had a sciences tricorder on a strap over his shoulder; because of the rotation, it stood out straight over his head.

Suddenly, the man walking next to him stumbled. He shouted "Help!" Sulu grabbed for him but missed. He drifted off into space, slowly at first, but with accelerating speed.*

"Mr. Scott—Jakobs slipped and is dropping away from us. Can you pick him up and beam him back to us?" Scotty said he would. "Everybody hold your places until Jakobs returns."

Sulu hauled the tricorder in and pointed its sensors toward the Klingon vessel. "The hull of the vessel is mostly aluminum and magnesium," he reported to Spock. "I guess that rules out magnetism." He switched to another setting. "The temperature is twelve degrees, same as the planetoid."

"Look at this, Mr. Sulu." One of the security men was kneeling, hand out. "This must be what tripped Jakobs."

---

*This is the way it appears to Sulu and the other two security men, but if you think about it you can see that the crewman was actually just flung off in a straight line, with constant velocity (the way a piece of rubber, dislodged, might fly off a spinning tire). Sulu is dropping away from *him*, since his boots keep him fastened to the planetoid's surface.

Sulu looked, but didn't see anything. He put his hand out and felt resistance. "Force field?"

Jakobs returned and explained what had happened: "I was walking toward the ship and tripped over something invisible, about here." It was the same thing; feeling their way along, they could tell that it was continuous for about a hundred meters, and followed roughly the contour of the vessel. It probably surrounded it completely.

The tricorder, though, detected no field other than the magnetic one associated with the Bussard ramjet.

Spock deduced what it was: "Check for the presence of metal." When Sulu did that, the video display gave out an alphabet-soup confusion of letters and numbers, with one line making sense: "ATOMIC (MOLECULAR) WEIGHT 1132.4963." The vessel was evidently being held inside a net of the same material that made up the doors and windows of the House of Education and Justice, inside.

They tried to melt it. The concentrated energy from four phasers produced a bubbling puddle of white-hot rock underneath the net, but the material itself was not affected.

Spock called them back, and in the transporter room the other two joined them.

Lieutenant Sydny was a young dark woman of arresting beauty: she did not like space suits. But until she put the helmet on, she could still reduce Sulu to jelly with a look.

"I don't suppose we will find any Klingons on board."

"Uh, no, no," Sulu said, staring at the floor. "The, uh, ambient temperature, you know . . ."

"The ship is too cold."

"Yes, um, exactly."

"It should be interesting, though."

"All richt," Scotty said, standing by the controls console. "She came back." Not wanting to make the same mistake twice, they had sent a passive probe into the Klingon vessel and brought it back. Evidently the net didn't have the same blocking effect on the transporter that the convex surface below did.

They put their helmets on and took their places. "Turn on your suit lights," Sulu said. They did, and Scotty bleeped them away.

Inside the Klingon vessel, the deck was covered with a centimeter-thick layer of bluish frost: frozen air. As they picked their way down a dark corridor, wisps of vapor swirled around them, the stuff being melted and evaporated by the heat from their boot soles. Twice they came to sealed doors; Sulu and Jakobs burned them open easily. The last one opened on the control room.

One Klingon had evidently survived to the very end. He was in a space suit similar in design to their own. Just before his death he had removed the helmet. His mouth and eyes were full of ice, his skin was frozen leather. The others, eleven of them, looked less pretty; they had evidently committed suicide together, and the cold preserved them in an advanced state of decomposition.

"Lieutenant Sydney," Sulu said.

She didn't respond immediately. "Yes, Mr. Sulu."

"Can you decipher the control board well enough to find the ship's log?"

"I don't know." She moved slowly past the frozen stare of the seated Klingon, and played her suit light over the control console.

"The lettering is strange, but the language seems about the same as modern Klingon. Here. They don't have a log, as such, but there is a computer entry mode that translates as 'lessons'—or 'teaching pains,' literally. I wouldn't know how to trace the wiring down, though, and separate the memory."

"I might be able to figure that out," said Ensign Masters, the antique-spacecraft expert Scott had recommended. "All right if I cut into it?"

"Go ahead," Sulu said.

It took most of an hour, working carefully with a microphaser. During that time, the three security men and Sydny checked out the rest of the vessel, taking pictures and measurements to pass on to Star Fleet Command. They found no other Klingon bodies, though the dormitory space indicated the normal crew was 113.

They beamed back up, and turned the "lessons" log over to the *Enterprise*'s computer.

PARTIAL TRANSCRIPT OF KLINGON LOG

(Note: some data erased by leakage of magnetic field through shielding. No dates were preserved, but the following excerpts are in chronological order, assuming the Klingon system recorded from the base of the crystal toward its apex.)

Suddenly our situation is quite desperate. None of the soldiers has been able to communicate from inside the planetoid, and attempts to call them back only result in overheating of the transport crystal.

In our extremity we have condescended to attempt communication with (the worms). They do not respond on any channel. We have sent fifty more soldiers down.

(Next day) Mortifying failure! I have given two fingers to the altar and still cannot find peace. My subcaptain has offered his head, good soldier. I cannot bear to record.

(Much later) Only we priests are left.

It grows colder.

In recording failure I risk blasphemy. I command all (not translatable) curses upon the putrid souls of any foreign curs who may see this, and pray (bitter) deliverance for future brothers who might learn from it.

To purify this act, I call for the heads of all surviving priests, now.

It is done. I live to watch them rot, my own most terrible penance. The facts are as follows.

We have been unable to contact the Father Ship because of the heathens' magnetic field. Over a period of (several days) we transported both companies of soldiers into the planetoid. Only then would the captain undertake the embarrassment of asking for reinforcements.

When we tried to drop back from the planetoid to call the Father Ship, we found we had been entrapped by a gauze of some apparently indestructible material. Attempting to pull free only resulted in deforming the ship, almost crushing it.

The heathens drew us in like (a fish on a line). The netting somehow drained power from the ship; when we touched the surface of the planetoid we tried to abandon the vessel, wanting to die fighting, but there was no longer enough power to transport us. Similarly, the captain attempted to explode the ship by warp overload, and nothing happened.

The captain and remaining crew, all except the priests, delivered themselves to space. We remained, to savor the terrible pain of defeat.

As (the worms) sucked the heat from our ship, we have all moved into the control room. It should stay warm here long enough for my brothers' heads to mortify, which is as it must be.

If any future brothers find this record, heed

me! This world is a bane! Do not attempt conquest—destroy it!

Turn our rot to ashes. Send us home to hell.

"A remarkable document," Spock said. "They
don't appear to have changed much over the centuries."

"I wonder how far they were from the planetoid,
when they got roped in," Chekov said.

Spock nodded. "A good point. We should stand
off as far as we can without breaking contact with the
confrontation team."

"I'm not sure about the transporter range under
these conditions," Uhura said, "but the neutrino communicators are definitely limited, by inverse-square
attenuation and weak-interaction noise. Maybe a thousand kilometers, probably less."

"What is the current separation, Mr. Sulu?"

"Between centers of mass, 231.59 kilometers;
from transporter to mean surface, 122.99 kilometers."

"Take us out to seven hundred, between centers
of mass."

"Aye, sir." His fingers danced over the console. He
paused, frowned, pushed the same button several times,
hard.

Resigned: "They've got us, sir."

Kirk and his men woke up soon after the Klingon wreck had been spotted; they listened in during the first hour or so of exploration, until the interpreter came back.

Their interpreter, whose name was W'Chaal, had grown more friendly the night before, as they exchanged questions and answers. He didn't actually *believe* their outrageous tale, but he was willing to concede that it was an honest delusion. When they started to talk about this business of a vessel wrecked "outside," though, his reply was gently firm:

"Please. For the sake of argument, I have accepted that black is white. Now you want me to believe that hot is cold. What next? Low is high? *Ven* is *ela?*"

"I suppose you're right," Kirk said, laughing. "Moore, will you persist in the delusion, and stay in contact?"

"Yes, sir."

"When do we get to meet this magician?" McCoy asked W'Chaal.

"He's downstairs now," W'Chaal said. "There are

certain formalities to be gone through, and he may have some business to conduct."

"What should we expect?" Kirk said. "Do you know this particular magician?"

"I have spoken to him. He is much like any magician." After Kirk's silence, he continued. "Reserved, cold, superior. Very corscious of his power."

"I take it his power over *us* is considerable," Wilson said. "He could have us put to death."

"Sent Below, yes. True death. Death without replacement." He paused, perhaps worried about his association with them, then added hastily, "But surely you have nothing to worry about. He must know all about you."

"I wouldn't bank on it," McCoy said.

"Last night," Larousse said, "you told us—"

"Hold it," Moore said, the communicator to his ear. "There's some trouble here."

Everyone was looking at him when the magician walked through the door.

"Stand, fools," the magician said. More than a head taller than Kirk, he was so different from W'Chaal as to be another species altogether: bulging veined muscles under a bristly stubble of black hair, wings of shiny black leather, head large and more humanlike, but the mouth too wide, grinning fangs. A medieval artist's vision of Satan.

"My God," Larousse said, standing. "He spoke to us in Klingon!"

The *Enterprise* had switched to emergency power conservation mode, normal lighting replaced by dim red safety lights. The turbolift moved slowly, and its doors had to be opened manually.

Spock slid the doors open and stepped out into the engine room. He blinked at the darkness. "Mr. Scott?"

"Over here, sir." The normal lighting of the ship was rather dim to Vulcan eyes; Spock was virtually blind now. He turned on a hand light and its beam found the Chief Engineer. Glak Son stood next to him.

"Any change?"

"No, sir. Whatever is draining power from us is doing it at a Warp Nine rate."

"And the rate increases, the more power we use?"

"That's right." He turned to Glak Sön. "Tell Mr. Spock what you calculated."

"At the present rate, the life support systems will continue to function for 18 days, 4.67 hours." The short, hairy alien was handy to have around, with the computer shut off. "However, if we have to transport everyone to the inside of the planetoid, we must do so within four days, 9.18 hours."

"Even that would only be a stopgap," Spock said. "Eventually, we would have to eat their food. Dr. McCoy found that it contains arsenic."

"I *like* arsenic," Glak Sön said.

"What we must do," Spock said, "is isolate the crew and all necessary supplies in as small an area as possible. Then shut down the life support facilities for the rest of the ship."

"Aye," Scott said. "We can set up the portable transporter in here, and close off the transporter rooms."

"Very well." He paused, then went on, almost talking to himself. "We can move down to the emergency bridge on this deck, and close everything above Deck Six. Move Medical down to the recreation area, and concentrate the crew on decks Eighteen through Twenty. Can the ship be rotated?"

"Rotated, sir?"

There was a slight note of exasperation in Spock's voice. "So that, when we come to rest on the planetoid's surface, we can take advantage of its rotation, and shut down the artificial gravity."

"Yes, Mr. Spock, I believe we can." Scotty's accent had all but vanished.

"Do so. Inform Lieutenant Uhura." Scotty went to the control console. "Can you recompute, Glak Sōn?"

"I would have to look up the exact function for the gravity generator's power drain," he said. "But this should roughly double both periods. About thirty days, or sixteen if we transport into the planetoid."

"Very well. We should have help by then." Uhura had sent a distress call as soon as they realized they were trapped. Static from the magnetic field kept them from hearing any reply.

It may also have scrambled the distress call. No one talked about that possibility.

Spock:

This is most uncomfortable. That such an emergency should occur under my command. But there was no lack of caution on my part. There were no data until we learned of the Klingon ship.

     Posit: Had I initiated a separation from the planetoid immediately upon finding the wrecked vessel, might we have evaded the capture?

     Inadequate data, of course. We might have been trapped soon after approaching the planetoid. Alternatively, it may be that our investigation of the wreck set in motion some automatic defense.

Subjunctive discourse is no substitute for logic. We must accept the problem as a given initial condition, and not concern ourselves as to its cause until more information is available. And then investigate the cause only as a possible avenue to solution—not as a tool for placing or dismissing blame! That is a purely human impulse, and a waste of energy.

Energy: the dilithium crystals, at least, are unaffected. Whatever the planetoid is doing to us, the net effect is a symmetrical draining of the matter and antimatter in our fuel supply. The more power we use, the faster they drain it. Thus:

$$\frac{dE}{dt} = \frac{\delta m}{\delta t}c^2 - \frac{\delta f\,(W, t)}{\delta W} - R(A)t - W,$$

and the only practical course at present is to minimize the last two terms of the equation, power output and radiative transfer.

Sulu suggested, and many other of the human crew must have entertained the idea, that we should attempt to penetrate the planetoid with concentrated phaser fire. Although I did suggest this earlier (if only to allow the confrontation crew to be beamed back), I believe that it would be the wrong course of action at present. The energy drain would be equivalent to many days of life support, and there exists the possibility that the phaser banks would not penetrate beyond the mysterious metal shell. It apparently is an almost perfect conductor of heat.

Besides, we may be at the mercy of the Chatalia for some days, even if the distress signal got through. If it didn't, it may be months before the Federation finds us (in which case we must find a way to make Chatalian food compatible with the metabolisms of the crew; otherwise only Glak Sōn will survive to be rescued.

So we must not antagonize them. Their experience with the Klingons can not have been pleasant; we bear the burden of proving ourselves pacifistic.

"I know some few words of your language," the magician continued.

Larousse had studied Klingon for one semester, twenty years before. "Not-to-be . . . language to ours. Human not Klingon. Use translator." Klingon didn't have a word for "please."

"What the hell is going on here?" McCoy said.

The magician indicated W'Chaal with a look and a flap of the wing: "He doesn't know Klingon."

"No! *Machine* translator!" To W'Chaal: "Give him the translator."

"It's blasphemy. Besides, he speaks your tongue."

"It's *not* our tongue."

"The ship," Kirk said. "Klingons must have gotten inside here."

"Silence," the magician said, which nobody understood. Larousse stepped forward and snatched the translator from W'Chaal. "Listen—"

The magician shouted "Guard!" (in behavior-enforcer language) and one stepped into the doorway. He fired his slingshot device; Larousse instinctively raised his arms to ward off the missile, and was struck in the forearm.

"Ouch!" Larousse jerked his arm and the dart fell to the floor—not a particularly impressive weapon.

Moore looked at Kirk, for an order. He shook his head. "Not yet," he whispered.

"Will you listen just one second?" Larousse said angrily. "You are speaking the language of our enemies. Our *enemies!* We are human, not Klingon."

The magician looked at him impassively, arms folded over huge chest. He didn't say anything.

"What are you talking about?" W'Chaal said plaintively. The magician gave him a slow glance.

Larousse took a deep breath. "From what we've been able to find out, many generations ago a Klingon vessel contacted you, just as—"

"*Quiet!*" The magician turned to W'Chaal. "Have you been listening to this sort of thing?"

"Yes, master. They have many strange delusions."

He considered that for a moment. "We will talk, later. It may be that you will have to be reborn."

"Your will, master."

"Die for hearing the truth," McCoy said. "They ought to get along well with the Klingons."

"Guard," the magician said, "the one in the middle." The dart caught McCoy in the abdomen; he cursed and plucked it out. "Okay, I'll keep my mouth shut."

"No, we did *not* enjoy the presence of you devils, the last time you came. You killed thousands prematurely. The memory of your attack upset all the world, waiting for you to come again. It took many generations to remove that memory from the *ven* and *lan.*"

"We are not Klingons—really!" Larousse insisted. "If you could see one, you could tell how different we are."

"I have seen many twenties of Klingons. The memory was not removed from the *ela*. You are Klingon."

Bones straightened his tunic, having examined the small puncture wound. "Don't you see, Larousse—from their point of view we do look identical. Like two different species of cuttlefish. Magician, do you have medical men, life scientists?"

"You will not direct questions to me."

"W'Chaal? Do you?"

The interpreter looked at the magician, who gave him no sign, one way or the other. "Among the magicians, there are those who practice life arts. Both *ven* and *lan* have families devoted to healing in addition to their main work, which is barbering and massage."

The doctor winced at that. "Well . . . the magician doesn't have to listen to this, but it might interest him. There are basic physiological and anatomical differences between Klingon and human. Surely someone must have examined at least one Klingon."

"Surely," the magician said.

"They have two *livers*."

"Doesn't everybody?" W'Chaal said.

"Humans only have one. Furthermore—"

"We'll count your livers soon enough," the magician said. "As for your physiology, you have just proven that you are Klingon. Otherwise that dart would have made you comatose. Two would kill you. Guard?" He appeared, aiming. "Give the middle one another." This one went for his face; McCoy stopped it with his palm, grunted, withdrew it.

"This is how you were able to take so many lives, before. Your long-range weapons worked, but ours didn't."

"Have you noticed," Kirk said, "that we turned over our weapons to you, voluntarily?"

"I said *you will not question me!*" He pointed at Bones. "You—stop that. What are you doing?"

Bones had turned the tricorders on, holding the point of the dart over its sensors. "Trying to find out what this poison is, to find out whether we will need treatment." He smiled. "Table salt, sodium chloride. No wonder it didn't affect Klingons. Or us."

"You will remain standing, while I address you." Bones stood up, slowly.

"It is you who should be grateful that you surrendered your weapons. If I thought you presented any danger to us, I would have had you killed in this cell. The information I can get from you is not worth anybody's pain or early death."

"On the contrary," Kirk said, "if you will only listen for a—"

"I may have you muzzled. Speak only to answer. Are you the leader?"

"Yes."

"I command the truth: how many of you are coming?"

"That depends on what you do. There may be only the five of us. If you endanger us, there will be more."

"You don't consider yourselves to be in danger?"

"Nothing we can't handle. Peacefully."

He was silent for a moment. "You do act differently. Before, you came simply killing. And most of the prisoners never talked."

"You see, we aren't the same. We aren't Kling-on."

"I prefer to think that it's a trick. At any rate, it will be different this time. We have your weapons from before, and we are in the process of investigating the ones you brought this time."

"You mustn't allow that," Kirk said quickly. "As we told W'Chaal, they are very dangerous. On the wrong setting, they will explode with great force."

"An obvious ruse. We have the most skilled artisans at work—" On cue, a tremendous explosion thundered somewhere below them. Flakes of plaster sifted from the walls and ceiling.

The magician didn't change expression. "Guards-with-spears. Kill all except the leader: that one."

Spock was doing several things at once, an occupation that suited him. The magician had just arrived at the cell below, and he was monitoring the conversation through Moore's communicator. At the same time, he was coordinating the transfer of all command facilities and personnel to the emergency bridge, and moving all other personnel and necessary supplies to the lower decks around the recreation area. Deck Eight was also kept open, both because of the large emergency transporter on that level, and because of the flora and fauna in the small park that made up the entertainment area.

The emergency bridge was crowded. Five security men sat on the deck, around the portable transporter. Sulu, Chekov, and Uhura sat at their stations; an engineering ensign sat in the command chair, running systems checks. Spock stood in the middle.

"Lieutenant Gary," he said to the security officer, "I think it would be better if you and your men would station yourselves at the transporter on Deck Eight. That way you wouldn't have to beam down one at a time, if trouble starts."

"Aye, sir." The men got up, stretching. "I'll detail someone to stand by to beam us down."

"At my order."

"Of course, sir." They trooped out with a subdued clatter of weaponry. The room was suddenly larger.

"Mr. Spock," the engineer said, "there's a redundancy here we could eliminate—"

The explosion was loud even through the communicator's tiny speaker. Spock stepped up on the transporter plate.

"Energize."

Spock materialized within touching distance of the magician, and touch him he did: dispassionately, scientifically, very hard, and on the jaw. The Chatalia fell back into the doorway, knocking over a guard, narrowly missing the point of his spear.

Spock drew his phaser and stunned four guards. He stepped into the corridor beyond, ducked a spear, and stunned another ten. Stepped back. "Are you all right, Captain?"

"So far, so good. We'd better get out of here."

"Agreed. This would be W'Chaal?"

"I am." The interpreter had retreated to the far wall and was doing his damnedest to press his way through it.

"We must ask you to come with us." To Kirk: "A hostage."

"We should take the magician, too. Can you handle him?"

Spock scooped him up and draped him over one shoulder. "Which way?"

They stormed down the corridor to the elevator. The door was closed, though, and there was no call button.

"Must be stairs somewhere," McCoy said. He sprinted toward an open door off to the right. Stopped short, staggered back. "My God."

People with wings don't need stairs. It was a straight drop of a hundred meters, with a skimpy-looking rope ladder dropping down the middle. The rope was about two meters from the edge, a scary distance.

They all looked cautiously down. "I must go last," Spock said. "I am by far the heaviest, with the magician. The rope might break." Five phasers materialized on the floor.

While they were arming themselves, Larousse said, "Hold it. W'Chaal, how do you call the elevator?"

He cocked his head to one side. "An elevator."

"No, not *what* do you call it. *How* do you call it?"

"Elevators don't have ears."

"Listen. If you want to ride the elevator down, how do you make it come?"

"Nobody rides the elevator down. You only ride it up."

"What if you have something heavy? You just drop it down the shaft?"

"Of course not. You leave it by the elevator, glide down, and ride back up."

"Worth a try," Wilson said. "Geronimo." He

jumped into the gaping shaft and snatched the ladder. It swung him around wildly.

Rather than going down stepwise, he bunched the ropes together in both hands, then wrapped them around his ankle, braking with the other foot, and slid down. "I'll try to get the elevator," he called back.

While they watched Wilson descend, Spock called the *Enterprise* and asked that they beam down two two-meter lengths of rope. "I apologize for the inconvenience," he told W'Chaal, "but we must immobilize your arms, to prevent your flying away."

"I understand," he said. "But I can't fly, really. Only fall gently. *He* can fly."

"Interesting." The magician was light for his size, and heavily muscled; he appeared to have at least twice the wingspan of the smaller alien. "For the time being though, I must ask you to submit."

The rope appeared and he tied up both aliens. While he was taking care of the unconscious magician, the faint sounds of some commotion drifted up the shaft.

Moore braced himself to jump. "No, wait," Kirk said. "Wilson can probably take care of it. If he . . . if they overpower him, they'll be waiting for you."

"Staying here, we are virtually invulnerable," Spock added.

"Until they haul out those Klingon weapons," Moore said.

"The weapons are centuries old. Unless they were properly maintained, I doubt that they will function."

The elevator doors opened a minute later, with a visibly shaken Lieutenant Wilson behind them.

"Hard show, sir?" Moore asked, as they got in.

"Not the fighting; I just stunned them all down. But it's a mess down there."

The bottom button took them to some subbasement; W'Chaal told them to punch the third, for the ground floor.

The phaser had evidently exploded near the elevator door. The floor was covered with purple blood. The force of the blast had blown several Chatalians to pieces. W'Chaal fainted dead away.

"This will be difficult to explain," Spock said.

Moore hoisted up the limp interpreter and swung him into a fireman's carry. "Let's get out of here!" He strode toward the door and slammed into the invisible barrier.

"Stand away," Wilson said, adjusting his phaser to the highest setting.

"That will probably have no effect," Spock said. "Not if the door is the same material as the net that is restraining the *Enterprise*."

True enough, the door was unaffected. "Aw, hell," Wilson muttered, and shifted his aim to the wall. It blasted out a hole slightly too small to drive an elephant through.

Outside, the street was deserted. A few Chatalia peeked from the upper-story windows of nearby buildings, but there was none on the climbing nets.

"Moore, keep a lookout above us," Wilson said. "Where to, Captain?"

"There." Kirk pointed to the vague outline of the magicians' island, hanging in the "sky" halfway to the zenith.

"Long way," Wilson said.

"About 169 kilometers," Spock said.

"At least we won't need a compass," Moore said. He was only half right.

Walking through the city was fairly easy, since the streets were laid out with checkerboard regularity. W'Chaal regained consciousness but remained mute when they tried to explain how the accident had occurred. He walked along with them, radiating fear. When the magician started to come to, Spock decided they ought to stun him back into dreamland—he might be more of a burden on his feet than on Spock's shoulder.

At the edge of the city they came to a broad, placid river, with no bridges in sight.

"How do you get across, W'Chaal?" McCoy asked.

He broke his silence. "You don't. It's forbidden."

"But we saw lan-Chatalia in the square. They must have come across."

"It isn't forbidden to *lan* or *ela*."

"And they fly, I suppose."

"That's right."

"That is not possible," Spock said. "The *lan* must supply food for the market, and by your own testimony they bring full-grown ven-Chatalia in, for replacement. Their wings would not be adequate."

"I didn't say they *always* fly. Sometimes they use boats."

Absorbed in the argument, they almost fell to a surprise attack. A spear struck Moore in the back, knocking him to the ground. Several other spears were in the air, but they were tumbling—evidently not balanced for throwing.

Some twenty Chatalia loped toward them; the

sweeping fire from four phasers dropped them all. Moore staggered to his feet, groaning. "What the hell hit me?"

Bones pulled up the back of his tunic; the wound was a cut about a half-centimeter deep by three long. "You're lucky. It must have been a glancing blow."

"Yeah—I sure *feel* lucky." Bones washed off the blood and closed the wound with the anabolic protoplaser.

"Are they all dead?" W'Chaal asked.

"Not unless some magician gets ahold of them," McCoy said. "These weapons can kill, but not the way we use them. This way, they only put people to sleep for a while."

W'Chaal kneeled down next to the nearest victim and stared at his face. "That's true."

"*All* of what we've told you is true," Bones said, sharply. "If you people weren't so damned . . . ignorant—"

"Cut it out, Bones," Kirk said. "W'Chaal, where do the *Ian* keep their boats?"

"On the other side, of course."

Patience. "When they're here. We know there are some here. Where would their boats be?"

"I don't know. That is not my family's concern."

"You keep saying that," Larousse said. "Are you really never curious about anything? Except languages?"

"Why should I be? The magicians are curious."

"In spades," Bones muttered.

"I guess we had better start walking, sir," Wilson said. "We'll come across a boat sooner or later."

"I suppose . . . W'Chaal, the water wouldn't be shallow enough to wade across, would it?"

"He doesn't know," Moore said.

"I don't, really. There might be some place where it is shallow—but you wouldn't want to wade through. There are fish and eels that bite."

They started walking, briskly. After a half hour they spotted a boat ahead; it took another half hour of walking (always uphill) to reach it.

It was a flat raft some four meters square, propelled by poling. They cast off and started across the "river"—it was actually a lake that girdled the planetoid, and had no current—and immediately saw why they wouldn't want to wade. A black eel, longer than the raft and almost as big around as a man, followed them halfway across, grinning.

"That is very strange," Spock said. "If I were to set up an ecology for a ship like this, I certainly wouldn't include large, dangerous predators."

"I don't know," McCoy said, staring at the toothy creature. "From what we've seen, logic isn't their strong suit. Maybe it's just to keep the peasants from swimming across."

"Or it could be that they wanted to preserve as many species as possible. Like Noah's Ark, in your mythology."

"Let me take that for a while." McCoy took over a pole from Moore; Spock relieved Wilson. The security men slumped to the deck, exhausted. They were about midway, and had at least two kilometers to go.

"I'd like to have the boat motor concession here," Bones said, straining into the pole.

"Actually, sail would work," Kirk said. "There seems to be a steady breeze."

Spock agreed. "It should be a permanent condition, the water being a heat sink. Unless they choose to superimpose another weather pattern—" The magician had come to, and was saying something. Kirk picked up the translator, which was lying at W'Chaal's feet, and took it closer to the magician.

"What did you say?"

"Where are you taking us?"

"Home. To the island of the magicians."

"No. You will not get there alive."

"He's a bombastic one, isn't he," McCoy said. "We're not particularly afraid of your weapons."

W'Chaal had been silent since getting on the raft. "That's not what he means—"

"Silence!"

"Master, if they are warned—"

"Silence."

"You don't have to obey him, W'Chaal," Kirk said. "We're in charge now. Would you have us die from our ignorance?"

"That would be fair," W'Chaal said. "The ones your weapon killed died from their ignorance, or so you say."

"I told you—" the magician began.

Even through the machine's translation, a note of defiance was evident: "It doesn't make any difference, master. By light tomorrow, we will all be dead."

"What the devil are you talking about?" Bones said, unconsciously brandishing the pole.

W'Chaal flinched. "As the master says, you must not be told. We all will die, and start over."

"Maybe *you* will. I don't happen to believe in reincarnation."

"That's true. You will probably not be replaced, for your aberrations."

"Tell me," Spock said, "you actually know you'll come back? You've seen it happen?"

"Of course. Many of my friends have been replaced."

"And they come back unchanged?"

"No, they start over. They know their family responsibilities, but don't remember their former lives—you wouldn't want to remember all of eternity, would you?"

"Clones," McCoy said.

"In all likelihood . . . magician, is that so? Do you make new Chatalia from the flesh of the old ones?"

The magician ignored the question. "You are a different kind of Klingon. Your skin and ears."

"None of us is Klingon. I am half-human and half—Vulcan. Humans come from the planet Earth; Vulcans come from the planet Vulcan; Klingons come from the Klingon Empire—many different worlds."

"Babble."

"I am constitutionally unable to lie, or speak nonsense. Your view of the world is wrong, if it is the same as W'Chaal's. Or are you aware of the fact that you live inside a small world, artificially constructed, that is moving through space?"

"I was told of your blasphemy. It is the same as the ones who came before—further proof that you are Klingons."

"Where do you think we came from, if not outside?"

"The future, of course. You are magicians from the future." He looked across at W'Chaal. "You must die for hearing that, little one."

W'Chaal shrugged. "I will die tonight in any event."

"How could we possibly be magicians?" McCoy said. "We're totally different species—even our body chemistry is basically different."

"Your pretense of ignorance is annoying."

"I wonder if that eel would come back, if you fell into the water."

"Threatening will accomplish—"

"That wasn't a threat. It was wishful thinking."

6

From the Captain's Log, Stardate 7506.5

This is Lieutenant Commander Montgomery Scott, commanding in the absence of Captain Kirk and Commander Spock.

We made contact with the planetoid at 7506.1074. In accordance with Mr. Spock's orders, I had the Enterprise's artificial gravity deactivated, to save energy while taking advantage of the planetoid's rotation. The sudden change to $0.479g$ made many of the crew ill, but all recovered in a few hours.

We have beamed down two heavy-duty phasers to the confrontation team. Both of the hostage aliens claim that all of them are in mortal danger, but they will not explain why. My suggestion that we send in reinforcements from Security was turned down by the captain. He agrees with Mr. Spock that the unfortunate phaser accident may have done irreparable harm to the Chatalian image of us, and we must avoid at all costs any action that might seem aggressive.

I do not interpret "at all costs" to mean sacrificing the lives of six crew members. There

are twenty-two heavily armed men standing by
in the emergency transporter room.

The opposite shore was a couple of meters of
gravelly beach, ending abruptly in dense jungle.
W'Chaal refused to get off the raft, but didn't resist
when Spock lifted him off.

"There must be a path," Kirk said.

Wilson squinted, scanning the uphill sweep of the
shoreline. "You'd think there'd be a loading dock,
too."

"Do you know of a way through, magician?"
Spock asked.

"Yes. I have flown over it."

"But you aren't in the mood to tell us," Wilson
said. The magician answered with silence.

"It can't be far," Spock said, "since the raft would
have taken the shortest crossing. I suggest that we split
into two groups, and search in opposite directions."

"Suits," Wilson said. "Come on, you." He grabbed
the magician by the arm.

The magician let out a brain-curdling scream and
forced himself from Wilson's grip.

"What the hell?" In the shape of Wilson's hand,
an angry purple blister welled up on the creature's
shoulder.

"Salt!" McCoy said. "The salt in your perspiration."

Wilson looked at his hand, then at the magician.
"I'm—I'm sorry. I should have thought of that."

"You will not touch either of us again." He looked
at Spock. "Why did your touch not harm the little
one?"

"Vulcans do not perspire. Our bodies have a more
efficient method of heat regulation."

"I do not know this first verb."

"Perspiring is something humans, and some other animals, do to regulate their body temperature. Special glands excrete a fluid onto the skin surface; when that fluid evaporates, it draws heat from the skin."

"Disgusting." He turned to Wilson. "I command that you stop doing that at once."

Wilson laughed in spite of himself. "They have no control over it, unfortunately," Spock said. "It is an automatic reaction to an increase in body temperature."

"This is all very interesting," Kirk said, "but I think we ought to get on with the business at hand. Moore, you go with Mr. Spock and Dr. McCoy, that way. Take the magician. The rest of us will go this way. First one to find a path gets shore leave."

"Very funny," McCoy said. They split up and started searching.

After a few minutes, Spock's group found an opening into the dense bush. They waited for Kirk and the others to join them.

It was a straight path of grass, cultivated like a lawn, some three meters wide. It dwindled to a thread in the distance, as the jungle gave way to square plots of farmland.

"About thirty or forty kilometers," Kirk said, looking at his watch. "I'm sure we don't have four hours of light left . . . I wonder—"

"I must say something," the magician said. "Though I do not in any way believe that you are telling the truth, I do admit that Klingons, as we knew them, did not have this perspiration-that-burns. So you may not be Klingons."

"You finally—"

"Shut up, Bones. So you're willing to cooperate?"

"I haven't decided. The thought is strong in me that it might be best if at least one of you survived to be studied. On the other side, once you are dead you will present no threat. I am not sure."

"Add this fact to your argument, then: if we die, there will be twenty times our number here tomorrow, heavily armed and angry."

"What you say is worthless, of course. However, my indecision is valid, and to serve it I think we should live through the night."

"That's impossible," W'Chaal moaned.

"No. Not with weapons."

"But the spirits—"

"They are not spirits, exactly. You must not hear this: go down the beach."

When the little one was far enough away, the magician started. "Let me explain. As you guessed, we use life to create new life; this art has been the primary function of my family for all time.

"Sometimes mistakes are made. Custom forbids killing these mistakes. We alter their eyes so that they shun the light of day, and put them in the jungle, here."

"So the jungle is full of malformed Chatalia?" Bones said.

"I think you use an improper word. We are forbidden to judge whether a mistake has resulted in an inferior being. Our legends say that the division of Chatalia into three species was the ultimate result of such 'mistakes.'

"And it is not only Chatalia in the jungle. We control the populations of certain large animals by . . .

your word was 'cloning.' Others reproduce without help, by an exchange of genetic material."

"You make it sound so sexy," Bones said.

"I don't know that word. The eel that followed our raft is the result of both cases: the ability to reproduce naturally, which had been suppressed, reappeared as the result of a cloning accident. It happened twice, many generations ago; an accident that also made them twenty times their normal size. Now they are a dangerous nuisance."

"Natural selection," Bones said, nodding. *"Un-*natural selection."

"You expect that we will be attacked by these 'mistakes'?" Kirk said.

"We will, both Chatalia and others. The competition for food is very strong in the jungle."

"I suggest, Captain, that we spend the night right here," Spock said. "At least our backs won't have to be protected."

"No!" the magician said. "That would be certain death. The water creatures gather at the outlet of this path, hoping something will be forced close to the waterline. And they can leave the water for short periods, to attack."

"Wait a minute," Wilson said. "He knows too much about this—magician, you *fly* over the jungle. The jungle creatures never bother your kind. So how do you know so much about how they attack?"

"I have seen it many times, at dusk, from the air. Many *ela* come here when it is time to die. They must die here, if they were responsible for a mistake."

"That is a rather extreme punishment," Spock said.

Wilson shook his head. "How do you suggest we defend ourselves?"

"We must move far enough down the path so that we are safe from the swimming ones. Then we kill the small one and place his body ahead of us on the trail, to lure the mistakes. As they come, you use your weapons to—"

"Wait," Kirk said. "Absolutely not. We don't like to interfere with people's customs, but we can't allow that. It's murder."

"I don't understand."

"Don't try to understand. We can't allow it."

"But he is already dead, ever since I told him things he mustn't know. This will at least make his body useful."

"Why did you send him away, then?" McCoy said. "It shouldn't make any difference, for him to learn the truth about these 'spirits.' "

"I am not cruel. I spared him the pain of reassessment." The sun dimmed rapidly; brightened, then dimmed again. Last night, that had happened just before it got dark.

"We must hurry," the magician said, and called W'Chaal. Kirk contacted the *Enterprise* and had them send down four more phasers, and a portable lamp.

Walking swiftly forward. Kirk outlined his simple plan. "Keep the weapons on 'stun.' We'll make a circle around the hostages and set up six fields of fire. Every fifteen minutes we rotate counterclockwise, for alertness. If you feel yourself getting sleepy, say so—Bones, you have stimulants in that kit?"

"Plenty. But let's hold off on them; people get

trigger-happy." The sun had dimmed from bright yellow to bright red, turning the jungle's green to dark gray against black shadow.

"This is enough," the magician said.

They stopped and formed up, scanning the dense growth for signs of motion. The arc-lamp threw long, grotesque shadows; Kirk had another beamed down to fill in.

"Maybe the light will keep them away," Wilson said.

"I don't know," the magician said. "We have never tried keeping them away." Spock gave Kirk a significant look: the alien was volunteering information without having been queried.

There was about ten minutes of silence, while the sun dimmed out completely. They stood tense in an island of harsh glare. Bright leaves and vines trembled in the constant breeze.

"Joke'll be on them," Moore said.

"Yeah?"

"Hell, I salt everything I eat. One mouthful and they'll keel over dead."

"You don't know how happy that makes me feel," McCoy said.

"Wait," Kirk said. "That's an idea—have the *Enterprise* beam—"

All hell broke loose.

Not watching overhead, they almost lost McCoy to a twice-too-big mistake-magician, who floated silently down with fangs bared. Their magician hostage shouted a warning; three phasers stunned it and it fluttered off to one side, unconscious. While it was still in the air, three smaller Chatalia attacked, on the ground. Wilson stunned one that had two heads and four arms, with rags for wings. McCoy's was hairless, white. Kirk's target had too many eyes.

When the flying one hit the ground it toppled over one of the lamps, and settled on it. Hiss of hair burning. Moore broke formation to push it off, and was attacked by a *ven* that had a large running sore instead of a mouth. He kicked it savagely between the legs, a questionable tactic against a sexless creature, but one that slowed it down enough for Wilson to zap the thing. Unfortunately, the beam brushed Moore, paralyzing his left side. He took one step and fell over.

Wilson ran to his side, blasting the jungle at a cyclic rate, heaved the magician off the lamp, and dragged Moore back to the circle.

They kept coming. A flying jellyfish that trailed glowing barbs. A *ven* that looked normal except for a flower growing out of its chest. A rolling ball of scales and teeth. A magician with no wings. A moose with spines and fangs. Two *ela* joined by a glistening tube of flesh. One of the eel-things, humping slowly along the grass, almost dead by the time it got to them.

The bodies piled up. Action slacked off while creatures dragged fellow-creatures, stunned into immobility, off into the woods to eat them alive. Every few minutes one would attack, scrambling over the heap of bodies. Others would recover from stunning and lurch closer, to fall again.

Moore fired from the ground until the numbness wore off; requested permission to change his setting to "kill"; permission regretfully denied. Something that looked like a hairy guitar with feet managed to get within an arm's reach without falling stunned; Moore bashed it over the head with the phaser's handle.

No one needed McCoy's stimulants.

Aboard the *Enterprise*, Scotty had deserted the temporary bridge to sit nervously with the 22-man force waiting by the transporters. He had made several suggestions to Captain Kirk:

Beam down a few men to spell them.

Sprinkle a ton of salt over the area.

Send down twenty-two men—or everybody!—and tear the whole damned jungle apart.

During lulls in the fighting, Kirk had answered "no," "no," and "don't be crazy."

From the communicator, amplified, came sounds of something snorting/meowing, then the phaser's bleat and a crash.

"Situation report," said an ensign, in a voice at once laconic and tense.

Moore replied, "Just another moose thing. Why don't you guys stop bothering us? This is nothing but target practice."

Scott let out a ragged sigh. "As if they c'd ken for sure that it won't get worse, suddenly."

Lieutenant Gary grunted assent. "They should at least let us send down something heavier than phasers. Like the portable disrupter field—then they could get some sleep."

"General Order One," Scotty said, half-listening. This was the standing order that Federation explorer parties must minimize the effect advanced technology has on more primitive cultures.

"Somebody should read *them* General Order One. We're flummoxed by their technology, not the other way around."

"Aye, richt." He was staring into the space over the transporters. He loved this ship, and especially he loved the engines—and here was a vampire, sucking the life from them. With uncharacteristic force, he said, "They'll pay for this. If it's the last thing I do, I'll see they pay for this."

7

When the sun came back on, Kirk's people and the two aliens were standing exhausted in the center of a ring of unconscious monsters piled two and three meters high. Kirk slumped to the ground, and so did the others.

"Bones, you can pass around your magic pills now," he said. "We have a good long walk ahead of us, if we don't want to spend another night like this."

"No pills," he said, opening his bag. "Hold out your arm."

"Joy," Moore said.

"If you hold your arm perfectly still, it doesn't hurt a bit."

"They've been telling me that since I was five years old," Moore said. "I don't believe in the Tooth Fairy anymore, either."

(The hypo fired a premeasured dose of medicine on a blast of compressed air. It didn't hurt if you managed not to flinch at the sound, but few managed.)

Captain Kirk tried not to wince. For obvious reasons, McCoy saved Moore for last.

They clambered over the heap of bodies—which smelled like a cross between a chemical plant and a zoo —and hurried on down the path, Moore and Wilson walking backward half the time, in case some beast decided to brave the light long enough for breakfast. As they revived, though, the "mistakes" made straight for the cool darkness of the jungle, very few of them stopping for so much as a mouthful of some companion.

"Are you willing to give us some suggestion as to a form of transportation more efficient than walking?" Spock asked the magician. "Besides flying," he added, without sarcasm.

Both the magician and W'Chaal were stumbling with fatigue; obviously, McCoy couldn't help them with his shots. "When we reach the lan-Chatalia domain," the magician said, "I should be able to find us a drawn cart. But I doubt that the little one and I will be able to walk that far."

"We will carry you when necessary," Spock said, "but the longer you can travel without help, the sooner we will be out of danger."

They managed about five kilometers. W'Chaal fell first, and the magician collapsed while Moore was hoisting up the other. McCoy offered another shot, but both Moore and Spock declined.

The air was still and the morning grew hot. Moore had light gloves beamed down, to keep his sweat off W'Chaal. As they labored along, they could hear others pacing them, behind the wall of greenery. The ones who weren't carrying Chatalia held their phasers at the ready.

They didn't dare seek shade during rest stops, which Bones insisted on, five minutes out of every hour.

The interludes weren't particularly restful, since the jungle rustlings stopped when they sat down. They could feel the eyes of patient monsters, waiting for dark.

As they neared the end of the jungle, several hours later, two of the creatures did attack, staggering blindly into the light, aiming at their sound and smell. McCoy and Wilson dropped them both.

Their first exposure to *lan* country was not impressive. Blue vegetables that looked like sick cabbages struggled through hard gray soil, in no apparent pattern. Most of them were dusty and wilted, and there was no sign of an irrigation system.

"They may have some virtues," McCoy said, "but farming ability isn't one of them."

"On the contrary," Spock said, not even breathing hard under his alien burden, "it may be very wise strategy. If the crops here were edible, they would only serve to feed the jungle creatures. It's quite likely they are poison."

"Hadn't thought of that," Bones said with just a hint of scorn. But the ground and plants improved over the next two kilometers.

As they were drawing near a village, Spock woke up the magician (who verified that they did plant noxious crops near the jungle, to discourage nocturnal roving). They were walking down a straight road of hard-packed gravel, flanked on both sides by rows of some low green bush with red fruit.

W'Chaal woke up too, and the first thing he said was to the magician. "How much longer will I be allowed to live?"

"You have special knowledge now, that is not *ven* knowledge. But since you can't tell it to any other *ven* in this situation, I don't see any reason you can't live until we reach the Island." Both of their voices had a strange echo to them, because of the way they were standing. They had solved the translator problem by having another one beamed down; each alien wore one on a loop around his neck. When they were about two meters apart, though, both voices were picked up by both translators, and the result was an unnatural echo.

"Perhaps we can convince you of the wrongness of this," Kirk said, "before we reach your Island."

"Save your breath, Jim," McCoy said. "You might as well try to talk Spock out of being vegetarian."

"The two are hardly equivalent," Spock said.

Kirk rolled his eyes briefly skyward. "Magician, how do we go about finding transportation? This cart you mentioned." The village seemed to be deserted, though they could see a few *lan* working in the fields.

"We look. When we find one, we take it."

"What about the *lan* it belongs to?"

"I don't understand."

"The farmer we take it from. Don't you suppose he might need it, for his farming?"

"He'll use another . . . wait. I think I see what you mean. That he might object to our taking 'his' cart."

"That's right."

The magician and W'Chaal looked at each other and made a sound that might have been laughter. "No, the *lan* don't have any property rights, unlike *ven*. It would be more proper to say that they belong to the property, at least for the *lan* who are farmers.

"If anything, any cart we find belongs to me, since I am the closest magician. As the lives of all of you belong to me."

In a low shed next to a tall cone-shaped building, they found several draft animals and two wagons. The animals looked like huge six-legged rats, tailless. After some trial-and-error, Kirk managed to hitch a pair to the largest wagon and back it out onto the road. He loaded a few bags of feed and got everyone aboard. They freed the Chatalia's arms, tying the ropes around their ankles instead. Neither protested, nor thanked them, but they stretched mightily.

Kirk wasn't surprised to find that he was the only one with experience in handling draft animals. His own experience was the result of a curious anachronism: his father had been a politically ambitious man, belonging to the conservative Back-to-Earthers. Part of his image (town mayor with an eye on the state senate) required that he do some token farming—the more primitive, the better. But he was a very busy man, so most of the actual work was done by young Jim, after school. Trying to coax corn out of eleven acres of bad soil had given Jim an intimate relationship with the south end of a northbound mule.

"Gee-*hah!*" Twelve legs rippled into reluctant motion. A bouncy ride at first, but it smoothed out. The hot sun, always directly overhead, made him drowsy as the effect of Bones's stimulant began to wear off. He could hear the doctor snoring softly behind him.

The road stretched out straight ahead as far as he could see. He wrapped the reins around his hands twice, just in case he drowsed.

A little groggy, Kirk untangled one hand and pulled out his communicator. "Sit-rep negative. This is Captain Kirk." He looked behind him. "Security's taking a nap. Is that you, Lieutenant Gary?"

"No, sir. Ensign Dunhill here."

"Well, you can report that everything is peaceful here, with most of the team resting. We're proceeding north in a requisitioned vehicle, at about fifteen kilometers per hour. How are things up there?"

"Cold, sir. We're conserving energy . . . uh, here's the lieutenant, sir." Voice change. "Captain, Glak Sōn's latest calculations give us three days and nine hours until we have to beam everyone down. At the current rate of power drain, that is. He requested that I ask you whether you foresee any unusual use of the transporter soon.'

"No, just food. No word from Star Fleet Command?"

"No, sir. Though I'm not sure we could pick up a message on normal subspace. I will talk to Uhura and report to you next sit-rep."

"Very well." He could call Uhura himself, but that way would save energy. "Over and out."

"I'm sorry I didn't answer that, Captain," Spock said from behind him. "I was meditating."

"Well, you needed rest."

Spock hesitated. "No, Captain. It was a time for meditation. Because of the high probability that our mission will fail."

"That we'll . . . die here?"

"There are many unknown factors. But most of them offer only various degrees of failure."

"Star Fleet will find us, sooner or later."

"I don't question that. But the vessel that finds us will probably suffer a similar fate. And the one they send after that one."

Kirk rubbed his chin. "So . . . even if they did believe us—even if they made us *kings* . . ."

"Even if we could modify the food so we could live on it, we may still be trapped here for the rest of our lives. Along with whoever comes to rescue us."

"Unless they come within three days and nine hours, and can be warned," Kirk mused.

"That possibility forms one of the few optimistic scenarios."

"Tell me another; I need cheering up."

"Obviously, one is that our small journey here is successful. That we find that our magician friend—"

"My name is T'Lallis." The magician seemed wide awake.

Spock nodded. "If we find that T'Lallis is not a . . . typical magician. That others might be more willing to accept our view of the universe; might even know how to free the *Enterprise* and refuel her. T'Lallis, you are a second-caste magician, aren't you?"

The alien touched his silver ribbon. "Of course."

"The first-caste ones may be the actual pilots of the ship," Spock said. "If so, we should be able to at least describe our situation to them. Whether they will help—"

"You may never meet a first-caste one. They are mostly plant managers."

"Planet managers?" Kirk said.

"They manage the plants. Horticulture."

"That's all they do?"

"Most of them. The second caste runs the world, and takes care of rebirthing. We obey the first caste, when they ask something of us. But that isn't often."

"Interesting," Spock said.

8

DISTRESS**DISTRESS**DISTRESS**
DISTRESS**DISTRESS**DISTRESS**

This is Commander Spock of the Starship Enterprise. We are in grave distress.

On Stardate 7502.9, we discovered a remarkable artifact: a gigantic space ship in the form of a hollowed-out planetoid, moving at sublight speed through the use of a Bussard-type interstellar ramjet. It is inhabited by approximately one million sentient beings, who call themselves Chatalia.

We beamed down a standard confrontation team, but found they were unable to return. A thin shell of some metal or alloy, with a molecular weight of 1132.5, somehow prevents the transporter from working both ways.

The Chatalia imprisoned the confrontation team. They evidently have forgotten that they are aboard a space ship—it has been under way for at least three thousand years—and do not understand the team's explanations.

Complicating the situation is the fact that, several centuries ago, the planetoid was attacked by a Klingon cruiser. They remember, and believe that we are Klingons.

We found the ruins of the ship on the planetoid's surface; a transcript of its log is here appended.

Evidently the Enterprise is suffering a fate similar to the Klingon cruiser's. The planetoid is draining fuel from the ship, by some unknown mechanism. The fuel loss is directly proportional to energy use.

A warning to rescuers: the Enterprise was trapped while 123 kilometers from the planetoid's surface. The capturing device is evidently in the form of a mesh of the unnaturally heavy metal mentioned earlier.

In less than a week, the crew of the Enterprise must abandon ship, and transport into the planetoid. We should be able to survive there for several months.

We recommend that rescuers attempt to hole the planetoid with phaser fire, concentrated in a small spot. This will enable the transporter to be used, and the air loss to the Chatalia should not be significant.

We cannot live inside the planetoid indefinitely. Not only are the Chatalia hostile, but their food cannot be assimilated by humans.

This message is being transmitted on Stardate 7504.966, from 119.70238^D, 689.4039 psc.; $—1.038572^D$, $—0.9966$ psc.; at a heading of 37.903^D, 0.0127^D; all with respect to Rigel.

This is the translation of the Klingon log. . . .

Contrary to the fears of Lieutenant Uhura and Mr. Spock, the distress signal did manage to penetrate the planetoid's magnetic field well enough to be picked up by a vessel.

It might have been better if the vessel had belonged to the Federation.

The Klingon cruiser was involved in a benchmark survey, rather like the one being done by the *Enterprise*—in fact, they were following the *Enterprise* at a discreet distance. No law against it, but they nevertheless remained silent on all communication frequencies.

They did listen, and very carefully.

"Lord? Have you come to a decision?"

Captain Kulain had let the transcript fall into his lap; he was staring at the viewscreen's black night.

Without looking at his lieutenant, he said, "There can only be one course of action. Implement it."

The first lieutenant raised a fist. "Survive and succeed!" The captain raised a fist at his reflection.

After the lieutenant left, the only other person in the room was the priest Kal. "Your enthusiasm is an inspiration to us all."

"Very funny, Kal. You of all people should share my reservations."

The priest picked up his copy of the transcript and looked at the last page. " 'Turn our rot to ashes. Send us home to hell.' " He hummed the first four notes of a religious anthem. "A pious man, that one. His memory will be revered, when we bring this log home."

Kulain stood, dumping the papers on the desk, and paced, his back to the priest. "If you desire that, you had best transmit the log on subspace. We aren't—"

"Kulain. I warn you, there are limits to brotherhood. You are skirting blasphemy."

"I am a realistic man. Practical. That is why I am captain, old friend, and you are priest." He turned to him. "This stinks of death, and you know it."

"So? We all die."

"And what better way," the captain said in an unctuous tone. "Avenge the memory of a lost ship and rid the Universe of Kirk. Accidentally." The Organian Peace Treaty between the Federation and the Klingon Empire forbade armed hostilities, though either group might wage war against a third party.

"Exactly." He leafed through the transcript, averting his friend's gaze. "Our weapons are much more powerful now."

"Let me spell it out in terms that even a priest might understand. We do have more powerful weapons, true—but no more powerful than the *Enterprise* has. Do you really believe that they didn't try to fight?"

"Human psychology is very strange. It's possible they would not."

"*Possible!* I fought these devils, Kal, before the Treaty. They worship soft and stupid words, but underneath they are ferocious. Mark me, they tried."

"I reiterate." He folded his arms across his chest and stared at Kulain. "So we die. We die fighting."

"Good philosophy but bad tactics." Into Kal's silence, he added, "We should send for reinforcements. Allow one ship to try destroying the planetoid, with others standing back to evaluate the results. Thus the loss of a ship might be an investment, not a sacrifice. In addition, the ship might be rescued."

"And its crew denied the opportunity to die in battle."

"In the first place, there doesn't appear to be any *battle* involved. It sounds more like dying of disease. In the second place . . ." He hesitated. "A warrior who is not killed can fight again."

Kal rose. "Kulain—"

"All right. I retract that."

"You have studied humans too closely. You begin to think like one."

"Was there anything improper in the order I gave?"

"No. But the way you stated it was less than . . . forceful."

An animal sound growled up from Kulain's throat. He strode across the room and jerked a ceremonial sword from its scabbard on the wall.

"Go ahead," Kal said. "Kill your only friend on this ship. Show me that you don't need anyone."

"Kal," he said, hefting the sword for balance, "hold out your hand."

"Mr. Scott," Uhura said, trying to control the excitement in her voice, "we have an answer on the subspace."

"Put it on th' screen." Swirl of multicolored snowflakes—interference from the magnetic field—over a vague manlike image.

"Captain Kirk?" the image said.

"Nay, sir, this is Lieutenant Commander Scott, commanding in the absence of superiors."

"My compliments, Mr. Scott. This is Captain Kulain of the warship *Korezima*. We thought it would be friendly to warn you that you are near a planetoid that we will be destroying, two days from now. We advise that you move off at least one hundred thousand kilometers, in your units."

After a moment of stunned silence, Scott said, *"We can nae move!"*

"Oh, my," Kulain said softly, "and we've already launched the nova bomb. Perhaps you should begin

whatever spiritual preparations you require for death."
The screen went blank, except for rainbow swirl.

Scott cut it off. "That pretty neatly forces our
hand. Mr. Chekov, try to find that bomb and trace
its trajectory. There's still a chance a Federation ship
may have picked up our message; they might inter-
cept it.

"Lieutenant Uhura, find Glak Sön and begin
preparations for transferring the crew. We'll want to
take a maximum amount of food—and have Nurse
Chapel confer with a chemist about the possibility of
modifying the alien food. There might be chemicals
we can beam down with us."

"You think the planetoid's metal skin will protect
us?" Uhura asked.

"Against a nova bomb? I dinna think so. Bit I
can nae see any other course." *Nivver did I seek command*. He reached for the communicator.

They were rolling through the lazy sprawl of a
rural town. The ambience was familiar to Kirk, even
though every detail was alien: too-tall buildings of
abode, with too much space between them, the space
filled with flowers instead of grass. A thing that looked
like a cross between a cockroach and a dog rushed out
of a house and barked at them. There were no children, but every adult they passed stopped what he was
doing to stare at them. Most of them had never seen a
ven, or an *ela* that wasn't flying—let alone a creature
from Earth or Vulcan!

Wilson and Moore had their phasers at the
ready, but either no one noticed the Chatalia were in
trouble, or they weren't disposed to help.

They had gone about fifty kilometers, and the force of pseudo-gravity had noticeably lessened as they got closer to the axis of the planetoid. "I wonder how long we'll be able to use the wagon," Kirk said. "It'll be floating by the time we get to the Island."

"I suppose it depends on the behavior of the animals," Spock said. "They will find it difficult to get purchase, before long."

"Reminds me." Kirk took out his communicator. "We'll have to have tractor boots to get around."

The machine bleeped. "Mr. Scott to Captain Kirk."

"Go ahead, Scotty."

"Sair, we have rill trouble."

"Do tell . . . what now?" Scotty filled him in on the Klingon threat.

". . . accordin' to Mr. Chekov and Glak Sön, we have aboot forty-six hours, before the nova bomb hits."

"That's within the time limit, isn't it? Imposed by the energy drain?"

"Aye. And with your permission, we'll wait until the last minute, to beam doon."

"I was going to suggest that. Help may arrive. . . . It would be far preferable for you to beam onto another ship."

Scotty was silent; Kirk knew him well enough to anticipate what he was going to say: "And don't let me hear any nonsense about 'abandoning ship'—"

"But *sair!*"

"Or abandoning us, for that matter. Your duty is quite plain." He looked at Spock with amusement. "It's going to be embarrassing enough, explaining how we managed to misplace the two top line officers, the senior surgeon, and the chief of security."

"Ensigns and linguists are easy to misplace," Larousse whispered to Moore.

"Easy to *replace*," Moore said. "That sometimes bothers me." Kirk gave him a withering look and a *shush* gesture.

Both Chatalia were listening with interest, munching on fruit they had gathered at a grove outside of town. Kirk asked for the tractor boots and dinner, then signed off.

A stack of ham sandwiches appeared, and a bowl of raw vegetables for Spock.

"I don't understand that kind of magic," T'Lallis said. "Does that come from the future?"

"It comes from the ship," McCoy said flatly. "From outside, not the future. Outside."

"What kind of magic do you understand?" Larousse asked. "What kind do you *do?*"

"Life magic, of course."

"Show me," Bones said.

"I may, once we get to the Island." He took a fold of wing-skin between his fingers and studied it. "When we do get there . . . well . . . I wish you would give up this talk about 'outside' and your *Enterprise* and such. Maybe they would let you live for a while."

Kirk cut off Bones's reply. "We've reached an impasse at that, T'Lallis. Both of us know we are telling the truth; both of us know the other is completely wrong. There's no need to talk of it anymore."

"Look at this," Bones said. He picked up the rind of a fruit W'Chaal had peeled. He had carefully torn it off all in one piece, a stiff spiral. McCoy pieced it back together, and held it with both hands, an irregular hollow globe. "Can you at least *try* to visualize it?"

"If only to help you understand our delusions," Larousse added.

"Right now, we're on the *inside* of the—"

"Trouble," Wilson said. Twenty *lan* rushed out of a building ahead, and formed two rows across the gravel road. They tilted long spears toward the approaching wagon.

"Can you say something to them?" Kirk said. "Otherwise, we'll have to shoot."

"I would," the magician said, "but they don't have an interpreter with them."

"W'Chaal, can you—"

"No." He sat up straight. "I am not a *merchant*'s interpreter!"

"If you hold the translator out toward them," Larousse said, "it will work in their language."

"Shoot them," he said. Moore and Wilson each gave a short burst, and the twenty fell like comic-opera soldiers. The draft animals froze up, refusing to detour over the flowers, so that they had to get out and stack the unconscious Chatalia on the sides of the road.

The sun blinked twice while they were doing that chore. "Do we continue in the dark, Captain?" Wilson asked from under a large alien.

"Unless there's trouble. We should be able to see the road all right, with the lights."

They could see the road, it turned out, but the road just stayed there. When it got dark, the animals folded up their dozen legs and were sound asleep in seconds.

Kirk got down and tried to coax them, with

no success. Then McCoy stepped down to help, with the light. When the light shone in their eyes, they dutifully stood up.

So they moved all night, standing three-man shifts: one driving, one guarding, and one walking along backward with the lantern swinging in the creatures' eyes. Since Kirk and McCoy were the only ones who could handle the animals, and Wilson and Moore were professional guards, Larousse and Spock spent the night either walking backward or dreaming about it (insofar as Spock dreamed at all, or even slept).

Spock

The only reasonable approach to this problem is to predicate success, and then work backward down the various logical trees that lead there.

The first thing that must happen is that the Klingon nova bomb be unsuccessful. There are three groups of scenarios that allow this:

1. A Federation ship intercedes. The presence of the Klingon vessel implies that *they* did receive our message, so this may not be too unlikely. That there would be a ship within forty hours' flight time is improbable, though.

2. The bomb malfunctions. Low probability; besides, they would only try again.

3. The bomb is of insufficient power to destroy the super-metal shell surrounding us. This is the most likely possibility, but is impossible to evaluate in ignorance of the metal's heat capacity. (There is the secondary possibility that the shell will remain intact, but will conduct heat so efficiently as to raise the temperature to a lethal extreme.)

Proceed assuming the third set of scenarios. We are alive here, but the *Enterprise* has been destroyed on the surface.

It is possible that the Klingons will be satisfied and go away, confident that life inside has been destroyed—or at least will be desirous of reporting so. However, it is more likely that they will transport a fighting force inside. The Chatalia were evidently able to vanquish them before, unaided. With our help it should be possible to do so with less bloodshed, although it is unlikely that any Klingon will allow himself to survive.

What happens subsequent to this series of actions largely depends on the magicians.

1. They simply execute us. This is not unlikely but is a trivial solution.

2. The first-caste magicians are the pilots, and are willing to help us. In this case, our survival would depend on

   A. Food supply. Strict rationing. If the local water contains arsenic, it can be removed by the Marsh process. It may be impossible to process the local food without sophisticated equipment.

   B. Finding an exit to the surface. Thus we can be transported to safety when the Federation vessel arrives. Although we would be unable to communicate with the vessel, they would certainly beam down an investigating team, once bio-sensors showed life.

3. They are the pilots, but are not willing to help us. Use of force a possibility, but not advisable; we can't fight forever, and we can't take and hold the entire planet with standard issue weapons.

Our best approach in this case would be to convince them that they need our cooperation. Even if the nova bomb has no effect on the inside of the planetoid, it will certainly destroy the Bussard drive. Federation engineers would be able to repair or replace it.

4. Finally, they may not be the pilots; the ship may be either totally automated or a derelict. In this case we must try to deduce its history, and thus its mode of operation, and in this wise find a safe way to breach the super-metal skin.

All of this speculation is likely to be futile. If the ability of the super-metal to resist phaser action is due (even in part) to an extremely high thermal conductivity, then the interior of this planetoid will in forty hours attain the temperature of a supernova— for only a minute fraction of a second, but that will be sufficient.

"Spock—wake up." Larousse handed him the lamp, then hoisted himself aboard the wagon and collapsed on the floor, half asleep. Spock had been meditating, not sleeping, but he saw no reason to correct the linguist.

He stepped off the wagon and drifted slowly to the ground. They were down to about one-fourth of regular gravity now. Paradoxically, it made walking harder, not easier—especially backward.

McCoy was taking over the reins from Kirk, who stretched and yawned. "Wonder how much longer," he said.

Spock made a quick calculation. "If we continued directly to the axis at our present rate, night and day, we would arrive in seven hours and ten minutes. We do have a body of water to cross, though, which may present novel difficulties."

"We find another boat," Bones said.

"There may not be any. I don't know what happens to a body of water in a rotating frame of reference, at one-tenth gravity, but it should be interesting. And perhaps not navigable."

"In which case?"

"I have considered various possibilities. As your proverb has it, we will cross that bridge when we come to it."

McCoy shook the reins and the creatures slowly got to their feet. He looked at Spock incredulously. "Did you just make a joke?"

"Not consciously. Was it a 'good' one?"

"Awful."

Spock nodded seriously and began walking backward.

9

Soon after light, the draft animals began mewling in fright or frustration. With each step they would float up into the air for a second in the drastically low gravity, and their progress was slow and jerky. Kirk unharnessed them and shoo-ed them off in the direction from which they'd come.

Wearing tractor boots, the *Enterprise* people didn't have any trouble getting around, but the Chatalia did. W'Chaal had never been in such high altitudes, and T'Lallis was used to flying, not walking, when in low gravity. They spent a lot of time in the air, each step, until Spock took each by an arm and hustled them along.

They walked at a severe angle, as if the ground were actually a steep hill, since "up" was only perpendicular to the ground when you were near the equator.

It took several hours to get to the body of water that separated the Island from the mainland. As Spock had predicted, it presented a formidable obstacle.

The surface of the water was not well defined— lumpy, actually. It seemed to be boiling slowly, though not from heat. Volumes of water as large as swimming pools would separate from the surface, hover a moment, and slowly slide back; there was a constant mist several meters above the water, which looked dense enough to drown in. A full circle of rainbow shimmered in front of them.

"Doesn't look like a boat would do much good," Bones observed. "How do you get cargo across?"

T'Lallis shrugged. "Boats . . . *air* boats, not water boats."

"How do these boats fly?" Kirk asked.

"The *boats* fly? How could a boat fly?"

"This has a familiar ring to it," Bones said.

"How do they work, I mean," Kirk said.

"One or more *ela* tow them, with cables. They are made light by magic."

"Your 'life magic'?" Kirk said.

"Yes. It's a plant called a *hrnii*. When you put the seed in water it grows into a ball, and the ball fills itself with lightness."

"T'Lallis," Spock said, "if you open a *hrnii* ball, does the air inside burn?"

"Yes, with a hot flame you can't see. As you must know."

"A plant that generates hydrogen," Bones said. "Have you ever heard of anything like that, Spock?"

"Only on decomposition," Spock said. "Never while growing. I think we will be very interested in your magic, T'Lallis."

"If we ever get over there," Kirk said. "Even if we had one of these air boats, we couldn't do anything with it."

"I could pull all of us, this short distance," T'Lallis said.

"No ... I would fear an accident," Kirk said with just a trace of sarcasm.

"Sir?" Moore said. "I have an idea. We could fly across ourselves."

"Have you taken leave of your senses, Ensign?" Wilson asked politely.

"No, sir. I've seen it done, on the Moon. Earth's Moon, on my last shore leave."

"I've been on the Moon a dozen times," Kirk said, "but I've never seen anyone *fly*." Wilson agreed, giving Moore a slightly dangerous look.

"Sirs, you've never been in Disneymoon, then."

"The amusement park?" Kirk and Wilson hadn't committed a frivolous act since getting their officers' stripes. "Do they fly there?"

"Now that you mention it," McCoy said, "I've read about that. It's a natural underground dome—"

"Bigger than the *Enterprise*, sir. You can fly for a long time, in the one-sixth gravity. Big lightweight wings."

"Was it hard to do?"

"Uh, I don't really know, sir. My, uh, girl was afraid to try it." Which had been a relief to Moore.

"What do you propose we use for wings?" McCoy said. "Have Scotty beam down feathers and glue?"

"It shouldn't be difficult to design wings," Spock said. "Learning to use them properly might be a different matter."

"Tourists use them on the Moon, sir."

"Park Tinney probably knows all about it," Larousse said. "She's a linguistics ensign, born and raised on the Moon."

Kirk nodded and flipped the communicator open. "See what Scotty says."

As a matter of fact, Ensign Parker Tinney had flown almost every weekend from her tenth birthday until the day she left the Moon for the Academy. She still had her wings, rolled up in her locker, just in case they had shore leave on a low-gravity planet.

The wings were lightweight metalweave cloth glued to hollow metal struts: big ones for the arms and little ones for the feet. They rolled them out on the Engineering Room floor and made careful measurements. Glak Sōn computed how the measurements had to be changed for each crew member below, and it took less than two hours to fabricate them.

"Park" Tinney volunteered to beam down with the wings and coach the men. Scott obviously didn't relish the thought of sending a wee lass like Tinney into danger while he stayed safe aboard the ship, but he couldn't argue with the necessity.

If all other things had been equal, it would have been easier to fly here than on the Moon, since everyone weighed less than half as much. But all things weren't equal. On the Moon, you could launch yourself by kicking off from a perch. On the Moon, flyers weren't encumbered by clothes; Park knew better than to suggest that these men confront their adversaries in the altogether (they did have to relinquish their boots, though, since you steer with small movements of the feet and toes).

Because of the foot-wings, you couldn't take a running start, but that turned out to be no problem. In the weak gravity it was possible to do a ten-meter standing high jump. Keep the wings close to your sides until you reach the apex of your jump, then tip forward, spread wings, flap like hell.

While the men practiced, Park had great fun doing

acrobatics. Both the Chatalia watched spellbound while she maneuvered—they had never seen true birds, since no other animal in the planet could fly, and the magicians only plowed through the air with brute force.

When everybody was able to stay aloft with little effort and make simple steering maneuvers, Kirk called them all down. Moore swooped in and braked to a feather-gentle stop; he had a natural talent for the wings. Bones broke one of his foot-wings landing, and remarked that he was lucky not to break an ankle. Park had a repair kit, though, and was able to straighten out the strut and reglue the fabric without taking the wing off his foot.

"I think our best strategy would be to stay as far from the water as possible," Kirk said. "We'll go back about a kilometer, and go for altitude. T'Lallis, can you carry W'Chaal?"

"Yes, but I don't see any reason to bring him along. He can die on this shore as well as the other."

"Bring him. We may have something to say about that."

Spock was thoughtful as they half-walked, half-glided back to their launching place. "Captain," he said slowly, "in the past you have joked with me for lacking imagination. I am afraid this is often true, and especially with the problem that confronts us now."

"Flying to the Island?"

"No, sir—the Klingon attack. There is a way that we might enhance the probability that they will fail. If it isn't too late."

"What is it?"

"Sir, the nova bomb may be a powerful weapon indeed, but like all omnidirectional weapons it suffers inverse-square attenuation: the farther away we can cause it to detonate, the less damage it will do to the planetoid and the *Enterprise*."

"Of *course!* We use the ship's main phasers to . . ." His brow wrinkled.

"As you see, it is a complicated problem. We must at any rate transport the crew, and their provisions, into the planetoid. The more power we allot to the phasers, the less power we have for the transporter and life support systems.

"However, we do wish for the crew to stay aboard the *Enterprise* as long as possible. Reconciling these various aspects of the problem requires the solution of a differential equation of at least order five; one for which I lack parameters. With access to the ship's records, Glak Sōn should be able to solve it."

"We'll see."

Scotty rubbed tired eyes. "Lemme see now. At 0947, we transport everybody doon, save one. At 0948, the one remaining—me—will lock the main phaser bank on to the bomb, and blast it. Then—"

"Attempt to blast it, sir." Glak Sōn was shivering. "There is an element of guesswork in the calculation. We can't know for certain how powerful the Klingon nova bomb is, nor exactly how vulnerable it is to phaser fire. This timing represents an optimum solution, but one based on intelligence that might be out of date."

"Intell—oh. *Spy* intelligence."

"But I still recommend, sir, respectfully, that we not leave a man aboard. It is so unlikely that the bomb will change trajectory abruptly—"

"That is my decision, Ensign," Scott said, a little sharply. He forced his tired brain to work. "Any calculation we can make, they can duplicate. They might foresee our logic, and arrange a course change immediately when their biosensors report that we have left the ship. This would protect them against a preprogrammed phaser attack."

Glak Sōn mumbled an apology.

"Ye've never fought them, lad—" (as good a term as any for a creature that changes gender every other year)—"so you can no' think like them." He looked at the chronometer.

"Gives us nine hours. Lieutenant Uhura, I'm going down to quarters for a while. If I'm not back by 0730, have someone come by an' give me a shake."

"Aye, sir." She smiled at him, and he thought complicated thoughts, and tried to think of something clever to say, and instead walked out blushing.

Back in his tiny temporary cubicle, Scotty poured himself a small glass of brandy, looked at it for a moment, and carefully poured it back into the bottle.

It had been a good decision to move back from the water's edge for a "running start," since there was a gradually rising thermal of warm air constantly moving from the land to the water. They rose swiftly, in a straight line at first. But the two aliens kept dropping behind, T'Lallis awkwardly holding W'Chaal in his feet, like a clumsy bird of prey. Park and Moore kept surging ahead—Moore delightfully surprised that he didn't feel the expected fear of height—and had to spill air and drop back frequently.

"Sort of fun," McCoy admitted as he drew alongside Kirk. "If they were smart, they'd sell this planet to Disney—buy a quiet little—"

"Where the hell are they?" Moore called back, beating his wings furiously to kill his forward velocity.

Both Chatalia had disappeared. In a few moments they caught sight of both: the magician a speck high above, the interpreter below, behind, falling.

Park folded wings around herself and did a slow-motion swan dive, and started swimming down through the air. In a couple of minutes she caught up with W'Chaal, whose wings were slightly extended by the rush of air, but not enough to slow him very much.

"W'Chaal! Glide! You can make it back to shore!" All he would have to do would be to turn around, facing the thermal, and flap a little.

"I know I can," he said. "The master told me to die, to fall into the water."

Glancing down, Park estimated they had about twenty seconds left. No time for argument, she grabbed a handful of fur in each hand and stuck out her elbows, which splayed the large wings out to their fullest extent, scissoring her legs for balance.

"No!" W'Chaal flailed out with both arms, striking her hard in the solar plexus. Doubling up in pain, she dropped him.

The curling-up reflex spilled all the air from her wings; she was falling as fast as he, and backward—out of control for precious seconds, until she could twist back around.

W'Chaal shouted something unintelligible and disappeared into the mist. Park splashed straight into a floating blob of water the size of a man and came out coughing and gagging.

Blinded, panic rising, half a lifetime of flying by instinct saved her. She twisted out flat, body stiff, wings full, until the coughing subsided. Feeling wet mist close around her, she ordered starved lungs not to breathe, and slowly sculled upward, toward light.

When the air on her face seemed dry and cold, she breathed cautiously through her nose, coughed twice, wiped her eyes. Pumped hard for altitude, glad that the wing fabric was nonabsorbent.

A shadow passed over her and she looked up to see Moore floating down. *"Get back, you damned fool!"* He came alongside and clumsily matched her climb rate—really not too bad, she had to admit, for a beginner.

"You looked like you were in trouble," he said.

"I'll give *you* trouble!" But she smiled.

They had gone about halfway, ten kilometers or so, when the magicians caught them, coming in from behind, lost in the glare of the sun. They enveloped the humans in a broad net of the invisible wire.

"Don't struggle!" Kirk said. "Hold your fire." Moore had taken his phaser out part-way, then reholstered it. Anyone they stunned would fall to his death.

Park had cut the backs of her hands, pushing away from the net. "What is it?"

"Microscopic wire," Larousse said, "like a razor if you press it. Try to relax."

"Looks like about thirty of them," Wilson said, shading his eyes. "I guess all we can do is wait and see what they have in mind for us."

His communicator bleeped. "Situation report, sir."

He worked it carefully off his belt, avoiding the wires. "Things are looking up," he snarled. "We're getting a free ride."

10

I have put Lt. Uhura in charge of the evacuation details, including logistical organization after transport. Following the advice of Cpt. Kirk, they will beam into the underpopulated and relatively safe farming area, where the Ian-Chatalia live.

Their first order of business, after securing the area and setting up a defensive perimeter, will be to conduct analysis of the local food and water. Ensign Amstel (Chem.) is confident that he can purify it, so that they can survive indefinitely. Otherwise, they have only 19 days' food (at normal ration of 2500 kCal/day) and five days' water (at 5 L./day).

A mass movement toward the magicians' island would not be practical, since we have only ten pairs of tractor boots remaining. These ten have been fitted to Security personnel, who have also been supplied with wings. They will serve as a rescue force, heading toward the island as soon as the perimeter is secure. What measures they take will depend on how Kirk and his team are treated.

At last communication, the team was in the hands of the magicians, having been trapped in a net while crossing the body of water that isolates the island.

The evacuation will begin at 0945.0, with the transporters being energized approximately every six seconds. Transfer of personnel and supplies should be complete by 0947.5, leaving me behind to deal with the Klingons.

—Lt. Cmdr. Montgomery Scott

At 0932 Scotty was studying the list of coordinates Glak Sön had worked out for him, alone in the control room. Uhura stepped lightly through the open door.

He looked up. "Problem?"

"No, everybody's in place. Crowded down there, though. I wanted to get away for a minute."

She broke an awkward silence, voice quavering. "I wanted to say—"

"Aw . . ." Scotty waved a hand feebly, looking at the deck.

"I wanted to say goodbye," she continued, "in case it is goodbye." She rushed on. "I've always liked you, Scotty, and I admire your courage."

"Shoo," he said, still not looking up. "An' I always . . . I ken ye to be a guid officer . . . a guid woman . . . I—"

Suddenly Scotty had his arms full of warm communications officer. For some time they didn't move or speak, Scotty standing with his eyes closed, overcome by her softness and the sweet smell of her. "Time . . . time ye shu'd be gaen doon," he said in a strange husky voice, new to his own ears.

Light chaste kiss on his burning cheek. "We'll make it," she whispered. "I don't know how I know, but we will."

Watching her leave, Scotty had time to regret a

few things he hadn't said in the past. As for the future, only the next twelve minutes were important. He sat down with the list and tried to concentrate.

Aboard the Klingon vessel, Kulain rubbed sleep from his eyes and smiled thinly at the rapidly decreasing numbers on the readout plate in front of him. "You'll have a medal for this, Karez."

The science officer nodded. "It was one of several possible courses of action. Probably the one I would have advised myself, if I were cowardly."

Or if you wanted the maximum number of soldiers fighting inside, Kulain thought. "Begin the evasive action now."

He switched on the viewscreen and stared at the image of the trapped *Enterprise.* "If they hope to save the ship," he said, "they should start firing about now."

Scotty propped the figures next to the viewscreen and turned it on. Glak Sön's figures were based on a "random walk" evasion pattern, which the Klingons had used in the past. Both hands on the keyboard, foot on the firing switch, he stared at the image of the nova bomb. There was about one twentieth of a second time lag, so he'd have to "lead" the bomb, the way a duck hunter aims ahead of his prey.

The image twitched sideways: Scotty picked the figure for that angular displacement off the sheet, typed in three quick digits, and stamped on the firing switch.

A pale thread of light touched the bomb. There was no visible effect.

Sweat springing out on his face, he waited for the next twitch, and did it again. This time there was not even the thread.

He shouted a single word at the console and kicked it, hurting his toe. Turned off the viewscreen and limped to the portable transporter.

"Energize," he said. A red light started blinking on the automatic control. Not enough power. If he tried to beam down he would simply be disassociated into random particles, never to be reassembled.

Maybe better than nine hours' waiting for a nova bomb. Which would do the same thing.

He started to call Uhura and then decided to wait a bit. There'd be a real circus going on down there now. Besides, he had a few chores.

He walked down to the Galley and got a few rations, then closed it off. Then to his quarters, to pick up a bottle of Denebian brandy—should last nine hours. Eventually he shut off life support for everything save the emergency control room and Deck Eight, where the trees and streams were. He had to conserve power, since it was still remotely possible that a Federation ship would come to the rescue and save at least him from the Klingon attack.

More likely, he would be the first one to die, by a fraction of a nanosecond.

In the control room, he flipped a few switches to enable him to take and receive all calls through his hand communicator in the entertainment area. Then he took the lift there, found a small glass of exquisite crystal, sat on the cool grass with his back against a tree, poured a drink, and sipped at it. Set it carefully on the ground.

"This is the *Enterprise* to Uhura, Jim; whoever's listening down there.

"There must have been some error in the calculations. Although we did hit the nova bomb, there wasn't enough power left to do any damage. Neither was there enough power to beam me down afterward.

"Glak Sōn, I don't blame you for this, no' in the slightest. Ye warned me—besides, your figgers for the random walk worked foin."

He chose his words carefully. "I can't talk long. This neutrino thing pulls thirty times the energy of a reg'lar communicator. If I call again it will be because help has come. I miss you and goodbye."

"I can not understand," Glak Sōn said, trembling with some alien emotion—perhaps not alien—"I included quite a large margin for error."

Uhura reached down and patted him on the shoulder, occupied with her own thoughts. "It must have been the data."

"I do not see how. I had to be so sure." He turned and walked away. "I liked him."

Four hundred people milling around in a field of blue cabbages, giving and taking orders. If they were Bantu, Uhura thought, they would do the sensible thing: sit and wait quietly for nine hours. If they survived the nova bomb, *then* would be the time to set up food and water distribution systems, dig latrines, assign "billets"; the only urgent things to be done right now had to do with the natives—set up perimeter guards, mainly. She also detailed some people to carefully harvest and stack the cabbages in their immediate area so they wouldn't be trampled.

She sat cross-legged on the dry ground and watched her orders being carried out. She had faced death before and had that pretty well sorted out, but

she didn't care for this feeling of impotence, knowing
to the minute and second when the blow would come,
unable to stay it.

At least there was a familiar African feeling of
paradox about it. Not "paradox," quite; there wasn't
any precise English word for it. It was sitting inside a
tiny ball where the sky was the ground, closed in completely yet lost in the vastness between the stars. It was
this placid, idiotically well-manicured cabbage field,
where they had all come to share the sort of death
usually reserved for stars.

It was the odd family-feeling she had, being in
charge of these hundreds of brothers, sisters, children
—having tacitly given up motherhood for the Federation and the *Enterprise* (to her family's disappointment) and now mothering the whole ship's brood.

It made her think of a tale she'd learned from her
great-grandmother's sister:

*The first man and woman lived happily in
Heaven.*

*One day God told them they were going to earth,
and asked whether they would rather have the fate of
the moon, or the fate of a banana.*

They were not sure.

*He explained: the moon grows, then wanes, then
dies. But it always comes back.*

*The banana, while it lives, sends out shoots,
which accompany it while it waxes and wanes, and
surround it when it dies. But it dies forever, except
that its children still live.*

*So we may always be reborn, they said, but live
and die alone; or we may share life with children, but
die one time.*

As you choose.

Which way is better? they asked.

I won't tell you. All of the animals have chosen one way. Since you are my favorites I saved you for last.

Which way did the animals choose?

God laughed. I won't tell you that, either.

The man wanted the moon's way, arguing from his head and his fears. The woman wanted the banana's way, arguing from her womb and her hopes. The man used words, and the woman did not: thus, they gave us life, and death.

Her great-grand-aunt wouldn't have been surprised to learn of the Chatalia, Uhura thought. Just people who chose the way of the moon.

11

They were only a few minutes away from the Island. "I guess we better put on the boots," Kirk said, wriggling his right arm out of the wing and reaching back to where the boots were stuffed under his belt. "Can we fly at all without the foot-wings, Ensign?"

"You can stay aloft," Park said. "You just can't steer very well."

"Can't draw and fire too well, either," Wilson said, "unless we give up the wings altogether."

"That's true," Larousse said, "but they'll probably disarm us as soon as we land, anyhow."

"Or try to," Wilson said.

"We'll have to assess the situation," Kirk said. "If we still had Scotty to bail us out with the transporter, we could surrender the weapons without too much worry. But these are the only ones we're going to get, now."

"If they were humans," McCoy said, "I'd say hand over the phasers and rely on their curiosity to keep us alive, at least for a while. But I'm not sure they really have any."

"And they sure kill their own kind easily enough," Park added.

"Wait," Wilson said. "Insurance—two of us still have two weapons each, since the phaser rifles were beamed down. I can hide the phaser in the top of my boot, and just surrender the larger weapons—Moore, you still have your phaser?"

Moore smiled innocently. "Already tucked away, sir."

"So we'll play it by ear," Kirk said. "If they obviously plan to kill us out of hand, we'll hold them off as long as the phaser crystals last." Everybody knew, but didn't mention, that the crystals would likely outlast the planetoid's inhabitants. "If they want to talk, but want us disarmed, we give up all but the two hidden weapons."

"Three, sir," Park said, blushing a little. "Mr. Scott insisted that I carry a backup." It was strapped to her forearm, under the sleeve of her tunic. "Should I give it to someone else? I've never used one, except for training."

"No," Spock said. "Since you are by far the smallest, they may think you are the least dangerous."

"But I *am!*"

They were close enough to land now to see their welcoming committee. Most of them were armed with spears. All were magicians; one had the gold ribbon of rank. One was T'Lallis—or might have been some other *ela,* with the translator around his neck. The only translator they had, now.

Free of the net, they drifted to the ground. There was virtually no centrifugal "gravity" here; they landed feet-first because of the tractor boots.

"Hell," Moore whispered, "we could take them with our bare hands." The magicians had spears, but needed their wings to move. They floated around the crew like ugly angels.

"I don't know," Wilson said. "This is their natural element." But it was hard to see how they might use their spears effectively, the points bobbing up and down as they approached.

The first-caste magician said something incomprehensible. T'Lallis swam over and held out the translator, and he repeated it.

"You are prisoners now. Any aggression will be rewarded with death." T'Lallis whispered something. "Put your hands in front of you and allow us to take your weapons."

Three unarmed magicians moved in behind them, to disarm them.

"T'Lallis," Kirk said, "tell them to leave our communicators."

"No. You can use them to summon new weapons; I saw you do it."

"Remember not to touch their skin," the first-caste one said. "What is in those bags?"

"This is medical equipment," Bones said. He pointed to the ones Larousse and Park carried, shoulder-slung. "Those are scientific measuring devices and food and water."

"Search them." The three looked through the tricorder kits and the food bag, and were evidently satisfied. They brought the phasers and rifles back to him, having missed the hidden ones.

The magician inspected one of the phasers. "This is what killed so many *ven* at the House of Education and Justice?"

"Yes," Kirk said, "because they ignored our warning about it."

He handed it back to the second-caste searcher. "How are you able to stand there, as if you were downworld, and had force at your feet?"

"Just magic," Kirk said.

"That isn't enough."

"Good! We can bargain. The more you tell us, the more we'll tell you."

The magician was silent for a minute. "We can try, perhaps. Tell me more about standing."

"We wear 'tractor boots'—"

"Nonsense word."

"I know. Since you don't have a word for it, the translator can't do anything but make up a word. I'll show you, though." He unzipped the boots and stepped out, drifting a couple of meters. Then he clumsily flew himself down and put the boots back on.

"I see how you do it," the magician said, "the things on your feet are sticky. I don't understand why, though. You can fly; why deny yourselves the freedom?"

"We aren't used to flying. Where we live there is always force at your feet."

"As with the *ven* and *lan*."

"Something like that; a different kind of force, though. My question: What do the first-caste *ela* know that the second-caste don't?"

"I can't answer that with all of these people around. I'm not sure I could tell you anyway."

"Send them away, and try."

"No. I think that would be dangerous. Ask a different question."

"May I, Captain?" Spock said. Kirk nodded. "A

small question. Are you aware that we are not Klingons?"

"We think you are a different kind of Klingon," he answered without hesitation. "The ones who came before acted differently. Which doesn't mean we can trust you."

"All right," Kirk said. "That seems a fair exchange. Ask another."

"This weapon." He took it from the second-caste beside him. "How is it that sometimes it kills and sometimes it only puts to sleep?"

"There's a dial," Kirk began.

"Nonsense word."

"Let me try," Larousse said. "There's a way you can tell it what to do. Normally, we don't want it to kill anybody. But it can kill by burning, or even explode itself, if you tell it the wrong thing."

"We have made animals like that." He weighed the weapon in his hand. "This doesn't live, though."

"No. It's a machine."

"I don't understand." He drifted over and handed it to Larousse. "Kill someone. Not me."

"What?"

"One of the second-caste."

Larousse looked at the phaser, then at the magician. "I . . . we . . . don't kill without reason."

"This is a reason."

"Not—not good enough."

"They're just security." Wilson and Moore exchanged looks. "They won't be gone long."

"Spopock," he said in Op. "Whopat shopould opI dopoo?" *Spock—what should I do?*

"What was that?" The translator was set up for English, of course.

"Gopive opit bopack." *Give it back.*

The magician sculled backward. "Try this: Guard, kill the little one."

One of the guards gave a flip of his wings and flew straight toward Park, spear stiff in front of him.

"Take 'em!" Wilson shouted. He and Moore fumbled for their hidden phasers, hampered by the wings. Park's was more accessible: she had it out just as the point of the spear drove into her abdomen.

She fired, and the guard exploded into a bloody purple blossom, only the head and limbs intact.

She gave a single grunt of pain, maybe confusion; the force of the blow was enough to break the hold of the tractors, and she sailed slowly away, tumbling, trailing a viscous ribbon of blood.

Moore and Wilson were back-to-back, down on one knee, firing. They stunned the armed ones first, and then the other guards. Then Moore stood up and faced the magician. He spun the force-setting wheel up to "9."

"Murderer." He took aim.

"Don't do it, Moore," Kirk snapped. "Maybe later."

McCoy dashed over to Tinney and gentled her to the ground. He opened his medical kit and used scissors to snip away cloth, leaving the spear head in the wound.

She was in grave shock—skin grayish, only the whites of her eyes showing, breathing in shallow rapid gasps. McCoy set his tricorder on "tomography" and looked at the wound from several angles.

"Bad," he said. "Retroperitoneal, opened the inferior vena cava. You guys have paramedic training?"

"Yes," Moore and Wilson said simultaneously.

"Have to move fast. Get on both sides here." He slipped the sterile field grid under the small of her back. "Listen once." He gave her an anaesthetic shot. "I have to make a rather long incision here. Vena cava's about eight centimeters in. You have to hold the lips of the wound apart while I dig; just pull gently on the skin, like this. Won't be pretty." It was already rather gruesome, red foam bubbling everywhere but "down," but became rapidly worse when McCoy jerked out the spear and went to work.

It took about sixty seconds for the scalpel to work its way through the various layers of muscle, fat, gristle; enlarging the hole that the weapon had made, so Bones could work the business-end of the anabolic protoplaser in close enough to heal the slashed vena cava. Another sixty seconds to close up. By that time McCoy's two helpers looked worse than the patient— slightly green under splashed red.

"She'll live. But she mustn't be moved, not for about a day."

"I'll stay and guard her," Moore said.

"No," Wilson said. "You're faster than I am; that might make a real difference if there's another fracas. Besides, I'm old enough to be her father. She wouldn't be embarrassed, having me care for her."

"Besides," Moore said, "it's an order."

"I was about to bring that up."

McCoy did a fair job of cleaning the blood off himself, and passed the rag to Wilson. Kirk was talking in a low tone, reporting the situation to Uhura. Larousse stood with the phaser in his hand, trembling some, covering the magician.

"I don't understand," he said. "It was set on 'stun.'"

McCoy was standing over the shattered body of the guard who had attacked Park. "Guess you couldn't see from where you're standing. It was Tinney's phaser that got him, not yours. She must not've checked the setting, or maybe it spun up to a high number when she drew."

"That's . . . something of a relief. I've never killed anybody. Not what I joined for."

"I don't think Tinney's killed anyone, either. Not even now. Isn't that true, magician?" He prodded the remains with his toe. "This one will be back in no time, right?"

"I don't know what you mean by 'no time.' His new body will be quickened soon, but it will be many twenties of days before he can resume his responsibilities. *Ela* learn faster than our lower brothers, but we have so much more to learn, since we keep our memories."

The magician paused. "Is this why you are angry with me? Is it really true, that you are never replaced?"

"Yes, it's true; yes, that's why we're angry! You came within a centimeter of killing that girl—"

"Nonsense word."

"—and she'd never come back." He turned from the grisly scene in front of him and looked at the magician. "Girls. A girl, or woman, or female, is the same species as a boy, or man, or male. The basic constituents of life are different, though. Your standard model girl is made of sugar and spice and everything nice. Boys, on the other hand, are made of sticks and snails and puppy-dog tails. *Kapish?*"

"I don't understand any of that."

"Well, it makes as much sense as this 'replacement' mumbo-jumbo. You clone them, don't you."

"Of course not."

"You know what a clone is, though."

"Certainly. We clone many varieties of plants and animals. It's not the same as replacement, though.

"Look at this, for instance." He pointed to a thick white ridge that ran diagonally across his wing. "This is a scar I got from your brother Klingons, ten generations ago. A clone of me, if we were to clone Chatalia —let alone *elal*—wouldn't have the scar. No more than it would have my memories, my individuality."

"You're talking about immortality, which we know is impossible." (Some humans had "serial immortality"—replacing organs as they wore out—but after a couple of hundred years you couldn't coax the cells to divide properly, and everything fell apart at once.) "I think you're deluded. Or lying to us."

"Magicians do not lie," he said.

"That may be so," Spock said. "Neither this one nor T'Lallis has said anything that was demonstrably untrue, at least according to their own view of the world."

"Let me try to explain. It is not that we live forever. We are replaced as long as we are useful. Whole families have been allowed to die out when their function has become obsolete; individuals are allowed to die without replacement if their behavior indicates that their future survival would be a liability to the rest."

"That still doesn't explain what you do," McCoy said. "How do you duplicate yourselves, if it's not cloning?"

"The Father Machine." The magician gestured at the torn-up body that floated near McCoy's feet. "That one, for instance, his name is T'Kyma. The next time I go Below, I will tell the Father Machine that T'Kyma is to be replaced.

"We go to the Father Machine every twentieth day, and sit with it for a while. When we die, or are so ill that we must be killed, the Machine produces a copy of what we were, last time we sat with it."

"Memories and all," Bones said.

"For the *ela*, yes. The *ven* and *lan* are replaced by a different Father Machine, which only reproduces the physical body. There are *lan* families that specialize in educating these new ones."

"I would like to see this Father Machine," Spock said.

"There are a lot of machines I'd like to see," Kirk added. "Will you take us to them?"

"Below?"

"Wherever. You were going to take us somewhere with these guards, weren't you?"

"Yes, and Below, as a matter of fact. But not to show you things."

"Suppose we go there now," Kirk said. "Armed."

Scotty had rationed the bottle, one drink every forty-five minutes, and was sober as Spock. He didn't especially want to be sober, but he did want to save enough for one final toast, watching the bomb come in.

In Scott's university days, in Glasgow, he had spent a certain amount of time in pubs. There had been a custom then, and may be a custom still, to determine who would pay for the next round of drinks: the boy who had paid for the previous round would stand (banging a glass on the table, for punctuation) and recite the first line of a poem, Scottish usually;

sometimes English. The one to his left had to supply the second line; the one to *his* left, the third, and so on. The first one to muff a line bought the table.

Scotty thought it a mark of a gentleman to allow others to pay for one's liquor—and a man who can memorize every line of a complicated technical drawing can memorize a few lines of verse.

To keep from drinking alone, Scotty had been for a couple of hours reciting those poems from twenty years ago, summoning up his young comrades. Pacing around the green.

Twelve minutes to go, now. He had to move back to the emergency bridge, warm up the viewscreen. As he stepped into the lift, he began a poem by Robert Graham:

> "If doughty deeds my lady please
> "Right soon I'll mount my steed;
> "And strong his arm, and fast his seat,
> "Tha' bears frae me the meed—"

He let that one go; it seemed inappropriate to celebrate chivalry when your foe was a cruel sniper. Riding the lift, stepping out, he was haunted by dark lines from Donne and Shakespeare, but he wouldn't sing of death, not now. Ten minutes.

He settled into the command chair and turned on the screen. It took him a couple of minutes, at lowest power, to locate the bomb. He watched it come closer, debating with himself, finally not calling Uhura.

With one minute to go, he poured brandy to the rim of the glass, and solemnly drank it off. He scowled at the bomb, growing visibly larger every second.

"Damn you," he whispered to Kulain. He knew

stronger language, but was saying what he meant. "God damn you to Hell."

The screen went impossibly brilliantly white.

The Magicians' Island was a bizarre landscape to walk through. The ground was dry clay that seemed hard as cement, but plants grew everywhere, and in no esthetic or logical pattern. They were all colors of the rainbow—leaves as well as flowers—and came in every size and shape, from small tufts of grass to tortuous coils of thorny vine in clumps the size of houses. As they approached the entrance to Below, the going got rough: thick matted jungle that they had to burn away by phaser. It wasn't designed to be approached on foot, but Kirk and his men had no desire to take to the air. Spock held the magician (whose name, they learned, was T'oomi) firmly by the arm, and pushed him along in front.

The entrance was a carved hole some five hundred meters in diameter. Its sides were black and smooth as if carved from obsidian; there were no steps, of course.

"You lead, T'oomi," Kirk said. "I can't really threaten you, since you believe you can't die." He wiped dirty sweat from his face, panting with the past hour's exertion. "But before you give any thought to escaping, or not cooperating in every way . . . think of what these weapons could do to the Father Machine. And the rest of Below."

"I understand," the magician said. "And I will be cooperative . . . but I don't think—"

"Captain!" Spock said, a queer note in his voice. "Look at the time."

Kirk knew what Spock meant before he saw the numbers. "We're alive."

"The shell must have worked."

"Scotty . . ." Kirk whipped out his communicator. "Kirk to *Enterprise*. Come in, Mr. Scott."

There was nothing but static. He put the communicator away. "Get moving," he said, and took a step toward T'oomi.

"Don't touch!" The magician flapped away. He hovered over the edge of the pit. "Follow me."

"We'll walk," Kirk said. "You stay right in front of us." They started fly-walking down the smooth wall, toward what looked like a dense garden below.

It took nearly a half-hour to get there. It was easier going than the jungle had been, but the illusion of constantly defying gravity was disorienting and tiring.

The half-kilometer-wide hole was essentially an air shaft for Below, which was a huge buried dome tens of kilometers in extent. A cold bluish light emanated uniformly from the featureless ceiling. They drifted down cautiously, phasers drawn, Moore with the heavy phaser rifle.

Below looked like a formal garden gone to seed. There were plants in neat circular and polygonal beds, but weeds and vines sprawled everywhere. The variety of sizes, shapes, and colors was as great as they'd seen above, but in this cool dim light it all seemed sinister.

When they came to the floor, they bounced. The tractor boots wouldn't hold. "T'oomi?" Kirk said. "What is this?" T'oomi just floated there, looking at them. "Spock?"

"Interesting . . . there are a few substances that repel tractor fields, but they are all metallic." The floor looked like a conglomerate of gravel and cement.

"It's more complicated than that," Larousse said. "Check the time."

Spock and Kirk looked at their chronometers, and the faces were blank. Kirk drew out his communicator and flipped it open; there was no bleat to indicate activation.

"Kirk to Uhura." Silence.

T'oomi said something in Chatalian, and the translator was mute.

"My God," McCoy said. "Nothing works down here."

From every direction, magicians were sliding toward them through the air. Most of them were armed.

12

Scotty had rubbed the glare from his eyes and pinched himself hard, and decided that either (1) he was alive, or (2) the afterlife was rather prosaic.

"Uhura to *Enterprise*. Come in, please!" The message was weak and full of static.

"This is the *Enterprise*. I'm all richt, Uhura!"

"*Enterprise*, come in, please." She didn't hear him. "*Please* come in!"

"Kirk to *Enterprise*. Come in, Mr. Scott." The captain's signal was even fainter.

"I'm here, Captain!" He was shouting. "The ship made it through!"

Disgusted, he turned off the communicator. There wasn't enough power to maintain the neutrino carrier wave.

He felt a cold chill that was simultaneously one of scary revelation and actual physical coolness. If there wasn't enough power to run a communicator, how long could the life support systems run?

It felt like the temperature of the emergency bridge had dropped at least ten degrees, since he'd seen the bomb go off. If it kept falling at this rate, he'd freeze solid before long.

He leaped out of the chair and ran to the turbo-lift. He would have to gather some food and water from the entertainment area. Other things. Blankets—

The lift didn't come. Not enough power.

Scotty forced the doors open. There was a gangway that would normally take him down the one deck necessary, but it was connected to the parts of the ship that were without life support. Fortunately, the elevator shaft was sealed, and there were rungs connecting the decks. He clambered down and forced open the Deck Eight doors. Have to move fast; get everything together and then shut it all down, everything but the Bridge. Pity about the trees.

There must have been two hundred of the aliens, all with the gold ribbon of first caste. T'oomi was talking to them in a loud orator's voice.

"Can you understand any of that, Larousse?" Kirk asked.

"Nothing useful. I understand the word for 'magician' and the word for us, or Klingons, maybe. It's a different language than the one T'Lallis used."

"Do you want me to make a break for it?" Moore suggested. "I can probably outrun them, in a straight line."

"If they just had the spears, might be a good idea," Kirk said. "But some of those in the back have bows."

"That doesn't mean they could hit me."

"Let's not take the chance." One Chatalia was swimming toward them, weaponless, but with an armful of what looked like bunches of celery, dark blue. "Get ready for something."

There were fiber loops threaded through the bases of the blue celery; the magician approached Kirk and slowly passed the loop over his head, the stalks hanging there like a vegetable necktie.

"Now," the alien said, "can you understand me?"

"Uh," Kirk said, nonplussed. "Uh . . . yes, I do. You understand me?"

"Of course." He moved to McCoy.

"What the hell is going on here?" McCoy tried to brush him away.

"Translators," Kirk said, but what McCoy heard was "Grunfoon w'kaiba."

"Oh, I get it." He cooperated, as did the others.

When Larousse got his, he said, "How did you do this?"

"I didn't do it. Don't you remember? The Father Machine made them. Last time you came."

"Wait. These work with Klingon?"

"Of course."

"Copan yopoo opundoperstopand mopee?" *Can you understand me?"*

"Sure." He swam away.

"They're *better* than ours," he said to Spock. "They don't have to be calibrated to one language."

"Je parle français," Spock said. *"Pouvez-vous me comprendre?"*

"I hear that in French," Larousse said, "but I understand French. *Wakarimasu ka?"*

"That, I heard in Vulcan. 'Do you understand?' "

"It was Japanese. What an incredible machine."

"Telepathic," Spock said, looking at the stalks

with interest. "Similar to ours, really, except for being plants."

T'oomi was talking. ". . . and when they die, it is always death-without-replacement. This is also suspicious.

"But I have been with them for some time, and a second-caste one who traveled with them for days agrees with me: they don't act at all the way I remember Klingons."

Kirk spoke up. "We are not Klingons. The physical similarities are superficial. Your scientists, your 'life arts' people, could examine us and tell you that right away."

There was a long ringing silence. "The Father Machine," someone in the crowd said.

"That would be possible," T'oomi said. He turned to the crew. "You might not survive it, though. The Father Machine killed every Klingon we sent to it. Without replacement."

"Do you know why it killed them?" Kirk said.

"Because they endangered the order of things."

"Not because they were . . . evil?"

"That word doesn't translate."

"Ah. I suppose we also upset the order of things."

"You certainly have. Whether that would cause the Machine to kill you, I can't know."

"Let me suggest an alternative," Spock said. "You know that my touch, unlike the others', doesn't harm you."

"So far as we know."

"Very well. My people, Vulcans, have a special gift called 'mind touch.' It allows an intimate telepathic connection between two beings, where there can be no falsehood, no slightest misrepresentation. Would one of you agree to enter into this with me?"

"Can others monitor this?" T'oomi asked.

"No. It's a personal communication, one-to-one."

T'oomi sculled toward him. "There is danger involved, though."

"It is painful to both. Not necessarily dangerous."

"I will try."

Spock's long, graceful fingers touched the alien's temples. Kirk grimaced, watching. He had seen this done before, and knew what a toll it exacted from his friend.

But as the minutes passed, Spock just floated there, a frown of intense concentration on his face. No sign of pain.

He let go of T'oomi, puzzled. "Nothing. Somehow, you must be capable of blocking the process."

"I haven't resisted. But I also felt nothing." He floated away, turning his back. "I think the Vulcan, as he calls himself, was lying. Like a *ven* or *lan*, or Klingon."

Kulain sat tensely in the command chair, and viewed the crystal again, perhaps for the twentieth time. It showed the nova bomb falling in toward the planetoid, dropping so it would detonate right beside the *Enterprise*.

"Slow it down, now," he said to the communications officer. "Slow it down as much as you can."

The image of the *Enterprise* took up nearly half the screen. The bomb came to within two or three hundred meters, and suddenly became a white dot, painfully bright, that began to grow. The fireball swelled until it touched the surface of the planetoid —and then it suddenly disappeared.

"Impossible!" Kulain raged. "Energy can't disappear like that."

The Klingon beside him, the ordnance officer, nodded uneasily. "The fireball should have grown to envelope the planetoid . . . and then grown ten times more. And take many hours to dissipate."

"So what happened?"

He frowned at the screen. "Magic."

"Lieutenant . . ."

"I'm serious, sire. It might as well be. The laws of heat dynamics are at the very root of all our science. This denies them. So 'magic' is adequate, as a functional description."

"I want a counterweapon, not a 'functional description.' "

"Of course, sire." He thought for a moment. "The first thing we have to decide is whether this defensive weapon was deployed by the *Enterprise* or by these Chatalia."

"If the *Enterprise*, their distress signal was a hoax to lure us in, goad us into attacking," Kulain mused. "Perhaps to test their device. And put us in a situation that might prove embarrassing in terms of the Organian treaty."

"If the signal was real, though," the ordnance officer said, "it does contain testimony that the Chatalia have some mysterious mastery over energy. Magic."

"Offensive word." He leaned back and closed his eyes. "What we need is a plan of action that would be appropriate in either case. Ideas?"

After a long silence, the officer said, "Perhaps I lack imagination. All I can think of is a direct assault, via transporter. Force the secret out of them, perhaps, before wiping them out."

Kulain hadn't changed expression. Now he smiled thinly and opened his eyes. "You are fortunate that your post does not *require* imagination. We have one nova bomb left, correct?"

"Yes, sire. But I wouldn't advise—"

"No, we won't repeat the same action. We use the transporter. Detonate the bomb *inside* the planetoid."

"But, sire . . . the bomb is too large to be transported."

Kulain tapped the side of his head. "Imagination, Lieutenant. We send it in piecemeal. We also transport a team of experts, to reassemble and detonate it."

"An ordnance team, sire?"

"Would you trust the cooks with it?"

"Right away, sire." The ordnance officer stood, rather slowly, and saluted. "Survive and succeed."

Kulain watched him go, then turned to study the crystal once more. Of course, he thought, there was another course of action consistent with either explanation: flee. Distressingly human thought. Maybe Kal was right. Obscene. But there's dark pleasure in thinking it.

The magicians had taken away their celery-stalk translators so they couldn't overhear, and were engaged in lively debate, presumably over what to do with them. T'oomi had remarked that this group comprised every single first-caste magician, which was a gathering that occurred only a few times per generation.

"If there's anything like a control room down here," Kirk said, "it's pretty well camouflaged."

"It's possible we are looking for the wrong thing,"

Spock said. "I have a theory: all of their machines may be in the form of plants—remember, T'Lallis said that 'tending plants' was the main activity of the first-castes."

"Plant machines, though?"

"It makes sense. Suppose you were planning a vessel like this, one that would be in flight for tens of thousands of years, maybe more. What would be your main concern?"

Kirk rubbed his chin. "I think I see. Maintenance. No place to get spare parts, and almost nothing will go that long without breaking down."

"Exactly. But if you are advanced enough in life sciences to create plants that duplicate the functions of your machines, then you can make exact replacements by simple methods of plant propagation."

Larousse joined them. "If that's so, it's possible that none of them *does* know they're on a spaceship. If they had a strong tradition that every plant is to be cared for and eventually replaced, thus-and-so . . ."

The chatter was quieting down. "It should be easy enough to find out," Kirk said. "Here comes T'oomi." It was difficult to tell one from another, normally, but T'oomi had the identifying scar on his wing. Another *ela* accompanied him, with their translators.

"T'oomi, tell us," Kirk said, "are the plants really—"

"We will talk later, maybe. First you go to the Father Machine. Follow me."

It was a nervous-making trip. Each of the crew members had a spear-carrying escort directly behind him, and a phalanx of bowmen followed. They flew very slowly.

As Spock would have predicted, the Father Machine was a plant, or a system of plants. It rose fifty meters off the ground, and was as big around as it was high. Blue-green leaves larger than a man, thorn-pointed, overlapped one another as do those of an artichoke, but with striking regularity. It looked like a cross between an artichoke and a spiral staircase, the size of an office building. As they approached, they could see motion: it seemed to be breathing.

They stopped near the top of it, and found that indeed it was breathing, in warm regular gusts. Its breath smelled disturbingly of rotten meat.

"What does this thing eat?" Kirk asked.

"Anything it wants," said T'oomi.

In the assembly area adjacent to the transporter room, Kulain was inspecting his troops. There were two groups: the ordnance team, with a heavy-weapons squad for protection, and a group of priests and scientists (heavily armed, for tradition's sake), who were to beam down to the ruin of the ancient Klingon vessel.

Kulain himself planned to beam aboard the *Enterprise*. Their sensors said that one man had stayed behind. Kulain wanted to meet him, to indulge his interest in human psychology; perhaps to kill him, in an appropriate way. Some way that would not be "aggression" in Organian terms.

"This will be the order of transport. First, the ordnance team, with their guard. The parts of the nova bomb will follow directly.

"You will go to the leading pole. There is no centrifugal gravity there, so it will be easy to handle the machinery."

He addressed the highest-ranking priest in the next

group. "Then you go, and you'll be quick about it. If we can believe the distress message from the Federation ship, we may be close enough to be snared by whatever trapped them." Kulain would leave right after.

Scotty sat with his back against the dais of the useless transporter, wrapped in four layers of blanket. In front of him, a small fire burned brightly, the only source of light in the emergency bridge room.

To his left was a stack of wood: uprooted saplings, branches hacked off larger trees (which he'd done with a tritanium axe from a cabinet of emergency fire supplies—it could slice through metal doors, and made short work of wood), and some chunks of exotic furniture. To his right, seventeen bottles of compressed oxygen. The eighteenth, he had propped between his knees, regulator barely cracked, nozzle pointing toward the fire. A forgotten bottle of brandy sat beside him, frozen to slush. It was forty degrees below zero. In the rest of the ship it was much colder.

Flickering at first, then solid, Kulain appeared. Scotty had his eyes closed, trying to rest.

"Human!" Kulain said, then coughed spasmodically. Klingons had slightly better tolerance to low temperatures than humans, but not this low. "Are you alive?" he croaked.

"Aye, the last time I took a readin' . . . though I ken *you* won't be lastin' long, in this bitterness."

Kulain inhaled sharply; frost in his throat cut off his reply. He unsnapped the flap of his holster.

"Don' do that." Scotty's outstretched arm bulged the blanket in front of him. "I'll blast ye away."

Kulain said something in Klingon, loudly. He flickered slightly, but didn't go away.

"If ye're tryin' to transport, give it up. Ye're stuck here."

"Stuck?"

Scotty nodded. "Mebbe for good."

The Klingon looked at him blankly for a moment, then seemed to slump. "Don't you shoot." He slowly drew his weapon and put it against his forehead. When he pulled the trigger, it made a sound like a tired kitten.

"This doesn't work, either?"

"Nope. Nor would this phaser, if it were real." The blanket dropped away, revealing a bare hand. "Ye're welcome to share these blankets with me, if ye'll take a turn at tendin' the fire."

"I'd rather die." He folded his arms across his chest.

"Suit yerself." Scotty drew the blankets around himself. "Fat lot of good you do your fatherland, frozen stiff. Hold yer breath until ye turn blue, I don' care."

A minute later, he said, "All right," through chattering teeth. He picked up a sapling and broke it in two (with a brittle sound like ceramic breaking), laid a piece on the fire, and set the other half nearby. The blankets encircled both of them, so long as they stayed shoulder-to-shoulder.

Kulain stared morosely into the fire. "I've never been so close to a human that I could smell him."

"You ain't no bloody bunch of posies, yerself."

13

"I will go first," Spock said.

"Wait—" Kirk was cut off by T'oomi.

"No. It must be a human. There are twenty twenties of you gathered in the gardens of *Ian*. We have to know what to do with you."

"I'll do it," Moore said. "I'm the most dispensable."

"Moore," Kirk said, struggling between logic and emotion, "I would never order you to . . ."

"I know, sir. Maybe that's why I can volunteer." He floated up toward T'oomi. "Besides. It looks like we're all dead, anyhow."

"Oracles," said T'oomi. Two magicians presented themselves. "Ready him—as well as you can, without touching his skin."

They told Moore to be still, and keep his arms at his sides. Then, only touching his chest, they pushed him toward the purple blossom at the top of the Father Machine.

One of the oracles whistled a series of notes, and the blossom opened. They guided Moore into it, and the petals closed around him.

After about ten seconds, the blossom expelled him violently, sneezing him toward the ceiling. Two guards took after him; he met them halfway, flying back down.

One of the oracles fit himself halfway into the blossom, head and shoulders sticking out. In a singsong voice he said:

"Not Klingon. Klingons taste good, have unpleasant minds. This one tastes poison, but his mind is neutral. Where is the one that claims to be a different species?"

Spock drifted over. "Can you warn it I'm half-human?"

"It knows," T'oomi said. "It knows everything about you that T'Lallis did."

"Will the communication be both ways?"

"No, the Father Machine only speaks through the oracle family." It had never encountered a Vulcan before, though. Spock decided he would try mind touch with it.

The inside of the blossom was white and shiny with moisture, like the mouth of a snake. Spock let them ease him inside. As it closed over him, he put out his palms and did the mental twist that would initiate mind touch.

He screamed.

"Don't fire unless they show some sign of aggression," Uhura said. About a hundred *lan* were approaching them, a silent mob. A dozen or so had spears, but many of the others carried farming tools that would make effective weapons.

Leading them was an unarmed ven-Chatalia, with the three blue ribbons of a no-caste interpreter. Uhura turned on the translator. "Uh, hello," she said uncertainly.

The mob stopped dead. A hundred whispering voices sounded like a cloud of insects chirring. The interpreter huddled with a couple of the spear-bearers, who talked to higher-caste spear-bearers, and relayed some message back to the interpreter. The little *ven* came forward, obviously intimidated by the tall black woman.

"We won't hurt you," Uhura said. "We welcome a chance to talk with you."

"I bear a message," he said.

"From?"

"From the farmers of this village, and their protectors. You are destroying their land. You must leave."

"We have been careful not to disturb the crops, other than the ones we harvested to make room."

"But your touching them made them poisonous on the outside. And the poisons from your bodies are spreading through the soil." True, the plants nearest the latrine had started turning green—probably not a sign of health, in a blue cabbage.

"But if we move, we'll only poison some other area."

"Then it would not be my problem any more," he said logically. Suddenly, he looked up.

Three magicians coasted down from the sky. One of them landed between Uhura and the interpreter. Ignoring the woman, he towered over the *ven*. "What in the name of Below are you doing?"

"These *lan*, mine, they have, the soil . . ."

"Didn't you come from the city?"

"Yes, master."

"Don't you know you are to take no notice of these magicians from the future? That they can harm you?"

"Yes, master."

"Do you know you have marked yourself for death without replacement?"

"Please, master." He dropped his voice. "You know how it is with these—"

The magician picked him up by the loose skin behind his shoulders and hurled him toward the spearbearers. "Kill him," he said, and turned to Uhura. "As for you—"

The magician, the interpreter, the "protectors," and about thirty of the *lan*, all fell over stunned. The rest of the *lan* stampeded back toward the village. The other two magicians took to the air; one of them pulled a long silver knife from his pouch.

He dove toward Uhura, but it was an unequal contest. Uhura calmly stunned him in midair—and he fell hard, landing on his head with a loud snap.

"Drop the other one?" a Security man asked, tracking the magician as he rose.

"No," Uhura said. "I think we've done enough damage, for today."

Nurse Chapel was leaning over the still form of the fallen magician. Uhura rushed over. "Dead?"

She nodded. "This is passing strange." Holding its top-hair by thumb and forefinger, she gently moved the head back and forth. It went in any direction, without offering resistance. "Would it be all right if I did an autopsy?"

Uhura hesitated. "I suppose . . . first let's put up some sheets or something. So the village doesn't see."

Uhura had no great desire to watch; she was playing a slow game of Owari with Sulu when Chapel finished. She walked up as if in a daze, still holding her bloody gloves.

"Incredible." She sat down. "I wish Spock were here."

Uhura rattled a handful of pebbles; looked at the nurse with curiosity and concern. "What did you find?"

"It's got no central nervous system at all. Just a suffusion of minor ganglia. No spinal cord, no brain."

The Father Machine ate Spock, dissolving him the way a transporter dissolves people, but not as quickly; and then recreated him, as a transporter also does.

Watching the destruction of himself was rather horrifying, Spock thought, but the opposite process was fascinating.

—You are trying to talk to me.

Yes. To tell you the truth, so you can pass it on to the magicians.

—I know all truth. The magicians have no need of it.

You know you are inside a spaceship?

—Laughing. I built it. I am the pilot.

Do you know that you are doomed?

—Still laughing. Really?

If your present course is not changed, you will come to rest in a volume of space light-years away from any star.

—I lived near a star once. It exploded.

But understand: if you don't have a star nearby, you will run out of energy. Eventually you will cool down, to nearly absolute zero.

—*Laughing. You need a star nearby, you mean. Then what will you do for energy?*

—You may have noticed. Your starship is low on energy. I drained it. I am in the process of draining another now.

But you can't count on starships showing up regularly, forever.

—I have other resources. Although it's boring, and takes all of my attention, I can convert matter directly to energy. There is enough dust between the stars to keep me alive indefinitely. In lean times, I can consume my own substance, and recreate it when there is excess energy.

As you consume the Chatalia?

—Occasionally, yes. As you suspect, they are not truly alive. They are toys for me; it pleases me to watch them.

Does it please you to watch us?

—In small doses, yes. You are putting too much disorder in the system now. I will have to be rid of you.

You would kill us all?

—I haven't decided. You seem fairly sentient. At any rate, I wouldn't have to kill you; if I ignore you, you will die soon enough.

Same thing. It was you who trapped us here.

—You who trapped yourselves. You weren't invited.

With that, Spock was suddenly in the open air, tumbling, two magicians chasing after him. They flew back to the blossom, where an oracle was fitting himself into the space Spock had vacated.

"How was it, Spock?" Kirk asked.

Spock answered sotto voce: "The Father Machine

claims to be the only sentient creature on this vessel—"

"But our biosensor data—"

"Were ambiguous. I have a theory . . ."

The oracle began talking. "I think I may let you people go back to where you came from. Two conditions: first, that you never come back here.

"Second, I am hungry for Klingons. There are a few here now. Send me the rest. You know what I mean."

"That would be murder," Kirk said.

"No, Captain," Spock said. "Allow me to take care of it."

"In fact, those few Klingons approach Below now. There has been some fighting. They brought a gift of energy."

The nova bomb they'd assembled was a blocky piece of gray metal, about the size of a shuttlecraft. They had pushed it through the air shaft with back-pack rockets; it would hit the floor of Below in less than a minute.

"Is that what I think it is?" Kirk said.

"Perhaps less," Spock said. "We should be in no danger. Unless there is a limit to the amount of energy it can absorb."

"Not much we can do about it, at any rate."

They both stared at the bomb's slow progress. Nine Klingons accompanied it, dressed in funereal space suits. As they passed out of the air shaft, their rockets fizzled out, and they showed signs of distress— their life support systems failing—until they could get their helmets off.

"Bring them to me," the oracle said. "Escort these others away."

The Klingons floated with stiff dignity, expecting to be vaporized any second. When the nova bomb crunched harmlessly into the gravel, they had a swift conference, then eight of them formed a Klingon Square, blasters out, while the ninth opened a plate on the side of the bomb and tinkered with it. All of them swam clumsily, without wings.

As the *Enterprise* crew passed over them, the Klingons found out that their blasters didn't function. They also tried them on the phalanx of spearmen that approached. Then they drew knives and formed in a line.

When the crew from the *Enterprise* glided into the air shaft, their guard peeled away, presumably to strike the Klingons from behind. Their tractor boots worked again; it was a relief to walk.

Communicator bleeped. "Kirk here."

"This is Mr. Scott, sir. We seem to have power. Would you like me to beam you up?"

"Check Lieutenant Uhura, see whether she has any sick or wounded. Otherwise . . ." He looked back at the Klingons, getting ready for futile combat; looked ahead at the weird sun that would float forever inside this eternally stagnant world. "Beam me up *yesterday!*"

14

Captain Kirk tried to keep a straight face as he stepped down from the transporter in the emergency bridge. It didn't resemble any bridge he had ever commanded: a smoldering campfire, a couple of uprooted trees, food containers scattered everywhere. A couple of empty brandy bottles. A Klingon.

"Captain Quirk, I prezhume?" A drunk Klingon. "I am Captain Kulain, of the war, warship *Korezima*." He folded his arms on his chest and swayed slightly.

He flickered. "Oops! Time to go. Goodbye, Mr. Scott." His brow furrowed. "Can't . . . think of the word. Ah. Thank you."

"My pleasure." The Klingon disappeared.

"Looks like you've been entertaining, Scotty."

Scott finished adjusting dials and turned to Kirk. "It's a long story, sir."

"A good one, too, I'll bet."

"They're not such bad folks, once you get to know them. Can't hold their liquor, though."

"How did you get him to take a drink? I thought they didn't do *anything* for pleasure."

"No' for pleasure, sir. For temperature regulation.

It was so cold we had to thaw out the brandy." He checked a readout. "Be at least five minutes before the transporter room's warmed up, sir. Would you like me to beam up Mr. Spock?"

"Sure. I want to see his face."

No satisfaction there. He stepped down poker-faced. "It must have been very cold, Mr. Scott. I'm glad you are all right."

He went to the viewscreen. "Can you put me in contact with the Klingon vessel?"

"Aye." He fiddled with some switches.

"Spock—are you actually going to deliver—"

"I gave my word, Captain. But actually . . ."

A dim figure appeared. "This is Kal, temporarily in command. Who calls?"

"This is the star ship *Enterprise,* Science Officer Spock here. I have a warning for you.

"The dominant creature in the planetoid below, which calls itself the Father Machine, has issued a challenge: it wishes to consume every one of you.

"I strongly urge that you not answer the challenge. None of your weapons will work in his domain and he may be able to prevent you from ever returning to your ship."

"Knives will work, though, and bare hands, no?"

"True, but you will be greatly outnumbered."

It was hard to read expressions through the swirling colors, but it looked like Kal had a smug smile. "Good." He switched off.

"You see, Captain. Nothing but the truth."

The Father Machine had returned enough fuel for them to reach Starbase 3. Kirk put the crew on light-duty status and everyone settled in to loaf for a week.

Several of the officers were sharing a bottle of Saurian brandy in the lounge. "I wish we could go back, in safety," Spock said. "So many questions unanswered."

"This rebirth thing?" Bones said.

"No, not especially. That's really just regeneration, with the help of something like transporter technology. Since the Chatalia are actually only extensions of the Father Machine. Like limbs."

"Seems pretty impressive to me," Kirk said.

"Other creatures do it," Spock said, "usually on a smaller scale. The real mystery has to do with *energy*. What the Father Machine does defies the basic laws of thermodynamics, and conservation of energy. Since he does *do* it, our laws are wrong. Insufficient."

Wilson came in and pulled up a chair. "Just came from seeing Ensign Tinney, in sick bay. Chapel says she'll be up in a couple of days."

"Don't suppose you've seen Ensign Moore," Bones said.

"As a matter of fact, he was there, too. He was reading to her." Bones rolled his eyes ceilingward but didn't say anything.

"I guess we owe you a real debt, Mr. Spock," Wilson said. "They tell me if you hadn't been able to talk to that overgrown artichoke, we'd all still be down there. Dead, probably."

"It was the logical thing to try," Spock said. "And really not unpleasant, compared to other experiences with mind touch. As I was just telling these people, I wish I could spend more time with him. It."

"You had a lot in common with it," Bones said, expressionlessly.

"It was not the similarities that made it attractive. It seemed to be logical, for instance, but valid logic is invariant from species to species."

Spock stared into space. "No, what was most interesting about it was its humor. I believe it was the only truly intelligent creature I've ever met that had a sense of humor."

After a moment of silence, McCoy said, "There you go again."

"What do you mean?"

"If anybody else had said that, I would swear it was a joke."

Spock arched an eyebrow at him. "One of us is learning something."

Author's Note

Since this is probably my last Star Trek book, I ought to take a page and thank the people who helped me with both of them: the Science Fiction League of Iowa Students, especially Sue Weinberg, who helped keep my stories consistent with the TV series (I was overseas when most of it was aired); Miss Sheila Clark, who supplied authentic dialect for Scotty; Dr. Gregory Benford, who helped me figure out what happens to bodies of water inside a planetoid such as the one in *World Without End;* Gay and Sydny, for quiet patience; Gene Roddenberry, who not only let me take liberties with his creations, but even suggested a few.

A SMALL CONTEST:

The day *Planet of Judgment* (Bantam Books, New York, 1977) came out, I realized with horror that there was a grievous mistake on the very first page. I waited for a deluge of letters.

Well, there were plenty of letters, but none about that. So it's not too obvious a mistake.

Here's a hint: it has to do with a word that

sounds similar to my name. If you see the error, write me care of this publisher. First two correct respondents win autographed copies of my first novel, long out-of-print in hardback, and presumably valuable.

This offer expires 31 December 1978, is void where prohibited by law, and is a cheap trick to make you read *Planet of Judgment*.

Finally, a matter that might be of interest to science fiction readers. To assure that the wording of the quotation beginning this book was correct, I picked up the telephone and called Arthur C. Clarke—who lives on an island in the Indian Ocean, literally halfway around the world. I heard him quite clearly, though my own voice generated a faint feedback echo, characteristic of communication via satellite.

Clarke was the first one to suggest the possibility of using satellites for global communication, in a *Wireless World* article in 1945. I wonder if he could have predicted that it would be commonplace, so soon.

And it makes you wonder what magics will be commonplace tomorrow.

—JOE HALDEMAN

Florida, 1978

PLANET OF JUDGMENT

STAR TREK®

ADVENTURES

"Unable to proceed. Shuttles seriously damaged. Not safe to land here. Some crewmen dead."

On a routine mission to Starfleet Academy, the *U.S.S. Enterprise* sensors detect the presence of a rogue planet in space, orbited by a sun no larger than a pea - a circumstance impossible to explain by any known scientific law. Assuming the star to be an artificial construct, a landing party is despatched to the planet's surface, and there becomes trapped. Spock leads a rescue mission, and becomes trapped in turn.

With two crewmen dead, and unable to contact Scotty on the *U.S.S. Enterprise* bridge, Captain Kirk must battle to solve the riddle of the planet Spock calls Anomaly - a planet where no equipment works and none of their science applies... a planet that cannot exist.

For a complete list of Star Trek publications, please send a large stamped SAE to Titan Books Mail Order, 42-44 Dolben Street, London, SE1 0UP. Please quote reference STA12 on both envelopes.